PRAISE
AND HER EL

"Bull [is] original and c   nes

BONE DANCE
"It's heady and it's fast, and it takes you weird places with style and gusto and fireworks. Great stuff."
—Neil Gaiman, coauthor of *Good Omens*

FALCON
The explosive story of Niki Falcon, a star-pilot empowered by a deadly, addictive drug . . .

"*Falcon* soars! Exciting, evocative, and entertaining. I couldn't put it down!"
—Chris Claremont, author of *FirstFlight* and *Grounded!*

"A taut and chilling SF adventure."
—Julian May, author of *The Many-Colored Land*

"Action, adventure, romance, high tech, and intrigue . . . of a very high order!" —Roland Green, *Booklist*

"Wide-screen science fiction . . . a novel with color, action, narrative drive, fascinating characters, density and verisimilitude of background; in short, it is A Good Read!"
—*The New York Review of Science Fiction*

"Scores a bull's-eye!"
—*Isaac Asimov's Science Fiction Magazine*

WAR FOR THE OAKS
A masterwork of dark urban fantasy, in which strange, unearthly beings wage war in the city streets . . .

"This book is one to read for the sheer wonder of seeing a master storyteller at work." —*Dragon*

"One of the most engaging fantasies I've read in a long time!"
—*Minneapolis Star Tribune*

"A solid book by any standards." —*Chicago Sun-Times*

BONE DANCE

A Fantasy for Technophiles

Emma Bull, P.J.F.

ACE BOOKS, NEW YORK

"Bright Street Beachhouse Back in Business Blues" copyright © 1990 by
Steven K. Z. Brust and Emma Bull. "The Undertoad" copyright © 1990 by
Lojo Russo. Lyrics used by permission of the authors.

This book is an Ace original edition,
and has never been previously published.

BONE DANCE

An Ace Book / published by arrangement with
the author and the author's agent, Valerie Smith.

PRINTING HISTORY
Ace edition / May 1991

All rights reserved.
Copyright © 1991 by Emma Bull.
Cover art by Jean Targete.
Edited by Beth Fleisher.
This book may not be reproduced in whole or in part,
by mimeograph or any other means, without permission.
For information address: The Berkley Publishing Group,
200 Madison Avenue, New York, New York 10016.

ISBN: 0-441-57457-2

Ace Books are published by The Berkley Publishing Group,
200 Madison Avenue, New York, New York 10016.
The name "ACE" and the "A" logo
are trademarks belonging to Charter Communications, Inc.

PRINTED IN THE UNITED STATES OF AMERICA

10 9 8 7 6 5 4 3 2

Dedication . . .

Cyn Horton gave me the matches. Elise Krueger held the candle while I lit it. The following umpty-ump thousand words are dedicated to both of them. Thanks, guys.

. . and acknowledgments

A book, like a building, needs a proper foundation; Tom Canty, Terri Windling, and Will Shetterly helped to lay the underpinnings for this one. But any doors out of true or stairs that lead nowhere are my fault.

I owe thanks to Jerry Blue, Denise Habel, Tom Grewe, Magenta Griffith, Mitch Thornhill, and Tony Taylor for their generous assistance with construction materials, to Howard Davidson for inspecting some of the wiring, to Tom Juntunen and Will Shetterly for help in hanging pictures, and to April Anderson for the secret blueprints of the Norwest Bank building. Still more thanks to Beth Fleisher, who understood when the tract house became the Winchester Mansion.

This edifice has been inspected by the Minneapolis Scribblies, for which inspection the author is darn grateful, you betcha. Additional building code compliance supplied by Cupertino Deconstruction: Jon Singer and Gordon Garb.

The section headings are paraphrased from Bill Butler's *Dictionary of the Tarot* (Schocken Books, 1978), a wonderful book for anyone interested in the comparative symbolism and interpretation of the tarot.

Contents

Card **0**

The Significator

Page of Swords

Crowley: The earthy part of air, the fixation of the volatile, the materialization of idea. Subtlety in material things, cleverness in managing practical affairs, especially if they are controversial.

Gray: A brown-haired, brown-eyed boy or girl. Possible understanding or knowledge of diplomacy, messages, or spying. Watch out for the unforeseen.

0.0: The stock exchange

The room was dark. The room was always dark, because it had no windows; it ought not to have meant anything. But the way the shadows hung like drapery around the desk; the way the crook-necked lamp cast its measured oval of light on the polished rosewood; the way the silence lay on the room, unbroken by the hiss of a gas mantle; the way the faint, faint smell of petroleum and electricity, like the odor of wealth itself, rose up from everywhere—these things gave the darkness meaning. Nothing in that room was incidental.

The customer sat behind his desk, in a chair so tall and wide it could have hidden two bodyguards. He leaned away from the light, and it from him. Maybe he'd read somewhere that hiding one's face made for psychological advantage in business transactions. He was welcome to think so. He already had the only real advantage: money. All the rest was costume and props.

The merchandise was contained in a flat metal box half again as long as a hand, which had once been white. I put it on the edge of the desk, just outside the pool of light. Then I laid one finger on it and pushed, so that it skidded across the shining wood and stopped in front of him.

His hands came up from under the desk and settled on either side of the box. Then the left one rose again, touched the metal, spread flat on it.

"The one I asked for?" he said. They were the first words out of his mouth since his door had opened and let me in.

"Look at it."

He scrabbled a little at the catch, his self-control momentarily breached. One hinge stuck, complaining; then the box opened with a *tic*, and a broken speck of metal skittered over the rosewood. Inside was another box, plastic. It was mostly deep blue, with a color photo reproduced on it, and the title. He was

3

familiar with the design, I knew. I'd brought him others like it, but
with different photos, different titles. He opened the second box to
reveal the videocassette. He touched the label as if it might be
fragile. "*Singin' in the Rain*," he said, and I could hear his
satisfaction—self-satisfaction, really. He closed the inside box,
and the outside. His hands returned to their guard positions, flat on
the desk with the tape between them, like brackets in an equation.

"Do the contents match the label?" His voice was strong now,
the voice that ordered that room and everything outside it.

"Yes."

"And is it really the original, or did you make a copy to sell
me?"

At that, I reached out, laid the same single finger on the metal
box, and slid it back across the desk to me. His hands curved like
little cats rising and stretching. But they didn't reach after the box.
He knew the Deal.

"You can look for it somewhere else," I said politely, "if you
aren't comfortable buying from me."

His mouth, perhaps, had gone dry. I liked to think so.

We stayed like that for a moment. He might have been
considering sending me away, but I doubted it. I had been
searching for this one, at his request, for six months.

Finally he pulled a narrow leather bag into the light and spread
it open. He shook the contents into his hand and lined them up,
and made sure I saw that the bag was now empty. That was
insulting, but not as insulting as his questions. Ten bright, round
bits of gold he laid out between us, each with a nice portrait in the
center, lovely examples of the coin-making art. Two hundred
dollars hard, precisely what he had promised. Such a memory on
that man.

I turned the line of coins into a stack with one hand and passed
the box across the desk with the other. I looked at the top coin,
then smiled across the barrier of light toward his face. "Remarkable likeness," I said. I made the money disappear, and hoped
he'd noticed; it was a response to his showing me there was
nothing left in the leather bag to steal.

"Another commission," he said, as if I had asked for one and
he was weighing the prospect. He needed this little dance to keep
from himself the knowledge that he needed me. "This'll be a hard
one."

"The last one wasn't exactly lying around like gravel."

He picked up the box that held *Singin' in the Rain*, and turned it over and over in his hands. At last, he said, "I want the Horsemen movie."

I laughed, which I hadn't meant to do. "No."

"Why not?"

"Because I've never seen it, that's why not. If anyone in the City would have seen it, I would, and I haven't."

"So you think it doesn't exist." There was chilly disbelief in his voice.

"I know the folklore. That some poor bastard made a sci-fi-B-movie in which psychic Special Forces soldiers took over the minds of evil brown dictators and won the war in South America. And that some folks who wore dark glasses in the nighttime arrived at his house, asked him *urgent* questions, and took him into custody. I've never heard if they let him out. I've never heard that the thing got video release. I've never even heard it proved that it was released, period. File the whole story next to Hitch-hikers, Comma, Vanishing."

There was a silence, in which I decided he was trying to figure out what that meant. If he asked, I was going to tell him to look it up.

"You sound as if you don't believe in the Horsemen."

Sometimes I feel a profound, crippling sense of loss for something I never had: the world, as it once was. I felt it then. "Of course I believe in the Horsemen. I just don't believe that someone had the bad luck to make a movie about them."

"You're turning down the job?"

I shook my head. "I'll look. I've been looking for years. But I'm not going to find it. Not now. It it had ever existed, do you really think there'd be a copy left unburnt?"

"Five hundred," he said.

I raised my eyebrows. "A thousand, hard. Be glad I don't ask for the hand of your firstborn and half your kingdom."

"No one'd give you a thousand for a goddamn movie."

"Then if I find it, no one will get it."

Long, expensive-sounding silence. "If you find it," he said finally, rustily, "bring it to me."

I smiled, and stifled the impulse to bow. We had not agreed on a price; but we'd agreed that his figure and mine marked the borders of a country we were willing to skirmish in later, if the need arose.

He opened one of his desk drawers, dropped *Singin' in the Rain* into it, closed and locked it. As sometimes happens when a great deal of money changes owners in an atmosphere of bare tolerance,

he suddenly turned hearty. He gestured toward a lower corner of
the room and said, "Down there, some people call two hundred in
gold a fortune, son. What do you plan to do with it all?"

I smiled; if he couldn't see it, he would still hear it in my voice.
"Oh," I said, "I thought I'd treat myself to breakfast."

And that should have been the end of it; but it may be that I
don't think clearly with a fortune in my inside pocket. "Have you
seen it?" I asked him.

He was startled enough to get in the way of the light. It made
him squint, his eyes lost in pasty white flesh. "Pardon?"

"*Singin' in the Rain*. Have you seen it?" Dancing over sofas,
hanging from lampposts, piling furniture on the speech tutor. Did
he have a secret passion for foolery?

"No."

"Then how do you know you want it?"

His answer was all in his face, scornful and baffled at once.
Money makes me ask stupid questions. He wanted it, of course,
because someone else didn't have it.

"Debbie Reynolds dies in the end," I told him.

Five minutes later I was in an elevator rumbling down from the
top of the tallest building in the City, with more money than I'd
ever carried in my life, literally surrounded by wealth and power.
And I was mostly sick and frightened with it. When I got outside,
onto the street, to anyplace that had ever been touched by sunlight,
I would be all right.

I went past the guard desk, nodded at the man who sat behind
it, and tried, as I went out the door, not to look as if I was rushing.
I turned right, into the cheerful morning pandemonium of the mall
market, and the tight prickling between my shoulders went away.

I'd done a good job, I decided on reflection. That building, that
office, that customer, always made me feel claustrophobic and
small, but I'd kept my mind on the Deal, and it had gone as I'd
meant it to. I might have sounded a little like Humphrey Bogart in
The Maltese Falcon, but there were worse roles.

I bought eggs and peppers and a few ounces of crumbly cheese
at three different stalls, and took them all to a grill cart and had the
proprietor turn them into an omelette.

After breakfast I would hail a bicycle cab and pay for the long,
long ride to the western outskirts of the City, where a culture-
vulture knew of a sealed-up basement holding the remains of a
video production business. It would be, by my standards, a perfect
day.

But it had chaos hidden in it. Cancers start that way: a cell or two, mutated, dividing, a secret for weeks or months until suddenly the transformation announces itself, and the whole organism quails in the face of it. The cells mutated that day, though I knew nothing about it for weeks.

Card 1

Covering

Death, Reversed

Waite: Inertia, sleep, lethargy, petrifaction, somnambulism, hope destroyed.

Gray: Stagnation. Failure of revolution or other forms of violent change.

Crowley: Transformation and the logical development of existing conditions thwarted. His magical weapon is the pain of the obligation. His magical power is necromancy.

.0: Gonna go downtown

I came up on my back in the dirt. The sun was hot on the front of me, but the ground under my body was cool. I'd been there a while, then. A white-blue glaring summer sky made my eyes water. My mouth felt like a tomb from some culture where they bury your servants with you.

I turned my head reluctantly, and found the river flats around me, deserted, smelling like dead fish and damp wood. Far away, across the baked mud and spilled cured concrete, a bridge crew worked. I could hear the cadence shout, faintly, and the crash as the weight came down to drive the piles.

I rolled half over and tried to decide how I was. This time, all I felt was a sore and swelling bruise on the side of my face. I remembered where I must have got it: in the street in back of Tet Offensive, where I'd gone for spicy mock duck and gotten two *Charlies petites* instead. The last thing I recalled clearly was one of the boss girls doing a snap kick, watching her heel come at me out of the dark. Probably about then that I went down.

Since the only lasting damage I'd taken was something I could remember, I must not have been into any nasty things during downtime. How long had it been? And what had I missed?

When I stood up, I had to revise the damage report. My skull was the Holy Sepulcher of hangovers. Oh, I must have been into some nasty things, indeed. I hoped I'd had fun. By the time I got to the street along the Bank, it was enough to make me sick.

I'd had thirty bucks in paper, but my pockets were empty now. If the boss girls hadn't gotten it, then it had paid for whatever had left its residue in my head. I wished I knew what it was. Not that I could resolve never to consume any more. Sooner or later I'd go down again, shut out of my own mind, and all the resolving I'd ever done would be as useful as a dome light in a casket.

The next plunge down would be number five. The first time, I'd

thought it was something I'd eaten, or drunk, or otherwis
consumed. The second time, I'd wondered if it was someon
else's malice, the *coup n'âme*. By the third, it had occurred to m
that it might be all mine. The effect of my colorful origin, arrive
at last to rectify a long-neglected error. But if that was so, wh
wasn't it coming closer to killing me?

I sat on the wall by the road, shivering in the sun. Suddenly
could imagine all the things my body might do when I wasn't ther
to stop it, and I felt so vile they might as well have happened
Maybe they had; they just hadn't left marks. I thought about
future full of blank spaces, and knew I couldn't bear it. If that wa
the future, I had to escape it.

The obvious method came to mind, despair's favorite offspring
It came so sharp to the front of my brain, so clear and desirable
that I made a quick little noise about it. I was down off the wa
and headed for the Deeps before I could think about what I wa
running (figuratively) from. The human animal, when hurting
prefers to go to ground in its own burrow.

In parts of town, I could have sat on the curb and held out m
hand, and after a while, if I looked pitiful enough, I would hav
the money to pay for a bicycle cab. There were still people in th
world who were superstitious about beggars, after all, and i
bruised, dirty, and disoriented couldn't elicit pity, then what wa
superstition for? But the Bank was lousy panhandling territory
People there lived by the Deal, like everyone else. They lived *we*
by it, however, and that affected their judgment. Even if they onc
knew the First Law of Conservation of Deals—that there are neve
enough to go around—they'd let it slip their minds. So they drov
past in their co-op's car, or trotted by under the twisted trees, le
by dogs that ate as much as I did, and assumed when they saw m
that I didn't do as much to earn my food as the dog.

Once, even in a place like the Bank, you could hold your han
out in a certain way, and people would understand that you neede
transportation. They'd stop their private cars and let you ride i
them, without asking anything in return. Unnatural, but true. I'
seen it in movies. But that was a long time ago. I staggered on, th
dogs barked, and their owners made what they thought wer
imperceptible movements toward one pocket or another. I wasn'
worried; I didn't think even a shot of ammonia in my eyes coul
make me feel worse.

By the time I got to Seven Corners market, the whole worl
seemed to flash colors in rhythm with my heartbeat. The flapping
shutter of my headache kept time, too. Seven Corners has neve

een a good place for my preferred sort of marketing: it's food, clothing, housewares, and the kind of services that go with those, mostly. So I didn't much mind having to make my way through it with my eyes squinted three-quarters shut. It occurred to me, dimly, that I might have more than a hangover.

The weight of the sun finally brought me to a ragged halt at the market's edge. I stood under an awning, supporting myself by propping my hip against a table, and pretended to be thoughtful about a tray of tomatillos. The next stall over had crates of live poultry, and the noise and smell were unlovely. A black woman with a serpent scarred from cheek to cheek over the bridge of her nose traded the vendor a bottle of homebrew for a white rooster; the vendor popped a little sack over the bird's head, tied its feet together, and ran a loop of string through its bonds for a carrying handle. The woman walked away, swinging a rooster too dismayed to struggle. *It gets worse*, I wanted to tell him, thinking of his new owner's scar.

I was waiting, I realized, for my wits to disappear into darkness. As if it would happen when I was ready for it. There would be some consolation in knowing what it was. Brain tumor, bad food, the heat? The heat would kill cactus. Perspiration was trickling out of my hairline, warm as the air, too warm to be doing its job.

The poultry dealer had a pair of doves in a wicker cage, velvety gray and sullen. Doves in paintings were never sullen. They seemed, in fact, to have managed a permanent state of exaltation, like the mindless fluttering ones around a chalice in . . . Sherrea's . . . cards.

I stood clouted with revelation amid the produce. I wanted knowledge. Sherrea claimed to call it up out of a seventy-eight-card deck. I didn't believe in the cards, but I might, if pressed, admit to uncertainty about Sher. A little mind reading, with tarot as its rationalization—however she explained it to herself, she might locate my missing memories. If she *was* a mind reader, if the memories were there, if there was any help in them. But I had to try.

The brown grandmotherly woman who sold the tomatillos was shooting ungrandmotherly narrow-eyed looks at me, so I turned to move on. But I missed my step and stumbled against one of her awning poles, rocking the whole canvas roof, and she shouted something about mi madre. That made me laugh. The sun hit me over the head with its hammer when I came out of the shade, and I stopped laughing.

The Ravine forms the western edge of the Bank, only a few
hundred yards from Seven Corners market. It's full of the cracked
pavement of an old interstate highway—still a perfectly good
road, in an age that requires less of its road surface and has no use
for the concept of "between states." From the lip of the Ravine I
could see the Deeps on the other side, hard gray and brown brick
and wood on the nearest structures, shading farther in to rose,
bronze, black pearl, and verdigris in spires of stone, metals, and
brilliant glass. The empress of it all, rising from its center, was
Ego, the tallest building in the City, whose reflective flanks had no
color of their own, but wore the sky instead—relentless, cloudless
blue today. The towers of the Deeps, rising in angles or curves,
were made more poignant by the occasional shattered forms of
their ruined kin. If I'd reached them as quickly on foot as I have
in the narrative, maybe I'd have no story to tell. Or maybe I
would. Coincidence is the word we use when we can't see the
levers and the pulleys.

The bridge over the Ravine was scattered with vendors who
hadn't found a place in the market. Very few had awnings, or even
stalls; they spread blankets on the scorching sidewalks, and kept
their hats and shawls and parasols tilted against the sun. The heat
rose with the force of an explosion from the road surface below,
and the whole scene wiggled in a heat mirage. Near the center of
the bridge, I stopped to press my hands over my eyes, trying to
squeeze the aching out of my head, to replace it with a firm sense
of up and down, forward and back. I shivered. Maybe the sweat
was working, after all. Except that I didn't seem to be sweating
anymore.

A warm wind brushed past me. No, it was the sudden breeze of
people going by. So why didn't they *go*? I opened my eyes. A
skinny arm reached out, bony fingers slapped my shoulder and
spun me around. Faces splashed with black and gray, stubbly
scalps, a flurry of ragged clothing—I was at the eye of a storm of
Jammers.

I've heard them compared to rabbits in the spring. Maybe the
people who do are afraid of rabbits. The Jammers were pale, thin
as wire, and as they danced their arms and legs crisscrossed like
a chainlink fence of skin and bone. They weren't dressed for the
heat, but I understand Jammers don't feel it, or cold, or much of
anything besides the passion of the drum in their veins.

The nightbabies, who every sunset brought their parents'
money down from the tops of the towers or from the walled
compounds of parkland at the City's edge, would follow a cloud

f Jammers like gulls after a trash wagon. They'd try to copy the
teps. But that dance has no pattern, no repeats, and the caller is
ie defect or disease that makes the Jammer bloodbeat and
ie shared mind that goes with them. The hoodoos claimed the
ammers as kin, but I never heard that the Jammers noticed. The
ightbabies pestered them for prophecies, for any words at all that
iey could repeat down in the clubs to give them a varnish of artful
oom for a few hours, until something else went bang.

But I didn't open fortune cookies, or feed hard money to the
Weight-and-Fate in the Galería de Juegos, or seek out prophecies
rom the Jammers. No one could prove to me that the future was
lready on record. And if it was—well, the future is best friends
vith the past, and my past and I were not on speaking terms.
'rophecy was a faith for the ignorant and a diversion for the rich,
nd I was neither. The Jammers couldn't know anything about me.

"Infant creature," sang one of the Jammers, "ancient thing,
ong way from home."

Lucky guesses didn't count. I could be, when I wanted, as close
o invisible as flesh and blood came. Nobody Particular in a street
ull of the same. It didn't seem to be working now. "Blow off!"
 shrieked.

"Barely a step away from home," piped another voice.

"On one side." A third Jammer.

Fourth: "And on the other."

"Ain't got no home at all."

"Have you no homes? Have you no families?"

They all seemed to think that was hilarious. Given that they're
upposed to share a mind, it was the equivalent of laughing at
ne's own joke.

By that time I couldn't tell if I'd heard any voice twice. "Get
.way from me," I said, "or I'm going to hurt one of you." The
art of my mind that was doing my thinking, far away from the
est of me, was surprised by the screech in my voice. "Maybe two
f you," I added, just to prove I could.

"You are the concept immaculate," caroled a Jammer, shoving
1er/his hollow face up close to mine. The skin, between streaks of
;ray paint, was opaque and flaky-looking; the breath the words
ame out on was eerily sweet. "You are the flesh made word.
Whatchoo gonna do about it?"

"Which way you gonna step?"

"This is the step, this is it, right here."

I folded my arms around my head, as if to protect it from angry
irds. "Go away!" I screamed, and now even my thinking mind,

cowering in its corner, didn't care if every living soul on the bridge saw me, and knew I was afraid.

"Step!"

"Step!"

I was closed in by a fence of bones singing in the voices of crows, and if I didn't get out *now* it would club me to my knees with my own secrets. I shut my eyes and punched.

They whooped, and it was a moment before I realized I hadn't connected with anything. I opened my eyes. There was a gap in the circle, so I bolted through it, through the forest of pedestrians and parasols, and if I hadn't stumbled over a blanket full of pots and pans and tripped on the curb, I wouldn't be writing this. Or perhaps I would. Those levers, those pulleys . . . Amid the ringing of aluminum and cast iron, I hit the pavement on my backside, inches from the path of the tri-wheeler that was scattering foot traffic to either side. The driver honked, swerved, and slewed to a halt.

The Jammers were yelling and—cheering? Who knows what Jammers cheer about? Had I just taken the going-home step, or the no-home-at-all step? Or did it mean anything?

The trike carried full touring kit and weather shell, and had a mud-and-dust finish from someplace where there used to be roads. When the hatch popped, clots of dirt cracked away from the seams and fell to the blacktop, and the driver unfolded out of the opening with startling speed and economy. It was hard to tell what pronoun properly applied under the tinted goggles, the helmet, the crumpled coveralls, and the dust. She or he was squatting next to me before I had a chance to think of standing up.

"Are you hit?" Quick, sharp-cut words, the middleweight voice cracking out of roughness into resonance. The skin on the angular jaw, under the dirt, had never needed shaving, and when the stained leather gauntlet came off the right hand, the battered fingers seemed relatively light-boned. I hazarded a "she." Those fingers grabbed my chin before I could dodge them.

Everything tilted forty-five degrees. My vision was clear, but for a moment I felt as if I were sitting on a slant with nothing to hold on to. Then the world snapped back to true. The driver's dark goggles showed me two views of myself, slightly bug-eyed. What *was* this hangover from?

"No," I said. "You didn't hit me."

She peeled off the goggles, snapped them closed, and dropped them into her breast pocket. Her eyes were black, and surrounded by clean tanned skin where the goggles had sealed out the dust that the tri-wheeler's shell hadn't. She was frowning, as if I'd confessed to something more offensive than not having been hit by the trike. Then bland and lazy good nature replaced the frown— no, was held up in front of it like a mask on a stick. "I could make another pass, I suppose," she said thoughtfully. "No? But you seem so offended."

"Not by your aim, honest. Excuse me," I said, and stood up. A bit too fast. She grabbed me around the rib cage.

"Whoa, Paint, old girl. It's *that* way that's up. Put one foot there, and the other—that's it." She stepped back, and I swayed, but that was all. "Now, is there someone to carry you away, or are you doomed, like a public works project in cast cement, to grace this bridge forever?"

It was true that nothing I'd said or done up to then had indicated I ought to be allowed out alone. "No. I'll be fine, I'm just going into the Deeps." Now there was a mindless utterance. Still, if I could reach the Deeps, I would be all right. Or at least, the burrowing instinct told me so. I looked around and realized that the Jammers were gone. I must have stopped being interesting.

She raised her eyebrows: delicate inquiry. "The D—oh, down-town." She swiped at a trickle of sweat on her forehead with the back of her wrist, then snatched impatiently at her helmet, yanked it off. The hair underneath was tangled, wet with perspiration, shoulder length, and very black. "I suppose your career as a caryatid will have to be cut short," she said. "I'm going that way myself." Glorious smile, hiding nothing, signifying nothing.

I had a dirty shirt, a dirtier pair of jeans, and a pair of sneakers, none of which I intended to give up. I had a few useful things in my pockets, but none that would turn to gold in someone else's fingers. So riding would entail racking up an obligation to a formidable stranger. But the thought of sitting down, closing my eyes, and effortlessly reaching the Deeps—no, I had no credit here. "No thank you," I croaked. "It's a lovely day for a walk."

Breath burst out between her lips. "Oh, Our Lady of Martyrs. I missed the odor of sanctity on you. Get in."

She meant it as one kind of blasphemy. It fell on my ears as different, and worse. Where were the lovely, familiar cadences of the Deal, the careful weighing of goods and considerations, the call-and-response of buying and selling? Hers was an alien and heretical language, for all that I knew the words. She propelled me to the trike, and I tried not to go. But I really did want to sit down under the shell of the tri-wheeler where the sun couldn't get me, even if I paid with the rest of my life—

She stuffed me onto the back seat as if I were her laundry, straddled the front seat, and slammed the hatch. In a moment I was surrounded by engine noise and the rattle of the weather shell.

Well, one more for the debit side of the ledger. "I'll pay you back," I said as loud as I could, doubting it was loud enough.

She turned in the saddle, passed a quick glance over me, and said mildly, "Good God, with what?"

We crossed the Ravine. My silence was fulminating; I don't know what hers was. She drove quickly through the hollow-hearted warehouses, briskly past the copper-roofed riverbank palace and surrounding defensible wasteland of the Whitney-Celestin families. Pedestrians and bicyclists kept out of her way, except for once, when someone belatedly driving a pair of goats toward the mall market claimed right-of-way. Her Creole was idiomatic, at least on the obscenities. I felt the back end buck and slide on the gravel as she braked. Something flickered on the surface of a gauge in front of her. "Oh, shut up," she said, and whacked a button with her index finger.

The trike was, by its nature, intensely valuable; but it wasn't beautiful. There was a wealth of dust and dirt under the weather shell, and cracked rubber and scarred paint, but that was all. Everything in my field of vision had been repaired at least once, with varying degrees of success and duct tape. I let my head rest on the seat back and closed my eyes. The pain behind my eyebrows was dissolving my muscles.

"Do you plan to tell me where I'm going?" came the honed and honeyed voice from the front. "Or do we drift like the Ancient Mariner? You don't look like an albatross."

"Well, you haven't shot me," I said, alarming myself. "Yet, anyway." I opened my eyes and saw through the roof window the hard, hot sky and the ruined exterior of the Washington Hotel. "Go past the last gerbil tube and turn left."

"I beg your pardon?" she said with delight.

"The pedestrian walkways over the streets. Gerbil tubes."

She gave a shout of laughter. "Christ, they still call 'em that. I haven't—" She shifted down, and the trike whined like an eager dog. "Here?"

"Yeah." I had a moment of disorientation, watching the immense wet smile of the billboard boy on the front of the Power Authority Building sail by over my head. Conserve, by all that's holy. You damn betcha.

"So, what do you think of the quality of life here? Are all the women strong and all the men good-looking?"

Ignoring the unnerving mixture of good humor and ferocity in her voice, I said, "I take it you're new in town."

"You can damn well give it back, then. I grew up here. But I've been gone ten thousand miles or seven long years, whichever comes first. Give or take what you will."

For the first time it occurred to me that my chauffeur might not have all her outlets grounded. "I see. Stop when you get to the fence."

"I'd be a fool not to," she said, and I realized she'd downshifted as I spoke. "Unless I wanted to end up coarse-ground." I leaned forward for a view out the windshield, and found the red-rust chainlink edge of the Night Fair before us. Quiet now, it waited for sunset. "What is that?" she asked, nodding at the fence.

I chose understatement. "A market. I can get out here."

I expected her to pop the hatch. Instead, she cast a leisurely eye over the neighborhood. I was close enough to see the shallow lines at the corners of her eyes, the dense black sweep of her eyelashes, the precise shape of her lips. Her earlobes were pierced, but she wore no earrings. No rings, no cosmetics, no ornaments at all; no personal touches, no sentiment. She reminded me of my apartments.

As if she'd heard the thought, she asked, "You live here?"

"No," I said blithely.

When it became clear that I wasn't going to add to that, she killed the engine and looked over her shoulder again. I smiled at her. In defiance of logic, I felt worse now that the noise and vibration had quit. "My heavens," she said at last, "a fount of information. Loose lips sink ships." I heard the latch over my head open; she lifted the roof off us, swung out of the driver's seat, and offered me a hand. "At least, come tell to me your name."

Likewise your occupation, and where and whence you came, I thought, my startled mind dropping the rest of the quote into place like a puzzle piece. Not mad—or at least, endowed with an interesting education, as well. I avoided her hand by pretending I needed both of mine to get out of the back seat. By the end of the process, it was true, and I leaned against the trike while my vision cleared. "Sparrow," I said.

"Come again?"

"The name. And since you've had your will of me . . ."

"Hardly that," she replied, laughing. But I thought I saw a flash of pleasure in her face, to find that I knew the beginning of her quote. "Besides, mine's debased coin. One of sixty or so is hardly the same as one of a kind, an original, a work of art."

"Do you think I was born with a name like Sparrow?" I said, pretending mild offense.

She swung her leg back over the front seat, her face good-humored and distant, and thumbed the starter. The tri-wheeler broke alcohol-scented wind, loudly, and came back to life. Then she looked up at me, her eyes half-lidded, her mouth half-smiling. "We're all born nameless, aren't we? And the name we end with has only peripherally to do with our family tree."

I turned to go.

"Wait; I forgot," she continued. "You were saying you'd pay me for this?"

Well, of course she'd remember. Things could only get worse, after all. "That's the Deal."

She took another up-and-down survey of me. "What's that holding your hair back?"

It was a braided leather thong with a few jet beads in it. I'd forgotten it in my first inventory, but it wouldn't have mattered—it wasn't fair coin for a ride from the Bank. "It has a lot of sentimental value," I lied, reflexes kicking in anyway. "I couldn't part with it."

"Yes, you could." And she held out her hand, palm up.

Once again she'd chopped through the rituals of the Deal with brutal simplicity, razored the pelt of civilization off an already dubious exchange. I felt mauled. I yanked the thong out of my hair and dropped it into her hand. Her fingers closed over it with disturbing finality, and she nodded. "Just so. I'll treasure it always. Goodbye, Sparrow, and watch out for the cats." With another vivid smile, she closed the hatch.

I watched until she was out of sight, and even until the gravel dust had settled. Then I went carefully around the corner to Del Corazón, to cadge five minutes on the phone from Beano.

1.1: A surfeit of transactions

Del Corazón smelled of frangipani and leather and Fast Luck incense, and was suffocatingly warm. On any day but Friday, it would have been closed against the midday heat; but some business is best done when other people sleep. Del Corazón was open, if not precisely for me.

Beano was an animated wax statue in the dim light of the shop, gleaming from a fine, even coating of perspiration. Sweat darkened the front of his tight red tank top like blood. I asked my boon.

He laid both his clean white palms on the glass counter, between a tray of glow dermapaints and a rack of patent leather garters, and gave me a long pink look through ivory eyelashes. "Nothing's free," he said softly. Beano never raised his voice.

I felt a sudden, incautious relief. I had escaped out from under the fairy hill and returned to the real world, safe at last. Nothing was free. Even Beano was a danger I was used to. I gathered my strength and flung myself into the fray. "Well, and five minutes on the phone is nothing. I'm doing you a favor, in fact. Beano, *mi hermano*, if I'm on it, it can't ring."

"Ain't but a hundred phones in the City. Don't ring very often."

"Yes, but I know how you hate to be disturbed on Fridays." I twitched my nose like a cartoon rabbit. "Mmm. What an interesting new smell. Almost like . . ." I let my voice taper politely off. *Graceless*, I thought, *but functional*.

Beano accepted three currencies: hard money, flesh and blood, and knowledge. He preferred the first two. I mostly used the third, often pointed in the opposite direction from the one he had in mind. Usually with a lighter hand, but I felt like the saint with all the arrows, and it was undercutting my judgment. (I'd given him money, too, when I had it, when I could afford it. But never the second alternative, never skin. Never.)

"Almost like what?" he said.

I pursed my lips. "No, forgive me, it couldn't possibly have been. And if it was, I'm sure it's perfectly legal."

Beano leaned down and opened the back of the display case. I watched his hard white hands, their backs veiled with sparse but surprisingly long white hairs, their nails long and thick and filed sharp, moving delicately over the merchandise. It was like watching a cave spider. The fingertips passed over knives with blades inscribed in Spanish, over a necklace made from the stuffed skin of a rattlesnake, fangs intact, over a pair of engraved silver clasp bracelets welded together, back to back, their inside curves studded with little spines. I looked away.

"Here," Beano said, and set something on the counter. I turned back. It was a little box, covered in dark red velvet and lined in black satin. Ranked neatly on the satin were six bone needles, their broad ends still flanged and rough and recalling the joint they'd once been part of, their long points polished bright. "Do you know what these are for?" Beano asked.

"No."

"Do you want to know?"

I swallowed, because I couldn't help it, even though I knew he'd see me do it. "No."

He slammed the cash drawer and I jumped. He clenched his hands around the edge of the counter; the muscles in his forearm showed like rope. "Someday," he said, "maybe I'll show you."

"Does that mean I can use the phone today?"

Beano smiled slowly. "Sure. Sure you can."

It's possible to miss things you never had. Pay phones, desk phones, cellular phones, hot lines to Russia—they're taken for granted in the old movies. Whatever it took to get a phone installed in those golden days, it must not have been as complex as the City's system of influence, blackmail, and graft. And it must have resulted in something better than A.A. Albrecht's collection of scratchy party lines.

The phone was on the wall of a room behind the shop, where the extra stock was stored. The thing on the front of the rack was made of paper-thin black leather and lined with rose-colored silk. The material was so light that it hung shapeless, unidentifiable. A garment, probably. But thin leather cords hung from it at intervals, and a strand of wire coiled down from one side. I tried not to look at it as I listened to the ringing of the phone on the top floor of Sherrea's building. Eight rings. If no one answered—well, I could try again later. But that's not how I felt. My pass with Beano seemed to have used up all my insouciance; suddenly it was desperately important to hear Sherrea's voice, even if it was telling me to go to hell.

And at last, the life-giving click. "Eyeah?" Not one of her neighbors, but Sher herself. She sounded gritty beyond what the noisy connection would account for. Of course, I'd woken her; it was barely past noon.

"Sher? It's Sparrow," I half shouted into the tube.

"Mmh? Whaisit?"

"I need a reading."

"Ah, shit. Whattaya think, I took a Hippocratic oath?" There was a moment's pause before she said, "Call me when the moon's out."

"Sher—" My mouth opened to dicker, to offer her all the inducements, mythical and real, I could call to mind. In that moment, they seemed frail and faded. I shut my mouth and tried again, and found myself saying, "Sher . . . please?"

There was another crackling pause. "What's wrong?" Alarm and suspicion mixed in the words, with suspicion leading.

"I just woke up on the river flats. Between now and nine-ish last night, I have a big gap where my life used to be."

Silence on the other end. She bargained hard, but not as fast from straight out of bed. I could hear her trying to figure out how much my desperation was worth. "Uh-huh. And I can help."

"Maybe," I answered as the dickering impulse reasserted itself at last.

"*Chica*, this is gonna cost you."

"I'm good for it, Sher."

"What do you mean," she said ominously, "you're good for it?"

"One of the things that happened while I was down is that my money went away."

"Get some more."

"It's, ah, in my other pants. Which are locked up in the Night Fair."

"Where are you calling from?"

"Del Corazón."

"What'd you give *Beano*?"

"Threats and promises," I answered.

Sherrea said some things in a language I didn't recognize. Then she said, "It's a long walk, and you deserve it. Or are you planning to scam a lift out of some poor bastard?"

Twelve blocks and four flights. Well, after that nice restful ride . . . "I'm walking."

"You're gonna owe me, Sparrow. Got that?"

"Yes, I'll owe you." I felt suddenly, grovelingly, indecently grateful. Another debit for the ledger—but to Sherrea. I'd never known Sherrea to deal in flesh and blood.

"Get here in less than twenty minutes and I'll cook your flat ass for breakfast."

It took me thirty. I followed the route around the east flank of the Night Fair, where spindly locust trees cast a little shade. Sometimes I had to cling to the fence, when the curve of the world became too much to climb. Sometimes I just sat on the curb and panted and clutched my head. Two little black kids with the copper earrings of the Leopard Society threw fragments of paving at me. I scooped a handful of dust out of the boulevard plantings, spit into it, and closed my fingers over it, chanting at random, bastard Spanish, Creole, Lao. Then I stared at the kids. They made a great show of nonchalance, but they left. Which was nice; what was I going to do when I blew my handful of dust at them, and they didn't turn into lumps of clay, or get leprosy, or whatever they expected?

Away from the Fair, the traffic was heavier. I dodged bicycles and the occasional motorbike, as well as pedestrians more determined than I was, which was all of them. A silver sedan with smoked windows and the insignia of a northside greenkraal nearly put an end to my problems out in the middle of LaSalle. I jumped for the center island as the tires squealed. All's well that isn't over.

And all the while I watched for a filthy tri-wheeler, listening for its clotted growling. I had no idea what I'd do if I saw it.

Sherrea's building was smooth dirty yellow tile and rows of too-small windows, with a door that used to be glass and was now rather more practical armor-gray steel. It was built in the last century, when prosperity must have excused ugliness. The halls had once been blank and identical, the stairwells featureless tubes of concrete block and iron stair rail. Now living ivy worked its way toward the sky at the top of the stairs, where someone had turned a trapdoor into an open skylight; wisteria cascaded down to meet it from the roof. Things peered from the leaves: grotesque carved wooden faces, old photographs of people who all seemed to be smiling, faded postcards. A painted snake twined up the stair rail: red, black, and yellow on the first floor; blue, gray, and green on the second; purple, green, and orange on the third; blue, red, and yellow on the fourth. Fat candles stood in former floor lamps on every landing.

The stairwell doors were numbered, as if the residents wouldn't be able to keep track when they came home. The "4" was an elongated green man in a loincloth, one arm held out and bent. By the time I climbed that far, I was glad to see him. The hall behind him was painted with frescoes of vacant Roman courtyards. Sher's door was the middle of a fountain; I knocked on a painted nymph's tummy.

Sherrea had her face on, and layers and layers of black and purple clothing. The astral colors of sorcerers, she'd told me once. Her black hair was wet and had been combed flat to her head, but that wouldn't last long. There was a cigarette between her white-painted lips, smoked nearly down to the filter.

Her big dark eyes got bigger when she saw me, and it made her look almost as young as she was. "Sparrow. Blessed goddamn Virgin," she said around the cigarette. "Get in here and lie down."

"I've been lying down," I said, thinking of the river flats.

"Not in any way that was good for you. You've got some kinda shit in you, *chica*. What is it?"

Either she really is psychic, or I wasn't looking my usual sleek self. "I don't know. I wasn't there when it happened. I've probably got some sunstroke as well."

"*Oya*. Well, you're not gonna sit in my living room like that."

She drew me a bath. She was prepared to drop me in it herself, but I declined firmly. She insisted that I leave my clothes outside the bathroom door, so she could wash them (an unexpectedly practical gesture from Sherrea). I did, and locked the door.

Her bathroom was the place in the apartment that looked most like hers. Dark—probably where she put her makeup on. Paisley shawls, ferns shaped like visitors from outer space, incense, brass bowls. Mismatched glass jars (from jelly and peanut butter and salsa, elevated beyond their stations) full of dried leaves and flowers and powders, with a combined scent that called to mind medicines and hot metal. The mirror was like a pool half seen through vegetation; it was swagged with velvet draperies dimly printed with flowers that all looked carnivorous.

I was in the bath for a long time. I might have even fallen asleep; I know that when Sherrea pounded on the door and shouted, "Did you kill yourself in my goddamn bathroom?" I sat up with a jerk, my heart slamming in my chest like a moth against a window. Water lapped over the side and splatted on the floor. It wasn't warm water anymore, I noticed.

When I stood up out of the tub, my reflection appeared in the velvet-hung mirror like a doppelganger in a forest clearing. There was just enough light for me to see the discolored lump on the side of my cheek. The rest of my face was an interesting ghoulish hue. Bloodless. I decided that Sher was jealous; she always tried to look like a vampire in training. No wonder the woman on the tri-wheeler, she of the sixty or so names, had thought she'd run me down. I looked as if she had, and then backed over me, too. I found a comb among the glassware and worked it through my hair, but I couldn't find anything to tie it up with.

I had to wear a bedsheet out into the living room. The sheet was striped in red, white, and blue, and I wondered what Sher did with it when it wasn't wrapped around a damp customer. I couldn't imagine her sleeping on it. The living room had a reprocessed nylon/cellulose carpet in green, and walls like the outside of an eggplant, shiny and dark purple. I don't know what color the ceiling was; it was draped with a parachute, suspended in tentlike folds and billows. The genuine item, complete to the stains and scorches and holes it acquired during the festivities just before the Big Bang. I don't know why Sher had it there. I liked to think it was an icon of the second Fall, a new apple. There were things sewn to it, and hanging from it: a child's mitten, a blue rosary, a half-melted 45 rpm record, a clutch of shiny foil-cardboard stars.

On one wall was a print in overwrought colors showing Saint Bob holding a broken guitar. The furniture was all cushions, except for a sofa that sat too low because the legs were lopped off, and a metal cabinet lying on its side, painted black and draped with a tapestry that seemed to be not quite a view of the Last Supper. The shades were drawn, and the room was dim and smelled of candle smoke and flowers. I felt a little guilty, adding the red-white-and-blue sheet to all that ambience.

I went to the window and bent the blinds a little to look outside. The shadows had swallowed up the bottoms of the buildings; it was nearly sunset. "How long have I been here?" I wondered aloud.

"Forever," Sher answered from the kitchen. She came in and sat down on a heap of pillows on the other side of the metal cabinet. She had a new cigarette pinned in the corner of her mouth. She set a glass of water in front of me and sighed. "I had to cancel three other appointments. I don't know why the fuck you come and bother me. It's not as if you believed in any of it."

"Of course I believe in it. You, as someone who has more insight into me than I do, use the cards to reveal my sins to me and make me meditate on them. It used to be called psychotherapy."

"That's not what happens."

"Well, if it works, let's not fix it." That, at least, I could say with perfect sincerity. There was no point in arguing with Sherrea over how she did what I hoped she was going to do.

"There's no food in the place," she said.

"That's okay." I didn't think I could eat, anyway. My stomach felt like a sink drain full of hair.

"No, it's not. You ought to eat before a reading, and leave some as an offering. It draws the energies to you." She shrugged. "Well, screw the energies."

"No."

She glanced up, the young look on her pointy face again.

"Let's do it right." On one thumb, I found a rough bit of cuticle, at the base of the nail. I bit it until it bled. "Offering," I said, and held out my hand.

"*Santos*, Sparrow." But she whisked the tapestry off the cabinet/coffee table, and from somewhere in all the black-and-purple, she produced a wad of white scarf. When she laid it down, it fell open to show the deck of cards inside. "Let a drop fall on the table—no, over there on the corner. I don't want it on the scarf." I squeezed a decent-sized drop onto the very edge of the metal, and blotted the rest on one of the sheet's red stripes.

She mashed her cigarette out on the side of the cabinet and began to shuffle the deck. It arced between her hands, over and over, two parts folding into one like a flower blooming backward in time-lapse. "Wish for something. D'you think maybe you were on polygons?"

"If I had any idea, I wouldn't have had to come to you."

She fanned the cards on the table, flipped one out of the deck onto the scarf, shuffled again. Page of Swords.

She said she'd found the deck in a *botánica* in Alphabetland. It was luridly colored, worse than Saint Bob, and the figures moved when you tipped the cards, like printed cardboard toys and kitschy postcards. The iconography was a schizoid blend of Christian saints, African deities, and pre-Bang SouthAm pop stars. The Page of Swords was Joan of Arc at the stake, holding a sword over her head. The flames leaped and Joan's head nodded up to look at heaven, down to study hell. "You don't know what you took. You really black out completely during these things?" Sher asked.

"I told you I do."

"You've told me lots of dumb shit. That was the seventeenth

card. Whatever you just wished for, you can't have. Cut the deck."

I wondered what it had been.

She snapped cards down on the scarf, growing the layout like a crystal. Joan of Arc's suffering was overlaid upside down by Death as Baron Samedi, all bones and grin and tall black hat, with a victim under each arm: a fat white man in a pinstripe suit, and an old black woman almost as thin as the Baron. The Baron opened and closed his mouth—laughing, I'd guess—and the victims flapped their arms. Beside him went a card showing a naked brown prettyboy holding a violent yellow solar disc in front of his hips. The rays of the sun rippled when the card moved, which seemed like a waste of technology.

Snap—an overdressed black man juggling two bags, each marked with a white star. That one was upside down, too. Snap—a grinning masked figure stepping into shadow at the back of the card, a fan of five bloody swords over his shoulder. In the foreground two more thrust, point downward, in a puddle of gore with no apparent source. Snap—a man and woman dressed in movie-medieval, she in white, he in red, hands clasped; a huge, well-fed cherub like a scrubbed pink pterodactyl hovered above. Snap—a nearly naked blond woman with a quarterstaff, blocking the attack of six ninjoids, also with staves. Snap—a dark-haired, dark-tanned man or woman, lying on his or her back on a beach. The posture I'd awakened in on the river flats. He or she had ten long swords for company, the points in the palms of the hands, the knees, the belly, the groin, the breasts, the forehead, and through the open mouth. I stopped paying such close attention. Sherrea laid three more cards down.

"Swords," she muttered, tapping her long purple index fingernail on the spiral made by the first seven cards. "Swords here in the country of flesh. There's fighting over this, has been and will be."

Between me, myself and I? I wanted to ask.

"Death, the Sun, the Lovers. Lots of major arcana. Your future's controlled by others. There's powerful people playing with it. You're gonna have to fight to get it back. And over here"—she slid the fingernail down the silk next to the upright row of four cards next to the spiral—"this is the country of truth. There's the Devil, the Star, the Tower. In the country of truth, where your spirit lives, your life still isn't your own. Other stronger spirits, or maybe gods—they've got the say in what happens to you."

A nice metaphor for my blackouts.

She touched the juggling man. "Something got out of balance in the past, yours or somebody's. Stuff that's supposed to shift around, change, grow—it's all gone stagnant and sick."

Sherrea looked up, but it was a blind look. "The air's not moving around you," she said, "but there's a wind that's trying to blow. Somebody's gotta pull the windbreak down." Her voice was changing. Now she wasn't looking at me at all; she was looking at the tops of her eye sockets. All I could see were the whites. I rocked slowly back from the cabinet.

"Sit still, *muñequita*," said the new voice. It was lower than Sher's, and thick with an accent that ought to have been Hispanic and wasn't. Sherrea's lips, making the words, moved differently than they usually did. Her face looked suddenly much older. "You afraid of me?"

Muñequita meant—I felt the infinitesimal shift of new knowledge. *Little doll.* I shivered. "I wouldn't say that. Not yet, at least. Who are you?"

A hooting laugh. "Nobody *you* know. Listen now. It's time you was doin' what you supposed to. You got work to do, and all you do is look out for your own self. You not ready to do your work. That's bringin' danger on you, and all the ones bound to you."

"Nobody's bound to me," I said firmly.

"You think that? Where you been, sittin' in a hole? You wait 'til *le Chasseur* comes. But you dangle those lives over the fire and that's all for you. I give you warning."

Sherrea's lips had drawn back from her nicotine-stained teeth in a big nasty smile. I stood up carefully. "Well, thank you. I'll be going, then."

"Sit down." I can't describe that voice. I sat down. "But you can save your ass. You gotta learn to serve, and let your own self be fed by the spirits. Serve the *loa*, serve all the people, and go hungry and cold yourself. Then all the parts of you gonna come together and make you well. But strong people want to keep chained what you gotta make free. There's gonna be blood, and fire, and the dead gonna dance in the streets. But if you give what I tol' you, the light of change'll shine in the tower of shadows."

I felt like someone who's gone to get a wart removed, and been told he needs radiation and chemo. I am not good at hungry and cold. "So what is it that I have to do?" I said.

"Donkey. Are you a little baby that I have to tell you right from wrong? You feel every day what you have to do, and you make like you don't. But don't ask what's in it for you. It's the ten of swords."

"All I want is to quit doing downtime."

Whatever was using Sherrea's mouth hooted. "My brother already said he'd help with that. You know my brother? Uncle Death?"

I clutched at my knees. "What am I trying to accomplish, at least?"

"To open the way, little donkey!"

"What're you frowning about?" Sherrea grumbled, pinching the bridge of her nose. She was back. Her eyes were where they ought to be, her face was her own.

"Is this your way of teaching me that I get what I pay for?"

"You don't like the way I read, don't ask me to do it."

"I don't mind your reading. It's your little friends coming to visit that gives me a sharp pain."

She was sullen. "So you got a visit from Tia Luisa, huh? Better clean up your act, then. That's for when the querent is in shit up to the chin."

She put out a hand to sweep up the cards. I put two fingers on hers, lightly, and let go. "Sher. I'm sorry. But four times, it's happened. I get some kind of physical trauma, not even enough to knock me out, and zip—I wake up someplace else, with the closing credits rolling, and I can't remember the rest of the movie. Something in my head is broken."

"Most people's heads are broken, Sparrow. So what?"

"So I need help. And I'm scared." That last escaped before I got my mouth closed.

She scratched her lower lip with her fingernail, watching me. "Okay," she said finally. "I'll try a clarification."

She picked up the cards, all except Joan of Arc, and shuffled them. "Cut," she told me, and I did. She picked up the piles and began to flick down cards. And slowed, and stopped, finally, with the fourth card, the grinning figure with the fan of swords over his shoulder. The third card had been the black juggler. The second had been the man with the sun. The first, Baron Samedi. Sherrea's hand hovered over the deck, not quite touching the next card. Then she pulled it, quickly, and slapped it down. The red-and-white lovers. She raised her eyes to my face. "Don't fuck with me," she said.

"Funny. I was going to say that to you." And I really was. I was angry. My vulnerability had slipped out into her hands, and she was playing me with it. I've seen card tricks; the randomness of a shuffled deck is an overrated quantity. But Sherrea's eyes were a little wild, and her hands were graceless and uncertain. In a haphazard flurry, she laid the rest of the pattern. All the same.

We sat in the dim room, staring at the ugly pictures. I was holding as still as I could, so that none of them would do their foolish dance of transformation. But my nose itched, and it made Baron Samedi laugh.

"I guess you better do whatever it was I told you to do," Sher said at last, and began picking up the cards, slowly, all her facility with them disappeared.

"You mean, nothing concrete?"

She shook her head. "If you can't *act* the way the cards tell you, then *react* that way. Make your decisions when it's time."

She lifted the last card, Saint Joan. Under it, at the precise center of the white silk scarf, was a spot of fresh, vivid red.

"Do what you were told to do." Sherrea's voice was thin. "And don't come back here until you're sure you're doing it." She lifted her face, hard as a marble goddess's. "The next move is yours."

I found my shirt and pants in her kitchen, stiff from the clothesline. On top of them was a thin leather cord with a little pendant made out of dark wood: two V shapes, overlapping point to point. I locked myself in the bathroom again and dressed, and after a moment shrugged and dropped the thong around my neck and under my shirt. The pendant felt just like wood.

When I left, Sherrea was still sitting in the living room, in front of the blood-marred white scarf.

Card 2

Crossing

The Sun

Waite: The transit from the light of this world to the light of the world to come. Consciousness of the spirit.

Crowley: Collecting intelligence. The lion, the sparrowhawk. Alcohol is his drug. His magical power is the red tincture, the power of acquiring wealth. Glory, gain, riches, triumph, pleasure; shamelessness, arrogance, vanity. Recovery from sickness.

2.0: A place for everything, and everything wired in place

Happiness, in the land of Deals, is measured on a sliding scale. What makes you happy? A long white silent car with smoked-glass windows, with a chauffeur and a stocked bar and two beautiful objects of desire in the back seat? An apartment in a nice part of town? A kinder lover? A place to stand that's out of the wind? A brief cessation of pain? It depends on what you have at the moment I ask that question, and what you don't have. Wait a little, just a little. The scale will slide again.

The beauty of the Night Fair was that no matter how one defined happiness at a given moment, it was usually available there. The price was negotiable, within limits. That's why the Night Fair endured: because we never stop needing something to make us happy.

The sun had set in a smear of indigo and orange when I reached that chainlink border. I twined my fingers in the fabric of the fence and felt bits of rust grind away under my grip. I was in my own country again. Here there were no gods but the Deal, no spooks but those that could be conjured for money at the buyer's request. I was safe from Sherrea's riding spirits, if not my own.

I traveled the fence line to the nearest of the three gates and found it open. The Night Fair was alive from sunset to full dawn. At any other time it was locked and silent, and no one climbed the fence.

What is that? she'd asked, and, *A market*, I'd told her. And an ocean is a large body of water, and hearts pump blood. The subtleties are lost.

What the Night Fair had been before I knew it, I couldn't say. Now it was ten blocks of the City, in various states of repair. There were places where buildings had been knocked down or burnt away, and in those cavities and in the streets were the market

35

and carnival places, the booths, the games of skill and chance, the
food and drink vendors, the rides, the freak shows. For less easily
granted wishes, one had to look to the buildings. There was no
directory, no skyway map, no Guide to Retailers. If one wanted
something in the buildings, one had to want it enough to go
looking. I was as confident of the Night Fair as any of its patrons,
but I went carefully when I left the streets.

I was so hungry I felt transparent, so thirsty that my own saliva
rasped in my throat. But that was a state I could change, with a
little currency. I could trudge to the other side of the Fair—but that
was a long trudge. Besides, I wanted to feel the Deal in action. I
had enough concentration left to do a little magic, if I could spot
someone who'd shell out for it.

The Fair was half-asleep, so early in the evening; some of the
stands were empty, and the ones that weren't were gaudy islands
without their proper context. The smell of cooking-oil lamps
seemed strong without the stronger smells of food and fuel and
humanity to bury it. But in a courtyard I found the kind of thing
I was looking for, or in this case, listening for. A fat Oriental kid
was running a duckshoot, and trying to catch custom with the
City-run all-dance broadcast channel playing through an old
Carvin PA speaker. Every bass note had the crunchy sound of a
ripped speaker cone.

He looked hopeful when I approached, less so when I pointed
to the speaker and said, "Sounds bad."

His mouth turned down at the corners. "Sounds okay to me."

"Ah. I guess you won't want it fixed if there's nothing wrong
with it." I half turned away.

"Why do you say it sounds bad?" he asked quickly, and I knew
it was going to be all right. The passage of arms was begun.

"Well, last time I heard that jam, the guy playing the giant piece
of cellophane wasn't with them."

"You mean that little noise?" He shrugged, and rather well,
too. "It ain't much. Nobody but an audiofreak'd notice."

"Must be an audiofreak convention in town. People are
crossing to the other side of the street."

He scowled. No patience. With more patience, he could have
been good at this. "What would it take to fix a little thing like
that?"

"The right person, and twenty hard bucks."

The kid spit to his left. A ward against liars. "Hell, I could get
another whole speaker for twenty."

"You couldn't get one of those for less than a hundred, and

you'd have to find one first. And you know it." Oh, he could have gotten something for twenty bucks. Maybe even that speaker, from someone who didn't appreciate its solid, deep-throated sweetness.

"Five," he said, one syllable of pure bravado. "Soft."

"Kid," I said, smiling kindly and leaning on the counter between the popguns, "have you ever heard the joke about the plumber and the little teeny hammer?" He was beaten. I could tell by his eyes. "Tapping, fifty cents; knowing where to tap, fifty dollars? Now, because I always enjoy telling a joke, I'll give you a deal: fifteen, soft." I should have held out for ten hard, but visions of carbohydrates were beginning to dance in front of my eyes.

It was a little tougher job than the plumber had. But I got the grille off and the cone out, and I carried a few things in my pockets that nobody else would have recognized as valuable. A roll of heat-shrink fiber tape, for instance; good for strain relief on cords, for covering spliced wire, and for mending tears in any stretched material. I covered the rip in the cone with a narrow piece and borrowed matches from the kid to shrink it tight. The speaker was not as good as new; one more fine and irreplaceable thing had slipped out of the world, and the world, as usual, hadn't noticed. But a normal human being could now listen to it with teeth unclenched. At least, if said party liked City broadcast.

I wandered off with a light head, a sense of duty done, and fifteen folding City-made dollars. The first food vendor I came upon did Chinese. After six pot-stickers and three cups of lemon-balm tea, I was able to see the world with less prejudice. After another block, a few smoked pork ribs, and a skewer of batter-fried vegetables, my sense of proportion was restored. I tallied the day's accomplishments. Today, after an impressively bad start, I had saved the life of one twelve-inch speaker cone, fed myself, and got all the way to Sherrea's under my own (I granted myself some poetic exaggeration) power.

Where I'd been made no wiser, and been told besides to start shoveling or don't show my face again. A fine friendly gesture. How was I to get my ordure in order if she couldn't even give me useful clues? My theories about her mind reading were a little shaken, too; I refused to believe that the afternoon's display of amateur theatricals had come out of my head.

In the deep, gritty voice that, looking back, I couldn't call male or female: *That's bringin' danger on you, and all the ones bound to you.* I wasn't bound. That would have been flying in the face of good sense, and I tried not to do that. Surely the pure voice of my subconscious would have a better handle on me than that. Sherrea—or her friend—seemed to declare that sacrifice was the road to salvation; but I wanted to fix a busted head, not a rotten soul.

But don't ask what's in it for you. It's the ten of swords. The card with the dark-haired figure on the sand, the upright swords.

I noticed that I had finished eating; or at least, I didn't seem to want any more.

By then, the joint was, as they say, jumping. Money, bright and folding, hard and soft, was running in its well-worn channels. Objects and services were passing from one hand to another, and by that alchemy were turned to gold, purifying with each transaction. The streets fizzed like charged water with noise, motion, and change. Here before me was the familiar exercise of my faith, the Deal. The exchange was only its sacrament, the symbol of its larger principles. Nothing Is Free. One way or another, you will pay your debts; better you should arrange the method of payment yourself.

This was what the woman on the tri-wheeler had blasphemed against, and why I feared her. Because she didn't know the Deal.

The Odeon was open. Under its optimistic, badly lettered sign, block-printed posters taped to the painted-over shop windows promised showings of *The Lady Vanishes*. I dropped my gaze to the doorway where Huey was sitting in his folding chair, taking tickets, and I shook my head and grinned at him. He rolled his eyes. This was shorthand for (in my case), "Huey, I happen to know that's a bad third-generation dub of the lousy non-Hitchcock remake that you're going to show on your crummy nineteen-inch monitor with a misaligned yoke and out-of-whack color," and (in his case), "So what? You don't come to no storefront vid parlor, anyhow." This is a conversation one only needs to have once; after that, it reels out again on fast forward whenever necessary, without further rehearsal.

In front of the Odeon's shabby blandishments, a herd of nightbabies clumped like a blood clot in the vein of the sidewalk. They weren't going in, oo dear meee, nooo. Only the crawlers do vid parlors. But it's sooo Deep ambie, y'knoow?

They were in High Savage, by which I decided they were from the greenkraals at the City's edge. The tide was going out on Savage; in the towers, Rags was the waxing mode. The nearest nightbaby swayed out in front of me as I came closer. She had a mud-painted face, multicolored mud hair, and an epoxy bone in her nose—or a real one, maybe, but that was considered gauche in some circles.

"Ooo, loook! It's a preeecious bit of street-meat! Let's take it hooome and waaash it, and see what it iiis."

That provoked a unison giggle from the group. I'd probably sold things to their parents. "Cinder in your eye," I said, held up my palm, and blew across it at her face. She dodged, and I laughed.

She gave me a quick, narrow-eyed look—wondering if she'd been had? She couldn't have been sure. The blood of the Horsemen had trickled over the continent—still did, though the Horsemen were dead. And where that blood was, where those genes came to rest, a skill might sprout: Sherrea's mind reading; the placing of a nonexistent cinder in someone's eye. But I had no inheritance from the wicked riders of the mind.

The mud furrowed and cracked around her eyes as she stared at me. Light reflected into her face for a moment, and I saw that those eyes were a peculiar flat, hard gray. She seemed older than I'd first thought, bones planed with years. "Use it while you can, honey," she murmured, so angry she forgot to drool over her vowels. I felt her watching me as I walked away.

I passed Banana Sam's Beer Garden on my way up-Fair, and heard a familiar half whistle, half call, high-low-high. And Cassidy's voice: "Little bird! Keeper of the fire! Come drink with meeeeee!"

He was already low in his chair, flushed and untidy. His wide eyes sank into their bruised-looking sockets like clams dug into the sand, and the bones below them lurched up against the skin as if to counterbalance. Frail strands of bleached gold hair had slid out of his queue and fallen around his face and ears. The pitcher in front of him had maybe an inch and a half left in it.

Resigned, I came to his table. "What's this 'little bird' riff, Cass?"

"The sparrow," he said, smug, dignified, and clownish. "Guarded fire for the Devil, 'til Swallow ripped it off and gave it to the walking dung beetles who started callin' 'mselves Mankind."

Cassidy always talked like a Taoist mystic with a lobotomy when he was drunk. "I take it tonight we're on the Devil's side?" I asked as I sat down. I poured the last of the beer into his glass, and drank off half.

"Hey!"

"You don't need it. Besides, you invited me."

"For company. You can damn well buy your own suds." He peered at me, as if through fog. "I don't owe you any, do I?"

I considered my answer carefully. But lying, after all, would have been a sin. "No," I said.

Cassidy looked long at the empty pitcher. "Well, hell. Make it a present, then."

I set the glass and its last swallow of beer on the table. What was left in my mouth tasted suddenly like soap. I leaned back in the uncomfortable wire chair, away from the table, from Cassidy's gesture, from him. I felt the need to wound. "I thought you were going to stop drinking at Midsummer." The picador rises dancing to his toes—*thump.*

The unfocused camaraderie vanished from his face and voice. "'S not Midsummer anymore." His sunken eyes were bright with resentment.

"Just curious. I don't care if you drink." *Thump*—a second pointed sentence between the shoulders of Cassidy's amour propre. No doubt the picador also thinks of it as self-defense.

Cassidy frowned down at his knotty fingers. There was a freshly scabbed cut on the back of his left hand, and I wondered, with a jolt of disgust, if he remembered how he'd come by it. In a few seconds that thought came back in my face. Well.

"How've you been?" I said, in lieu of apology.

He shrugged. "I've been like me, I guess. Like last night, only sweatier."

"Did I see you last night?" I asked after a moment. My spine felt as if someone was about to hit me there.

"Course you did," he said, looking hurt. "I bought you a drink."

"That was nice of you. Where were we?"

"The Merciful Trap. Don't you remember?"

"Let's pretend I don't."

He'd had too much beer to notice the way I said it. "And you think I have a drinking problem. Yeah, you were burnin' it last night. Dancing, buying rounds. You asked the band for a bunch of songs I never heard of." He smiled at me. "They threw you out when they poured one round more than you could swap for."

He hadn't had too much beer. He must have watched my face shut up during that recitation, and known that it was an even trade for my unkindness. "Ah. I'm surprised you'll be seen with me after that."

"I'm savin' your reputation," he said. "Hey—will you introduce me to the redhead? The one with the shoes?"

"What redhead?" I asked, frightened.

"Oh, hell. You really don't remember? Or are you just being a shit? When they tossed you at The Mercy, she went with you. And the guy dressed in gray, too, with the silvertones. They were worried about you."

I wished I'd had the sense to be worried about me. But I couldn't have. I hadn't really been there. "What was I drinking?"

"Beer."

"Was I taking anything else?"

"How should I know? You weren't even drunk when they threw you out. Just kind of warmed up. You were maybe a little crazy, but not like you were dosed."

"Such fine distinctions. If I wasn't drunk, why don't I remember anything?"

That startled him. "I don't know. Hey, are you just saying you don't remember so you don't have to introduce me to the redhead?"

I smiled. "Me? The one who guarded fire for the Devil? Would I do a thing like that?"

"Like what?" said Dana from behind me, in her whiskey-liqueur voice. Of course; what was Leander without Hero? Cassidy was drunk, so it followed that Dana must be within striking distance.

She trailed a hand across my shoulders as she came around the table, sat in the chair between us, and laid her palm over Cassidy's long, sharp-boned fingers. Dana couldn't talk to anyone without touching. For someone like me, an acquaintance with Dana was a torture akin to water dripping slowly on one's forehead.

"Cassidy thinks he's found a chink in my obliging nature."

"Shut up, Sparrow," Cassidy said. Oh, Cassidy. I could have told her it was *three* redheads, and Dana wouldn't have cared.

I'd have said Dana took her style from Bette Davis movies, if I thought she'd had access to them. Maybe she practiced in front of a mirror. Those Dana had access to. Her suit was metallic brown, fitted close to her tiny waist and just-ripe hips. Her silvery-blond hair fell forward over one shoulder, the end knotted off halfway down her breast with a black velvet ribbon. Her skin was smooth and faintly, rosily tan, all over her face and throat and disappearing between the lapels of her jacket. She had a super-natural artifice about her that made one want to pour water over her head just to test the strength of the illusion.

It occurred to me suddenly that it was a remarkably expensive

illusion. The fabric and tailoring of the suit suggested the money
that the nightbabies, in their mud and rags, pretended not to
have. What was it that Dana did, when she wasn't disturbing
Cassidy?

"So, did you see me out carousing last night?" I asked her.

"No. Were you?"

"Cassidy says so."

"Then it must be true." She riffled a fingertip over Cassidy's
jutting knuckles, as if they were piano keys. Cassidy looked
overwrought and a little ill. Alcohol and unrequited love will do
that. Dana's attention remained on me, the intensity turned up
full. She'd caught a whiff of the bizarre; her nose never failed her.
"Did you have a bang time? You don't usually get radded up, do
you?"

I would *not* tell Dana about the blackouts. The genuinely
freakish always moved Dana to pity. She would exclaim over me;
she would advise me, with relish; she would recommend the
counsel of her friends, who were legion; and worst, she would pet
me. Then Cassidy would probably be sick on the table. "I woke
up today feeling as if I'd missed my own funeral," I said. True,
so far as it went.

Dana shook her head. "Is something troubling you? You
shouldn't zero yourself out, sugar. You could dig yourself a hole
awful fast." She clutched my shoulder. "You're so thin already."

"Like coiled steel."

She let go. Her coral liptint was faintly luminous; when she
pressed her lips together, they made a glowing rosebud in her
face. "Well, at least if you ruin your health, you'll have your
friends."

"Whew," I said.

But she wasn't done. Now she was squinting at the bruise on my
face. "And where's that from?"

"I walked into a door."

Her eyebrows lifted. "I only want to help."

"Then it's too bad you weren't there when I met the door."

Cassidy, who had looked hurt, now looked affronted as well.
He was busy, since he had to be affronted for two; Dana wasn't
doing her share. I hadn't the heart to watch him work so hard for
long. "Well, it's been an interesting day, and I'm past helping,
that's all. I got sunstroke, rode around with a madwoman,
square-danced with Jammers, and was spoken to in tongues. Bare
civility is the best I can do."

I spotted my mistake, and cursed myself for a boiled-brained idiot. Dana's eyes, and Cassidy's, were opened wide. Cassidy's lips parted as if there were a membrane of soap between them and he meant to blow it into a bubble. But Dana got the words out first.

"*Jammers!* Sugar, did they say anything?"

I closed my eyes, took a breath, let it out. "I don't remember," I said.

Cassidy shook his head, very grave. "You should try to. Jammers are kind of like holy innocents. They say what the universe wants you to hear."

My pal, the helpless drunk, wanted to interpret my oracle. Maybe he was giving up on interpreting Dana. I steepled my fingers and studied them, to keep from meeting Cassidy's eyes, and said brightly, "Is there anyone in this damn place taking orders, or is it help yourself tonight?"

"Oh, Sparrow, come on," Dana said. "Was it scary?"

Well, that was my opening. I could make a great story out of it—Dana would love it.

"It was like walking through a cloud of human-sized gnats. It was annoying. They stink." That would have gotten me nine eggshells on my doorstep from a hoodoo, but I didn't think the Jammers would mind slander. And Dana's sense of romance could never tolerate bad smells.

"Y'know," Cassidy said, "the Jammers are the only people who aren't alone." I looked at him, but his eyes were on some middle distance over my shoulder. "I mean, none of us can know what's going on in each other's heads. We all agree"—he shrugged, hunting words—"on what color the sky is. But how do we know we're seeing the same color? That's lonely, man, that's *cold*." He shook his head.

"But the Jammers are supposed to be in each other's heads all the time, right? So there's always somebody who knows exactly what it's like." He stopped, and blinked.

It was one of those moments of genuine, unalloyed thought that sometimes came on him, appearing out of his mental mists like synaptic ghost ships. I found that my gaze had fallen on Dana, and that she was watching me with the idle patience of a cat.

I stood up. "I have to go. I'm sure you two have a lot to talk about." Cassidy's bleak and startled face was a rebuke. I pushed the glass across the table to him and strode out, heading up again.

I didn't get far; Dana's confiding, confining hand on my arm

stopped me. "Sparrow," she said, low against the background
noise of the Fair. "You can't be alone all the time, honey. If you'r
in some kind of trouble, and I can help, you come to me, hear?

Perfect skin, flawless hair, costly clothes, and the time t
involve herself in other people's business. If throwing money an
influence at the problem could solve it, she probably *could* help
"Thank you, Dana," I said. "But there's really nothing wrong.
This time when I moved off, she didn't follow.

Maybe secrets are toxic to the organism. Maybe, when kep
long enough, they always produced the intellectual and emotiona
nausea that had suddenly made me want to match Cassidy drin
for drink. Born alone in our skulls; living alone there; dying alone
With the grave, then, to keep the secrets. For a moment I'
wanted, desperately, not to be alone, the way people in hiding fo
too long will dash out into daylight, in front of the guns, just t
end the waiting.

I walked through the Fair: shrill and brittle and tawdry,
savorless night with anger lying just under its curling edges. /
while ago this had been my country, and I'd returned to it relieve
and glad. Now it was as welcoming as a carnival midway. Give u
your money and get out. Strings of bulbs giving half their rate
light reflected in puddles of what might have been water
Hucksters called from their booths as if everyone's first name wa
Hey.

*There's gonna be blood, and fire, and the dead gonna dance ii
the streets.* The dead should feel right at home.

I bought a ticket on the GravAttack, hoping that speed and spin
fear and adrenaline, would wash me clean. The closed whee
smelled of rust, sweat, and hot alcohol from the generator; m
fellow rubes shrieked; pitch-dark alternated with flashes of light
and centrifugal force mashed my back into the padded bay. I fel
as if the wall of my body cavity would give way and let my organ
out—but my mind wasn't so fragile. My mood survived the rid
undisturbed.

So I unfolded my last paper portrait of A. A. Albrecht an
bought a ride on the Snake's Tail from a vivacious man dressed in
tinsel. The drops fell on my tongue from the little tube in his hand
It tasted like spearmint and red pepper. In five minutes the Nigh
Fair stretched from sea to sea, shining.

I was turning the pages of a rotting paperback at a junkstal
(each newsprint page crackled brightly as I turned it, like static
electricity in the dark) when a hand closed over my arm. "Hello!
said its owner. "How are you?"

He was tall, with a great, fine white smile that was only a little enhanced by the Snake. He wore a lovely silver-gray suit, like a politician or a talk-show host. His hair, which curled, was a delicate pink, like the inside of a shell. His skin was fine-textured and pale. Over his eyes and ears he wore a pair of silvertones, which would be making his world as bright and beautiful as mine, except that his would be real and mine was a hallucination. My spike of jealousy confused me. So did the feeling that I was supposed to recognize him. "All recovered?" he asked, his fingers tight on my wrist. He was pulling me away from the junkstall.

I didn't recognize him—but of course, this was the man in gray that Cassidy had mentioned. Still in gray twenty-four hours later. An affectation. I scorned affectation. I tried to scorn him.

"No, no," he said, laughing. "Myra'll have my ass if you scoot away now. We've got us a conversation to finish." He pulled me toward the middle of the pavement. Why was he laughing? He was hurting my wrist. At the end of the block where the crowd thinned, I could see a woman standing under a pair of oil lamps. Her hair was the color of dark cherries.

The air went out of my lungs. It had been knocked out, I realized. Riding the Snake's Tail does that, sometimes, reverses cause and effect. I was sitting in the street, and the man in the silvertones was no longer attached to my wrist. Now he was holding on to someone else, who seemed to be having trouble standing up. He had stopped laughing. The someone else was creasing the lapels of the lovely gray jacket, but other than that, I got no clear impression of him. Next to all that silver and gray and fragile pink, the newcomer seemed like a dim spot on my eye. Down the block, the woman with the cherry-colored hair was coming toward us.

"Jesus, I'm awfully sorry," said the newcomer, who was still having trouble standing up. "I really don't—oh, jeez! God, I'm *really* sorry."

The man in gray had fallen. A noise like a blast of whiteness came from behind me, and I realized it was a truck horn. Then the truck was between me and the man in gray, and the other one, who'd been having trouble standing, was half dragging me across the street.

I was beginning to feel like a snatched purse. The Snake was tapering off a bit, and I could almost conceive of events outside my mind that might be urgent, so I pulled against his grip.

"Stop that," said my new companion, in such an ordinary voice that I did. He hurried me up four steps and pushed me down into

a hard seat. Just before a pair of doors flew open before me ont
darkness, I realized I was in a car for the haunted house ride.

I tried to bolt over the side, but the stranger pulled me back.

"Don't worry," said his voice, unaccountably pleased, near m
ear. "There's nothing here that's not dead."

2.1: You have to invite them in

A skeleton dropped, phosphorescent with grave mold, in front of us, and was snatched away just before its toes brushed my face. The man next to me said, as if he hadn't noticed, "You don't want to go back out there yet, anyway. Those two'll be right behind us."

The corridor ahead was misty white with webbing; a hundred little movements, of things the size of my fist, scuttled in the haze. I ducked just as the car plunged sharply about four feet. It put my stomach directly under my tonsils, but we passed untouched under the things. I was reasonably sure they weren't real, anyway.

The car flung around a corner, where a woman in white rotated at the end of a rope. Her face was swollen, purple, and authentic. My self-control was feeling gnawed at. "What is this?" I said.

"It's a rescue. We kinda slow tonight? Here comes our stop."

The tunnel in front of us was an illusion, painted on another door that swung open and pitched us into a hall of mirrors. The stranger yanked me out of the car as it took a ninety-degree turn, and I fell full-length on the floor. I could hear the next car hurtling through the doors, so I scrambled. A mirror yielded before us; I caught a glimpse of us before it folded back, our faces strange and wild in the dim light. Then we passed through stuffy blackness and out into the sharp-edged gloom of the Night Fair.

We ran for perhaps six blocks. I had no choice; his hold on my wrist was adamant, though not painful. We stopped when I stumbled for the third time, my breath sore in my windpipe. We'd reached the chainlink border of the Fair. He let the wire stop him and rolled until his back was against it, propped up on the fence. He was panting, too, and clutching his left side. His eyes were closed, his face set in concentration. I dropped onto the curb and took inventory of him. Not every stranger rescues me from the pink-haired, bug-eyed monsters. Or whatever he'd just done.

47

He was a little sharp-featured, but a wide mouth and dark thick eyebrows saved his face from austerity. His hair was foxy brown, glossy in the oil-lamp light. I could imagine people telling him he was handsome. Bad for his character, probably. He had a tapering, athletic look, and long legs. I was surprised at how much the six blocks seemed to have taken out of him. He looked more durable than that. He wore a polished cotton jacket in the style the SouthAm mercs had affected, back before the Big Bang. It might have been that old, too; the glossy finish had dimmed along every surface subject to friction.

He opened his eyes, and they seemed to take a moment to clear, as if he'd been in pain and it was passing away. His eyes were darker than I'd expected, piercing as the stare of some fearless animal. They fastened on me and he grinned, wide and crooked.

"Well, thank you," he said.

"What?"

"Never mind." With the whole of his mobile face, he was laughing at me. He just wasn't using his lungs.

I folded my arms over my knees, as if I was prepared to stay where I was in spite of him or an entire migratory flock of gray-suited, pink-haired men. "So, what the hell did you do that for?"

He looked confused for a moment. Then he dropped down onto the curb next to me, stretched out his legs, and leaned back on his elbows. "Nothing personal. I'm figuring to get to heaven on the strength of my good deeds." His grin was strictly nonporous; nothing would get past it.

I looked at him, my mouth partway open in case some telling comment came to mind, and waited for the explanation that was owed me. He would realize it soon, that he owed me.

"Okay, okay. But you gotta keep this to yourself, all right?" He shifted on the pavement, settling in for a long chat. "I'm an agent from the United Network Command for Law and Enforcement. Those folks back there are ops of the Nic government in exile. See, they thought you were one of our guys." He shook his head. "Probably figured to torture you for the location of our headquarters."

I made my eyes big. "Then if they try again, I just have to click my heels together three times to get away?"

"You got it."

"Who the hell are you?"

"Oh! I'm sorry." He smiled and stuck out his right hand. "Mick Skinner. Call me Mick, or Skinner, or whatever you want."

He had a quarter twist of accent that I thought might be Texas. There was no guile in his face, only an alert sort of sweetness (except for those eyes). It annoyed me. Either Mick Skinner was the village idiot, or he didn't rate me high enough to deserve a little cunning. Unless that was the most thorough cunning of all.

Then I recalled that the people in the City who would know his joke could be numbered on one hand and leave fingers left over. Only a few more would have gotten mine, about the heels. But he had.

Stiffly, I said, "If you work for the City, I just live here."

He smiled the impenetrable grin. "Hell, no. I just *got* here. Not long ago, anyway. It's not a good thing to work for the City?"

"Depends on the work." I stood up. "From the samples you're giving out, I'd say you're a traveling fertilizer salesman."

"And you're not buying."

"You want something to grow around here, try sprinkling some truth on it." I looked at him expectantly.

"Ooo-kay." The truth, to judge from his face, gave him less pleasure. "They thought you might be me."

I waited for something more; when it didn't come, I said, "Gosh, we *do* look so much alike."

"They don't know what I look like. They're hunting on the basis of something else."

"What?"

"Just something else. Last night I—in the bar, you did things they thought were a giveaway. So they bagged you."

In front of the brownstone that edged the sidewalk was a ruined wrought-iron fence. I caught and held it to keep me still. Last night. My whole downtime seemed to have been in the spotlight last night, illuminated for everyone but me. "You mean they expected you to order drinks you couldn't pay for and get kicked out of a club?"

He seemed to find that quietly funny. "Nooo. That was when you began to act like somebody else to throw 'em off the scent. Too late, though."

Now I had motives, too, out of my control, beyond my comprehension. I wished that the curb was twenty feet high, so I could throw myself off it. And drag Mick Skinner with me. "What else do you know about last night?"

A swift look up into my face. It wasn't startled or guilty or meaningful at all; it was just a look. "Nothing," he said.

"And how do you know it?"

"I was there."

"The hell you say. In what capacity?"

"An observer of the human condition."

I figured out, then, what his eyes reminded me of. I'd once seen a pet wolf, tame as any dog, loyal and trusty and true. But around the eyes was an incipient feral craziness, a sense that this animal didn't figure the odds like a real dog did. Skinner's eyes made his most earnest expression seem ironic.

I pushed off from the railing. "Sure. I'll go find the guy in the gray suit and ask him."

"No!" Skinner sat up with a wince. "My God, don't go making deals with those people, they'll peel you like an onion. Your one chance now is to make sure they mark you for an innocent bystander."

I was shaking. Maybe it was anger. Maybe not. "You listen to me. You have no business knowing one goddamn thing about my life. You have no business giving me advice. If I bump into that guy again, I'm going to tell him what you look like and where you are. Then you'll all be out of my hair."

Skinner scrubbed at his face with both hands. My getting angry hadn't scared him. "Well, for your sake, I hope it's that easy. Jesus, I'm beat. You from around here?"

He spoke as if the question were friendly, the answer inconsequential. But that line of inquiry is one of my least favorite. "No," I said. And, "Indiana," I lied.

"Kee-rist. You came up the river? When?"

"Long time ago. I don't remember it."

Skinner shook his head. "Last time I passed that way, you had to be careful somebody didn't eat you. I didn't mean that far back, though. D'you live around here?"

Now, what was I supposed to make of that? "Yes and no."

He worried that in his head; I took pleasure in watching him do it. "Let me put it this way. I need someplace to crash tonight. You know anybody might lend me a corner?"

The Snake is a strange set of chemicals. You think it's worn off long ago; when it really lets you go, you think someone opened a trapdoor under your feet. Suddenly you see the world with the ghastly accuracy you took it to escape from in the first place. In the middle of Mick Skinner's speech, I fell off the Snake's Tail. All distortion, illusion, alteration of mood, emptied out and left me beset with a clear head. With it, I recognized several things:

First, that I wanted to go home.

Second, that Mick Skinner did not owe me. I owed him. I didn't know what the man in gray had wanted; but my wrist still ached where he'd had hold of it. I had been given a drug the night before by someone who was not concerned that I have a good time on it. And tonight I might have ended up in something vile, if this bastard hadn't carried me off like a bandit stealing a chicken. The obligation might have been forced on me, but I couldn't deny that I had one to Skinner.

Third, that Mick Skinner had just asked a favor of me.

With a strong sense of martyrdom, I accepted all three revelations. "You have any problems with tall buildings?" I asked.

He looked up, startled, shaken out of a focused expression that looked like an exercise in mind control. "Hell, no."

"Some people do," I added, hopeful. But of course, none of them were him. No mercy for me tonight. "Come on. I owe you." I turned and headed up the street, not waiting to see if he followed.

The possibility had crossed my mind, as I spoke, that I was going to commit suicide after all, that I'd chosen my method in showing a stranger where I lived. I didn't trust Mick Skinner. But like that wolf, there was something straightforward about him, that was part of his alienness. He would do what was smart, what made sense. I just had to keep watching him for signs of hunger. That, at least, was the rationalization.

A block later, he said cautiously, "And I was beginning to think you didn't like me."

"Did I say I liked you? I said I owed you."

"No, you don't. They thought you were me; it was my fault. I'd have felt bad if they got hold of you. Purely selfish on my part."

"Philosophical tail-chasing," I muttered. He walked beside me in contemplative silence, as if he hadn't heard me anyway.

The only break in that silence happened at the sight of the car. It was long enough that in parts of town it might scrape walls when it turned, black enough to have been cut from Death's own tailcoat. The windows were black, too, the windshield one-way, the engine no louder than snow falling. It appeared like a cruising shark at the end of the street, and Skinner swatted me into the deep shadow of a courtyard entrance. "Back!" he whispered.

"What are you—"

"Turn your face away!" The black car swept slowly past.

"What was that?"

"Trouble," Skinner said firmly, but would say no more.

There were a number of places around the City where I could spend the night. There was a room on the second floor of the Underbridge, behind the sound balcony; it even had its own outside entrance. There was a squat in an underground garage, which was more comfortable than it sounded. But there was only one place I thought of when I heard the word "home."

On the south side of the Night Fair there was a rose-red sandstone office building, dating from the far end of the twentieth century. It was over half empty, like many of the buildings in the Fair. On the third and sixth floors, the windows were wide, many-paned arches set in ornamented openings like baroque half-moon picture frames. On the seventh floor, jutting from the mansard roof, were dormers with arched tops, like wide-open cartoon eyes. It was an interesting structure.

Home was a corner of the seventh floor, and the rooftop, somewhat. Or, certain things that were mine took up space on the roof. The stairway that rose out of the lobby inside the front doors was railed with ornamental cast iron, and wrapped level by level around the open center of the building to the third floor. Where it stopped. The back stairs were nearly rotted away; it would have been safer to climb the sandstone bare-handed than to try them. The lobby elevator was ruined; the car was jammed in the shaft between the second and third floors, and the cables were ripped out. The doors were boarded shut.

I was the only tenant above the third floor, because I was the only one who knew where the service elevator was, and that it worked.

I saw the place with Skinner's eyes when I brought him in the side entrance. The shabby grandeur missed being romantic and fell back on pitiful: the broken black-and-white marble floor, the gouged oak wainscoting, the bits of mirror clinging to the wall above it. The hall smelled like cooked cabbage, and I heard an old-man voice behind one door, singing a pop song with only occasional reference to the tune. The huge brass light fixtures were all defunct; instead there was a swagging of wire from the ceiling, with a bulb every twenty feet. It was dim, but it worked, and no one there could have afforded the juice for the original wiring. Still, it depressed me suddenly, and I blamed Skinner for that.

I unlocked the door to the basement stairs, and led Skinner to the service elevator. He looked around dubiously. I wasn't inclined to offer him reassurance, so I turned my back on him, dug a pair of wires out of the seeming ruins of the control panel, and crossed the bare ends. I kept what I was doing out of Skinner's sight. If he missed killing me on this trip, I didn't want to have shown him how to get upstairs and try again. The cage shuddered and began to climb at an irregular pace, mostly very slow. But silent; I'd used a lot of lubricants to ensure my privacy. Inside the elevator was the inspection certificate, light brown with age and dated 1995. Skinner looked at it and made a clicking noise with his tongue.

"Is this the only way up," he asked, "or are you doing this for my benefit?"

"You could still find room on the sidewalk for tonight."

He shook his head, smiling faintly. I didn't seem to be scaring him.

We ground to a halt on the seventh, and left the box of the elevator. High above the rest of the tenants' cooking and living, my hallway smelled like decaying building: dusty, dry, abandoned. I fumbled with locks, and opened the door onto the darkness of what had been a reception area. It was an empty room; a last defense against anyone who broke in. Sound bounced off bare walls, the light switch didn't work—anyone would have concluded that they'd picked the locks for nothing.

I thumbed a box in my pocket that had once opened garage doors, and the bulb lit in the corridor behind the front room. Skinner jumped. "This is it," I said sourly. "Enter freely and of your own will, and leave something of the happiness you bring."

He laughed. A lot of people wouldn't have gotten that one, either.

I walked the streak of light from the open doorway and was home. The left-hand room must have held supplies, once; it was just big enough for my wadded-cotton mattress and a chest of drawers. The middle one, which was larger, I'd turned into the living room-and-kitchen. The dormer windows were covered with black felt (a light in the top floor might have attracted attention). I'd hung a sink on one wall, stealing water and drainage from the john beyond it, and had a propane stove on a metal cabinet and an old RV propane/electric fridge next to that. There was a wooden desk that served as countertop and table, and things to sit on, including a leather-and-chrome armchair that looked like a compound slingshot, and a shabby upholstered wing chair. There was also a shelf unit of books, enough to be convincing. I went in and lit the gas lamp over the sink.

Skinner stopped in the doorway, and I watched his gaze go straight to the books. He walked forward and began to read the spines. He touched one now and then, never actually taking a book down. I found myself almost wanting to show him the third room.

"*Pale Fire*. I haven't seen a copy . . ." His eyes and fingers wandered on. "*Four Quartets*. 'The Lady's Not for Burning.' Oh,

God, *The Prisoner of Zenda*." Suddenly his drawl thickened to parody. "Land sakes," he said, "have you *read* all these?"

My insides gave a leap of anger. He'd betrayed me into a momentary thaw of attitude, only to dump the resulting ice water over my head. Then I recognized the familiar sound of self-ridicule. My books had caused some failure of reserve in him, and he was only repairing the damage. "Have *you*?" I asked.

He was a little white-lipped. "Some of them," he said.

"If you walk off with one, I'll rebind a few in your hide."

He ran his thumb down a ragged Britannica spine. "What do I do to get a little slack around here?"

"Sorry, all out of slack."

He squeezed his forehead between thumb and fingers, which almost hid his face and the turned-up corner of his mouth. "Guess I'll just get some sleep, then."

"In here," I said, and stepped back into the corridor. He followed. I showed him into the little bedroom, and lit the candle on the dresser.

"What about you?"

"I'll sleep in the next room. The sink works like a sink, the icebox works like an icebox—if there's anything in it; I don't remember—and the toilet, which is through there, works like a toilet. Whatever you do, don't smoke in bed, and don't wake me up."

I was in the corridor already when he said, "You don't remember anything that happened last night, do you?"

No. But I never said so to you. "What makes you think that?"

He was standing in the half-open door, that vitreous grin in place, eyes alight and untrustworthy. "Because I do remember."

"What's that supposed to mean?"

"Just that I know. You ever want to find out what went on all those times you can't recall—just ask me nicely."

With that, the bastard shut and locked my bedroom door.

I could have broken the door open, I now realize. Or apologized lavishly through it, and begged for an explanation. Under ordinary circumstances, I'm sure I would have. Instead, I stared at the blank wood until the insides of my eyes hurt. Then I walked down the corridor to the third room, the one I didn't show him, unlocked it, went in, and locked it behind me.

(Mick Skinner knows about last night, said my head.)

The third room was accessible through the false back of a closet. It was the largest of the rooms I called mine. It no longer had windows; sunlight does damage, and the sun, at least, I could stop. The heat, too, though not so thoroughly; the thermometer at the duct from the swamp cooler on the roof showed 78 degrees. This was the only room that wasn't furnished like a thrift-store campsite. The steel shelving covered most of the wall area, the chair was meant to be sat in for eight hours at a stretch, and the light, when I needed it, was strong and steady. This, after all, was the terminus for the cable that came down from the roof, from the batteries that charged off the windmill disguised as a rusty roof vent.

(Mick Skinner knows what happened to me, said my nerve endings.)

I moved around the room touching things—my talismans, the trappings of my sect. More books: the ones I needed to keep that room working, and the ones that would disappear (and their owner with them) if it were known I had a copy. Thought-contraband in fiction and nonfiction. The video monitor: fifteen inches, with three switchable levels of resolution. The record/playback hardware: three videotape decks; a video editing board; three audio cassette decks, one digital; a CD player; an eight-channel reel-to-reel recorder; a turntable, probably used in a radio station; two 120-watt amplifiers from the middle of the last century, probably likewise, but heavily modified for my purposes; a six-channel audio mixer with EQ and other enhancements; two pairs of headphones. And the diamond: a studio-quality recording CD unit and a case of blanks.

(Mick Skinner knows . . .)

And, of course, the archives. They were mostly copies; I'd sold the previous generation of each one after I'd dubbed it, to collectors rich enough, crazy enough to own something rare and powerful and useless. Then I'd taken the money and spent it on hardware, and on more product, and the media to record it on.

Audio- and videotapes, their mylar bases fragile with age. Vinyl audio disks, brittle as porcelain. Audio CDs, their information becoming vague as if with senility. Two thousand movies, four thousand albums, music and words and pictures like voices whispering from a sweet, sunny past, degrading every time they were played.

It ought to have been depressing—just as every day should be depressing, because it leads to the grave. On bad days I sat in the next room and thought about the value of the plastic tape shells alone to a reprocessor, never mind the mylar, I could be rich. . . . But they were like slaves on an underground railroad, outlaws I hid from the sheriff. Who'd keep them alive, if I abandoned them?

(Mick Skinner knew about . . .)

I sat in my valuable, comfortable chair and contemplated the possible distractions. I'd found a new CD two days before; I'd check that over. I rolled the chair over to the rack, powered up the CD player, and plugged headphones into the amplified jack. The insert under the scarred plastic of the jewel box was a faded drawing of five bemused-looking people sitting or standing around an immense antique car with a startling paint job. It was only one page, front and back, with a ragged edge—there had been more, once. The name of the group wasn't familiar. I cleaned the silver rainbow disk, set it in the tray, closed the 'phones over my ears, and put my feet up.

The first cut opened with a sweet whine of fiddle, the *tsk* of a cymbal, a muttering of bass. Two women's voices traded lyrics, as if they were telling each other a story.

Pretty Tommy Belmont was shooting up in back,
Fixing up his hair and digging through his pack.
He said, "All I want is for you to cut me a little slack."
He never even knew what I was saying.

Angela the dancer said she never heard the shot.
Maybe she was lying, and maybe she was not.
She keeps 'em coming in, and that keeps the party hot,
And she says there isn't any point in praying.

Hunched in my chair, I almost laughed. So much for the sweet illogic of a sunshine past. This could have come from Here and Now, from the clean irreducibility of the Deal, from the hard surfaces of the Deeps. Two skips—I'd try another cleaning.

Then the second song began. None of the reckless flourish of the first one; this opened with a plaintive swell and ripple of guitar notes and a shivering fall of chimes. Fingers long since dust slid evocatively on strings corroded, snapped, discarded, on a guitar broken or burned or somehow lost long, long ago, and a voice slid like the fingers, hypnotic with its power of life-after-death. I'd been disarmed by that first song, cynical and safe.

Out in the light of the dark city scene
Pushin' and shovin' and blowing their horns
Only the pigeons are enjoying the view

The concrete is cold and the street is alive
But the only thing you hear is that voice inside
So you step off the curb . . .

A dead woman sang about isolation, and faced me down with mine.

We were all of us alone in our heads, Cassidy said. Living and dying alone in our unbreachable heads, our indefensible bodies.

The Jammers were mad. The Horsemen before them had breached the unbreachable, gone mad, and pressed the red button on the Tree of Knowledge of Good and Evil.

But the tarot flickered garish on Sherrea's coffee table, thick with the major arcana, saying, The issue you have raised is largely controlled by others.

There's something in the air tonight,
I can see it, but it's just out of sight . . .

And Mick Skinner knew about the blackouts.

The disk played on in my headphones, unattended. Eventually I noticed the silence and the smell of warm circuitry. I was curled up tight in the chair; Sher's pendant was poking me in the chest. I unfolded, painfully, and turned things off. Then I sat in the dark, thinking hard about nothing. Eventually I fell asleep in the chair.

The sun couldn't wake me in the archives, and the chair was made to be comfortable. But it was a chair, not a bed. My knees got stiff at last from being bent, my neck got sore from being turned, the circulation slowed in my right arm, and I woke up.

I peeled a corner of the felt back from the living-room windows, squinted out, and found it midmorning. The Night Fair would be sealed, stagnant around the base of the building. I'd go back to sleep until sunset. The Night Fair in sunlight loomed as an unknown, unnatural land, and I wasn't going to brave it today. But before I slept, I'd look in on Mick Skinner. If I was lucky, he'd have slipped away.

He hadn't. I'd had a hopeful moment when I found the bedroom door unlocked, but he was there. His cotton jacket and a broken-down pair of boots were on the floor by the mattress. He lay on his back under my blanket, his limbs neatly arranged, staring at the ceiling.

Without blinking.

Once I'd taken a step into the room, I was sure it was true, but death is a diagnosis that can never go untested. I jabbed his shoulder. Then I felt for a pulse in his throat. There was none, and his skin had the same chill on it as the top of the dresser. But his flesh was soft, and his arm, when I lifted it, limp. Didn't rigor mortis set in as the body cooled? Maybe he had some disease that produced this convincing catalepsy. Who would know—and how could I find them, in the Night Fair in daylight?

I began to examine him for some kind of damage. Perhaps a blow to the head? Nothing. He'd clutched at his side the night before—

Under his shirt, just to the heart side of middle, between one ridge of muscle and the next, there was a hole. Not a large one, not a fresh one, and not healed. I stared at it for a while before I rolled him over. There was a corresponding hole in his back. They were the entrance and exit wounds made by a bullet, and since they hadn't been dressed, treated, or healed, they must have killed him.

Sometime before we'd met.

It was only a few steps from the corpse to the door; easy to do walking backward. I closed the door. Then I stumbled down the corridor and out into the building hallway. I locked my front door, methodically, watching my hands work. I went down in the freight elevator, climbed the basement stairs, and slipped out, at last, into the silent street. Somewhere in the sleeping Fair I had to find someone who could help me get rid of Mick Skinner.

Card **3**

Beneath

Two of Pentacles, Reversed

Crowley: The Lord of Harmonious Change overthrown.

Gray: Inability to handle many things at once; disruptive change; harmony at the expense of change.

Waite: Enforced gaiety. Simulated enjoyment. False news.

3.0: The goddess and the girl next door

It was already as hot as it had gotten the day before, and promised to be one of the arid ones. The street smelled like scorched tar, and the sidewalk glared where the sun hit it between the building shadows. Nothing moved, not in the hard light, not in the shadow. In a thousand years, when planet-hopping archaeologists discovered the ruins of our civilization, the photos in some alien *National Geographic* would look like this. They'd be silent like this, too. The Dead City: remarkable state of preservation.

I was reminded of my houseguest. So I moved on, briskly.

Once I began to penetrate the heart of the Fair, I had to stop again. Hadn't I had a nightmare like this once, before I'd been lulled into thinking that there would always be enough people?

The food vendor's booth on my right was empty; it had been stripped down by its operator at closing, at dawn. I reminded myself of that: It had been open just hours ago. The turquoise paint on its corrugated metal sides was peeling in places, fading all over. "Mariscos" said the hand-painted letters, above a portrait of a shrimp. The word was bleached from red to pink, the shrimp to mud-green. The counter was gritty with dust. The booth had had an awning once; I saw the rusty brackets above the service pass-through. The iron barrel chained to the wall had no trash in it.

In front of me, a Ferris wheel rose against a chromakey-blue sky. Or rather, the geometric bones of the wheel were there, black against the light, thickened at the joints, flanged at regular intervals by the vertebrae of the seat buckets. The flesh for those bones was darkness and little lights and noise, and that was gone. There was rust and grit here, too. I sniffed, trying to smell alcohol or ozone, and got nothing but sun-heated metal and concrete.

61

It was the light, of course it was the light. When I stayed at my place in the Night Fair, I rarely went there before dawn. If I did I went there to work, then sleep, then wake up when the Fair woke. I'd never seen the Night Fair at midmorning. But I couldn't shake off the conviction that everything I saw had been transformed—that this was not the Ferris wheel I'd seen last night but one a thousand years older, a thousand years broken and silent.

"Sparrow," said a voice behind me, and if I'd been my namesake, I would have been halfway across the City in a breath.

Context is everything; wrap enough strangeness around them and familiar things become unrecognizable. It was Dana's voice firmly attached to Dana's person. She leaned in the entryway of a brown brick building. She wore a dressing gown printed with herons and palm fronds that reached almost to her ankles, and a pair of little-heeled slippers of a sort I'd only seen in movies. Her pale hair was loose and brushed back to fall straight down behind her. She'd been standing there awhile; there was half a cigarette in her fingers, and the stub of another on the porch at her feet.

"You okay, sugar?" she asked with a quirk of the lips, and I realized I hadn't said anything yet.

"Fine. I'm fine. What are you doing here?"

More quirk. "I live here. Upstairs. You act as if I caught you trying to steal that thing."

I shook my head. The sense of unreality, Dana in mid-necropolis, had doped me.

"No snappy comeback?"

"I guess I'm just not a morning person," I said finally.

"That's better. So what brings you out?" She laid the cigarette between her lips and took a long pull. She looked disturbingly undressed without lipstick.

The cigarette wasn't hand-rolled, and I thought I could see a tobacconist's mark printed on the paper. Luxuries, rarities, and indulgences: Dana surrounded herself with them.

She had offered me her help. Here was a problem that might yield to wealth and contacts. If she really had them. And where else was I likely to find a solution?

". . . I need a favor."

Dana let the smoke out of her lungs and watched me through it. "Anything I can do?"

I suffered a rush of doubt—had I ever been out of balance with Dana, on the owing side of the Deal with her? Always too many debts. I pushed the corners of my mouth away from each other and hoped it looked like a smile. "I have to dispose of a corpse."

From her face, I might have just shed my skin. She whispered something and spit left. Her eyes slid away from me, then back. "I guess you better come in."

I followed the swirl of her hem off the porch and, sunblind, into the building's front hall. The smell of last night's lamp oil hung around my head as I climbed the stairs. Very old marble ones; each tread was scooped out and shallow in the middle, as if the stairs had been a watercourse. The second-floor windows were shuttered, but on the third-floor landing, light fell on us like a malediction in shafts of dust. It was very hot in the hall.

Dana pushed open a door and sauntered in. I had never been in a place Dana called home. This one was so much hers that I found myself shying on the sill like an animal at an outstretched hand.

We were in a lavishly cluttered, languorous room, where the light filtered through slatted blinds and folds of lace. The unmade bed beneath one window looked right and proper, as if the linens weren't woven to lie flat, but would always form those shadowed valleys, that textile refuge. There were rugs on rugs, so that even Dana's heeled slippers were soundless. The chairs were strewn with things: clothes, magazines, single shoes, embroidered towels, gloves, strands of beads, and a box spilling tissue and printed with a shop logo rarely seen in the Night Fair. On the kitchen table was a bowl of full-blown roses, and I smelled rose incense, very fresh. The room was sleepily warm, and all its colors were indistinct.

Dana swept a robe and a cedar box off a kitchen chair and onto a footstool. "Have a seat," she said. "D'you want some tea?"

I wanted, in fact, to leave. "No," I said, and sat down in a cloud of disorientation. "I want to move a corpse."

"Well, if it's already a corpse, then there's no hurry."

"In this heat?" I wanted to break this slow, hypnotic atmosphere with something crude. But the imagined stink of decay couldn't hold out against the incense. I looked around and found it still burning on a wicker table half curtained with lace. There was a figurine there, too, draped with veiling, surrounded by an oval mirror, a shell comb, and nine pink candles. Maîtresse Erzulie, the queen of love. At the foot of the statue was an apple, cut apart and fastened back together with straight pins. The skin at the cut marks was just starting to pucker. I thought of Cassidy the night before, suffering in silence. What was Dana asking for, so early in the day? What lay under Erzulie's dominion that Dana didn't have?

She stood at the counter, filling the kettle from a stoneware jug. Her hair fell straight down, between her face and my eyes. From behind it, she said, "This body, is it . . . Did you kill somebody?"

Her voice was smaller than it usually was. When I didn't answer immediately, she pushed back the hair curtain and darted me a glance. I read her expression: If I *had* killed someone, well, the world was tough, and she was tough enough to live in it, wasn't she? I realized suddenly that I didn't know how old she was. A confusion of feeling smacked me from the inside, understanding, pity, tenderness. My thoughts leaped away from all of them.

"No," I snapped.

"Oh." She was trying not to be relieved. She moved out of sight behind me. I heard a cupboard open; then her fingers stroked my shoulder. "What kind of tea do you want?"

I shook my head, as if to dislodge something (which didn't work). "There's a dead person in my apartment. I don't know anything about him, except that there were people after him that I don't want after me. For all I know, they're not the only ones after him. I don't want his debts, I don't want the blame, and I don't want any tea. What I want is someone who can make him disappear."

Dana shrugged. "Dump him on the sidewalk."

"No. I mean *disappear*. I'm connected to him already. I don't want City security stopping by. And the people who were after him saw me with him. If he turns up dead, they'll come straight to me. You know the ritual for splitting with someone, when you draw a line across the threshold with a knife after they've passed? I need the real-life version. Just tell me if you know someone who can help."

"Easy, sugar. While the tea's making, I'll go call somebody." She gave me a sweet, indulgent look. "You see? It's not so bad, having friends. Nobody can be by herself *all* the time. So who is—was—this character?"

"I don't know," I said, trying to decide if that was a lie or not. "It was just—sometimes you bump into people."

"And take them home," she added sourly. I wondered if she disapproved of my recklessness, or was only jealous of some imagined intimacy.

"Well, in this case, he got the worst of it."

"What kind of tea?"

"Will you—Earl Grey," I said, because I hadn't seen Earl Grey tea anywhere since . . . Someone, once, had given me some, but I couldn't remember who, or when. A long time ago.

She laughed and pulled a stopper out of one of a cluster of tins on the counter. The smell, very strong and fresh, added itself to the incense and unlocked a memory. At the edge of a town in what had been Ohio, in a farmhouse kitchen full of dirty dishes, a fast-talking man with piercing eyes behind thick glasses, who told stories as if they'd been corked up in him and my arrival had broken the seal—he had poured tea into a cup for me. The dark liquid had spun and swirled, and wide-eyed, I'd asked, "Why does it smell like that?"

Dana dropped some of the tea in a china pot and lit the gas under the kettle. "Be right back," she said, and whisked out the door.

"Wait!" I yelled. "Wait . . . You don't have a private line, do you?"

She stuck her head back into the room and smiled. "I'm discreet, sugar."

Without Dana, the room was much larger. Still, nothing in it seemed quite in focus. I stared at the wide-open roses in front of me. Down the hall I could hear, barely, the rise and fall of Dana's voice as she talked on the phone. Finding me a corpse-removal service. I could probably have done it myself, if I wasn't so rattled. But no—the telephone; this apartment, uncontestedly hers, filled with luxuries; the shop logo on the box; the tea—Dana had connections, of a sort I would never have expected. I knew people, from deals, from the Underbridge, but I couldn't call them connections.

She came back in. "Where's your place, sugar?"

"Why?"

"They'll meet us there."

I told her, because I couldn't see any way not to. She went back down the hall.

When she returned, the teakettle had begun to hoot. She did appropriate things with kettle and teapot, and brought all the paraphernalia to the table.

"Shouldn't we go?" I asked. If my privacy had to be invaded, it seemed better to get there first and prepare the ground.

"Drink your tea." She poured, through a strainer, into two thin china cups that matched. For some reason, I thought of Sherrea, with no food in the house. I drank my tea, with milk in it.

It was beginning to catch up to me that I hadn't had enough

sleep. That would explain my inability to concentrate, the distance everything seemed to recede to. Dana watched me over the rim of her cup, wearing her purring look. The angle was flattering.

"Why do you treat Cassidy so badly?" I asked suddenly.

"*Do* I treat him badly?" She sipped tea. "I don't think I do. He's one of my best friends, honey."

"That's not how he thinks of you."

Left shoulder up, eyebrows raised, mouth pursed—it was such a graceful expression of regret that I couldn't tell if it was genuine. "I can't do anything about that."

"You could stop giving him encouragement."

"I treat him just the same as I treat you."

"Ah, but I'm not your type."

"Neither is Cassidy."

"You should tell him so."

She laughed. "Oh, Sparrow, honey, when did you start up in the lonely-hearts business? I thought you didn't mess with romance." She put the emphasis heavily on the first syllable, and grinned.

It was true; it wasn't my place, my right, or my business. I turned my teacup around between my hands. I hadn't had caffeine for months. I could almost feel my blood vessels narrowing.

"Cassidy," she continued, "is having himself a fine time. He'll collect just enough heartbreak, and then he'll get tired of it and give up. In the meantime, he's getting a little excitement, and not taking any harm. D'you want anything to eat with that?"

I shook my head. Dana pushed my cup gently down on the saucer and filled it again. It was time we left. I pointed to the wicker table and the draped figurine. "I didn't know you were hoodoo."

She raised her eyebrows again. "Sugar, we're all hoodoo, aren't we? Or whatever works."

"What makes you think it works?"

"That it *does*, I suppose. I mean, you turn the fire on under the pot and it boils, doesn't it?"

"Does it? What are you asking for?"

She smiled. "None of your damn business."

This time she didn't refill my teacup.

There was a car in front of the building when we got there: long as the course of history, black as a killer's thoughts, and damnably familiar. "Wait," I said, reaching for Dana's arm. I missed it.

"They're here. That's the car."

I watched her cross the street to the front door, and followed slowly after. Someone who'd been looking for Mick Skinner was about to find him. Or maybe Mick Skinner had successfully avoided someone he didn't want to see. It all depended on your point of reference. Mine, I decided with a sinking feeling, was too close to the action. But there wasn't much I could do now.

Two figures commanded the ruined grandeur of the lobby. One was a teak-brown man, nearly seven feet tall, carved with muscle and shining bald. He wore narrow trousers and a sleeveless double-breasted tunic with silver buttons; tunic and pants were black, and suggested a uniform without insisting on it. He had a baroque pearl hanging from his right earlobe. His arms hung loose at his sides, his hands open; he looked as if he was thinking about matters several miles away. On the floor at his feet was a leather case with a handle, like an old salesman's catalog case.

The woman next to him seemed small only in contrast. She had to be the owner of the car—she belonged in something that long, that black, that silent. She was black herself; I'd never seen skin so dark. She wore a long dress, almost to her ankles, of dull dark blue chiffon over a dark blue slip. Her hair was hidden under a sheenless black scarf wrapped close around her head. Her long, angular face was interrupted by sunglasses with dark lenses and matte-black frames. Even her lipstick was black, and didn't shine. I was afraid to look at her fingernails.

"*Chérie*," she said to Dana with regal near-warmth. Her voice was low and hoarse. Against all that darkness, Dana, in a hyacinth-blue dress, looked like a faded print.

"*Bonjour, Maîtresse*," said Dana, in a startling schoolgirl voice. I glanced at her face and found an expression there to match. "This is Sparrow, who . . . has the problem."

I was about to say something snappy—mostly to banish the urge to bob or tug my forelock—when I realized that the black woman had gone very still. I couldn't tell what held her attention because of the sunglasses. I shot a look over my shoulder.

"Sparrow. *Bonjour*. What is your age?"

My heart gave one powerful beat and seemed to quit. "Old enough for most things."

"Where have you come from?"

"I don't think that's relevant."

"Sparrow!" Dana said.

But the black woman shrugged. "Keep your secrets, then, if you feel better. It doesn't matter. Take me to this dead man."

"Shall I call you Mistress, too?"

"When you need to call me anything, I will tell you what it will be," she said pleasantly.

Gosh. Since there were no more channels for the small talk to run in, I led them all to the basement.

Again, I stood in the elevator in such a way that no one else could see what I did with the loose wires in the control box. I knew it was a delaying tactic; one of them could, with enough incentive and time, duplicate the process. I hated knowing that. Three more people who were aware that the elevator was not broken down. Mick Skinner seemed to be doing me all his disservices posthumously.

The apartment door was still locked. The apartment, when I opened the door, was quiet as—well, perfectly quiet. Dana came in after me, followed by La Maîtresse and the large man. He closed the door after himself, which made me uncomfortable.

When I opened the bedroom door, I knew immediately that something had changed state. Mick Skinner's mortal remains were where I'd left them. But the body seemed altered; maybe in its color, or the texture of the skin. I stepped in and plucked gingerly at the wrist I'd lifted before, and found that this time rigor mortis worked. "He's different."

Dana was standing in the doorway, staring. The woman pushed her gently out of the way and came to the bedside. "How?"

"Well . . . deader," I said.

I found myself staring at my reflection in the sunglasses, long enough to realize that my way with words had not impressed her. "I need more room," she said at last. "Can you give it to me?"

"Oh. Yes, down the hall."

"Mr. Lyle. Bring him, please."

At that the big man came forward and took the body off my mattress with no apparent effort. I led the parade to the next room, wondering what she needed space for. Dissection, maybe. I ought to tell her I didn't have a garbage disposal. Mr. Lyle laid his burden tidily on the floor, and went back to the hall. When he returned, he had the leather case. He gave the woman an inquiring look.

"Yes," she said.

He took candles out of the case. Lots of candles, in black. They all had something sticky at the base, and stayed upright when he placed them on the floor—one at the top of Mick Skinner's head, one at each shoulder, at each wrist, at the outside of each knee, at the sole of each bare foot. He reached into the case again and came up with a tin box. I craned my neck when he took off the lid; the contents looked like flour. When he began to dribble it on the floor in fine lines, I realized that of course it *was* flour, and he was making the *véés* with it.

I turned to Dana, who sat cross-legged on the floor out of the way, her skirt spread out around her. "Maybe I gave you the wrong impression," I told her. "I said I wanted the real-world version."

"Don't bother them when they're working, sugar."

"Does it bother them if I talk to you? I want him disposed of, not raised from the dead."

"We will dispose of him," the black woman said behind me. "When we are done with him."

"I'd think the whole world was as done with him as could be. He's dead." The *véés* were going remarkably fast, for drawings done in flour; there was one elaborate triangle at the corpse's head already, and another taking shape at its feet.

"In an ideal world," the woman said fiercely, "the dead are left in peace. Do you live in an ideal world, do you think?"

I wasn't even tempted to answer that.

When the *véés* were done, Mr. Lyle stepped back, and the woman began to take things out of the leather case. An unmarked bottle of clear liquid. A shot glass. A little dark glass vial. A square of red silk, embroidered around the edges. She spread the silk over Mick Skinner's chest, with points toward his head and feet. Then she poured some of the liquid into the shot glass—the smell of high-proof drinking alcohol reached me—and set the glass in the middle of the square of silk. After that, she began to light candles.

She was speaking, and so was Mr. Lyle—in unison, I realized only after a moment, because their voices were so different I had trouble listening to both at once. Hers was low and smooth; he might have had some damage in his throat, to judge by the whistling, broken, breathy sound of it. I didn't recognize the words, or even the language, but the speech had a dance rhythm. I had to work to keep from swaying. Dana wasn't bothering. Her eyes followed the woman in black, and her shoulders moved freely with the words.

It was taking a long time to light nine candles. The room was already warmer, and the points of light swam in halos before my aching eyes. By the time there were nine of them, bouncing in their golden auras, the speaking seemed to have a tune, and someone was patting a drumbeat on the floor. The woman produced the dark vial, unscrewed the cap, and held it over the corpse's closed mouth.

"Elegguá," she said, as if to someone in the room. "Find this man for me, and see if he has something to say. Exú Lança, somebody fooled you when you closed the way behind this one. Let him through to speak to me, and I will see that the joker is punished in your name. Papa Ghede, this is your daughter asks you this, and it is right that you give it to me."

I wanted to rub my eyes; they burned with tiredness, with the candlelight, with not blinking enough. But I didn't want to move. It was important not to move. Someone might notice me. I wanted to see what Dana was doing, but that would have meant turning my head. The candles, the singing, the beat, were narrowing the world alarmingly. The woman let a drop fall from the vial onto the corpse's lips.

Silence. Silence as if the air had turned to mercury, heavy, thick, and poisonous. The candles burned straight up, not moving. I was watching Mick Skinner's lips so hard, I thought I might be sucked into his mouth if they opened. The whole room might; the space behind his teeth was such a vacuum, it would take the whole room to equalize the pressure. I thought I felt a drop of sweat crawl from my forehead, past my ear, to my jaw.

The liquid in the shot glass burst into flames, and the glass shattered.

I was halfway to the sink for water before I realized I wasn't holding still anymore. The teakettle was full, and I grabbed it. Nothing we did in this room could harm the contents of the other, of the third room, except fire. Except fire. I bolted back toward the mess on the floor.

But when I tried to fling the contents of the teakettle on it, I couldn't. I looked down and found two huge brown hands closed around my wrists. "That will only spread it," Mr. Lyle's whistling voice said above me. "Look."

The corpse was burning. The black, oily smoke of it rose straight up and stained the ceiling. But where the flames should have splashed around it with the burning alcohol, there was nothing. The nine black candles stood untouched, like everything outside them. I couldn't even smell the smoke.

The woman was on her knees, bent double, and Dana hovered over her, her hands stretched out and falling a little short of La Maîtresse's shoulders. Then the black-wrapped head lifted. The woman looked straight into my eyes and said, *"He wasn't there."*

The sunglasses had come off. Below the line of the scarf, at the bottom of the sweat-marred forehead, were her eyebrows, two arcs of silver metal inlay in her skin. I hugged my teakettle and stared.

"He wasn't there. Where has he gone?" She rose and advanced on me, her eyes very wide under those bright, motionless brows.

I edged around the smoking corpse. "Who?" I croaked.

"The one who was in there. *Le chevalier,*" she spat. Her hand snapped sideways and down, toward the body.

"He's dead." Even in my own ears, I sounded hysterical. "What do you expect?"

On the left, around the pillar of smoke, I saw Mr. Lyle moving carefully toward me. Dana was on my right, looking back and forth between me and the woman in dark blue on the other side of her.

"You are an ass, an ass," the woman said to me. "Where is he now? Tell me, or I'll wring it out of you like water from a rag."

I didn't kick Dana, exactly; I pushed her hard with my foot. She stumbled into the black woman. And I threw the teakettle at Mr. Lyle, and plunged for the front door.

It seemed to take five minutes to turn the knob and pull the door open, half an hour to run down the hall, with the sound of footsteps coming fast behind. The elevator control box took a week, and I looked up from the crossed wires to the sight of the doors closing on a huge brown hand, with an angry face behind. Two fingers stuck through the rubber door seal, so I bit them. They disappeared and the car lurched downward.

The opposite wall of the elevator was farther away than usual. So was the ceiling, and the floor. I rubbed my eyes. The light in the car was fading. I knew, suddenly, what was happening. This time, for the first time, I had some scrap of warning. And it didn't help a bit.

I went down.

Card 4

Behind

Seven of Swords

Gray: Possible failure of a plan, arguments, spying, incomplete success, unstable efforts.

Crowley: The policy of appeasement, which may fail if violent, uncompromising forces take it as their natural prey.

4.0: What friends are for

. . And came back up, easy as a swimmer who rises, breaks the water's surface, and opens eyes and mouth to the air. I opened mine to the night. I heard the churning, guttering sound of water moving over something; smelled a faint odor of dead fish, beer, perfumes, and old smoke; and saw row after row of little electric lights, swinging vigorously on their strings overhead. My Hyde persona had brought me to the street in front of the Underbridge and dropped me off. I was standing up, my feet wide apart on the uneven concrete. Finding myself so suddenly in charge of my own legs almost made me fall off them. I caught myself on an iron stanchion that marked the edge of an old parking lot.

The Underbridge had been a generating plant for electricity once, stealing force from the water dashing past the river dam. Electricity was still generated there, but on a much smaller scale. Now the river ran spotlights and a few tubes of neon and the sound system and the video projector and these festive strings of lights outside the building. When the river was low in midsummer, we snuffed the outside lights and the neon, and kept the volume down and our fingers crossed. Yes, we; the operation of the Underbridge was the only thing I did in which I identified myself as one of a group. I didn't do it with very good grace, but even so I recognized the Deal in action. I got to work with the skills I'd been born to; I paid with my independence. Fair's fair.

This was the first time I'd come back up without discomfort or outright pain somewhere on or in me, and in a familiar place. So it was a minute or two before I panicked. What time was it? How had I gotten here from the Night Fair on the other side of the river, and what had gone on while I did? Were Dana and her friends still here? Had they found the third room? No, they couldn't have, not without knowing to look for it, and even Dana wasn't aware of my collection. Had they found and braved the stairs? If they had,

75

maybe they'd all broken their necks. But if they'd made it to th
ground floor, they might be in pursuit of me even now.

A frantic look around told me they weren't, at least no
immediately; nor was anyone else. Then I realized that for all
knew, it had been months since I went down. By now we migh
all be best friends. I hated this.

The moon had risen down the river, above the Bank. Tha
would make it about nine o'clock. It was a furry squashed sphere
near full, veiled with converging clouds. The wind was coo
emphatic, and from the west. The Underbridge would soon b
packed, then: we were going to get a storm.

Robert was doing the door, his dark curling hair loose over hi
thin shoulders and his antique T-shirt with the London subwa
symbol on it. He turned one corner of his mouth up and nodded a
me.

"Didn't know you were coming in tonight," he said.

I had to clear my throat—how long since I last talked? I *hate*
this—before I said, "Just lucky, I guess."

"You or me?" he asked, perfectly serious.

I wasn't prepared to answer that, so I didn't. "Actually, I forgo
what day it was." I shrugged for de-emphasis.

"Oh," said Robert.

I cursed him in my heart. "Um, what day *is* it?"

With the infinite patience of someone used to dealing with
drunks, musicians, and techies, he replied, "Sunday."

I'd lost a day and a half. It could have been worse. It could hav
been a lot better. But I relaxed some. "Who's here?"

"Theo, so far. Spangler. There might be somebody else i
later."

And now me. Gracious. Hadn't anyone been watching th
weather? Robert on the door was a waste. The Underbridge wa
his creation, and if there'd been three of him, the place would
have run best if he'd done it all himself; he was that much bette
than anyone but me—and I had unnatural advantages. For him
screwdrivers didn't slip and solder went on like a liquid kiss. Hi
fingers would brush patterns over the sound board's faders, dab a
the EQ, and one song would segue into the next out of the mai
speakers like pleats in a single piece of fabric. I knew I ought t
offer to take over the door, but I didn't want to be the first thing
anyone coming to the Underbridge would see.

I looked past Robert into the main room, all three stories of it
The long windows showed me the Deeps across the river,
silhouette against the mounting clouds, speckled with lights in the

owers. The reflected moon stuck to one of Ego's faces like a dab
f wet silver; then a tail of cloud stroked across it, like a finger
rawn through the puddle. I'd once referred to the windows as the
assive video system. People paid to come and dance under that
iew, and more of them paid to do it when the City cowered under
ghtning and thunder. A great show, and it didn't cost us a thing
o put on.

Over by the beer taps were a dozen or so clubbers, looking lost
nd embarrassed in all the empty space. Someone was tending
ar, of course, but bartenders were not included in Robert's or my
ally. At the other end of the room up by the screens, a tall wooden
adder, spraddle-legged and spindly, stuck its head up into the
onfusing darkness of the rigging. A beam of light on the dance
loor changed color and position. A monotonous stream of
omment and obscenity rolled gently down from the ladder top.

Robert tilted his chin toward the ladder and grinned. "He's been
t it since before sundown."

"I'll go see," I said. "It always makes him feel better if
omeone asks."

I walked to the bottom of the ladder, warily; solid objects had
een known, at moments like this, to follow the stream of sound
hat fell from the ladder. "Hullo, Spangler. What's it this time?"

"Oh, nothing, we just lost another fresnel, that's all, there's no
oddamn fucking way in the *world* I can get it working by
howtime, if *ever*, and the whole lighting balance is *fucked* at this
nd of the room because we're running out of goddamn units *I can
ill in with.*"

"It's beautiful," I said.

"Shows what you know." He did, in fact, drop a crescent
vrench, but on the other side of the ladder. By the time his feet
vere on the rungs at my eye level, my heart rate was almost back
o normal.

"I take it you don't want to say something like 'Hi, Sparrow,
iow's it been?'"

He jumped the last three feet to the floor and gave me a
lisgusted look. Spangler was not exactly the youngest crew
nember, but he claimed the distinction, and it would have been
ounterproductive to contest it. Half his brown hair was long and
vorn braided beneath his ear; the rest of his head, from forehead
o nape of neck, was shaved clean and tattooed with Japanese carp
nd water lilies. Whenever the shaved part went to stubble, it
ooked as if the pond had an algae problem. "I know how it's
een," he said. "Wonderful. You never have anything go wrong."

"Not a thing. If you like, I'll try to trip on my way upstairs. I wasn't in the habit of airing the details of my life here, either

Spangler shook his head, even more disgusted. "Help me wi this fucking ladder first."

I did; then I pulled myself a beer and took the stairs behind th bar two at a time to the sound balcony.

"Robby?" Theo's voice came around the door as I opened it

"Nope. Me."

"Sparrow!" he said, surprised and pleased. "What're you doin here?"

He'd been cleaning one of the cassette decks; a stick with cotto wadded around it was in his right hand, straight up like a littl torch. There was a hand-rolled cigarette balanced and glowing i one corner of his mouth, and I could smell Theo's mixture o tobacco and marijuana. The air itself seemed to tremble, full of th light of the dozen mismatched candles that he always lit on th balcony.

"I'm watching you undo your work," I replied.

He took the cigarette out of his mouth, looked at it, an grimaced. "Well, that's why I'm cleaning the thing."

"If I answered that, this conversation would get damne recursive."

"Instead of just redundant. Glad you're here, man. We shoul be able to do some groovy stuff tonight, if we get the crowd."

Theo's favorite movies were *Wild in the Streets*, *The Dagge and the Rose*, *Easy Rider*, and *Leary*. They'd affected hi vocabulary. He seemed to glow a little in the semi-gloom; he wa wearing a white cotton jacket whose previous owner had bee either a waiter or an orderly at an asylum, and a collared knit shi under it. The VU meters from two tape decks and the mixin board reflected in his wire-rimmed glasses, and Spangler's floo lights turned his brown bob to auburn. I found myself wonderin what less appropriate things shone on him when he wasn working. I'd known Theo for about four years, and I had no ide where he lived, or what he did before the moon was up. I hadn seen anything strange in that before, but suddenly I was aware o it, and it bothered me. Paranoia, maybe—downtime erasures walking dead men, vampire hunters, and why shouldn't I wonde who my acquaintances were when I wasn't there?

"I may not stay the whole night," I warned him.

"That's okay. Maybe Liz'll come 'round later to fill in." One o his heels tapped furiously at the leg of the chair he sat in; h seemed unaware of it, as if it were run by a second brain.

After a moment I said, "Also—sometime—some people may ome looking for me." *Well, spit it out.* "I'm in a little trouble."

He closed the door on the tape transport and stared at me. It was nnerving to find myself the single focus of all that energy. Somebody *noticed* you? Sorry," he said, in response to my xpression, no doubt. "Bad trouble?"

"No, no. Annoying. I just don't want to be found."

"Nothin' easier." Theo stood up, ambled past me to the door at le top of the stairs, and kicked it shut with a crash. The candle lames leaned wildly. "You're working, man. Can't be dis- irbed."

"That's the idea, anyway. But these people may have connec- ons beyond those of mortal men."

"City connections?" He was rolling the cotton swab hard etween his fingers.

"I was thinking of the kind that are supposed to result from acrificing small animals. But yeah," I said, remembering Dana's partment, "there may be one or two of those, as well."

Theo nibbled his lower lip. "That's not good. If it was just the *rujo*, you hire another *brujo*. But we bugger the City over here nd we're done, you know that."

I sat down at the console and powered up the two video decks nd the A/B switcher. "They need us. We're part of the circuses ide of the equation."

He sat down next to me and stared into my face. "What we have ere," he said in the voice of the warden in *Cool Hand Luke*, "is failure to think straight. We generate electricity by the grace of iod and A. A. Albrecht. I don't know about God, but Albrecht an shut us down anytime he wants."

"Theo, what can they do to us? Reroute the river?"

Theo shook his head, sadly. "The City controllers license the ardware, sell the fuel, own twenty-five percent of the metered utput and tax the rest, no matter how you make it. What do we lo if the inspectors confiscate the generators?" He waved a hand t the quaking flames around the balcony. "Light candles and ing?"

I knew all that. It was why the wind turbine on my roof was lisguised as a vent, after all. But the Underbridge had seemed— till seemed—too big, too important, too visible to be at the mercy f the City. "There'd be a stink if we closed."

"There's people lined up to run places like this. If the City loses us, they just hand our permit to the next guy, who'll keep

his nose cleaner than we did. And the nightbabies all just move o
down the block. Be damned hard on Robby, man."

I knew all that, too, I suppose. "It's okay," I said. Outside th
windows, the moon had drowned in the cloud bank. I felt—it too
me a moment to figure it out. Lonely. "If anything happens, I'
keep it away from here."

"Sorry, Sparrito," said Theo.

I shrugged. "Maybe nothing will happen. Let's do some good.

I had color bars on monitors one and two, and zip-all on numbe
three, which meant that either the third monitor was evil-eyed o
the camera in the rigging was. I hoped it was the monitor. Th
camera was one of maybe five I'd seen in my life, and that onl
because I'd been looking. It had full remote capabilities and
twenty-X zoom, and I suspected it of having been made to militar
specs and used to spy on SouthAm dictators. But who am I t
judge?

I jiggled connectors, and finally crawled out on the edge of th
balcony, lay on my stomach on one of the crossbeams, and, b
reaching as far as I could, managed to poke at the camera jack
themselves. The camera swung on its mount, and I grabbed at th
beam.

"Watch the fuckin' *lights*," Spangler shouted from somewher
below me. Serve him right if I fell on his head. I wiggled my wa
backward off the rigging, and checked the monitor. Live, tah dah

"I hate it when you do that," Theo observed.

"D'you ever wonder what it was like when this stuff was new?
I asked him, waving at the mixer, the tape decks, the video gear

Light turned the lenses of his glasses opaque pink. "Crowded,
he said, but his voice made it mean more than that.

The house lights were down, the room was dark, and thunde
muttered from miles away. I slapped a tape in one of the decks an
faded the image up on the projectors, on both screens at the othe
end of the room. At the edge of my vision I could see Theo's han
on the mixing board, bringing up sound as I brought up my video

"So, don't let 'em catch you, okay?" Theo said mildly in tha
last moment as it got too busy to answer him. I don't know wha
I would have said anyway.

Strange scratchy sounds moved through the room, hung o
moaning bass notes like the lowing of cows lost underwater. Th
image I'd grabbed to start with was the old black-and-white tes
pattern and countdown spinner: nine, eight, seven, six . . . A
one it froze and began to melt, iridescent color oozing slowly ou

of the monochrome rings and crosshairs. Theo would have called the effect "trippy."

Suddenly Theo segued to his other deck, pulled in something that went *thump-thump-thump* against a harmonica that went *chigga-chigga-chigga*. So I switched sources, too; because I knew how Theo's mind worked, I had a bit ready from a fifty-year-old war movie that put the viewer nose to nose with an assault rifle on full auto. Pull back on bronzed beefcake sneering under his visor, spewing hot lead at whoever it had been that week, *budda-budda-budda-thwakow!* I grinned at Theo: That for your *chigga-chigga*. He grinned back and poked the pan controls as a flute riff seared the room and sent me back to my decks for the next image. We were just warming up.

On most nights our partnership would snag on some piece of equipment; something would fail. Everything we had was old, and hardly any of it was built for the kind of industrial-weight use we gave it. The regular after-closing ritual turned the sound balcony into a repair shop where we fixed anything that had broken during the show. But that night, we had the hoodoo working.

Christopher Lee sank his fangs into someone just as Theo cranked to a horrible reverbed wail from Morticia just as lightning shattered the air between two clouds outside the window. Uma Thurman, with a look that would melt glass, stretched out a glimmering hand to the Beast in the Forman remake of *Beauty and*, while Theo raised a Zimbabwean singer's plaintive high note into the rafters, while blown rain broke the view outside into a moiré pattern. Lightning lashed at the City like artillery; Ego's top was lost in cloud, but the hits on the obelisk shape of the Foshay looked like pointing fingers. Theo put both decks to work at once, overlapping and cutting between something that was entirely percussion and something else that was all singing. I took a feed off the camera, panning the dance floor in dizzy swoops, then zooming in on anyone who took my fancy.

I had a lot of people to choose from. The place seemed to have filled up suddenly; but that only meant I'd been absorbed in what I was doing. Then, on one of my video strafing runs, I noticed a hand waving, an oval of face looking straight at the camera. I zoomed in, startled. "My God," I said aloud, "it's Sher." Sherrea's pointed chin and big, shadowy eyes, under a mass of black-and-purple headwrap, filled my monitor. Just then she turned to glance at the screens and saw her own profile ten feet high. She turned back to the camera and gave me the finger.

"What?" Theo asked.

"It's someone I know," I said, loud enough to be heard this time. "I didn't know she ever came here."

Theo looked over at the monitor, where Sher was now making some shrugging, inquiring motion. "Oh, Sherrea," he said, nodding. "Groovy. Take the mix, and I'll send her up. I need a break."

And he left, while I was still trying to ask how he knew her, and trying to figure out why I was surprised that he did.

One person can handle all the hardware on the balcony; you just can't do as much, and it's not as much fun. I cued up the next song: "They Want My Four-Wheel Drive," by Los Blues Guys, copy of tape courtesy of my archives. I'd gotten the original from someone who'd brought it from northern Texas, who knew the recording engineer and half the band members. A fine example of the new record distribution system.

Much of the material at the Underbridge was of my providing. It was another thing I weighed on the scales of the Deal: Robert provided the opportunity and a cut of the door, and I repaid him with fresh antique marvels for the customers. Besides, like most collectors, I couldn't quite keep it all to myself. I needed some appreciative audience to ooh and ahh over the gems.

I was showing the car chase from *The French Connection* when Sherrea came up. It had taken her too long, and I wondered if Theo had waylaid her and mentioned my personal problems. Joke on Theo—she had the advantage of him on a few points.

" 'Lo," she said. "You want me to take audio or video?"

"You know how to run these?" I asked. I had assumed she was a technophobe; most *adivinos* were. Or at least, I thought they were.

"*Santos*," she sighed. I'd never heard anyone sigh that loud before. "You hardware heads all think you need lessons from God to do this. Next time your significator's gonna be the High Priestess. Audio or video?"

"Video," I said weakly. "Theo's had the tunes all night."

She slid into the chair in front of the A/B switcher, pulled her headwrap off in a heap, and began rummaging for tapes. I began to think of the 27 Various, Reptile Zoo, and pre-detox Lilly Guilder. Or—what kind of music did Sherrea like, anyway? The candlelight caught the embroidery on her rusty-black denim jacket: silks, beads, and metallic thread in Celtic knots, runes, warding symbols. They didn't seem to have worked against the weather; her shoulders were damp. "How's the storm?" I asked.

"Just rain, but a helluva lot of it. Theo says somebody's after you for something."

Good guess, me. "Did he say that? Not exactly. It's nothing serious."

She popped a tape into the B deck and turned to me. "Sure. Robby says you showed up white as a bar of soap and looking like you slept in your clothes. Nothing serious."

Well, I *had* slept in my clothes. I noticed, too, that she called him Robby. I felt as if I were looking in the window of some place I used to live in. "Spangler dropped a wrench," I said.

"Oh, excuse me for asking. I just figured if there was something I could do, maybe you'd like to mention it." This sounded like Sher being acerbic, which she did often. It also sounded like Sher being hurt. I looked up and met her eyes. Sher wasn't the sort to avoid eye contact at a moment like that. But I was.

"It's no big thing," I said, changing the tape bias on one machine, then changing it back. "It's taken care of."

She brought up B deck: a series of shots of the head of a daisy, a chambered nautilus that came apart into animation. There were fractals right after that, I knew. I ought to cue up something trippy. "Sparrow," she said, "if you really don't want anybody to give a shit about you, say so, and we'll just let you go to hell."

I almost cracked wise. If it had been any conscious impulse that stopped me, I would have overridden it. "It's important to me," I said instead.

"Why? What's so private that you have to make an enemy of the whole world to keep it that way?"

Just for that instant, I was tempted to tell her.

But Theo came in, a beer in each hand, and kicked the door shut behind him. "Who needs a fresh one?"

"You take it," I said. "It's my turn for a break." Then I caught a look at the third monitor. The camera, which wasn't feeding to either screen, was on the front door. I saw Robert leaning on the frame, a pack of nightbabies newly arrived and staring just in front of him, and behind them a head of pale curly hair, a big white smile, shades—no, not shades.

I grabbed the camera remote and zoomed in. Dana's friends hadn't found me. The other ones had. It was the man in the silvertones.

At the corner of my eye I saw the shift in room light that meant the picture had changed on the screens. "Sher, no!" I cried, but it was too late. The camera feed was up on the left screen. I panned the camera away so fast it must have made the drunks sick, and

Sher hit the switcher, but it was too late. I'd seen him look at the screens. He knew somebody on the balcony was watching him.

Sher was chalky, and her eyes were big. "I'm sorry," she said faintly. Theo stood as still as I'd ever seen him.

"I have to go," I said. "I'll use the back stairs."

"And we're gonna handle it?" Theo asked politely.

Sher looked at him. "Yeah," she said. "We are." She stood up and stretched, flexed her hands, glanced over the edge of the balcony at the dance floor.

"Then I guess we are." Theo shrugged, picked up a heavy flat-bladed screwdriver from a box by the sound board, jammed the blade between the stairway door and the door frame, and pounded it in as far as it would go. "Door's sticking again. Bummer."

"I'm sorry." And I was, but I didn't know what to do.

"Get out of here," Theo said to me, his face blank as tape leader. I plunged through the door in the rear wall of the balcony and shot the bolt home.

I said before that I had a place at the Underbridge. This was it. I passed through without really registering it, beyond deciding that nothing in the closet-sized space could help them find me: a mattress, a couple changes of clothes, a toothbrush. Maybe the barrenness of my life-style would move them to pity, and they'd leave me alone. I began to feel more than guilty. The guy with pink hair seemed like a dangerous sort, and I was leaving Theo and Sher to make my apologies. Well, what could I do? I yanked open the outer door and stepped onto the fire escape.

It was raining steadily, steamily, and everything shone. Somewhere many blocks away, a fire alarm was wailing. I heard the Underbridge's sound system from the open front door. Water gushed over the dam in the river in front of me. The storm, stalking away to the east, gave a long, low rumble like an empty stomach. I hoped the accumulated noise was enough to cover the sound of me running down all those metal steps.

I ran down most of them, actually. Five of them I fell down, loudly, because I forgot that things are slippery when wet. And the last three I skipped entirely and just jumped to the pavement. I was feeling hopeful when something small and hard settled against my skull over my right ear, and a cheerful female voice said, "Darlin', you must think we're awfully thick. Were you hoping we'd forget to look for another exit?"

I stood very still, because I had a suspicion about the hard thing over my ear, and wondered if I should tell her that no, the forgetting was all on my side, thank you. Because, of course, I'd known that the man in the silvertones had a partner.

"Put your hands behind you," she said. When I did, something closed around my wrists. *Handcuffs?* No, these people were not City security, I knew that. What was happening here? What had I done?

"What do you want with me?" I asked, and there was more than a hint of a wail in my voice.

She came around in front of me. Yes, that was a gun she had. Under the mannish hat she wore I saw her hair, the dark cherry color I remembered from a distance in the Night Fair. Her skin was translucently pale, the complexion of the rich. Money made an excellent sunblock. Her eyes were cold, flat gray, and familiar—oh.

"You were with the nightbabies. Outside the Odeon," I said. I was forgetting to breathe, which broke my sentences up. "With the bone in your nose."

She looked pleased. "Very good! I didn't even have to do the voice for you. Now—who are you, at the moment?"

I stared at her.

"All right, I don't think your other half is a good enough actor to do that brain-damaged look. You're still the little scavenger, whatsits . . . Starling? Sparrow."

Behind me, I heard the steel door slam and feet come pounding down the fire stairs. "Well, damn it, Myra," the pink-haired man said, "sometimes I feel like your damned bird dog. You can do your own flushing and chasing next time."

He was simmering with something: adrenaline, anger, speed, maybe all of them. I could feel it behind me, and it made the skin on my back want to crawl around to the front of me for protection.

"Dusty, honey," the red-haired woman—Myra—said, "I let you have all the fun while I stood out in the rain, so what *are* you complaining about?"

I cleared my throat and said, "Did you . . . was there anyone here when you passed through?"

Dusty came around at last into my line of sight. He might have been studying my face. Then he smiled his huge fluorescent smile. "That'd bother you, if I hurt somebody? No—messed up the real estate some, but the tenants, they're all safe and sound. And I know where to find 'em if I need to."

"What do you want?" I said again, and this time I was pleading in earnest. "Is there something you want me to tell you? I'll tell you. You don't have to hurt me—you don't have to hurt anybody."

"That's good," said Myra. She took me by one elbow and pulled me toward the packed-dirt service drive by the riverbank. The rain had turned the dirt to slurry. I hadn't realized it would be so hard to walk with my hands stuck behind me.

I could feel the major arcana at work, the cards that said someone else was in control of my future. I was in terrible trouble, and yet it seemed to stand a polite distance from me. All I had to do was be propelled around, by these people, by another set—simple. They would make me do what they wanted me to do, right or wrong. I had no choice, and no responsibility.

There was a little electric delivery van parked in the drive, painted dark maroon with "Kincaid Adjustments" on the driver's side door in gold. I wondered if I was going to find out what the inside looked like. I could start yelling, I thought, and hope someone came to see what the problem was before they could club me senseless and make me disappear. Silly. Who would come?

The red-haired woman pressed me against the van's front fender and over the wet hood; then she hooked her foot between my ankles and forced my feet apart. She was going to pat me down. A long, uncontrollable shudder went through me. "Dusty," she said, "take this and cover her."

"Her?" said Dusty.

A loud voice, behind and above me, said, "Stand back from the truck. Sparrow, move away from 'em."

It was Theo's voice. I'd never heard him yell before. He was at the head of the fire stairs, with Sher beside him, and he, too, had a nice little gun, which he'd pointed at Myra and Dusty.

Oh, Theo, no. Didn't he remember his own advice? Didn't he know he was making the Underbridge look damned uncooperative? Didn't he have the sense not to do this for someone who'd never done anything for him?

Dusty still had Myra's gun. So he smiled and snapped it upward. I was lunging headfirst toward him, not sure how I'd gotten there or what I was going to do, when someone exploded the whole volume of air around us. At least, it sounded like it.

I was lying in the mud, deaf, looking at the toes of Dusty's shoes. My nose was full of the smell of fired gun. I couldn't get up, because my hands were behind me, so I rolled over.

Dusty still smiled, with the pistol in his hands pointed at the fire stairs. Theo stood where he'd been, wearing the archetype of expressions of surprise. Sher was flattened against the door at the top of the stairs, her eyes showing white all around, her face colorless. Everything was—I looked back at Theo. His attention was fixed on his right arm. It looked as if someone had spilled ink inside the sleeve of his white jacket, and the stain was spreading. I saw his lips move. Was it something profound? All I could think of that needed saying was, *I'm sorry*, and it wasn't his line.

Then someone back by the van said, "If you try that with me, I'll cut you in half, Peppermint," and I thought, *Have we had enough drama yet tonight?*

I struggled to sit up, and found myself looking at Myra. She held an automatic rifle that I realized must have come from the van, was pointing it at Dusty, and seemed ungodly pleased with herself.

Card **5**

Crowning

The Lovers

Waite: Trials overcome.

Crowley: Various twin deities. His weapon is the Tripod. His drugs are ergot and abortifacients. His powers are to be in two or more places at the same time, and prophecy. Analysis, then synthesis. Openness to inspiration, intuition, intelligence, second sight.

5.0: One hundred stories without a punchline

"Myra?" said Dusty with a quaver.

Myra surveyed us all with the same smile. "God, I love tableaux. *Les Enfants du Paradis* meet *The Untouchables*. Peppermint, hold that toy of yours by the barrel and fling it toward the river just as hard as you can. *Now.*" He did, and after a moment, there was a splash. "There's a good boy. Lie down."

"What the hell is going on?" Dusty's voice was like a skin of ice over deep water.

"Allah has sent the change wind, and the world's turned arse over ears. Now do what you're told."

"I ain't gonna lie down."

"Yes, you are. But you have a choice as to whether you do it alive or dead. I have no preference, myself."

Dusty sank slowly to his knees in the mud, and finally lay on his stomach. Myra reached into the little van and started it, fiddled with some things in the cab, and stepped back. The van lurched forward into the darkness, toward the river. In a few moments, there was a crunch.

"Pity," said Myra. "I was hoping it would sink. Now, as for you two," she went on, turning her attention to Theo and Sher.

Theo had come to himself enough to clamp his hand over the wound in his arm, but he looked as if he would like to fall down. Sher was keeping him from doing it, and staring narrowly at Myra.

"Who are you?" Sherrea asked her.

Myra's eyebrows went up. "Child, you frighten me. Bright young people always do. Take your leaking comrade back through that door, lock it, and don't come out again. Will you do that for me?"

"What're you going to do with Sparrow?"

"I am going to take Sparrow home, and you will damn well have to take my word for it. Get inside."

"What home?"

I was, after all, a confirmed bird of passage, but I hadn't thought that Sherrea knew that. Myra said, "If I wanted you to know, I'd invite you along."

Sher was glowering from under her hair, a pixie with a bad attitude. "I'd rather she didn't shoot you," I croaked.

"You don't belong to them," Sherrea said savagely. "You never did. And you don't now." Then she turned and pulled Theo inside.

Myra walked over to me and hauled me up by one arm. "Your standards of personal grooming never cease to impress me," she said, giving my mud the once-over. "Peppermint, stay there until I come back for you, and if I find you've twitched a finger, they'll mistake your corpse for a screen door."

He still had the silvertones on; their blankness gave his face extra malevolence. He said, "When I kill you, I'm gonna make you remember tonight."

She looked down at him, the rifle pointed at his jaw. "Probably," she said, her words slowed by the weight of some personal meaning. "I have a damnably long memory." She took my elbow and drew me stumbling toward the parking lot.

The dust was rinsed away, but the thing parked at the pavement's edge was recognizably the tri-wheeler from two days before. We stopped next to it, and Myra dug in her raincoat and pulled out a little chromed key. She poked it into my jeans pocket. "The cuffs," she explained. "I'd ditch them now, but you're so much more manageable this way. Get in."

She'd popped the weather shell open, and I stood staring, a sickly colored light dawning in my battered head. In the driver's seat of the tri-wheeler was the black-haired woman who owned it, she of the many names. She sat slumped, her eyes half-closed, her mouth slack, her hands dead on her thighs. Inert. Gone.

"Oh. Oh, hell," I whispered. I glanced at Myra, back again to the black-haired driver.

Myra sighed. "Never mind; I'll do it." Before I could struggle, she grabbed the back of my shirt and the waistband of my jeans and swung me in behind that uninhabited body. Then she turned the driver's limp hands over. Twined in the fingers of the left one I saw a strip of braided leather thong and black beads: my hair tie. Myra laid the rifle across the black-haired woman's palms. I must have made a little noise, because Myra turned her flat gray gaze n me. "Sorry," she said. "When you booked your seat, you should have specified 'no shooting.' "

Myra walked away from the tri-wheeler, about a dozen feet. Then she turned around. Her face was blank.

The hands that had been limp closed around the rifle and raised it, pointing it at Myra. And above the rifle, the black-haired woman's face was alive with the pleased expression that Myra's features had worn moments before. Myra looked like someone who had gone to sleep in the basement and woken up on the roof, which I suppose wasn't far from true.

"Myra Kincaid, you make me wish there were disinfectant for the mind," said the black-haired woman. "Are you confused? Of course you are. The short version is that I'm not on your side, I'll shoot you if you take *one more of those steps*, and I'm stealing your friend here. For the long version, ask your brother. He's around back."

I saw Myra take a breath; then, as if that had broken a spell, her face contorted, and she screamed, "Who the hell are you?"

"I'm the thing you're a pale shadow of," said the black-haired woman, and started the tri-wheeler. "Come see me again when your permanent fangs grow in."

Myra took another step, and I steeled myself against the sound of the rifle. But the weather shell slammed down instead, and I was thrown against its scarred window as the trike launched and U-turned.

The driver said loudly, "If I'm lucky, her brother will kill her first, thinking she's still me, and ask questions later. But God knows, I haven't been that lucky yet."

"I know what you are." The words popped out of my mouth as soon as I opened it. Maybe they'd been sitting there too long.

"Do you?" she said, all polite inquiry. "How nice. I was afraid, for a moment, that you might disappoint me."

Once there had been people who stole the prerogatives of the *loa*, who forced their way into other people's minds and possessed them. They were a fantasy from silly novels and B-movies come alive. They were harnessed to the military—but who harnesses gods? In the end, they betrayed their side, betrayed everyone: they pushed the Button. Over half a century ago.

"You're a Horseman," I said.

The three wheels rattled and slammed over a street of potholes and patches, a typical street in this rough, hollow new world. The one she had made.

She stopped at the bridge to the Deeps and turned, and smiled a smile that made my skin creep. "Aren't we all supposed to be dead?"

I nodded. Somewhere in the back of my head, where I couldn't get to them, I felt facts begin to fall into line.

"Good. It would have been so confusing, otherwise. Now, shall I return the favor?"

"I don't—what?"

"Well, you see, I know what *you* are."

We stared at each other for perhaps ten seconds, which is a very long time. For the rest of the trip to the Night Fair, I tried not to move. It hadn't worked with La Maîtresse and Mr. Lyle; but this time I was hoping for better results than simply not being noticed. This time I meant to disappear entirely.

The gates of the Night Fair were open, the lights on, the party rolling forward in its habitual way. She stopped at the first opening in the fence and said, "Give me directions."

I stared at her, all my possible responses shooting like scan lines across my mind: fill the screen, overwrite, overwrite.

She laughed. "As I've said once tonight, I have no preference. But I thought you'd rather I asked, since we'll get there whether you help or not."

I wanted to ask which of the major arcana she was. There was a gas lamp on one of the gateposts; it sent light skidding over the side of her face, across her nose, but it missed the eye socket. There was a little scar, barely more than an indentation, near the corner of her mouth. It might have been from a childhood injury, long forgotten. Oh, little laughing gods, of *course* forgotten—her body couldn't have been more than thirty. It was an injury *from someone else's childhood*.

"Keep going," I said in an ugly, clogged voice. "There's a closer gate."

She took the handcuffs off as soon as we arrived. My wrists hurt, but I didn't rub them. She kept the automatic rifle with her; I couldn't imagine what she meant to use it on, since she didn't need it for me.

There are no similes for the way I felt, leading her into the building, into the elevator, standing across from her in that little box as it lurched quietly toward the top of the building. Maybe it says enough that I didn't try to hide my wire-crossing from her.

What had it been like for Myra Kincaid? Had she known that her body was being stolen? Had she struggled? Or had she missed it all, and suddenly found herself awake, face-to-face with the comfortless smile of the *loa*? Make the elevator work, Sparrow; or she'll mount you, and sink her spurs into you, and have every scrap of knowledge out of you, of that, of anything. *Let her fight me for it*, I thought. But there were the wires in my hands, and here was the elevator quaking around me. Maybe a reputation for coercion was the best coercive tool of all.

Open the elevator doors, unlock the apartment door—no, it was already unlocked, because I'd bolted out of it with the key in my pocket and a large man close behind me. I didn't feel anything at the memory. Through the dark front room, then, into the hallway.

I wasn't numb after all. Because at the end of the hall, the doors to the third room stood a little open, spilling light and music, and I felt a shock of cold on my skin, and a scream blocked up in my throat.

I think I took the black-haired woman by surprise; I was through the hall door and the inside one as well before anyone could have stopped me. A man sat in my comfortable chair, his back to me. The song was Richard Thompson's "Yankee Go Home." I had an absurd, precise recollection of it; it was on disk, and the insert was inscribed to someone, in blue ink, in a pointy, idiosyncratic hand. Then the man swung around to face me, and smiled.

"I love this one," he said. "Brings back a lot of lousy memories."

I'd never seen him before. Maybe in his mid-twenties, with smooth, glossy brown skin, long hair bleached to chestnut-brown that was braided all over his scalp and twined with bright green thread and tiny copper fish charms. Wide mouth, heavy straight brows over large round black eyes. A compact, slender body in a yellow cotton shirt and loose gray trousers. But he was wearing Mick Skinner's jacket, and smiling Mick Skinner's self-mocking smile, and I knew who he was. And what he was. The facts were assembled now, because the driver of the trike was not the only person who ought to be dead and wasn't, and Myra Kincaid wasn't the only person with a chunk missing from her memory. Mick Skinner knew what all my missing pieces were.

Of course he did. He'd been me while they'd happened.

Now he was somebody else, but it was still him, using my best-kept secret, my archives, my sanctuary. It was as bad as using my body.

"How the hell many of you *are* there?" I squeaked in his uncomprehending face.

His eyes went past me then, and narrowed, and his smile faded. The black-haired woman had come in behind me, the damned rifle leveled—*Chango*, if she pulled the trigger she'd chop the hard-

ware to bits. She didn't pull the trigger. She just stared with the
same narrow-eyed concentration at him.

"Frances?" he said at last, as if he couldn't breathe.

"Hello, Mick," she said. The rifle never wavered. "I wondered
when it would be you."

He puffed air out through his nose—a substitute for laughter,
maybe, though he wasn't smiling. "You're still a woman."

"'Again,' actually. Didn't *you* go through a few learning
experiences getting out of the goddamn stinking jungle? Or have
you kept your boyish charm ever since Panama?" She had an edge
on her voice and manner now, blackened and smoking and too hot
for safety.

He shook his head, as if shaking off insects. "Fran . . . Jesus,
would you put that gun down?"

"No, I don't think I would. Why aren't you dead, Mick?"

"Well, why the hell aren't you?"

"Because I have the morals of a shark. On the basis of personal
experience, I'm forced to assume the same of you."

Mick's new mouth pressed closed, crookedly. Then he said,
"We all did. There wasn't one of us I'd trust to feed my dog for
a weekend. But that was a long time ago."

"As long as that?" Her smile was really only a baring of her
teeth. "Heavens, Mick, did you think we'd *evolve*?"

It took him a moment to rally. "Learn, maybe? Change? People
do." But his voice was fainter, battered down by her manner.

"And lucky they are, too. But we're not people. We're sharks.
It's our nature. We can't stand to see clear water without a little
blood in it."

"Fran, can't you—"

"What are you doing here, Mick?"

"Pardon me," I said, and I was as amazed to hear my voice as
they seemed to be. "If neither of you minds, we could have this
conversation in the next room just as well. And if you're going to
shoot him," I added to the woman named Frances, "I wish you
wouldn't do it in here."

She stared at me, then took in the room with a quick shift of her
gaze. I think, until then, she hadn't really seen it. "Bless my
soul," she said at last. "It's the lost graveyard of the Sonys."

"If it was only a graveyard, I wouldn't care," I replied, though
I hated to do it. "They all work."

She looked the room over again, this time with more attention.
Then she looked at me. I could almost hear her thinking, though

not well enough to know in what direction. "Lead the way," she ordered. So I did. She gestured Mick Skinner out behind me.

I walked into the middle room. The teakettle was lying on the floor in a small puddle; most of the water seemed to have disappeared between the floorboards. That, and a black smudge on the ceiling, were all that were left to remind me of La Maîtresse and Mr. Lyle. I took the kettle to the sink and started pumping water into it. There was a calm and reasoned dialogue going on in my head, something like:

This is a ridiculous thing to be doing.

The whole business is ridiculous. What should I be doing that would make more sense?

She might shoot me.

For making tea? I suppose she might. She might shoot me for not making tea.

In other words, I can't fix things no matter what I do, so I might as well do anything at all.

I think I'm so scared I can't feel it.

When I turned back to face my houseguests, Mick Skinner was standing by one felt-covered window, watching me, bemused and a little alarmed. And he *was* Mick Skinner; I was surprised at how easy it was to think of him that way, independent of his looks.

The woman, Frances, was perched lightly on the arm of the leather slingshot chair, the rifle comfortable in the crook of her right arm, its barrel tracking Mick Skinner. A casual sweep of that arm, and both he and I would be perforated at the waist.

She said, "I haven't forgotten the subject before the committee, even if you have. What brought you here, Mick?"

"I came back for my jacket."

"No, no, answer the exam questions fully; you've no idea what we're testing for. This city, Skinner, you idiot, just now, for what God-damned *purpose*."

He looked steadily at her, his face baffled and hurt, and resigned. "Do you still have purposes?" he asked. "I used mine up. I just move around, Fran."

"Why move here?"

"I'd never been here, so I came. I had a notion to go on north and try to get into Canada."

"A pitiful and profoundly moving story," she said. I hadn't realized I'd been hoping she'd believe him until I felt my spirits fall. "Let's explore a promising side passage, shall we? What's your connection to our chum here?" She tipped her head toward me.

Mick Skinner, inexplicably, was silent. "He rode me," I told her, and stopped. The bald statement of it, out loud, sickened me; and it didn't answer her questions, or mine.

"Oh, my downy chick, my sweet hatchling, I *know* that. I knew there was one of us here by the stink of it. When I laid hands on you, there on the bridge, I got the smell of Horseman in my nose so strong I thought I'd gag with it.

"Did you know that, Mick? That we leave a trail behind us, a spoor of possession? It's related, I think, to the way we recognize each other in some other poor bastard's body. And I thought, when I got a whiff of this one, that it was damned familiar."

"I couldn't help it," Mick said. He sounded as if the words were being squeezed out of him. "I had . . . some bad rides. I didn't know what happened the first time. I didn't make the switch, it just—"

"Don't, please, spare us the gory details," Frances said pleasantly.

"The body I was on got hit by a car," he said. I could tell—I thought I could tell—he hated doing it. "And suddenly I was three streets over, on Sparrow, being pushed out a door." I had been in danger of being thrown *through* the door; if he had, by skill or fortune, spared me that, I owed him something. "I only stayed long enough to find another ho—another body."

"What was wrong with that one?" Frances asked, pointing at me.

A muscle worked in Mick's jaw. "He wasn't done with it."

Frances raised her eyebrows.

Mick Skinner's eyes closed, and his long brown hands clenched. He was . . . ashamed? Of *not* taking me over? "I can't not do it. Every time the choice comes, between dying and taking another horse, I jump for the horse every goddamn time. I can't let go of living. But I try to find people who *have* let go. You find somebody who's about to eat a bullet, you hop on, take the gun out of his mouth—it's almost with his consent, isn't it? It doesn't feel so fucking *evil*."

"But it happened more than once," I said. I couldn't bring myself to say it again: *You rode me*.

"I couldn't get a solid ride. Sick people are hard. Crazy ones are harder. Jesus, the last one I got on a second too late, and he was *dead*. I didn't think that was possible." He looked up at me, apologetic. "And you were such a good fit. I kept being pulled back. I didn't mean to be."

At that, Frances began to laugh. She rose from the arm of the chair and came over to me. She still held the rifle as if she meant to use it. "Heavens, yes. Fits as if it were made for you. And with every convenience built in. Of middling height, to avoid drawing attention. Strong, young, resistant to disease, toxins, and bad food. And eminently hiddable."

"Fran," said Mick with great care, "you don't have to mess with Sparrow."

"No, I don't. But I want to. Do you know, Mick, that by my reckoning there are only three Horsemen left? I'd thought it was two, until you surfaced, which only shows you that I may be a hair off in my figures." She was close enough for me to see the gloss of sweat on her skin. "Only the real sharks survived the witch-hunts after the Big Bang. And I found that each passing year pruned them further, leaving only the crème de la crème of sharkdom.

"Now, Mick, my old friend and partner, if there are only three of us left, and my theory of natural selection is correct, mustn't we be the three meanest sons of bitches in the valley?"

Mick shrugged, not too unconvincingly.

"And yet—I remember you, Mick. You weren't a nice person—"

"We were all shits," Mick interrupted.

"—but you didn't have the real, cold-hearted taste for blood. Now, how could someone like that have survived for years in a world that will not suffer a Horseman to live? By apprenticing himself to the biggest shark of all, the Daddy Killer of the whole toothy race, that's how. The slayer of cities, the drowner of worlds, the pusher of Buttons. Let me tell you why *I'm* in this city. I've come to pay a long-delayed call on the Prince of Sharkness."

The stove burner hissed in the silence while Mick and I worked out what that meant. "Who?" Mick said finally. His voice was a colorless whisper, and all the blood had deserted his face for parts unknown. "Who was it? My family lived in Galveston."

"Excessive, Mick. Too much pathos. Add the dog that was your boyhood companion, and I'll throw you off the stage."

"Who did it, Fran?"

She was grave when she said, "For to see Mad Tom O'Bedlam, ten thousand miles I've traveled."

Mick Skinner stared, his round black eyes open as wounds. His lips formed the first letter twice before any sound came out. "Worecski? Tom Worecski pushed the Button?"

"He was the mastermind. He assembled the clique, and convinced them they would be humanity's saviors. The clique, hubris-ridden idiots, have made permanent amends. Now there's only Mad Tom."

Mick put one unsteady hand behind him, found the wing chair, and sat in it. "It *would* have been Worecski. My God."

The teakettle was rumbling, I realized, and I stepped toward the camp stove to turn it off.

"No," said Frances. She took hold of a lock of my hair and pulled me to a halt. "We just got to the good part."

I stood very still as she fingered my hair, tugged it lightly, tucked it behind my ear. I would *not* tremble like a nervous dog.

"As I was saying about our specimen here, all the conveniences. The apparent genetic inheritance, for instance. The ruddy tan, the black hair and dark eyes, the bone structure"—she tapped my cheek under my right eye—"nothing there to raise an eyebrow anywhere from Oklahoma to Tierra del Fuego. Indigenous Western Hemisphere genes. Just what you'd want for sneaking around down below Texas."

Mick Skinner's eyes were on us, but I wasn't sure they were seeing anything. I wondered if his mind was somewhere in drowned Galveston.

"Another handy thing about those genes is that they're commonly associated with a lack of facial hair in males."

My resolve was all for nothing; I was shivering in little, uncontrollable bursts. Frances was studying my face as if I were a painting, or something else that couldn't stare back. She prodded my jaw lightly. I was more aware of her hand than the rifle.

"And there, Mick," she said, "we come to the real artistry. This face, this pleasing architecture that would be handsome on either sex. The gothic arches of the eyebrows and the nostrils and the lips, echoing each other. That's a work of art, that is, a work of trompe l'oeil."

"He hates to be touched, Fran," said Mick.

"A nice balance of bone to flesh, too. Seems a bit sturdy one minute, a bit frail the next. The Adam's apple, that was tricky. See?" She pushed lightly with her thumb to raise my chin. "There isn't one, but there's sort of a suggestion in the angle of the neck. Marvelous. There's a lot here that's done with suggestion, in fact."

Mick said, "Stop it."

"The silhouette of the torso, for instance." She drew a line with her index finger, slowly, from my collarbone to my stomach. I closed my eyes. "Tapered, but not excessively; narrow at the waist, but not too much. The tits weren't a problem; within tolerance for a flat-chested woman, as long as the shirt never comes off."

"Frances," Mick said in a voice that would have stopped a train. It stopped her hand on the first button of my shirt.

"Yes?"

"I got real tired of watching people be tortured. Give me another thirty years to work up a taste for it. He hasn't done anything to you."

She was suddenly full of focused intensity, like a magnifying glass held up to the sun. "His mind?" she asked Mick gently. "Or the body? You and I, we've learned to consider them separately."

"Do you think he's Tom? God damn it, Fran, I've been in there. I would have known—"

"Two things: I have only your word for that; and if it's not Tom," she said in a voice like a breeze off an icefield, "why do you call it 'he'?"

Mick opened his mouth, and closed it.

"Because if you've ridden this body," said Fran, with horrible satisfaction, "you must know it's not male."

"Or female," Mick said faintly. "It's—oh. Oh, my God."

"Christ, Mick, if you really *were* surprised, I'd think you were a drooling idiot. Non-sex-specific bodies aren't exactly thick on the ground."

"It's a *cheval*," said Mick, huge-eyed.

"Very good, class." She brushed loose hair back from my forehead and studied my face. "A mindless, soulless, sexless shell, genderless as a baby doll," she said to me—at me—whoever she was talking to, it wasn't me. She didn't believe I existed. Oh, tricky Legba, she was going to kill me, and she didn't even know I was there. I stepped back, and she matched me as if she'd read my mind. She probably had. "A crisp new brain without a tenant. A bottle made to be filled by one of us, empty brass waiting to be turned into a bullet. A shiny new horse to be offered to the desperate Horseman, in the vain hope that he or she will prefer it over the nearest infantry grunt. A domestic animal bred and broken for one of us to ride. And that means *one of us is riding it*. If his intentions were good, why the charming masquerade?" Her eyes were strange and wild, and I couldn't look away from them.

"What if he—she—doesn't know?" Mick said desperately. "What if it's one of us, but messed up, so he doesn't remember?"

Her fingers twisted in my shirtfront, and she thumped me back against the kitchen wall. "Run for it, Tom," she said softly. "Or plead a bit, or try to kill me. Do anything you like, except move to skip off this body. That, I won't allow."

My vision wavered with tears, and my knees were buckling. I

wanted to reach out and grab her shoulders, to hold myself up, to beg, but I was afraid to raise my hands for fear she'd pull the trigger. She was going to pull it anyway. My knees hit the floor, and the tears spilled over. What a horrible, shameful, pointless way to die. "Please," I babbled wetly, "I'm not who you think I am. I'm not *anybody*."

Mick Skinner said fiercely, "Fran, if you don't stop, I'm gonna hit you. And you're gonna have to weigh whatever's kept you from shooting me against that."

"Maybe I just wanted an audience," she replied. There was a distance in her voice at odds with the violence in her eyes. "Shall I tell you how many people's bodies I've ridden and lost, or used up? I can't remember. But I took them all to get Mad Tom Worecski. I'll kill that many again before I let him get away from me."

"It's not Worecski," Skinner shouted. "You want to know for sure? Ride him—it—oh, God damn! Ride it and see!"

She stood over me, her face wild. The muzzle of the rifle was almost against my lips. Then hot white pain blossomed in my chest, my head, pierced my eyes and ears and made me deaf and blind. Consciousness didn't slide away; it just stopped.

And was back. I had barely enough warning to turn my head before I threw up. My head was too heavy for my neck, and both of them were too much for my shoulders. I slumped against the wall. That hadn't been anything like before, when I'd been . . . when Mick . . . I couldn't think it, I'd be sick again.

Frances was still in front of me, her feet planted wide, the rifle in her hands. She was the color of raw bread dough, and her face and arms shone with sweat. She shook her head and turned away, walked across the room to the desk, and laid the rifle on it. Then she braced both hands on the desktop.

"He's not there," she said, her voice muffled. I wondered if it was her voice or my ears. Mick stood watching her, and I thought he might be preparing to do something, though I didn't know what. "But one of us has to be riding. The *chevaux* were empty, no personality, no mind. Just a carcass. It's a *cheval*, but there's a mind on it, so it must be one of us. But it's not Tom Worecski. And if it's not . . ." She straightened up, and her right hand reached, shaking, for empty air. ". . . then I don't know where he is."

Slowly, tidily, she folded up; Mick caught her before her head hit the floor.

5.1: Sweet memories are the paradise of the mind

"Oh, Frances, you never did know much about people. Including you." Mick turned to me, and there was nothing on his face to say that he didn't spend every day in scenes like the one we'd just played. "It's only exhaustion," he added.

It took me a moment to realize he was talking about the woman in his arms. I wanted to say something rude, but couldn't mobilize more than a stare.

"She was always like this. Like a damn guided missile—once she launched herself at something, she couldn't stop or slow down or change direction. We used to call her Redline. I'll bet she hasn't let this body sleep for a couple-three days."

He got her over his shoulder and stood up with a grunt. "I'll put her on the bed."

"No."

He stopped and blinked at me.

"She was about to shoot me in the face. Leave her where she fell. If she gets a crick in her neck, I'll cry buckets." Then I remembered that the crick would be in someone else's neck. But Frances would feel it. . . . Papa Legba, no wonder they'd gone nuts.

Mick frowned, but lowered Frances gently back to the floor. Her black hair had swung forward when he'd picked her up; strands were caught in her eyelashes and over her lips. Mick smoothed them back, his long brown hands light and careful, as if he were afraid of marking her skin. "She's not . . . It sounds stupid, but she's not so bad. For one of us. She was crazy, but she wasn't vicious."

The taste of bile was still in my mouth, and I was shivering steadily. "Which were you?" I asked. "Crazy, or vicious?"

He settled back on his heels and shook his head. "We were all crazy. God, how long d'you think *you* could stay well adjusted after you found out you could possess people?"

"I'm the possessee. You tell me." I got up slowly—I felt as if I'd lost blood, I was so weak—and turned off the fire under the kettle. It hadn't boiled dry, which was my only proof that it had not been hours since I filled it. I rummaged for tea on the shelves and found chamomile in a jam jar. Fine with me; my nerves could use soothing. I caught myself reaching for the teapot, and took down a mug instead. While the flowers steeped, I cleaned up after myself.

"If I leave for half an hour, will you be here when I get back?" Mick Skinner asked, which forced me to admit to myself that he was still in the room.

"Where are you going?"

"Thought I ought to fetch some food, before things shut down at dawn."

He was relatively new to the City, but he knew the Night Fair's schedule. "Did you steal that out of my head?"

"What—oh. Yeah. I needed it this morning, when I . . ."

When he'd ridden me last. "Do you have all my memories now?"

"No. Don't get so damned excited. I get at a hor—a person's memories just like they do. I have to fish for 'em. Sometimes what I'm concerned with brings one up, but it's usually not that easy."

I settled carefully into the wing chair, cradling my mug in both hands. I felt as brittle as one of my fragile old tapes, yanked into motion between pinch rollers, around capstans. If one reel balked: snap. I angled my head at Frances, limp on the floor. "Is that why it felt like she was killing me, when she made her little trip in?"

He rubbed his forehead and finished the gesture by smoothing his hair. The copper fish chimed lightly. "She was in a state. Instead of opening a window, she broke the glass with a hammer, I guess."

"In other words, she didn't have to do that. Heck, I feel lots better."

Mick's front teeth met, sharply. "Look. There's a limit to how much apologizing I'm going to do for Frances, but I'm not going to trash her for you, either. We went through hell together—and if that sounds like a cliché, it's not. We were friends. If she's nuts, I know why. And there's nothing she's done that I haven't done, too." He stood up, a series of precise movements. "I'm going for food. If you're not here when I get back, I promise not to give a goddamn." And he left.

The tea had cleared the foul taste out of my mouth, and had stopped my shaking. I could probably make my way out of the building now, and lose myself in the Night Fair. I remembered, suddenly, the thong from my hair that Frances had held outside the Underbridge. She'd found me then. But maybe she was done with me now that she'd gouged out knowledge and found I wasn't what she wanted.

Oh, snakes and scorpions. Of course I couldn't go. The archives were all the hostage anyone needed to hold me. Without them, what did I have to Deal, except fast talk and falsehood?

"Excuse me," the pale thread of a voice came from the figure on the floor. "Can I borrow two pennies? The man with the ferryboat won't take my I.O.U."

She hadn't moved, except to open her eyes. Those were fixed on me, large and black and smudged underneath with the driven weariness that, I now realized, had been there all night.

"You're not going to die," I said. It would be harder than that to squeeze sympathy out of me.

"Ah. That explains it. Though I can't imagine why I'm not."

"Because there's a cure for overwork. More's the pity."

She closed her eyes at that. "Do you know, I think I agree?"

I stood up with a lurch and went to pour more water into my mug.

"For what it's worth—which I suspect is not a lot—I'm sorry," she added. "When I have a little more energy, I'll endeavor to grovel, if you want."

"Don't put yourself out on my account." I thought about going into another room. But it would have looked, and felt, like retreat. And there was the possibility, small but non-zero, that if I stayed I might be able to make her uncomfortable. I sat down again. "So, did you have a nice time? Did you get everything you wanted?"

"Out of you? No, since what I wanted was to find out you were Tom Worecski. Does it make you feel better, or worse, to know that you went through that for nothing?"

"Only from your point of view. It makes me feel better that I'm still alive."

"Ah, yes. Everyone's first desire. To stay alive."

I suppose what happened was that we were both made uncomfortable. At any rate, the conversation faltered there.

It was she who broke the silence. "You were in Louisiana?"

At the word, I remembered: waking disoriented and empty of

thought, chilly and stiff-limbed, to a steady sound I didn't recognize. I'd struggled up on one elbow, discomfort in my eyes until I'd realized I could rub them with my fingers and the feeling would go away. Running water, that's what the sound had been.

I flinched and splashed my tea.

"I *am* sorry," Frances said. "Whatever that was, it was probably my fault. Memory is like silt, sometimes. It may be a while before it settles."

"No. I just—I didn't know I remembered it."

"What was it?"

"The first thing I ever . . . Coming up, the first time."

She looked amused. "The first time for what?"

"No, the first time for anything. When I woke up."

"It can't have been the first time, you know," she said. "You must be one of us; riding a *cheval*. You've mislaid your identity, but it may turn up."

"You're the one who went through my head with a crowbar. Didn't you find it?"

She frowned. "No. Nothing older than a bunker down south."

"How much of that did you sample?" She winced; at my tone, I suppose; so I added in the same one, bright and pointy, "Not that I object. I just don't want to bore you with things you already know."

I must have reached the limits of her apologetic mood, because she said, "If you bore me, you'll know. I'm going to get off the floor and sit in this chair. Unless you plan to shoot me if I do."

And that, I swear, was the first time I remembered the rifle abandoned on the desk. In her hands it had been a malevolent, ticking presence. Out of them, it was a paperweight. Something had happened in the room, something I couldn't fathom, that had made it unlikely that any of the three of us would shoot the others.

She settled into the slingshot chair like an old woman, and the leather creaked. "What happened to Mick, by the way?"

Had that last been too casual? Was she worried? If so, what about? "He's gone to get supplies to restore your depleted self."

Frances looked up at that. "Has he?" she said mildly. "If he has a yen to play Saint Theresa, he can lavish his talents on a more appreciative audience."

"Since you've proven you can take care of yourself."

"Given the state you were in when I made your acquaintance," Frances said, "you should talk."

I shrugged. "I couldn't help it. Your pal Mick left me lying in the sun."

"And you warped. I understand. Tell me about Louisiana."

"It's very wet."

"No, I mean waking up in Louisiana."

I stood up again. I was beginning to feel spring-loaded. I talked to the sink, put my mug in it, and turned around. "Why in ell do you want to know?"

"Maybe I'll be able to figure out who you are."

"I know who I am."

Her eyebrows went up. "Really."

"All right. I don't, particularly. But are you surprised that I'd ather be the palace eunuch than one of the great boogeymen of ur age?"

"If we were only boogeymen," she said, echoing my earlier vords, "no one would care." In the way she spoke, I heard again vhat she'd said to Dusty: *Probably. I have a damnably long nemory.* Indeed. Nobody should have one that long.

"*Have* you ever done anything that Mick hasn't?" I asked.

"Did he say that?"

"More or less."

She laughed a little. Then she said, "He was mistaken." She aised her eyes to mine. "But don't tell him. He'll find out ventually."

"Are you going to kill him?"

"The future is a land unmapped, from which no expedition has eturned. I don't think so. He had nothing to do with the Bang. trange as it seems, he is, as these things go, a passable human eing."

"Are you going to kill me?" In spite of my conviction, it eemed reasonable to ask.

"I told you I was sorry. No. I'm not."

"But you're still going to get this Whatsisname."

"Yes," she said, "I am. In the best tradition of vigilantism, I've illed all the appointive offices myself: judge, jury, prosecutor, nd she-who-pulls-the-trigger."

"It's a long time since the Big Bang," I said uncertainly. I'd een almost at ease with her for a few minutes—or pleasurably ineasy, caught up in the heightened reality of verbal sparring. But ier last declaration reminded me of the woman she'd been before he fell down.

"Sparrow, Tom Worecski is responsible for more deaths than Hitler. Does time wipe that clean? How much time? Does emorse? I don't know if he's sorry for murdering millions of eople and making large areas of the Western Hemisphere uninhabitable, but tell me, how sorry ought he to be before I say 'Oh, never mind, I guess that makes it all right'?"

I stared at her, and she stared back. "Is that what I'm supposed to say when you apologize?" I asked.

She pressed her lips together. "Point to your side. But believe me, Tom has to die. And I have to do it. There's no one else."

"Chango, you could assemble a posse in five minutes if you told 'em what you wanted them for."

"And shall I tell them how I come by my information? That I know Tom from way back, that we worked together, et cetera? No. There really is no one else."

This time she didn't sound as if she took pride in the fact. Or maybe the phrase meant something else, now. She sat staring at her strong hands crossed in her lap, as if images of the long, terrible, unchangeable past were shining up between her fingers.

I pumped the teakettle full of water and put it on the flame. Then I dumped the rest of the chamomile in my chipped enamel teapot and went back to the wing chair.

"Louisiana *was* wet," I said. "And getting wetter." I told the whole story without looking up. I had never told it to anyone. I'd been so careful never to even want to tell it that I'd mostly forgotten it myself. After all, no one else I knew remembered being born.

I'd heard the sound, rubbed my eyes, and recognized the hiss and bubble as running water before I'd seen anything. My vision had been slow to clear; the room revealed itself with each blink, each scrubbing pass with my fingers. The lighting was bluish and uneven. I was surrounded by metal boxes, large ones, with tops that caught the light: glass. I squinted past the reflections into the nearest one.

A dead, sunken face, a shaved head, a mummified naked body. There was a corpse in the box. There were eight boxes in the room, all alike. When, frightened, I turned my eyes away, I saw my own legs and feet, attached to the rest of me, bordered by a box with an open glass lid. I began to scream. I don't know why; it was an instinct toward terror, a dread of being just like the eight dead things in the room. And of course I was, but for one small detail.

I scrabbled out of the box and fell, and learned that I couldn't breathe in water. There was almost three feet of it on the floor. I dragged myself up the side of my resting place. On the walls above some of the coffin-boxes, red lights flashed. Warning, alert, something needs attention, system failure. It babbled through my

ead. Later I knew I'd understood the purpose of the lights, but
ot then.

I had a sudden clear knowledge, like another instinct, of
electrocution and the conductivity of water. I staggered clumsily
through the flood (the strangeness of that came to me later: I was
born knowing how to walk) to a door (sight of it, and the word
springing into my head, *door*, and the understanding of what it
did), which I pounded and pushed on. Finally I found a lever in
the wall next to it, which turned.

The door crashed inward on its hinges. It and the water that had
leaned on it for—years?—threw me back into the room. One of
the mummies floated past me, upward; another followed it. The
water had broken the boxes open.

And then, when I had to know it, I knew how to swim. I lurched
toward the ceiling of that underwater charnel house, sucked air out
of the rapidly diminishing space there, and kicked out against the
pressure, toward the door.

I learned eventually that it was the water of Lake Pontchartrain
I was struggling against. The place where I came up, under a full
noon with mist rising white from the surface into the cooler air of
a midsummer night, was Bayou St. John. Three weeks later a
hurricane added it all to the New Orleans basin.

"How long ago was that?" Frances asked after a little space of
quiet had settled between us.

"Fifteen—almost sixteen years, now."

She leaned her head back and smiled. "Mmm. If I'm right,
you're eighty or more. If you're right, you've barely reached the
Golden Age of Skepticism. Either way, you hardly look it."

I don't know what I'd expected from the first person to hear that
story, but I found Frances's response oddly comforting. Just
another bizarre, life-threatening adventure. How many of them
had she had? I went to pour hot water into the teapot.

There were a few cookies, bought maybe a week ago in the mall
market, in a tin on the shelf. They weren't fresh, but they had
refused to go stale, either. I carried the tin, along with the teapot
and my other mug, over to the desk and set them on the corner
nearest her. She looked at the two mugs and said, "Entertain
often?"

"I only have an extra for when I'm too lazy to wash the first
one. If you were me, would you have a lot of close friends?"

"In my own fashion, I'm under the same constraints. And
you're right, I don't. It's a furtive little life, but it's all mine." She
chewed carefully. "Better already. Butter and sugar, in sufficient

quantity, will cure anything." She ate and worked on her tea as if that were all she could concentrate on, and maybe it was. I'd done my talking; I was prepared to sit, and watch, and see what happened.

At last she set the cup down and slid her hands over her face. "Thank you. God, I'm tired." She closed her eyes, and I wondered if she meant to fall asleep there. Then she said, "If we'd been left to our own devices, I think none of the Horsemen would have willingly been within a hundred miles of each other. As predators go, we were more like tigers than wolves. Forcing us together like that just made us worse."

"That gave you a taste for the furtive life?" I asked.

I expected her to ignore me, or, more likely, to turn one of her phrases that sounded impressive and gave away nothing. Instead, she said, "Christ, no. If it gave me a taste for anything . . . no, only a distaste. For myself, among other things." She sighed and tipped her head back against the chair. It was harder to see her expression now. "What a damned waste of human potential it all was."

"Turning Central America into an archipelago wasn't enough of an accomplishment for you?"

"Is that the proper ambition of humankind? We had—we were like gods." She gave a gasp of uncomfortable-sounding laughter. "We *were* like gods. Think of Zeus: He could turn himself into a shower of gold, and all he wanted to do was to cheat on his wife. We played savage practical jokes, ruined lives, and wreaked vengeance. That was our contribution to society."

"Why did they keep you?"

"Who?"

"The army. Or whoever."

"Why did they keep the stealth bomber? I'm sorry," she said when I shook my head. "You don't know what the stealth bomber was. Or you don't remember. I suppose they'd spent too much money on us. Though, to be fair, we did exactly what we were meant to do, as long as we felt like it."

"Which was?" I knew, in a vague way; but something told me that Frances discussing the past was a rare commodity. It seemed a shame to let her stop now, when, if she kept on, she might get to . . . something I wasn't even sure I wanted to hear.

She drew her feet up in the chair, folded her arms over her knees, and propped her chin on her crossed wrists. "Objective," she said crisply. My experience of lecturing professors was all from actors on video, but she reminded me of those. "To provide

busy intelligence and advice to El Presidente de la República
Banana. Old-fashioned method: feed fake dispatches and phony
coded orders to *his* intelligence staff, and hope they don't realize
was too easy to get. Newfangled method: mount a Horseman on
is Jefe de Seguridad, maybe another on his Secretary of State.
Not only do you get hand delivery of your bogus information; you
also get a highly placed double agent with an impenetrable cover.
Qué bueno, sí? And that, of course, was only one of our many
uses."

"Did it work?"

Her grin was feral. "Sometimes. And before you ask, we'll
leave the exceptions decently buried, thank you. Since they
ranged from the deeply shameful to the utterly horrific."

"Why didn't you just take the presidentes over and declare
peace?"

"It may be," she said, looking insufferably patient, "that you
are fifteen, after all. Because the cabinet, the generals, and the
God-damned janitorial staff would have blown El Presidente's
brains out and declared a change of government. Do you think a
nation wages war because of one person in a big leather chair in
a nice office?"

"Having never lived in a nation," I said, "I wouldn't know."

Frances turned her face away, as if I'd slapped her. "Don't
worry, you're not missing much. A wretched anthill of peaceful,
productive, useful life with hardly any invigorating biting and
scratching. Where people flossed once a day and mowed the lawn
on Sundays."

I watched her, and said, "It wasn't your fault."

One emphatic black eyebrow went up, and her straight mouth
crimped with irony at the corners. "Thank you, I feel ever so
much better. I suppose my sense of social responsibility makes up
in vigor what it lacked in timeliness."

"Could you have stopped them then?"

She paused to think about it. "Yes. Which is why I'm so
assiduously stopping them now. Have been stopping them. It's my
penance. Hail Mary, Full of Grace, the Lord Is With Thee would
be easier, but it seems a shame to waste all that good marksman-
ship."

My hands closed over the arms of the wing chair. "You mean,
it's not just this Tom Whatsisname. You're hunting them all
down."

"*Have* hunted. Past tense. I'm nearly done."

"All the Horsemen?"

"God, no. Besides, the populace at large has mostly taken care of that. I only wanted the refined gathering that thought, for their various reasons, that lobbing one in would be a good idea. The populace did take care of one of them, as it turned out. I dispatched four more." She spread her hard, browned fingers in the air between us. "And all the perfumes of Arabia canno sweeten this little hand. Well, not specifically *this* hand." Then suddenly: "That bothers you, doesn't it?"

I swallowed, with an effort, and said, "That I'm sharing a room with someone whose life's work has been to find people and murder them? Why would you think that?"

"Whatever you're good at, it's not sarcasm. They were four people who had never done a decent thing in the world and never would. They were the highest accomplishment of a subset of humanity who gloried in degradation and cruelty, who saw everyone—even each other—as lab rats and Judas goats."

She was so calm. Maybe she'd lived long enough with righteous anger that it had smoothed into something else. But it drove me to say, "What's the matter? Were you jealous?"

She leaned forward, and there was something in her face that made me shiver. "I had nothing to be jealous of. Listen and be made wise. Once upon a time in New Mexico, there was an MP named Stedmon. One dark night he annoyed me. I don't remember the offense. The next evening he walked in on an edifying scene involving his fiancée and four men from his unit. Four being the most I could collect, from my vantage point on his fiancée, on short notice.

"Then there was the Great Parachuting Lesson, considered by my fellows to be one of our best gags. I mounted my victim in a bar off base and dismounted in midair, just when he ought to have opened his chute. He was a little disoriented at first, I'm afraid, and as a result broke his legs.

"The four people I killed could have matched both of those for cruelty. In fact, any Horseman could have. Every sane community kills vermin and rabid animals."

She jerked to her feet and strode to the other side of the room. I hadn't noticed until then how small an area the lamp illuminated; she was an arrangement of light and dark near the door. Then the arrangement moved, and I knew her hands had gone up to her face.

"I'm very sorry," she said. Her words were blurred, as if by her fingers. "I told you I'd developed a distaste, which was under-stating it a bit. I'm not proud of those incidents, and I apologize or telling them as if I am. Or for telling them at all. They're over half a century old."

She was not going to get to it, the thing I was afraid of. I didn't have to worry about it. So I was alarmed when I found myself saying, "And what was I supposed to be for?"

I heard her take a steadying breath, and saw her hands come down. "Did you know you had something to do with us?"

"Not at first. Never mind."

She stood very still; then she came back into the light in a few strides and squatted beside me, looking into my face. "You didn't know, did you? Until tonight, when I said so?"

"Everything in the damned bunker said 'Property of U.S. Government' on it," I said bitterly. "I figured they just hadn't gotten around to stenciling me. And I didn't think anything hidden that well had been meant to do anybody any good."

"You were meant to do us some."

"That's not much consolation for having been hatched full-grown out of a box."

Her black eyes widened, and she said, "Would you rather not have been hatched at all?"

I stared down at her, silenced.

She rose again and began to pace the room, in and out of the darkness. "I think the most elementary purpose of the *chevaux* was to reassure everyone else. Regular forces pointed out—and rightly, too—that if any of us were wounded or threatened with death, we were likely just to steal the nearest available body. Those of our friends and allies, for instance. The solution was to have untenanted and highly desirable bodies available as a bribe to keep us from devouring our own side. So they grew the *chevaux*."

I repeated, a little numb, "Grew them."

"Well, of course. Did you think you were made of bicycle parts? The *chevaux* were organic; hence, grown. Brought to maturity and then held until needed, probably in those boxes."

The boxes in which, abandoned, support systems failing slowly, eight costly, empty shells had been left to decay. Nine. But one of them had risen like a horror-movie menace to walk a changed earth, where even the living tried to avoid the sunlight.

"They customized them, too," Frances continued. "After all, a brain is a terrible thing to waste, when you can store useful skills and information in it. Languages, codes, computer programming, volleyball rules, flirting with a fan—whatever the brass considered useful. Who knows. God and you, I suppose."

"Electronics," I said thickly. "Why am I neuter?"

"I'm not sure. I think . . . the *chevaux* could be modified by the rider."

"They could *what*?"

"I told you, I'm not sure. I never met one before you. Christ, I don't think any of them were ever deployed."

"Deployed. Amazing. Feels just like being alive."

"Life can be defined as that which admits of no comfortable acquaintance with the cemetery. By that definition, you're more alive than I am." The resonant voice was smooth and bitter as unsweetened chocolate.

"I don't know," I said, examining my filthy shirt. "I look as if I might have just dug myself out with my fingernails."

That seemed to amuse her. "You could go change, you know."

"I would have. But . . ." My voice slipped away from me.

"But it would have meant leaving Mick and me alone in here. And," she said slowly, "it would have meant undressing with strangers in the place. In the whole secretive fabric of your life, your body is the most private thread. Because it's the outward sign of all your secrets."

I wondered if I was pale. "Gee. Do you read minds?"

Frances snorted. "No, I attack them, stun them, and bolt them whole, like a constrictor. And I'm sluggish while digesting."

"I think you need sleep," I told her, shaking my head. "And food."

"I always talk like this. Almost always. It whiles away the tedium of the decades. But speaking of food, where the hell is Mick?"

A good question. He wasn't as familiar with the Night Fair as I was, but the place was full of things to eat. If he wasn't picky, he could have been back in twenty minutes. Unless—well, why not? Why shouldn't he have taken the opportunity to bolt before Frances came to and started waving her rifle around again? Even in the vulnerable and addled state I'd been in when he left, why should I have expected him to do anything else? The way he'd caught Frances as she fell, brushed the hair back from her face, was no evidence to the contrary.

I looked up to find Frances's eyes on me, her hands curled tight on themselves. "Pack if you're going to," she said softly. "We're on the street in ten minutes."

"What?"

"Mick is the only person besides you and me who knows where I am. And who I am."

I gaped. "He wouldn't—"

"Wouldn't he? Maybe not. But even so, could he keep it to himself if someone asked him strenuously enough? Or, perhaps, *didn't bother to ask?*"

I swallowed, to no effect, and said, "You've been looking for this guy for years. You think he'll find Mick Skinner in an hour?"

"I can't afford to believe he hasn't."

"I'm staying here." I managed not to drop my eyes from hers.

"No, you're not," she said agreeably.

"They don't want me. None of them want me. They want you."

"What I did to you tonight," she replied, each word evenly spaced and without emphasis, "was nothing. Tom O'Bedlam or anyone who serves him will separate you from your desire to live and any last complacent conviction you may have about the privacy of your own mind as easily as tearing rotted cloth. Knowledge of me will gush out of your brain and your mouth and a hundred other openings that he'll make just for that purpose. I suggest you come with me."

"What can I tell him? 'Well, yeah, there's this woman, right now she looks like this, but that might have changed; and she wants to bump you off, but you knew that already.' "

"Sparrow," she said, and stopped, and began again. "It didn't occur to you that I might have *your* welfare in mind and not mine?"

I frowned at her, and she returned my gaze, her eyebrows raised. "Why would you?"

"Thank you, I have retained a few dried-out shreds of human decency, I think."

"That's not how things work around here."

It was her turn to frown. "Pretend you're someplace else, then. Go change, and gather up anything you need, within limits."

"Where are y—we—going?"

She leaned on the corner of the desk. "Away."

Do you still have purposes? Mick had asked. *I used mine up. I just move around.* I couldn't go to Dana, obviously; and I couldn't go to Cassidy, because I didn't know where that was. If I went to Sherrea, I might involve her—

Oh, no. Think. I already had. Sherrea and Theo, Theo with a hole in him, and at the bottom of the stairs the woman Frances had ridden, Myra, and Dusty, whose craziness had come off him like heat off a griddle. Who'd pointed out, smiling, that now he knew where to find Theo and Sher if he needed them.

"When you . . . when you rode that red-haired woman out back of the Underbridge. How much of her brain did you pick?"

"Not much. I was busy, you'll recall. Why?"

I didn't ask them to get involved. I didn't ask Theo to follow me out of the building with a gun. He knew better; he'd told me so. "The two people I was with. They were still there. . . ."

Some buttress of self-containment slipped loose, for an instant, behind her face, and was restored just as quickly. "If you're going to suggest we go back," she said, "I'll save you the trouble. No."

"Why the hell not?"

"Because if it's not the first place they'll look, it's the second."

"You think Myra and Dusty work for Tom Whatsisname."

"Worecski." She sighed. "I didn't, when I thought you were a better prospect. Whole hours ago. Now I'm forced to confront the notion that I backed, as it were, the wrong horse."

"They were after Mick Skinner."

"Were they?" she said, startled. "Why? Do you know?"

"No." I thought about the confrontation behind the Under-bridge, before she'd arrived. "But they knew that he'd—that I'd been him part of the time."

"Now that would suggest a surprising familiarity with the process, wouldn't it? Hmm. Go change."

I did. I locked the door of the bedroom, and felt no more comfortable about it than I'd expected to. Another pair of jeans, another shirt, jungle boots; it didn't take long. I hid folding money in each boot, and coins in a bag around my neck. When I dropped the cord over my head, I realized there was already something there: Sherrea's pendant, the two overlapping V shapes. If it was protective, it was doing a rotten job. Maybe it only worked for people who believed it would. What did I believe in? The Deal; it wouldn't make much of an amulet. I threw a few other things in a rucksack and went to submit myself to the will of Frances.

She looked me up and down. "That must have been a tough decision."

It was my turn to make my eyes wide. "Would you prefer the evening gown, or the tuxedo?"

Frances gathered up her purloined rifle. I locked the archives and doused all the lights. We rode down to the first floor in silence. Frances, it seemed, was thinking. We got all the way to the tri-wheeler before I finally asked, "Where are we going?"

"To the Underbridge," she said. "I've had second thoughts about renewing my acquaintance with everyone involved. Mount up."

I looked at her sideways. Frances just smiled.

Card 6

Ahead

Seven of Wands

Waite: Discussion, wordy strife, negotiations, war of trade.

Gearhart: The individual against the community; one against many. Unequal odds.

5.0: The house of the spirit

The nights are getting shorter," I shouted over Frances's shoulder as we rode. "Mind the east." The sky there was a dense and velvet cobalt, over solid rooftops and shattered ones, over the feeble lamps and torches of the Fair.

"Very nice," said Frances.

"That means the gates close in an hour or so."

"It does?"

Well, there; that was one thing I knew that she didn't. "That's why they call it the Night Fair."

"What happens after that?"

"Nothing. Lively as a mausoleum. The hours are shorter in the summer, but it beats staying out in the sun."

We were threading a narrow, noisy, busy strip of pavement bordered with vendors' stalls. She braked as a huge, hairy gray dog shot out from between two of them and hurtled across the path, its bony joints rolling. A smooth, loam-black face topped with a brilliantly colored cylinder of a hat thrust itself in front of the windshield. *"Las bujías, señora,"* it said, showing small white teeth and a raised hand full of spark plugs. *"Para todas las máquinas, señora, y muy baratas—"* Frances growled with the throttle, and the face disappeared as we lunged forward. I peered back through the weather shell, and couldn't find a sign of the bright hat.

"Not to be critical," I told her, "but if we'd gone to the gate we came in by, we'd have missed the crowds."

There was a pause before she said, "I was hoping we might find Mick."

"The place is a warren. We could pass him a dozen times in the next ten minutes and never know it."

"Ah, but *he* would," said Frances harshly. There was a fierce,

119

fruitless rev from the throttle. "Have you noticed many of these here tonight?"

"What if he's gotten into trouble?"

"In other words, what if he hasn't come to us because he can't?" She turned the trike into the mouth of an alley and, to my surprise, killed the engine. Her shoulders rose and fell with her breathing. Finally she said, "We *do* all want to survive. I've been doing it for a long time, in difficult circumstances, and I've done it by suspecting everyone unfailingly. I'm afraid it's a habit now."

Her habits didn't account for why we'd stopped here. "Does that mean that you *don't* think Mick Skinner is in league with the devil?"

She twisted to look at me. Her eyes didn't look focused. "Of course I do. I told you, it's a habit." She turned away again.

After a moment I said, "If you'll open the shell, I'll get some food. The stall's right there; I'll be in sight the whole time."

She didn't answer, but she groped for and pulled the lever that popped the shell. I scrambled out past her as best I could.

The smell and sound and sight of chicken frying was a swooning sensual overload; I wondered, for an instant, if that was how a caress seemed to most people. I was suddenly vague and giddy with hunger. I had always worked that way: not needing to eat all day, until I needed it desperately, like an engine that runs smoothly through a tank of alcohol and stops without warning when it's gone. What string of adjectives had Frances hung on me earlier? Strong, resistant to disease and poisons . . . She could have added cheap to operate, and rarely needs refueling. I bought chicken ("*Picante*," the old woman warned, her hands fluttering, her accent terrible, "*picante*") and fried potatoes and okra and buttermilk biscuits and two long bottles of homemade pear nectar. I tucked the bottles under my arm and juggled the hot paper-wrapped parcels back to the trike.

Frances sat where I'd left her, but her wrists were crossed over the instrument panel, and her forehead was pillowed on them. Her hair had fallen forward to sweep and scatter across her near forearm. Relaxed, that arm looked surprisingly thin, and the pointed bones in her elbow seemed frail and vulnerable. Out of character.

Sometimes wisdom arrives first in the pit of your stomach. That was where I felt it then, a little slippery twist. Of course it was out of character. That wasn't Frances's arm.

I already knew that this body didn't belong to Frances; but now I *really* knew it, all the many-sided shape of it. There was no relation here between the shell and the spirit, no way to judge from outside, except by the crude language of action and expression, what the person inside was. The body I was looking at was the life story, in fading ink, of a person I'd never met.

Who was she? Would she approve of this vendetta she was being ridden on? I'd awakened, over and over, in strange places with bits of my past gone, and it had nearly driven me crazy. How long had Frances ridden this woman? Would she wake up in a new city, maybe years since her last memory, and do any better than I had? Would she get the chance to wake up at all?

The exhaustion belonged to the stranger's body. The driving passion, the mind under the lash, belonged to Frances. Both needed to eat and rest. Both would suffer if they didn't. Whoever was entitled to judge between them, it wasn't me.

I said, a little loudly, "Well, if you didn't like spicy chicken, you should have *said* so."

"I love spicy chicken," she said, and sat up. Her face was composed, and I knew I wasn't supposed to notice, or at least to comment on, the weariness in it.

So I said, "At the Underbridge, there's a place where you can catch a few hours' sleep."

"I'll be fine once I eat. Now, can we eat?"

"You're welcome," I replied, and began to set bundles on all the flat surfaces. There weren't a lot of these, on or in the trike, but I ate leaning against the outside, which left her the passenger's seat as a table. "Eat the okra first," I warned. "It's terrible cold."

And that was the last conversation for a few minutes. Except for the rattle of the paper, we were a speck of silence in the Night Fair's tapestry of noise. I stopped chewing to listen to it. I felt like an alien object in the world-body, something it had encysted because it couldn't cast it out. Or was it Frances who had been isolated, and I was simply standing within the radius of the effect?

"Wish I had some coffee," Frances said at last, around a bite of biscuit.

I stared at her. "Nothing easier. Give me ten bucks, and I'll be back sometime tomorrow with about twelve green coffee beans. *If* someone, somewhere in town, has managed to lay hands on a sackful."

She smiled, wry and surprisingly genuine. "I know. I think that's the rest of my penance. To get to where coffee grows, it's a thousand miles over bad roads full of unpleasant people. I hear there's a slope near Taos where they've discovered it does pretty well, but strangers within half a mile can expect to be shot at."

"Is coffee worth shooting people for?" I asked.

"Or getting shot at for? Have you never had it?"

"No."

An indecipherable expression crossed her face at high speed.
"In that case, I suppose not. But I wish I had some, all the same."

Headlights appeared and bobbed in front of us, blinding, as a
car turned into the other end of the alley. "Bother," Frances said,
and began to clear wrapping paper away from the ignition.

"Stay where you are, please," said an air-filled whistling ruin
of a voice behind me.

I was drinking the last of the pear nectar. As I lowered the
bottle, I reversed my grip on the neck, smacked the glass against
a sign post as I turned, and ended crouched in front of Mr. Lyle
with a broken bottle in my hand. I was probably more surprised
than he was.

He was smiling, in fact, 'way up at the top of his great height.
I'd forgotten how unreasonably large he was. "Teakettles, bot-
tles—do you always fight with your drinkables?" he asked. And,
"You should turn 'round and have a look before you use that.
There are things you don't know."

I did not, of course, turn around. "Frances?" I called.

"I don't—" I heard the *clunk-squeak* of a car door opening.
"Ah. I see," she said. "Sparrow, before I decide how to manage
this, tell me, who are these people?"

I was frantic to look behind me. People, plural; the woman must
be there. I tried to figure out what Frances wanted to know.
"Night before last, Mick saw their car and avoided it," I said
slowly. "Then yesterday, when Mick left his last body at my
place, I went to someone—someone I thought I could trust—to
help me get rid of it. She brought these two around. They were
pretty peevish when they found out Mick wasn't resident any
more."

"Is that true?" Frances asked, but not, I realized, of me.

"It is so, absolutely," said the other familiar voice, the rough,
low-pitched female one. I could hear that she, too, was smiling.
"A careful witness, that one, who draws no conclusions. But it is
not all that is so."

"What do you want?" said Frances.

"That we should help one another, maybe."

In failing tones, with a fortune in skepticism, Frances said,
"And this, I take it, is symbolic of your good intentions. My
God."

"And which one is yours?"

I couldn't bear it anymore. I looked over my shoulder.

The long black car had pulled out of the alley at as much of a
agonal as it could manage; it blocked the sidewalk as well. The
oman Dana had addressed as "Maîtresse" stood in the open
assenger's side door. Her costume yesterday must have been
asual wear. Now she was a different kind of formidable: black
aede pumps, long dark legs, a black sheath dress of dull nubby
lk, a fur stole white as a cloud of talcum, long dark neck rising
at of it. Her face, under a black-and-white turban, seemed
ounger than it had yesterday. And still, nothing shone or sparkled
aywhere about her except her immobile silver eyebrows.

Behind the wheel was the dark-skinned person in the bright-
atterned hat, the one who'd peered in the windshield waving
park plugs. Beside the driver was the big gray dog.

The back door on our side was also open. And on the back seat,
ad lolling down as if it had been propped against the door before
opened, entirely unconscious, was Mick Skinner's new body.

Then one of Mr. Lyle's big hands closed around my wrist, and
e other plucked the bottle away, sent it flying to smash on the
dewalk. His fingers closed around my upper arms, pressed them
my ribs. It felt as if he might flatten me between his palms like
oftened wax. He half walked, half carried me to the car and
oked me in the back on a rear-facing seat opposite Mick. I shot
cross to the other door and tried the handle. No response, and no
ck in sight. The driver with the bright hat turned and smiled at
e through the glass between us.

"If you will come with us," the woman said to Frances, "we
ill go to a safe place, where we may talk. You will not come to
arm."

Frances nodded toward the back seat of the car. "How do I
now you have him, and not just a body?"

"He is there," the woman with the eyebrows said. "You know
"

"Yes." Frances's voice was low, but I heard her.

None of us moved, and time seemed to keep us company. I was
aiting for an explosion of violence—soon the rifle would come
p in Frances's hands, there would be lots of noise, and we would
robably all die—or a ripple of the bizarre—soon, now, Frances
ould possess one of them.

Slowly, Frances got out of the trike. Her face was full of
esigned and weary disgust, and her hands were empty.

"Leave the key," the woman said. "Etienne will drive your
ehicle after us." Etienne—the one in the hat.

"If Etienne wrecks it," said Frances, toward the driver, "I w
eat Etienne's liver. If I have to come back from the dead to do it

Etienne smiled and nodded, as if he thought that was reaso
able.

Mr. Lyle gestured Frances into the back, and she slid onto tł
other rear-facing seat. Not for Frances the indignity of beir
tossed in like a piece of luggage. He pushed Mick's unresisti
body farther along the upholstery, and closed the door. Som
where inside it a lock chunked.

Mr. Lyle took the driver's seat, and the dog wagged its ta
once, briskly. The trike did not explode when Etienne started i
As we pulled into the street, I watched its two close-set headligh
swing and settle in behind us.

Frances had rescued me once; against all reason, I had expecte
hear to do it again. "You didn't shoot them," I said finall
watching her.

She'd let her head drop back to rest against the glass partitio
and her eyes were closed. "No. I didn't."

"Or ride them. Or even drive the hell away. Why not?"

"You sound as if you're taking it personally." She opened h
eyes and rolled her head to look at me. The lights of the trike sl
and shuffled over her face, and I saw her eyes clearly for
moment, all pupil. "I found, on examination, that I couldn't affor
it." She turned her face back toward the roof and closed her ey
again.

Her nose was short, and tilted up a little at the end. But ther
it wasn't her nose. "Are you ever going to let her back out?"
asked sharply.

"Who?"

"The person whose body that is."

I thought she wasn't going to answer. The pause was attribu
able, perhaps, to thinking. "No. Either way, no."

"Either way?"

But that, she didn't answer.

Outside it was dawn, a light so fragile that it seemed a stron
wind could break and scatter it. On the edges of the City, peop
would be gathering the things they would bring to marke
peppers, poultry, straw hats, water jugs, fabric dye, burn oin
ment, door hinges. On Loring Common, the milking would ł
finished; the heavy-shouldered, lyre-horned cows would be ploc
ding out of the shed to graze. The milk would be on its way
market soon. I was on my way to . . . where? Someplace saf
where we could talk. What if I had nothing to say?

The long black car passed out of the gates of the Night Fair. Somewhere in the City Theo and Sher were alive, or dead. Myra and Dusty and Dana and Cassidy were doing whatever they pleased, or could get away with, or thought they had to. To them, for now and maybe forever, the three people in the back seat of the limousine were irrelevant. I wedged myself in my corner of the car and wrapped my arms around me. I wouldn't, had I been asked, have said I was cold.

In the morning light, the Schmidt beer cap sign looked as if it had been painted on the sky behind it. The suspension bridge, its cables looping like the flight of swallows, ran above and below us. If La Maîtresse hadn't intercepted us, we'd have gone this way anyway; the Underbridge was on the other shore, east along the river.

Then the car slowed and turned, and I straightened up and pulled my gaze down from overhead. We'd turned off—not on the other shore, not quite as far as that.

I stared, and breathed, "We're on the island."

"I know," Frances said. Her head was up and her eyes open. "What, then?" She must have understood me from my voice; hers was low and level. I saw in her face the effort to focus her mind, to gather up her scattered reserves and hold them ready.

"The place has unreasonably high ju-ju levels. For instance, they say if you don't belong, or weren't invited, you won't be able to turn off the bridge onto this street."

"The ultimate private subdivision."

I shrugged. "Don't believe it, then."

"I almost do, actually. This always was an oddity sink. Maybe someone's found a way to use it. Do *you* believe it?"

"I've never had business on the island." That was true. There was no reason to mention the times when, on the way to or from business elsewhere, I'd intended to test the folk wisdom, and forgot the intention until I was on the other side of the river. I wished I'd been paying more attention to where we'd turned off.

"I've been here," Frances said. "Before. . . . The row houses look the same. I wonder who lives in them."

We were on an old brick street that followed the edge of the island. To our left, the river ran gold in the morning light. The row houses were on our right, a handsome old block of gray stone and long windows, glossy doors with brass hardware. We drove past. Trees hung heavy over the road and shrubbery grew up between them, making a dim green tunnel. Sometimes we saw an opening, with a dusty gravel drive; sometimes a house and yard behind the weathered pickets of a fence. Once three chickens scrabbled out of the road in front of us, scolding.

"It was always a little wild," Frances said softly behind me. "But never so wild as this."

I thought I knew what she meant. People lived here; but it was as if the land had gathered itself around them, veiling and swaddling them, hiding them and the signs of their habitation. If I hadn't been on the outside of it, it might have seemed benevolent.

The car turned and nosed up to a peeling wooden double gate in a piebald wall of round stones and mortar. Ivy and clematis were turning the wall into a hill of shifting green starred with crimson. There was a flash of yellow on the other side of the gate, and it swung open to reveal an elderly woman in a yellow dress. She made a half bow to the car in general. The people in the front seat smiled at her. Since my window was one-way glass, I didn't feel I had to.

Then we were on the other side of the wall; and if what we'd passed through was wild green, this was its civilized cousin. It was solid garden on either side of the gravel drive. There were fruit trees and flowering ones; the dense, druglike smell of mock orange and butterfly bush, strong even in the car; a mass of tall orange and yellow flowers like a streak of fire; grapes hanging heavy and green on a long arbor; the red cones of hot peppers set like jewels in their bushes. There might have been paths or terraces of grass, but I couldn't see them from where I was.

And in the middle, a somber monarch in some highly ornamental court, was a three-story, sprawling wood-frame Victorian house. It was mostly dark green, trimmed in black, brick-red, and yellow. Once, maybe, it had been of modest size, before the gables and dormers and bays, the additional rooms and entire wings. It should have been awful; instead, it had a sort of rhythm, as if half a dozen dissimilar people had agreed to dress alike and dance in figures.

"I would swear," Frances said, "this wasn't here when I left."

"How the hell long ago did you leave?"

"I know. That house is a lot older than I am. Still. . . ."

By that time, the car had stopped at the broad front porch, and the tri-wheeler had pulled up behind us. Mr. Lyle got out, the dog following with a great lazy spring, and opened the passenger door for the woman. He performed the same office for Frances, as his—employer? partner?—went briskly up the steps, the sound of her heels uncompromising on the wood. She turned at the top.

"I think," she called back, "that you should carry your friend.
will be more work than it would be for Mr. Lyle, but it will keep
ou from trouble."

Frances stood in the angle of the open door and looked in at me.
he seemed torn between amusement and frustration. "Let us, by
ll means, be kept from trouble. Would you like the head or the
et?"

"The head," I said. "His feet will be lighter."

"Don't be chivalrous. You haven't the plumbing for it." She
ood back to let me out. Mr. Lyle was nearby, his distance nicely
dged: too far for us to surprise him, but close enough to stop us
 we did something rash.

"But I've got the energy." I grabbed the inert Mick under the
rmpits and dragged. "I thought you had to eat a poisoned apple
 stay under this long. What do you suppose they did to him?"

"Not, I hope, an apple, or one of us will have to kiss him.
erhaps if we're very good the lady with the alarming eyebrows
ill tell us. She might even tell us where she got the eyebrows.
od *damn it*!" she said suddenly, then pressed her lips closed. It
as the only leak in her supernatural self-command. It wasn't so
ad for me; I didn't expect to be able to control the situation.

Since I'd picked the head, I went up the steps and into the house
ackward. I don't suppose the effect would have been much
oftened if I'd gone in face first.

The coved ceilings were fifteen feet high, all of them, and the
all and the two parlors to either side were outlined and orna-
ented in glossy walnut. In one parlor, the walls were the color of
hilled butter, and painted ivy climbed out of the baseboards and
ined around the window frames. In the other, the paint was
umpkiny; beneath the ceiling molding was a frieze two feet high
f Egyptian kings and queens and gods and all their attendants and
ccessories. The door I'd just come through was double, and
ostly stained and leaded glass. It was flanked by a pair of
enches that looked Middle Eastern, piled with pillows covered in
frican cloth. Under my feet was a carved-pile Chinese rug;
nside the door of the ivy room was a stone carving that might
ave been Mayan; on the hall table was a shallow reed bowl that
as almost certainly Native North American. I didn't want to be
bvious about looking, but I had the impression that the place
ent on in that style: a world government of interior design, rich
n a way that couldn't be achieved solely by money.

And one thing more. Around the edges of the rug, the parquet
loor was bordered with inlay in many woods. It ran across the

bottom of the door, along the walls, and continued unbroke
across the doors to the two parlors. In it I saw designs and figure
I almost recognized, from Sherrea's cards, from the *vévés,* fro
amulets. If the border was continuous behind me, too, the
whoever stood in the hall would be well protected. Or nice
contained.

"Mr. Lyle," the woman said from behind me, "would you tak
him now, please?"

Mr. Lyle had come in after us. He nodded and smiled, an
gathered Mick up and over his shoulder.

"You should rest," the woman said. She stood at the foot of th
wide walnut staircase. "Then we will talk. Come with me."

Frances might have been made of stone, if stone could shru
She walked stiffly toward the stairs. Mr. Lyle, behind me, sai
"After you." So I went.

We climbed to the third floor, turned right down a sho
hallway, right again, and stopped halfway down another ha
carpeted, lighted by a window at one end. The walls were yello
and the trim was white. It's hard to feel apprehensive in surround
ings like that, but I did. After all, werewolves only grew hair
the full moon. The woman opened a door and stood aside for M
Lyle to pass. Then she went to the next door in the hall and open
that.

"Yours," she said to Frances. "If you need anything, pull th
bell."

After an instant's hesitation, Frances inclined her head and we
in. I didn't hear any loud noises.

I, of course, got the next door. It was open, and the woma
waiting for me to go in, when I said, "Do I need to call yo
anything yet?"

A look crossed her face, something like embarrassment. "I'
China Black," she said. "Though there are many other things t
call me, even respectful ones. Is it respectful to call yo
'Sparrow'?"

"It's the only name I have."

She nodded. "Until you have another, then." She turned an
walked to the joining of the two halls, where Mr. Lyle waited fo
her. I heard them a moment later, going down the stairs.

I looked back at the open door. Apparently it was not going t
be locked behind me. I went in.

It was a very nice room. It had sloping, papered walls and
large dormer window. It was so honest and pleasant and innocer
that I felt a rush of panic. I hurried to the window. It was neithe

barred nor locked, and looked out over the gardens we'd just driven through. I thought back over the orientation of the stairs and hallways. I must have missed something; I hadn't expected this to be the front of the house. I opened the window and sat on the bench under it to examine the rest of the room.

There was a bed, with a high carved head and foot, and a dresser with a round mirror. On the dresser was a pitcher and bowl, soap and towels. *Any minute the porter will bring my luggage up,* I thought wildly. Across from the dresser was an armoire. I got up and flung its doors open. A sudden movement, a person—a mirror on the inside of one door. I closed the armoire and sat on the bed until my pulse settled down. On a table next to the bed was an oil lamp and a box of matches. One doesn't supply a prisoner with the means to burn down the house. Unless it's impossible to do; I thought of the inlay in the hall.

"Comfortable?" said Frances from the door, and I jumped.

"I see you're not resting."

"No. I've reconsidered the wisdom of keeping from trouble. I want to know what happens when we try to walk out."

"You should have just made a break for it back in the Night Fair."

"Oh, I expect to be stopped. But I think it would be instructive to know where, and how. Care to join me? We could say we were looking for the bathroom." She seemed relaxed and casual, leaning in the doorway; but I suspected she wasn't.

"No."

"Care to join me anyway?"

I looked sharply up at her.

"I find I'm reluctant to leave you behind," she said. "I think you'd best come along."

The bathroom was at the end of the hall, perfectly agreeable, with a tub big enough to drown in. We continued to retrace our route, left and another left. But we didn't come out at the top of the stairs.

"Over there," Frances said softly. She pointed down the corridor. I saw the turned walnut newel post and frowned.

At the landing, instead of turning left to the next flight, the stairs turned right. "The back stairs?" I muttered.

Now Frances was frowning.

We might eventually have reached the first floor, but we couldn't tell. We might have passed through the basement on the way to it. The halls were graciously appointed, the stairs were ornate, the rooms we peered into and passed through sunny and

innocuous and even a little bland. And at last, without ever going
up a flight of stairs that I remembered, we turned a corner into a
hallway with yellow walls and white woodwork and a window at
the far end.

"Oh, Lord," Frances sighed. She was pale and inclined to lean.
"Shall we make book on the next scene? We open the doors to our
rooms and find ourselves sleeping on the beds. We open the doors
and find the pits of hell. Or someone with a sword, who kills us.
Or a bag of gold."

I stalked to the door of mine and wrenched it open. "Or the
room, just as we left it."

"Could we have been drugged, do you think?"

"I'm too tired to think. I'm going to take my damn boots off and
lie down. If you want to explore, have fun. Don't wake me." I
didn't actually slam the door. It had a bolt, so I turned it.

The sheets, of course, smelled like lavender.

5.1: A shedding of skins

The curtains were blowing lazily at the window; the breeze was lukewarm and smelled of the garden. A shaft of light gently cooked the floorboards. I didn't remember falling asleep, but it must have happened. There was a distinct feeling of afternoon in the air.

I sat up and swung my bare feet to the floor, and thought, *There's more changed than the hour*. It might have been the light. It might have been that the filter of weariness and alarm was thinner. Or maybe Frances was right: Maybe somehow we'd been drugged, and it had worn off. But the room seemed different.

Had the wallpaper been like that, before? Hadn't the bedspread been a little threadbare? For that matter, had there been curtains? I couldn't remember. The room seemed less determinedly reassuring and more . . . exotic? Not quite. Well, I'd been awfully tired.

I put my boots back on and cleaned up a little at the dresser. When I tried the door, I felt an instant of fright. Then I remembered I'd locked it. At least nobody had been hanging curtains while I slept.

In the hall, on the floor by the door, I found my canvas pack. So the porter *had* come up. I dropped it in a ladderback chair that I didn't remember, either. The corridor was quiet. I thought about trying Frances's or Mick's doors; then realized I didn't know why I'd want to.

When I came out of the bathroom, the enormous gray dog was waiting in the hall. It rose to its feet and gave that articulate single wag of its tail. Then it turned and went to the junction of the next corridor, and looked back.

"Don't tell me," I said aloud. "The old mine caved in, and I have to come rescue little Timmy." The dog, mercifully, did not

131

respond. I could test matters by trying to walk back to my room
but why bother? I followed the dog.

A left turn, and a left, and I was at the top of the stairs. It was
as annoying as *not* arriving at the top of the stairs the last time I
tried it. At the bottom of the stairs I was in the beautiful front hall.
The dog trotted into the ivy parlor. I thought it seemed a little
smug; given the success Frances and I had had at reaching the
same place by the same route, I supposed it had a right. I heard
voices and clinking in the parlor: low, even voices and the noise
of crockery used as its manufacturer had intended. It seemed, if
not safe to go in, at least the next logical step.

Everyone looked up when I entered, including the dog. Everyone was China Black and Mr. Lyle, Frances and Mick. They were
sitting on a pair of cushioned wicker couches that faced each
other, one team to a couch. I had just begun to wonder which team
I was on when I looked past them.

The far wall of the parlor held a log-swallowing fireplace
surrounded by painted tiles and complicated woodwork, sur-
mounted by a mantelpiece with what seemed a hundred un-
matched candlesticks on it, and a huge, gold-framed mirror over
that. On either side, taking up the rest of the wall from side to side
and floor to ceiling, fronted in leaded glass, were bookshelves.
Full bookshelves.

I made the circuit around the couches without exactly seeing
them and stood in front of the right-hand case. What was probably
the complete works of Mark Twain, in leather. *The Jungle Book.*
The Encyclopedia of Folklore. *Treasure Island*. Shakespeare.
Yeats, Piercy, Eliot, Woolf. Halliburton's *Book of Marvels*.
Grieve's herbal. Stephen Jay Gould and Martin Gardner. And
those were the ones I recognized. Who were Gene Wolfe and
Alice Walker and Kenneth Roberts and Jane Austen? Maya
Angelou and John Crowley and Zora Neale Hurston? And there
was another bookcase on the other side.

"I knew you'd do that," said Mick's voice, and I jumped. I
really *had* forgotten there were other people in the room.

"I'm sorry," I said, and yanked my eyes from the books and
back to the pair of couches. "Excuse me."

China Black's face was uninformative, but Mr. Lyle was
smiling broadly. "That's only part of the collection," he said.
"The rest is in the library. I'll take you there when we've finished
tea."

Chango—the rest. "Do you have any"—I fished in my memory
for the name—"Márquez?"

"All of his, I think," said Mr. Lyle gravely. "One of my favorites. Now, sit down and have some tea."

I saw a wicker chair with a cushion that matched the couches on one side of the fireplace. I carried it over and set it firmly down with its back to the bookcases. Which meant the seating was now U-shaped, with me halfway between the two couches.

Mr. Lyle hadn't meant tea; he'd meant Tea. On the low table that separated the couches was a brass samovar, a plate of sandwiches, a bowl of dark muffins the size of dandelion puff-balls, a tray of cookies with specks of something in them, and a bowl of strawberries. There were also two cups. I looked to see who else hadn't gotten tea yet, but Mick, Frances, China Black, and Mr. Lyle were all holding theirs. Maybe the dog had decided to wait.

The tea was mint, the sandwiches were cucumber and basil, the muffins were carrot, and the specks in the cookies were caraway. Then, I didn't think that was significant. Tasty, but not significant. Now I wonder: How much of what I ate at that meal came from the garden that held that house like a cupped hand?

"You are safe here," China Black said, "as long as you are our guests." She was stern and distant, the patron of some church that put mercy after judgment. Her voice was roughened a little, as if from hard use. "It seemed to me we must have safety before we could speak freely. But now I would like to know why you are here." And she looked at Frances and Mick.

Since her attention was elsewhere, I studied her over the edge of my cup. She wore a long, sleeveless olive-green dress, and a headwrap of green and yellow. Her nose, in profile, was high-bridged, and the nearest eyebrow shone like a streak of sweat. Her eyes were almond-shaped and sleepy-looking. I didn't think she was sleepy.

"I'd like to know why you ask," said Frances, smiling blandly.

Trust Frances to put all this amicability to flight. She watched us over her teacup like a panther eyeing a herd of antelope.

China Black was unruffled. "Would you like my credentials?"

"It's a start," Frances said.

Our hostess—was she our hostess?—seemed almost pleased. "This is a city divided in power. There is A. A. Albrecht, who sits at what he thinks is the heart, and tries to keep the flow of power all one way, all toward himself. He does not know, or care, perhaps, that the City is an organism, and that without its circulation, it will die. I am a *houngan*; I was chosen by the snake thirty years ago to serve the spirits, and the living. I and those like me try to keep the City's lifeblood flowing in spite of Albrecht."

"I thought if you were a woman, you were a *mambo,* not a *houngan.*"

"Once, if you were a woman, you could not be a *houngan.* And once, if you were a woman, you couldn't be a soldier." The look she gave Frances was probably meant to be quelling.

"Power is most things to most people," said Frances. "When you talk about power in the City, do you mean money? Politics?"

"I mean energy," China Black replied.

Frances's expression made me think again of predators. "The ju-ju kind?" she asked with a hint of distaste.

"Not usually. Like you, he has little interest in the spirit." China Black's teeth flashed, just for a moment. "He wants to control electricity and fuel. If your vehicle was powered by methane, he would have it confiscated, because in the City no one may use fuel he does not profit from, and he neither makes nor taxes methane."

While China Black and Frances eyed each other, I stole a glance at Mick. He was leaning back, legs crossed at the knee, cradling his teacup. He didn't look relaxed. He was waiting for something, and until it came, there was no way to tell what.

China Black put her teacup down and said to Frances, "What is your name?"

"Frances Redding."

"And you are . . . ?"

Frances raised her eyebrows. "Female? A Scorpio?"

"You know what I'm asking."

"Then I'll bet you know the answer."

"Then it can do no harm to tell it to me."

Frances's jaw worked a little, as if she might be biting the inside of her lip. "I'm a Horseman," she said.

It might not have surprised anyone in the room; still, there was a moment of silence for the enormity of the fact.

"And so are you," China Black said, turning suddenly on Mick. He started, looked up with a jerk. "Yes, ma'am."

"What brought you here?"

"Impulse," said Mick, with a shrug. "Nothing particular."

After a moment China Black turned to Frances. "And you?"

Frances leaned forward and laced her tanned fingers together. Meeting China Black's eyes, she said, "I came here to kill someone."

"Ah. In the interest of the general welfare, I think I am entitled to ask who."

"His name is Tom Worecski. He's also a Horseman. He was the leader of the group that betrayed . . . that started the exchange of things that go bang."

"That betrayed humanity?"

Frances shrugged. "It seemed, on reflection, a little melodramatic. And not quite true. I think the grudge belongs to the Western Hemisphere."

"The world is not so large that half of it can afford to ignore what happens to the other half. I would let it stand at 'humanity'— but maybe I am an unforgiving old woman. And maybe you are, too."

"Maybe. If, when I find Worecski, I decide he's become a saint, I'll see if I can forgive him."

"You haven't found him? Then why do you think he's here?"

Frances rubbed the space between her eyebrows absently. "I've trailed him here. I followed the wreckage he left behind him over the years—he's a great one for wreckage—and the little personal motifs. That's all we had as identities, once we found that the relationship between body and soul was tenuous.

"And Tom would want a city. He'd want plenty to work with, to run roughshod over. He wouldn't be out in the bush, or settled in some farm village."

"What if you're wrong, and he's changed?"

"Then I won't be able to find him, will I? He'll be safe. But I don't think he's changed."

China Black set her cup in front of the samovar and turned the spigot. A fresh wave of mint smell curled around the room. "And why do you trust me with all this?"

"Because I suspect it doesn't matter. I think he knows I'm coming, and if he does, none of this is news. If he doesn't, it still won't matter. He won't run; Tom always loved a fight."

"You know him very well, then?"

Frances's face was still. "We went to Killing People School together. It produces a wonderful camaraderie."

"Why were you after me?" Mick asked suddenly of the opposite couch. "You followed me around that night, didn't you?"

"Maybe we didn't know we were following *you*," China Black replied with a large and uncharacteristic grin. "Maybe we thought we were following your *body*."

Mick opened his mouth; then the expression seemed to fall off his face. "Oh," he said.

He settled back into the cushions again, as if he were satisfied. But I'd seen the line that had appeared between his brows for a moment, and the unhappy little twist of his lip. I wondered if anyone else had.

"You said we might be able to help each other," Frances said. "Now you know what I want. What about you?"

China Black's attention moved slowly from Mick to Frances. "I am not so sure, now. What do you know about the spirits, the *loa*?"

Frances visibly squashed her frustration. "I've heard of them."

"They are not gods, though they're like them; and they are not ghosts, though they're like that, too. The European churches prayed to gods that rarely spoke, and then only to a few. The spirits speak all the time, and we don't pray to them any more than you would pray to your grandmother. We live with them. They are part of our family."

"'Our'?" Frances said.

"If you asked, you would find most people of the City—of the streets—know them. The *loa*, the saints, the spirits, the ancestors. There are many names, but you would find the principles similar, and the way they shape the world. The people in the towers don't think about the spirits. They don't know how the world is shaped. And so they give it a shape, and try to make everything fit it. They separate the right from the left, the man from the woman, the plant from the animal, the sun from the moon. They only want to count to two. Ah!" China Black snorted and shook her head. "I have been a teacher so long that I fall into it, so!"

She drained her teacup and stood, and began to walk slowly up and down the room. "You don't believe. You are like the people in the towers; it is your past they live in, not seeing that it hurts us all. But these things don't wait for you to believe in them. Chango, the young warrior with the sword, came among us while we danced. He said that from his quarter, the south, one of his own would come, limping. Oya Iansa, Lightning Woman, came and said that change would arrive from the west, but would not know its own nature. And Eshu drank white rum and smoked a black cigar, and laughed until the tears poured down, as he told us to duck when the *marassa* met, and joined the *dossou-dossa*, and the three of them, like a three-pointed throwing star, broke all the windows in the tall buildings in town. Tell me," China Black said, turning back to the couches, "do you see anything of yourselves in that?"

Mick leaned forward to set his cup down; the angle and a sudden sweep of little braids hid his face from me. He didn't answer. Frances said, "Since I didn't understand much of it, no, not really."

"The *marassa* are twins," I said. "Real-world ones, and spirit-world ones; you have to figure out which by context, I guess. Their hoodoo is unity and polarization, innocence and malice both at once. They share one soul. The *dossou-dossa* is the child born after twins. Actually, it's *dossou* or *dossa*, depending on what sex the kid is. And in the spirit world, it's the neuter principle, the third point on the hoodoo triangle that connects the male and female points." I looked at Frances and thought, *Don't say a thing*.

She might have understood, or not; her face didn't change. "My, that was encyclopedic. Do *you* believe? I'm forgiven because of my great age, it seems, but what about you?"

After a moment I shook my head. It seemed rude to deny the operating system of our—hostess? Who owned this house, anyway?—in her own parlor. I was annoyed at Frances for making me do it. "Knowing it is a survival skill. She's right. If you mention any of those names on the street, the people you're talking to might tell you they use a different name, but that's the most denial you'll get."

Frances pressed her lips together—to keep from smiling? "This must be a hard town for atheists."

China Black said, "But I told you, they aren't gods. You don't believe," she added, and looking up, I found she was now talking to me. "But you have sworn by Chango, haven't you?"

"Me?" I shrugged. "It's swearing, not invocation. You pick up habits from your neighbors."

"If you were hoodoo, maybe you would swear by somebody else. Chango is not the master of your head. That's Legba's symbol around your neck, you know."

My hand went to my throat before I thought about it. Sherrea's pendant was lying outside my shirt. "No, I didn't know."

China Black nodded. "It is always in Legba's *vévés*: the figure for androgyny and metamorphosis. It is why Legba and all his cousin spirits keep the gates and the crossroads. Do you like practical jokes? Legba is a trickster."

She seemed to want a response, but I couldn't think of one. The gates I worked had to do with semiconductor technology, and in the last few days I'd discovered I had a positive distaste for change. As for practical jokes, it could be suggested that I *was* one. I certainly wasn't going to take up the matter of androgyny with her.

"So your information was that three people—or maybe four—would appear, join forces, and raise whatever passes for hell in this pantheon," said Frances thoughtfully. "You think we might be them. Pigs might get pilot's licenses, too, but I don't think so."

China Black didn't seem insulted. "How so?"

"I've come to raise a very limited and specific sort of hell, in a localized area. You found the three of us in close proximity because what I'm about to do would be likely to splatter on Mick and Sparrow if they're nearby. Far from joining forces with them, I was hoping to get them out of range before I started."

"That's very noble of you," said Mr. Lyle, his dark face exquisitely grave. It had been so long since he'd last spoken that I jumped a little.

Frances, equally grave, ignored him. I saw Mr. Lyle smile out of the corner of my eye. "If you think the text of all these messages from beyond is that you should help me," Frances said to China Black, "then you could hide Mick and Sparrow, and tell me about anyone highly placed and crazy enough to be Tom Worecski on his horse."

Beside me, Mr. Lyle made a dreadful sound. It was laughter, I realized, genuine merriment distorted by that broken voice. "You're trying to force the world into a shape. You were a soldier. Do you know the saying 'No battle plan survives contact with the enemy'?"

Frances turned to him, her face very still. "More so with some enemies than with others," she said at last. "Yes. Point taken. In the meantime, shall I plan on help from you, or hindrance?"

"We cannot help you," said China Black. She stood very straight by the fireplace, once again the stern, judging image. "We were warned, I think, of your coming. The *loa* never said we were to serve your cause."

It was the word "serve" that did it. China Black had received no instructions. But Sherrea—or a voice in her mouth—had given some to me. They couldn't be connected to this. If they meant anything at all.

The front doors rattled under three solid blows. Frances was on her feet, the butter knife held low in one hand. I'd risen, too, I realized, but my hands were empty, and I was wondering about other exits.

The door banged open, and a voice yelled, "China? Where are you?"

"Ti-so!" China said, her grim look melting. "Come quick!"

The intruder appeared in the door, disheveled and wide-eyed. It was Sherrea. She wore a black tank top and purple harem pants that looked like a pair of collapsed dirigibles, and a gold-shot sash around her hips that flailed the air behind her. Her neck and arms were hung with amber.

"You see, I have found them for you!" cried China Black, looking nearly as smug as her dog had.

"Sparrow!" Sher crossed the room in a leap, stopped before me, and put a light hand on my arm. "Are you okay?"

I nodded, because something stiff in my throat kept me from speaking. Her hand slid off my arm.

"*Gracias, mi hermana,*" Sher said to China Black, beaming. "Was it a bitch to do?"

"Oh, no, they were wandering around the Night Fair like old women on market day."

"Were you?" Sherrea asked me intently.

"No."

"That's what I thought. The old crow just wants to save it up 'til she can make me feel guilty about all the work she did."

"Pah! I would never be so stupid. I know you have no conscience at all, so!"

They were friends. They were *good* friends. I felt as I had at the Underbridge, when I heard her call Robby by his nickname, when I discovered she knew Theo.

". . . Theo!" I gasped. "Sher, where's Theo? Is he okay?"

She blinked and turned to China Black. "You didn't explain?"

"There were more important things to discuss."

"Sure. I bet you forgot," Sher grumbled, scowling. She sent that glare at Mr. Lyle next. "*You* could have said something."

Mr. Lyle grinned. "I had no chance, little sister. When she gets like Iansa with her horsetail, what can poor mortals do?"

"I apologize," Sherrea sighed. "These two would tell a gopher how to dig, but a little thing like saying whether your friend's alive or dead—"

"Is he?" I blurted.

"Dead? Nah. Theo's upstairs—or he's supposed to be. Resting up. If he comes downstairs before tomorrow, I'm gonna kick his butt."

"Get your pointy shoes, then," said Theo from the doorway. He was smiling and rumpled and pale, and his right arm hung in a black cloth sling. "I was cool with it, 'til somebody broke down the door. Then I got curious. Hey," he said to me, and the smile was wider.

"Hey," I answered. He looked embarrassed. I felt embarrassed.

I wondered if he had any idea why; I sure didn't. "Oh, Cha—here, have a seat." I moved quickly away from my chair.

China Black frowned. "We need another cup. I'll get one."

As she disappeared into the hall, Frances studied Sherrea. "I think I misjudged something a few hours ago," Frances said. "I'm sorry if I seemed patronizing, back on the riverbank."

Sher shrugged. I watched them size each other up, and realized, with a jolt, what Frances was reacting to. Sher and China Black weren't just friends. They were peers. China Black, with her limo, elegant clothes, haughty manner, and easy power, behaved as Sherrea's equal. The Sherrea I thought I knew, the *adivina* with the cheap cards and the melodramatic apartment, barely older than I actually was. What had I missed?

I was irritated. It was another change, another upset to my delicately balanced routine. I found myself suddenly too grouchy to converse. I would have dropped into my chair, but Theo was in it.

"Here," Sher said. She'd dragged two low-backed chairs to the other end of the tea table. That was irritating, too: the second-guessing, the attention, the proximity.

"Thank you," I said, and sat down. She gave me a sideways glance, filled the last clean cup for Theo, and sat, too. Then China Black returned with a cup for her.

"I bet everybody's told everybody everything," Sherrea said. "But would you mind telling it all to me, anyway?"

"Starting from the Underbridge," Theo added across his tea.

I didn't feel like talking, but they were looking at me. Well, I was the one they knew, not Frances or Mick. Chango—or who-ever—it seemed strange that they didn't all know each other. *I* knew them, and until a few days ago, I would have described myself as knowing no one and happy about it.

I started from the Underbridge and didn't get far. As I came up on the image of Mick in the archives, I realized I was in trouble; I should have started earlier and explained Mick. But I couldn't explain Mick, because that would mean telling about his dead body, and revealing that he was a Horseman, which wasn't mine to tell. And then there were the archives. I dragged to a hand-waving stop.

"They're Horsemen," Sherrea said briskly, nodding. "I knew that. Which one was riding the redheaded woman?"

I stared at her.

"It was the only thing that explained what happened. What did *you* think, that she was having a religious conversion?"

I gave up on chronology and explained Frances's vendetta against Tom Worecski and our interception by China Black and Mr. Lyle.

"How did you sandbag Mick?" Frances asked. "It's a bit of a trick to get one of us unconscious before we think to jump horses."

Mr. Lyle nodded. "You have to be very slow, or very fast. In this case, it was speed. And one can't suspect every large, friendly dog one sees."

Mick half grinned, sheepish, at Frances. "He distracted me."

"I'll remember that. Too bad it wouldn't work on Tom; he hates dogs."

Sherrea folded her knees up under her chin and wedged her feet on the chair. "So you want to find a guy who could be anywhere and look like anybody, who might not even be in the City. Why not give us a *hard* one?"

Frances turned her hands palm up. "It was the best I could do at short notice."

"*Ti-so,* this has nothing to do with us," China Black said urgently.

Sher looked up at her. "How can you be sure? It has something to do with Sparrow."

China Black's gaze went from Sherrea to me, and narrowed. She tapped a finger against her lower lip. She looked as if she were planning to move furniture, and I was a sofa.

Sherrea began to push empty dishes and the samovar to the far half of the tea table. Mr. Lyle caught the muffin bowl as it was about to heel off the edge, and stacked it and anything else in danger on the tea tray. Then Sher pulled a wad of electric-blue silk out of her sash. It fell open when she put it on the table, in a way I recognized. I wondered if anyone else there knew it was a new cloth, and knew why.

Given my last reading from Sher, I wanted to volunteer to take the dishes to the kitchen. Unfortunately, I didn't know where it was. I lifted my eyes from the cards to the rest of the audience. China Black was haughty and nervous; Mr. Lyle was calm, as if this was the logical progression of the conversation. Theo was leaning forward and peering. "Groovy cards," he said. "Where they from?" Mick was looking, and looking blank. But Frances was sitting straight-backed on the edge of the couch, her face frozen.

"Could we forgo this, do you think?" she asked. "It's silly."

Sherrea raised her eyes to Frances as she shuffled. I watched her small-boned, purple-nailed hands working over the cards, *flllllllt, flllllllt,* as she said, "This won't take long. And we promise not to tell anybody you did something silly." *Thump*—she set the deck on the silk and cut it into three piles. Then she snapped the top card off each pile and onto the table, face up.

"Oh," she said, and stopped. Her head lifted again, and this time her eyes went to Theo. "Well, that was easy."

Theo leaned even more. "What did—oh," he breathed.

The Tower, the Ace of Pentacles, and the Emperor. I looked at Sherrea.

"For the question-and-three-cards, you want to be pretty literal-minded," she explained. "Which means he's in a tall building, the one associated with the most money and power; and either the building is owned by, or he's in the company of, or he *is,* the bossman of the temporal reality."

"Or all of those," I said, staring at the three cards. "You mean, he's in Ego? With Albrecht?"

She turned again to Theo, so I did, too. He looked like old ivory. "He is," said Theo, barely audible. His glasses reflected afternoon sun; I couldn't see his eyes. "Oh, shit. He sure is."

Frances's icy posture was melted. It had been replaced with the hunting-animal intensity I'd seen before, and that was turned on Theo. She hadn't spoken, but she was waiting.

"What?" I said. "How do you know?"

"My dad's goddamn advisory officer. I know those two freaks who were after you at the Underbridge—they're goons of his. Oh, shit, shit, it makes too much sense."

"No, it doesn't. What does this have to do with Albrecht?" But as I said it, I knew.

"That's my dad," Theo replied.

China Black sat down suddenly. "Ah," she said with a look at Sher. "This would seem to be our business, after all."

The assembled multitudes were in the parlor, listening to Frances plan her murder, no doubt. I wasn't with them. I'd found, after a few more minutes, that I needed a walk in the garden.

The front door didn't object to the idea, and the path didn't lead me back to the porch as I'd half expected. It was a brick path at first; then it became a trail of slate flags in a stream of silvery creeping plants. In the shade of a cluster of trees, I found an ornamental pond with a boulder beside it for sitting. So I sat.

I hadn't been there long before Sherrea said behind me, "I know just how you feel. Hey, *you've* been doing this to *us* for years."

I decided I wasn't up to a heated response. I'd try Frances as a role model. Chilly. "I don't know what you're talking about."

"Oh, *fuck* that," she said, and sat down with a bump on the grassy bank. "You're pissed as hell that you've known Theo for years and he never told you who he was. And that you've known me for about as long, and I didn't tell you I was an accredited kick-ass *bruja*. In fact, you've had your nose rubbed in it that life has been going on outside your skin and nobody was filling you in on the details, and it bothers you *a lot*."

At the side of my boulder, almost hidden in a tuft of tall grass, was a thin-stemmed little plant with a cluster of deep pink flowers. The color was so vivid it seemed to vibrate. I pulled it. It had no fragrance. There were short oval leaves climbing in pairs up the stalk. I began to strip them off, starting at the bottom.

"So now you know how all your friends feel," Sher continued.

"Not quite," I said. "You haven't had any sudden revelations about me."

She glared at me. "I've had plenty about you. Half of 'em I found out by accident and the other half by putting things together, and every time I found the kind of thing friends tell each other, it made me feel like shit. Because you hadn't." Sher dug a stone out of the grass and lobbed it into the pond; I watched the rings of water pulse out toward us as she talked. "If you'd wanted to know anything about me, or Theo, you could have just asked. But then we might have asked *you* something, and whenever we did, you'd slither out of it until it was pretty clear that you wanted us to keep our distance. Now you're mad because we did. Were we supposed to keep giving our little secrets to you and never get anything back?"

"That's not true!" Careful, careful. Chilly. "I've always kept even-up with you. I know the Deal."

Sherrea looked at me as if I'd sprouted antennae. "Damballah, you can bite me now," she muttered. "For instance," she went on, stronger, "there was when I found out you weren't a woman."

The stem bent in my fingers.

"There's one you can pay Theo back with; I don't think he's been disillusioned yet. He still talks as if you're a guy, anyway."

"Make up your mind," I said. It came out thin. "Which am I?"

"My mind has nothing to do with it. When I figured out that either you were both or neither, I started watching for it. You do a chameleon thing—maybe it's not even conscious—that makes you seem female when you're with a woman, and male when you're with a man. Like you take on the local coloring. In a mixed group you kind of shift around. I was still trying to figure out if you were natural or technological when the Horseman showed up. Then I knew—I just did—that they were in it somewhere. And I was afraid she could control you with it, so I said what I did to you."

"You said . . . I'm sorry. I can't remember."

"That you don't belong to them. Never did, and don't now."

I blew air out through my nose, like laughing. "Maybe I don't now. But as far as 'did,' you're wrong. I was a custom order."

"No." She rose and brushed nonexistent grass off her trousers. "I'm the kick-ass *bruja*, and I say so. You never did."

I'd peeled all the leaves; now I had a bare, battered stalk with a little cluster of magenta blossoms. "What kind of flower is this?" I asked suddenly.

She stood with her hands in her pockets, her feet planted. She didn't answer immediately; then she said, "Why do you want to know?"

"I don't know." Inside each star-shaped circle of petals was another ring, little bristly projections, like eyelashes around a circular eye. It still didn't smell like anything. I tossed it on the water, where it wandered until it disappeared along the bank.

"I'm going back to the house," I said, and slid off the boulder.

"Can I go with you?"

"It's a big house."

She didn't flinch; she just closed her eyes for a moment.

6.2: Time stands still on the road

Altogether, my stay in that house was four days long. It seems longer; not because time dragged, but because of things I did, of things I looked at, of conversations I had. It seems strange that they all happened butted up against each other in four days. Maybe time, during those days, ran the way the hallways did when Frances and I'd tried to find our way out. The hallways themselves, after that first surreal morning, remained where they were put.

Mr. Lyle had promised me the library, and delivered when I came back, still snappish, from the garden. It was another long-windowed room on the first floor. The heavy moldings around the door and windows, the shelves, the pedestal table, were oak; the chairs were high-backed and upholstered in a dark fabric full of birds and flowers. The shelves were anywhere the windows weren't, except for the floor and the ceiling. The rug under the table and the smaller ones by the windows were deep red, figured with detailed geometric medallions in many other colors. There were lamps on brackets and on stands by the chairs, and a huge oil and candle chandelier over the pedestal table. Reading after dark, it seemed, was expected.

I was impressed, but I was also in a lousy temper, and not inclined to show I was impressed. I began to read spines. I'd been caught off-guard in the ivy parlor; it would be a good deal harder to make me gape now.

Part of the collection might have been acquired in reaction to the events of the last hundred or so years: all the books in the Foxfire series, for which I had a sort of uninvolved respect; several works, theoretical and not-so, on global warming; a delectable variety of how-to books on solar and water and wind power, and the attendant wiring, storage, water heating, and whatnot. (The latter were shelved in plain sight, which nearly

145

ruined my resolution. How secure was this house, its land, this island? Any City deputy who got a glimpse of those books would burst a blood vessel.)

The rest of the shelves, the majority, had been filled by the process of finding a book that looked interesting and bringing it home. The finders, I hoped, had been plural; there was a point at which diversity of interest became multiple personality, after all.

Eventually, under Mr. Lyle's benign eye, I found the works of Gabriel García Márquez. I took a volume down at random and pecked at the beginning. And began, after a little, to grin.

"Which?" said Mr. Lyle.

"You've read this one?" He nodded. "The bit about the maid shaking the pillowcase, and the pistol falling out and going off."

"You read Spanish?" he asked after a moment.

I looked up and closed the book. The title was *Crónica de una Muerte Anunciada*. "Is that so odd?"

"Some. It's the lingua franca, or one of them, but most of the people who use it can't read it. Many of them can't read at all."

I remembered my mood suddenly. "I don't imagine it bothers them. As long as they can count."

"No, they're perfectly happy. They have no idea there are things like this out there."

He might have been talking about the Márquez book, or the library, but I saw something in his hand, and turned to look. It was one of the books on wind-powered generators.

I put the novel back and stood where I was, my arms slack at my sides. "I saw them the first time."

"I was watching you when you did, too. Once you remembered that you shouldn't react, you had a very good stone face. What does this mean to you?" He gestured again with the book.

"It's illegal as hell to have it," I said, my eyes wide. "Isn't it? Any of those books."

"And that's what impressed you? The wickedness? Maybe it was. But tell me, why is it illegal?"

Well, there was a limit to how brainless I could be expected to be on the subject. I said, "In a town where the City controllers have an energy monopoly? Information about free, unregulated, untaxable energy? Heck, I can't imagine."

He smiled. "And don't you know anyone who buys untaxed methanol? Or has a portable generator with no registration tag in the cellar?"

I raised my hands and opened them; the international symbol of

elplessness. "Afraid not. If you're looking for households to
aid, I guess you'll have to find your own."

"My own would be a good place to start. But you've forgotten,
think. I rode in your elevator."

I had forgotten. "*My* elevator?" I asked, blinking.

"Up *and* down. I was glad you'd left the call button working on
our floor, after I had a look at the stairwell. But it took us half an
our to make it run from inside."

If it had ever occurred to me that I'd be escaping from my own
oor, I'd have torn out the damned call button. If I'd realized I'd
e facing this exceedingly large person who held a copy of
Running on the Wind like a smoking gun with my fingerprints on
t, I'd have jumped off the roof before I let him ride in *my* elevator.

I walked past him to the window seat and occupied it. There
asn't a chair nearby, and I thought he'd have to stand. "All
ight," I said. "What, do you need your VCR repaired?"

Mr. Lyle sat on the rug at my feet. It was like being attended by
folded cast-iron pillar. "A twelve volt to AC inverter, actually.
an you do it, do you think?"

This time my blink wasn't for show. "Good grief. You're not
idding. You use wind?"

"Solar panels."

"Wind's better," I said absently. "Or water. You can't replace
hotovoltaics anymore, unless you know about a warehouse I
aven't found." Then I woke up "Chango, *anyone* can spot a solar
anel! If you want to get busted, why not just carry the damn thing
owntown?"

Mr. Lyle's smile was benevolence itself. "You don't understand
he island. Besides, the City can't afford a helicopter."

Of course. The building that held my treasure house stood in
lain sight of Ego and her tall sisters. The spinning vent on my
oof had to pass daily inspection. Who would see anything here?
his was one of the tallest buildings I'd seen since we left the
eeps. "I don't have any tools with me."

Mr. Lyle shrugged and stood up in the same motion, as if his
houlders pulled the rest of him along. "Come see what we have."

So I was shown through the dining room, the kitchen, the
antry, and, finally, into the power shed, opening off the pantry.
was a little disappointed. There were enough tools, but no more,
nd they were only of reasonable quality. The inverter was all
ight, but I had one rated for twice the load, and another hidden
way, still crated, for when the first began to show its age.

This wasn't the opulent marvel that the rest of the house was;

this wasn't the magnetic center of anything, for anyone. While took the inverter apart and assaulted it with multimeter probes, asked Mr. Lyle, casually, what they ran off it. Answer: a pump some lights, some fans, a couple of recharging units. No audio, n video? A shortwave radio. So this wasn't Paradise, after all.

Mr. Lyle must have seen something in my face. He sai gravely, "There are so few disks and tapes left, and they cost s much, that it's easier to fall back on other things. Books, and liv music, and theater. There's a lot of that on the island."

"Anyone recording the music?"

He looked at me as if I hadn't spoken a language he knew.

"The trouble is finding blank tape stock. It would be great t videotape the plays, but there was never as much tape or hardwar for that, so it's hard to get. I think we've lost the movie biz fo good."

Then, appalled, I shut up. Enthusiasm had possessed me for moment, tricked me into an openness as foreign to m as . . . well, as any number of things. I'd be giving guided tour of the archives, if I went on like this.

The output off the inverter seemed steady. I put the cover plat back on. "Hand me the lamp and we'll test it."

The fluorescent tube clinked like microscopic bells and lit. Mr Lyle stared at it, pleased, and the light sketched chilly blue-whit highlights over his bare scalp, down his nose, along his upper lip and across his chin like a scratchboard drawing on the brown o his skin. "My first name is Claudius," he said. "Feel free to us it."

As if I'd earned it by fixing the inverter—but that didn't rin; true. Before I had time to reconsider, I asked, "What happened t your voice?"

"I used to sing. I was proud of it. But when I was fifteen, I wa involved in a cocaine deal that went a little astray. I was shot in th neck."

"Chango." My eyes, before I could stop them, went to a spo just below his face, but the band collar of his shirt hid most of hi throat.

"It was hard to forgive that fifteen-year-old boy for ruining my voice. But you *must* forgive yourself. I never forgot; that woul have meant unlearning the lessons that made me wiser than him But I forgave."

"Well, there," I said brightly, and put the screwdriver away "All done. But I still think you should switch to wind."

As we retraced our steps to the front of the house, I waited for him to return to the subject. I was relieved when he didn't.

The person I least wanted to talk to was Theo, so I was unreasonably annoyed when he was consistently somewhere else all afternoon. When I found China Black in the kitchen and mentioned him, she raised her hands from a pile of lettuce and looked at the ceiling. "Your Frances has him, *cher*," she said. "She is making him draw maps and remember the number of steps in all of Ego's staircases."

"She's not my Frances," I said, without heat. "But I wish her luck. Theo's doing all right if he remembers to go home when we turn the lights off." That was spite; Theo was perfectly acute by any normal standard. Now *I* could tell her how many—

I could, too. I could tell Frances all manner of useful things about Ego, that Theo was unlikely to have noticed. Number of security people on the front and back entrances, day and night; old fire exits; corners that stayed dark, even when guards passed with their lamps . . . Theo would never have gone into those windowless rooms wary of the absence of light, as I had, frightened of the power that could swallow me with impunity, that dimmed my life to nonexistence just by being there.

Frances was planning her damned murder. *Santos*, I could take the point for her, with a videocassette in my hand. All I needed was a faked label for—what was the supposed name of the stupid thing? —*Hellriders*. The Horseman movie. I sold video to his old man, for gods' sake. Did he know that? He had to.

"Are you well?" said China Black.

I'd forgotten I was in the middle of a conversation. "Yes," I said. There was a leaf cast aside on the counter, brown around its red-and-green edges. I picked it up and turned it between my fingers and thumb. "Dana called you 'Maîtresse,'" I said suddenly.

China Black went on tearing lettuce. "Shall I answer the question you want to ask? I am teaching her, for her safety."

"Safety?"

"I may be too late. Pombagira may already have her."

"Who," I asked with a stirring of unwelcome alarm, "is Pombagira?"

"She is the wife of Eshu. Some call her Red-eyed Erzulie. You will see her in the bar, in the whorehouse, wearing her tight red dress, smoking her cigarette. She likes liquor and blood, and in her service there is power and money, but no lasting joy."

I pleated the lettuce leaf, and heard the center rib pop with each fold. "You can't Deal with joy," I muttered, but she heard me. She turned her back on the counter and stared at me.

"No. You can *Deal* with power and money, and shame and pain. Do you want your friend to have those?"

"I have no friends," I said, and walked blindly away.

Pantry, power shed, garage. I stood staring at the limo, barely visible in the near darkness; the sun was dipping its toes in the river, to the west, and the garage windows faced east. Did Albrecht have a limo? Had Theo ridden in it, to the Underbridge, even, and dusted the smell of wealth off at the door to keep the secret? But it had been no secret for Sherrea. Just for me.

I didn't want to think about either of them. I hoped Frances the Serial Killer was scaring the wits out of Theo, along with the information she wanted. Was *this* why Albrecht wanted the Horseman movie? Not because it was rare, but because he had a damned good reason for wanting to know about the Horsemen, no matter how unreliable the source? Because he was suffering an infestation of Tom Worecski?

Or maybe he was a willing accomplice. I thought of that money-pale face in the light of his desk lamp, the profile repeated on the coins he gave me. He'd sent me to find a copy of *Singin' in the Rain*. Maybe Gilles de Rais would have loved *Singin' in the Rain*. But if A. A. Albrecht was delighted with Tom Worecski, why *had* he wanted the Horseman movie?

My thoughts were as productive as peas in a rattle: they made a lot of noise, and went nowhere. My eyes had adjusted enough to see the garage door, so I left by it.

Evening, in that garden, seemed to bloom like one of its plants. Clinging to the garage wall was a vine with flowers like the bells of trumpets, milk-white and luminous in the dusk, lavishly scented. Bats rose in a translucent cloud from the eaves of an outbuilding and set to hunting with brisk, irregular darts. A slow spark fired and disappeared in the shrubbery across the grass, and another: fireflies. I crunched along the gravel path to round the garage and see the last of the sunset.

It was down to turquoise, watery gold, and indigo. "Going someplace?" said someone behind me.

"Nope." I glanced over my shoulder. It was Mick Skinner. I wasn't familiar with the timbre of his new voice, though I noticed that he'd brought the hint of Texas with him when he'd switched bodies. The light warmed his features, delicate and angular under the well-kept copper-brown skin. The whole body was well kept,

I realized, and young. "Was that one trying to kill himself?" I
asked.

"What?"

"Your new ride. This is going to be a real growth experience for
him, right?"

"Jesus," said Mick, "who put a burr under your sa—"

It took me an instant to remember the end of the expression, as
it had him. The sound I made was a substitute for laughter. "Let's
do 'em all and get it over with. Shall I take the bit between my
teeth? Or you could look a gift horse in the mouth."

He looked away.

"I haven't any horse sense. I kick over the traces. I'm mulish.
I'm given to horseplay, nagging, and feeling my oats. Have we
locked the barn after the horse got out, or is this a horse of a
different color?"

"Stop."

"Whoa?"

"*I'm sorry,*" Mick said. "Whatever it was I did. Only I'm
betting it wasn't me."

I sighed. "Well, the thought of you doesn't lead me to
remember several years of my life with vague embarrassment."

"What?" he said again. "You're starting to sound like
Frances."

"That's almost an insult." I turned and walked back to where he
stood. "Are you part of her invasion plan?"

He lifted one shoulder. "I don't know."

"Why are you still here, then?"

"Why are you?"

"I don't know. Sorry, that wasn't meant as mockery. Last I
heard, you and I were to be protected."

He looked out toward the sunset, which was gone. "Would *you*
join the invasion?"

Here was the opening to say that I knew Ego, that I knew
Albrecht, that I'd be useful. "I can't imagine why."

After a moment he said, "Because nobody's as good at looking
out for themselves as Frances thinks she is."

That was nearly as hard to figure out as the sentence of mine
that he'd complained about. "Then maybe she'll get killed. Ask
anybody in this household if they'd weep at the thought."

"*I* would."

"Then go pick up your flamethrower and enlist."

He smiled, reluctantly. "I don't think a flamethrower would
help."

"Whatever. What *does* she have to do to get Worecski?"

Mick scuffed the gravel, drawing patterns in the pale stone with his toe. "It's all brute strength and speed. At least, it always was. Christ, two Horsemen in a head fight is an ugly thing. You can keep somebody from switching rides, from shifting to a new body, if you move on him fast and hard, as if you're gonna ride *him*."

"What do the real owners of the bodies do while all this is going on? Referee?"

"They're not necessarily there," he said with an odd expression.

"Where are they?"

"A Horseman seals up the host personality and uses the rest of it: memory, conscious and unconscious motor control, learned skills. But . . . if you've got a horse you want to keep, and you want it to stay where you left it when you ride somebody else . . . it's easier if the host isn't there anymore."

I felt a chill. "You kill it." He could have killed me.

"It can happen by accident, if you ride too long. The personality dwindles away, like a candle going out. But you can snuff it right away, too, if you need to. If you want to." He dropped his gaze to the path.

I wanted to ask him if he'd killed the young man who'd taken such care of that pretty body. I was afraid to know. "So Frances will try to take Worecski over. What happens if she does?"

"Oh, she won't," he said. "She just needs to hold him there while she blows his brains out."

"Chango." When my voice was entirely mine again, I said, "But if she's—won't she blow her own brains out, too? Effectively?"

"Timing's everything," he agreed. "If she pulls back too early, he can skip before she kills the body. If she doesn't pull back in time, it's blammo, brain for rent."

Unless that gave the brain back to its original owner. Did Mick believe that Frances had killed her host? "You don't talk as if this is hypothesis. You . . . People have done this before."

"Yes," he said, mildly surprised. "I told you, it's called a head fight. Not too many people actually got killed, but that was usually the intention."

"Frances has done this."

"Oh, yeah. It must be the way she got the Horsemen she was hunting, too. She was always good. Strong and fast. But Tom was strong and fast and bugfuck *crazy*. I don't think Frances can take him. Without help."

"This doesn't sound like something you can do by committee."

"We could distract him," said Mick. He was hard to see in the dark. "We could do that much." He sounded as if he were arguing with something I couldn't remember saying.

It was cool, out near the river after sunset. Mick was wearing his jacket, the one he wouldn't leave behind in my apartment. I shivered and rubbed my arms.

"Then you can," I said. "Have fun. If this is a remake of *High Noon*, she's not Gary Cooper. She's not the good guy."

"Who is?" he asked, as if the question wasn't rhetorical.

"Forget it. I'm square with Frances, and I'm sure as water runs downhill not going to try to get killed just because I *can*."

"You still hold it against her, that bit back at your place."

"No, I told you. We're square. If I owed her, it would be different, but I don't owe her anything. Do you?"

With a crunching of gravel, he turned back toward the shrubbery. He came out of the shadow of the garage and moonlight fell on him. I caught up to him where the path bent.

"We all slept with each other," he said. I wasn't sure what he was talking about, at first. "We had a lot of contempt for normal people—or we said we did—and besides, some experiences are so strange and strong that they force you away from anybody who doesn't share 'em. When we wanted to get laid, as opposed to when we wanted to prove something, we turned to our own kind. So Frances and I have gone to bed with each other a few times." He pinched a branch end off the nearest shrub and toyed with the leaves, creasing them along the veins. "I think, for Frances, that's all it was."

I knew it wasn't the sort of statement one was expected to answer. I said, "If that was supposed to make me understand, let me remind you that's not a motivation I have much experience with."

He looked up sharply. "Haven't you ever liked someone? Respected them? Been their friend?"

Had I ever . . . "No," I said. "So if you tell me it makes you want to get killed for no good reason, I'll have to take your word for it."

He dropped the twig. "I was going to tell you dinner was ready. I bet we've both missed it now."

We had, but there were leftovers. I felt a little like a character mistakenly let loose in *Beauty and the Beast*, in that house. All one's needs provided for, and no staff in sight. And a strong suspicion that one ought not to try to leave. Mick took his dinner away with him; I sat in the kitchen with mine, at a wooden table

with a scarred top, under a hanging kerosene lamp. It was anoth
of the house's comforting rooms, full of simple objects and t
smell of garlic. Or maybe the damned house just thought I need
comforting. I cleaned up after myself and found my way up t
back stairs without incident to my allotted room.

Of all the things that might legitimately trouble me, one seem
to take precedence, but I couldn't quite grab hold of it. I yank
off my boots and lay down on the bed, staring at the wall th
sloped over it, the part under the roofline that was almost but n
quite the ceiling. The wallpaper was full of flowers and leave
like everything else in the house. Who was the gardener? Chi
Black? It seemed out of character from my first sight of he
vampiric in dark blue chiffon and sunglasses, on the first floor
my building.

Bingo. The tea party, when China Black had told Mick Skinn
that they weren't looking for him, they were looking for his bod
But in my apartment, China Black had asked . . . no, it wasn
conclusive. She'd asked, more or less, to be allowed to speak
the previous occupant, and there was nothing to tell me for su
who she thought that might be. Then when she failed, and was
furious, she'd said, *He wasn't there.*

If there was something about Mick that ought to be passed o
she or Mr. Lyle would do it. If it didn't need to be passed on,
didn't want to know it. After all, plenty of people around that t
table knew things about me I was glad they hadn't said.

I lived on City time, staying up until dawn and sleeping throug
half the day to avoid fighting with the sun. So I was surprise
when I woke to a mild blue morning sky in the window. I hadn
remembered falling asleep, which I'd done in my clothes on top
the comforter. I really had to stop sleeping in my clothes. The ha
was quiet. I thought of that bathtub suddenly, the one big enoug
to drown in. I dug my clean shirt out of my pack and headed f
the bathroom.

If I'd been in *Beauty and the Beast*, the hot water would hav
been waiting for me. I found the sight of the empty tub reassurin
But there were towels in the cupboard, soap in the dish, and
didn't even have to pump the water up by hand. Of cours
not—the inverter was fixed, the pump was running. There'd bee
a hand pump in the kitchen, so that even when the electric one wa
down, no one would have to haul water from outside. One casset
deck and the place would be a pretty supportable prison. I braide
my wet hair and went downstairs.

The kitchen was deserted, but there were signs that someon

ngular or plural, had already had breakfast. I found some ftover muffins and carried them with me as I wandered.

I wouldn't explore the house; it would look as if I were hunting or company. I went outside again instead. Hidden in the gardens eyond the garage, I found the chicken yard, the rabbit cages, and ie beehives. There was a wooden shed that I knew from the sweet ickory smell was the smokehouse. Past that, down a wooded ail, in the center of a broad ring of old trees, I found a circular ne-story building that I couldn't identify at all.

Half the building didn't have walls; there were only the roof illars, peeled trunks maybe six inches thick, to mark where the alls would be. The floor was dirt, packed smooth, and feature-ss as if swept. On one side, where the wall started, there was an mpty raised platform. There was a center post for the roof, rising ut of a cement footing. Beyond the center post, at the back of the ircular room, it was dark; but I made out another platform, with squarish bulk on it like a table or a chest, and irregular points of ight. There was nothing to indicate that I ought not to go in.

The center post was painted. It reminded me of the stair railings ı Sherrea's apartment building, the colors twining one after nother, yellow, red, black, green, and white. The walls were ainted, too, with murals. They were simple and stylized, angular nd almost abstract—the antithesis of Sherrea's cards. A muscular oung black man, smiling, wore a red cape and carried a curved word, and seemed to be walking through fire. A naked woman, vide-hipped and heavy-breasted, her curly blue-black hair falling o her ankles, poured water from a jar under her arm. An old, fat lack man sat cross-legged and grinning, as if his erect penis were he best joke in the world. Two snakes twined upward, facing each ther, as if dancing on their tails. Between the figures, tying them ogether, explaining and keeping secrets, were the *vévés*.

The square bulk was an altar, draped in scarlet and purple, and he changeable lights were candles. They reflected off the rest of he altar fittings: glass bottles, a mirror, strings of beads, a silver owl, two tall vases with flowers in them.

I backed away and bumped into the center pole. The whole vide, unwalled space was closing in on me, pressing my skin gainst my muscles, muscles against protesting bones. I heard my reath entering and leaving in bursts. The back wall wavered nder my eyes.

I heard a voice, not loud, but I didn't see the speaker; I smelled zone and a thick, watery odor, like the banks of a pond. My

tongue was thick in my mouth. A ball of panic swelled in m
chest.

A voice—the same one? *Come with me.* I felt an arm arou
me, guiding me. Then I was sitting on the grass under the tree
and a glass was pressed against my lips, holding something th
gave off fierce fumes. I swallowed, almost prepared for it: run

The face above me belonged to China Black, as did the voi
that said, "Well, *cher*, are you sickening for something?"

I took the glass of rum from her and had another sip. "What
that?" I said, nodding at the building.

"It's the *hounfor*." I must have looked blank, because sl
added, "Where we dance, and call the spirits."

"I'm sorry. I suppose I shouldn't have gone in."

I thought, if she could have raised the silver eyebrows, sl
would have. "Why not? There's nothing there to harm anyone,
do harm to. Were you afraid?"

"Not until . . . No."

She studied me; then she took the glass out of my hand. "Hml
Come along. Yes, back inside, nothing will happen to you."

We came to the center pole, and she laid a hand on it. "This
the *poteau-mitan*. The spirits rise through it to us. The altar look
pretty, and we do our work there, but this is the source." Sl
stopped at the altar. "Kneel here. On the platform, yes."

"Why?" I said.

Her dark face radiated tried patience. "Because it will make m
happy. You do not believe in this. So what can it do to you?"

I knelt, which put everything on the altar at eye level.

China Black lit a new candle. "Legba," she said, her voic
peremptory, "are you listening to me? Here is one of you
children, Papa Legba, a child of the crossroads. Are you watchin
out for this one, Papa?" She took a rough gray stone off the alt
and handed it to me, along with the glass of rum. "Take a little an
rinse your mouth with it," she said. "Then spit it on the stone.
I did. She set the stone back on the altar. Then she handed me th
mirror I'd noticed. "Do the same to this." After I did, she took th
mirror from me and set it on the altar to reflect my face. Distorte
by the rum, the image reminded me of Frances's catalog of m
features, back in my apartment. I shivered and closed my eyes.

"Legba, you were thirsty, and we gave you rum. Now you se
your child, Papa," China Black said. "You will watch over thi
one, and play your tricks on the enemies of your servants. And w
will make a meal for you, to show you we are glad that you hav

listened." She tugged me to my feet, and led me out of the *hounfor*.

"Nothing's free," I said as we walked up the path. But I felt a nagging disappointment.

China Black stopped and stared at me. "Most things are free," she said. "You have much to make up for, that is all."

"What is Legba to me, or I to him?" I smiled when I said it, though.

"That is exactly what I mean."

I made a gesture meant to include the *hounfor*, the gardens, the house. "Was most of this free?"

The look she gave me had irritation in it, and surprise, and a little of something else that I liked less. She shook her head and continued up the path. I followed her back to the house.

She put me to work. As long as I was there, she said, and knew about these things, I could look over their electrical system. I reminded myself that I was getting free room and board, whether I wanted it or not, and climbed up to the roof to look at the solar panels. If I hadn't known better than to stay out in the sun that long, I would have found an excuse to be there all day. I could see the whole island, green and dotted with rooftops, and the silver-gray brilliance of the river around it. The suspension bridge looked like a fistful of streamers, tying the island to the City, and the City dozed upright, glossy and geometrical. I had locked the doors and covered my tracks; the archives were safe and would wait for me, as they always did.

There was a printing press in the basement. I should have known there would be. It was a hand-operated one; more than that I couldn't tell, since that wasn't the medium I specialized in. I recognized type cases, though, and the apparatus for laying out a page. I had to squeeze around it all to get to the circuit box.

I was in the cellar when Sherrea stuck her head around the door (I jumped) and said, "It's lunch. Are you done?"

"Mmm."

"Well, you may as well stop to eat it, since it's there. Theo's been asking where you are."

It occurred to me that Theo could have done a lot of what I'd found to do today. He was a friend of Sher's, and Sher seemed to run tame here. Had Theo been here before? Or had he been, was he still, an unknown quantity, as I'd been before Mr. Lyle—Claudius—surprised things out of me in the library?

The dining room, paneled and bay windowed, was awfully full of people. China Black and Claudius Lyle, Frances, Mick,

Etienne, the old woman who'd opened the gates—yesterday? Was
that all?—Theo, and now Sher and me. Sher's hand lifted, as if it
wanted to settle on my shoulder, and dropped again. "Don't
worry," she muttered, "I'll protect you."

"I'm fine."

"You're half out of your mind, and hiding it damn well. I've
never seen you in a group larger than three people."

She was right, of course. Maybe it had to do with the
chameleon nature she'd commented on, or maybe I was afraid that
if I talked to more than two people at a sitting, they'd compare
notes and find out all my secrets. The tea party in the parlor had
been, before this, the largest intimate gathering I'd ever been in.

"What's the old woman's name?" I asked.

"Loretta."

"And the dog's?"

"What?"

"The dog's name. If I'm doing this, I may as well do it all the
way."

Sher grinned. "Eustace."

"You're not serious."

"The hell I'm not. It was six months before I could call him
with a straight face."

The food was laid out on the buffet, which meant I'd be spared
having to ask anyone to pass the whatever. The whatever
consisted of the crown jewels of southern cooking: ham and
red-eye gravy, corn bread, hoppin' john, string beans, and sweet
potato pie. If Frances didn't get on with her murder soon, she
wouldn't fit into Ego's elevator.

Following Sherrea got me either exactly what I didn't want, or
what I did, depending on which interpretation of my wants I used.
I found myself at a corner of the long table, with Sher on my right
and Theo, at the end, on my left. He smiled when I sat down and
pointed to the sling on his arm. "Temporary lefties get to sit in
state, man," he said. "Makes me want to ask the meeting to come
to order."

I stared at the sling, stupefied. He hadn't told me anything about
himself. I hadn't told him anything about me. But he'd stood on
that landing in the rain and taken a bullet from one of my would-be
kidnappers. He—and I—made less sense than ever, but something
heavy lay on the scales between us. I had ignored that, yesterday.
How could I?

"Does it hurt?" I asked.

"Oh, yeah. I keep forgetting and reaching for things." He

pulled a hand-rolled smoke out of his shirt pocket. "But hey, we have the technology." It was a red-and-orange paisley shirt. I wondered it it was his. Probably.

I would have offered to cut something up for him, but the ham was fork-tender.

As it turned out, I wasn't the quietest person at the table. Mr. Lyle mentioned that I'd recommended wind power, and engaged me in a pleasant argument about the efficiency of aging PV cells and the availability of good bearings. The woman from the gate, Loretta, was sitting across from me; she scowled and shook her head.

"Everybody 'long the river ought to be runnin' off communal-owned hydro," she said sharply. "Doesn't make efficient sense *or* economic sense, all this sneakin' around for power that rightly belongs to everybody or nobody. No point arguin' over it, either, with that horse's ass Albrecht sayin' it's all his."

I glanced at Theo, but he seemed to be concentrating on his plate. For all I knew, he thought his father *was* a horse's ass. How should I know? I had no idea what family feeling was like.

"Why hydro?" I asked.

"Frees up the rest of the stuff for folks without running water nearby. Though the way you talk, I could run a goddamn dance hall on old bicycle parts and a car battery." I was about to protest when she smiled at me, and I decided I didn't need to.

I talked; it was Frances who was quiet. Her face was pale and pinched, and sometimes her fork would pause in midmotion, and her eyes would lock on nothing at all. I was halfway through dessert before I understood. She was afraid.

Did she share Mick's doubts? Was she wondering if she was fast enough, strong enough? Or was she only worried about getting in and getting out?

I could tell her the number of steps in all the staircases. But she never looked at me. Had Theo told her that I had knowledge she could use? Had he realized, yet, that I did?

Theo was pushing his chair back. "Can I talk to you?" I asked.

Sunlight flashed on the lenses of his glasses. "Sure. C'mon upstairs."

I caught sight of Sherrea as I rose from the table. She looked pleased.

Theo had a room on the second floor. It was larger than mine, but it had the same character; it was a guest room, not a regular habitation. "Heck of a house," I said, to see how he'd respond.

"Scared the shit out of me," he said, dropping lightly on the bed and prying his sneakers off one-handed. "When Sher brought m▮ here, right after that Frances hauled you away, and I saw this bi▮ old house with the lightning going off behind it . . . I though▮ she was checking me into the Bates Motel, man."

He knew I'd understand the reference. I would have used it wit▮ him, secure in the same knowledge. I looked into his face, the pal▮ face of a confirmed nighthawk or a rich kid, and said, "I'm not ▮ man."

The light on his glasses interfered with his expression, but ther▮ was no great surprise in the lines of his mouth. He wa▮ nice-looking, I realized suddenly, by any standards. "It's just ▮ figure of speech," he said.

"I'm not a woman, either."

He sat quiet for a few moments. Then he said, "Oh. Tha▮ explains some stuff."

I don't know what I'd expected. Or wanted. "What stuff?"

"Well, Sher and I once, when we'd had a lot to drink, had thi▮ discussion. I said . . . that I felt, sometimes, like I had a crus▮ on you, and it made me uncomfortable. And she looked at me lik▮ I was nuts, and said she didn't know why it would, because yo▮ seemed like someone it would be pretty easy to have a crush on▮ I was really embarrassed, and I laughed and said maybe for her▮ but you weren't, like, my type. Then we both looked at each othe▮ funny and changed the subject. But that was when I realized tha▮ maybe I didn't know what sex you were, and maybe Sher didn'▮ either."

"She figured it out," I said thickly.

"She didn't tell me." He gazed steadily at me through the top ▮ of his glasses as he said it. He was telling me that Sher ha▮ respected my privacy; and that he had, too, by not asking.

I sat down on the edge of an armchair across from the bed. W▮ had the window between us, lighting both our faces. The▮ conditions for perfect vulnerability had been established. So I tol▮ him everything I knew about what I was.

"Far out," he said when I was done. "In fact, about the farthes▮ out I've ever heard of. But none of you can figure out if you've go▮ a Horseman in your head?"

I shook the body part in question. "I want to say I don't. I'▮ sure I don't. But how would I know? For a while Frances though▮ I was Tom Worecski, and I can't even say for certain that I'▮ not."

"No," Theo said softly. "I'm pretty sure where he is. He'▮

calling himself Frederick Krueger. Some joke, huh? I never got it 'til yesterday."

Freddy Krueger, with a handful of knives and the ability to turn dreams to his advantage. Who died at the end of every movie and came back again and again. Some joke. "Is he that bad?"

"I'm scared of him. I think my father's scared of him."

"And your father's never even seen *Nightmare on Elm Street*, unless he bought it from somebody else. You knew I sold videos to your father?"

"Hell, yeah. That's how you wound up at the Underbridge."

After a moment I said, "Pardon?" Well, this wasn't supposed to be painless.

Theo must have understood. "I'm sorry," he said. "I don't—look, my dad and I don't get along. I mean, if he was just a guy I knew, I wouldn't like him. And contrary to popular belief, being A. A. Albrecht's kid is not the coolest thing in the world. I make a *point* of not telling people. So I couldn't just march up to you outside my dad's office and tell you about the Underbridge. And I couldn't ask you to sign on, anyway. It's Robby's club."

"So you asked Robby to ask me?"

"So I told Robby that you might know the stuff we needed, and that he should check you out. I told him where he could leave a message for you."

"You knew all this about me?"

He flung his free hand out to one side. He would have flung the other one, too; I saw him wince. "You were *interesting*! All right? D'you know how many other people care about this stuff? Electronics and old video and recorded music?"

"We're throwbacks," I said. "No, you're a throwback. I'm sort of a throw-forward. If that cigarette you showed me downstairs has marijuana in it, would you be willing to share it with me?"

He pushed his glasses back up his nose and poked his hand through his smooth brown hair. "It'll put you on your butt. It's high-test stuff."

"You'll be amazed."

"I'm already amazed. Let's get petrified instead."

We'd passed the thing back and forth twice, in near silence, before I said, "Did you tell Frances I knew my way into Ego?"

Theo looked insulted. "Hell, no."

"Why not?"

"Because I figured if you wanted her to know, you'd tell her."

"Are you going back with her?"

He shook his head. "I think she wishes she could ask. But,

man, I've talked to Kru—Worecski. And I'm staying right here 'ti
it's over. I've got a good excuse." He tapped the sling.

"I owe you for that," I said softly.

He gurgled. "Heck, I didn't do anything. And now I've got thi
cool dueling scar."

"But you tried. And you didn't have to."

He looked at me owlishly. Finally he grinned. "You're a
asshole," he said happily.

"*In cannabis veritas.* Don't fall asleep with a lit joint."

"Can't," he sighed, leaning back against his pillows. "W
finished it."

"You're no fun," I told him. "Guess I'll just go away."

I felt relaxed, but not at all absentminded; Theo *would* hav
been amazed, if he'd still been awake. I finally found France
outside, on the broad covered porch that faced the driveway. Sh
was sitting in a wooden chair with her feet on the porch railing an
the chair balanced on its back legs. She didn't move when I cam
out the front door.

I dragged up another chair, its back to the railing so I could se
her face. "Last night, Mick tried to talk me into going with you."

"I hope he didn't spend a lot of time on it." Her gaze move
idly over the distant edge of the garden.

"Why?"

"Because I won't take you. Or him, or anyone else."

For several minutes we sat in uncompanionable silence, whil
I tried to talk myself out of doing the inevitable. Was it inevitable
I thought of Theo, recuperating upstairs from the wound he'
received on my behalf. Even if Frances left the City now, lef
Worecski undisturbed, he could never go back to Ego. He ha
stepped between Myra and Dusty—Worecski's servants—an
their quarry, and they would remember. And how long would it b
before Theo let slip that he knew who and what Worecski was?

But if Frances killed Worecski and left town, Theo would b
safe. I would be safe, too. Frances would be gone, Mick woul
leave, Myra and Dusty would take their orders from someone else
and I could go back to something like the life I was used to.

"If you get Worecski, will you go away?" I asked, to be sure

For the first time since I'd come onto the porch, Frances looke
at me. "If I kill Tom Worecski, you'll never see me again. M
word of honor, for whatever that may mean to you."

I took a deep breath and sighed it away. "The guard shift at th
front door changes at midnight," I said. "They get sloppy then
The only working security camera is on the front door, and i

doesn't pan anymore, so it covers a pretty small area. The fire
stairs are great for getting out, but they won't do you any good
getting in; the doors lock from the stair side on all the floors. So
you want to go up in the elevator, which, as long as I'm with you,
is no problem."

Her eyes narrowed. "Then I have a problem."

"Because you won't have me with you? Bet you five bucks,
hard."

"Do you know what Tom would do," she said, her voice low,
"when he found out what you are? My God, he'd love it. It would
be horrible. You, of all people, are not going in with me."

This wasn't supposed to be painless for her, either. "What can
he do to me that you and Mick haven't done already?"

A muscle fluttered in her jaw, but she didn't turn away.

"Did Theo give you a good technique for getting in?"

"He couldn't," Frances said, as if she hated to.

"I can. Unfortunately for both of us, it needs me to work."

She spread her fingers like a fan across her forehead. At last she
said, "Why?"

She didn't mean, "Why does it need you?" *Because something
has twined you and me and Mick Skinner together, and the only
way to get free seems to be to go forward.* But I didn't say that.
"I'll tell you my idea. If you come up with a better one that
doesn't involve me, I won't complain."

I told her. I told it again to Mick Skinner, to explain why he
couldn't be in on it. I told it to Theo when he woke up, because,
however different his view of Ego was, there were observations of
mine that he might be able to check and correct. And I told it to
Sherrea, because she insisted on it. With each iteration, it became
more and more the shape of the future. The plan.

It required me to spend that afternoon in the cellar learning the
ways of movable type, and sent Theo and me to the Underbridge
for a day and a half of hard work making equipment do things it
wasn't designed for. Frances probably spent the time cleaning
guns; I didn't ask. On Thursday afternoon we came back to the
house on the island. I went up to my room, to try to get some of
the sleep I was going to lose that night.

When you're lying in a room that isn't yours, on an uninhabited
floor of a house that isn't yours, trying to fall asleep in spite of the
rat maze your mind is running and the sick feeling growing in your
bowels, you discover that your hearing is marvelously acute. I
heard Frances's door open and close, and something—shoes?—
drop to the floor.

Later (it seemed like fifteen minutes, but it might have been three) I heard someone knock there, and Frances's voice. Then someone else's. The creaking floor, and the door opening. Voice, voice, the door closing. The intermittent rise and fall of conversation from Frances's room. Then quiet.

That's what I heard with my ears. But the other things, what I didn't hear, or maybe heard with other ears than mine; and what I didn't quite see, and didn't quite feel, but thought I saw and felt all the same—

I can't describe it. I can half explain it: Mick had been in my head several times. Frances once, but she'd been there. Frances herself had said that there was a connection between a Horseman and the horse, a link that remained after the contact was broken. That the connection became relevant just then might have been an accident. I wanted it to be. I didn't like to think that either Frances or Mick could hate me so much, or be so cruel without cause.

I lay on my side hugging my knees, biting the inside of my mouth, while Mick and Frances made love in the next room. I didn't move until Sher knocked on both doors and said it was time to go.

Card **7**

Fears

Ten of Swords

Waite: Death, pain, desolation. Advantage, profit, success, power, and authority, but all transient.

Douglas: Desolation and ruin, but with the idea that it is a community, rather than individual, tragedy.

Crowley: Reason run mad, soulless mechanism, the logic of lunatics and philosophers. Reason divorced from reality.

Case: End of delusion in spiritual matters.

7.0: Off to see the wizard

"Well," said Frances, "have we forgotten anything? Hot dogs, pickles, potato salad, ants—you did bring the ants?"

"Frances," I said, not for the first time, "that's enough."

The trike was parked on the apron of an unused garage door, in a service drive between Loondale and the empty Gilded West tower. That put it near our preferred exit route. We'd circled Ego on foot, and were now on the opposite side, at Ego's front door, where the guard station was. It was five minutes to midnight.

"I suppose we'll have to do without the ants." She tilted her head back and looked at Ego's top, where the ring of white lights shone smugly, and running clouds edge-lit with moonlight made the view look like the opening shot of a horror movie. "Use it while you've got it, Tom. And so will I. May the best fiend win."

"Is the best one more fiendish, or less?"

"When we finish this, you have my permission to tell me."

"If I still can."

She looked at me, and opened up a moonlit death's-head grin. "If I can hear you."

"On that jolly note—it's time." I headed for the doors as Frances tucked herself in the shadows of the door embrasure. She wore something dull and dark and snug, with a pocketed vest of the same stuff. The fabric didn't make any sound when rubbed against itself. Motionless, out of direct light, she disappeared.

I pushed through the door and squinted under the bare bulb at the guard station. There were two men there, swapping gossip as their shifts overlapped. One I'd never seen before: an earnest-looking youngish man with short, sun-bleached blond hair. The other, a big man with a heavy red beard and a Santa Claus belly who occupied the desk chair, was a regular on the midnight-to-eight shift. I almost smiled at him. He did lousy work.

"Hey, look who's here!" he called, leaning back. The desk

167

chair screeched on its base. "It's the handyman! Albrecht keepin'
up his service contract, huh?"

"You'll have to ask him," I said. The blond man curled his lip,
whether at me or at his fellow guard I couldn't tell. Seeing that, I
tried a shot at random. "Is that a blackjack in your pocket, or are
you just excited about working with this guy?" I said to him.

The curl became a full-fledged sneer. He turned to the red-
bearded guard. "I gotta go, Shoe. Got a date out at the pier."

"Tell him hi for me," I said to the blond one's departing back.
Shoe thought that was funny.

Good. Down to one; now to move him around. "You want to
call up to Mr. A. and let him know I'm here?"

"Let him know *who's* here, boy?"

"D. W. Griffith," which was the name Albrecht knew me by.
"Tell him I've got the one he wants." In my hand was an
unmarked box, something nobody would identify as a container
for a videotape. Just like always. Everything had to be just like
always.

"I bet you do," said Shoe. He went through a door behind the
desk. There was a little pane of glass in it to watch me through,
but the door kept me from hearing whatever he might choose to
say to the person upstairs.

I dropped the videotape. Swearing, I went to my knees in front
of the desk and bumped it farther under. Then I reached beneath
the desktop and twisted the door camera's coaxial cable loose from
the wall jack, where it connected to the monitor upstairs. I was
careful not to break the connection entirely; I wanted streaks and
snow, not a blank screen. Frances came through the door like a
patch of black fog, under the guard's window, and around the
corner to the elevator. I popped the coax back on. *Never use
quick-connect jacks on security equipment*, I thought as I came up
smiling from behind the desk with the unmarked box in my hand.
I had time to dust off my knees and straighten my collar before the
guard came out.

"So, what's in the package?" he said, and my bone marrow
turned to brine.

"You'll have to ask Mr. A. about that, too, won't you?" I hoped
my voice was firm and pleasant. Hadn't I been passed? Did they
know somehow that there would be a break-in? If that elevator
moved without authorization, hell, in condensed form, would
break loose.

"Maybe I will. You're supposed to get your ass up there. You
know the way."

The release of fear was almost harder to bear than the onset. I couldn't answer him, snappily or otherwise. I walked at what I hoped was a leisurely pace down the hall and turned the corner.

Frances materialized from whatever surface she'd adhered to. I poked the button, and the scarred bronze doors in front of me opened. There had been lots of elevators there once; the sealed-off openings for their doors were all that were left. Frances stepped in next to me as I pushed the button for the top floor.

I sagged against the wall when the doors closed. I could feel sweat wandering down my spine and chest and rib cage. I couldn't think of anything to say that wasn't swearing.

Frances had a pistol in her hands; she was mounting a silencer on it with quick motions. "If I were you, I'd save my emotional collapse for later. That was the easy part."

"For you, maybe."

"Could they have seen you drop the box?"

"Upstairs, you mean? No. The camera only covers the area right around the front door."

"Then there isn't anything to connect with the snow on their monitor. Good." She seemed to be content with the pistol, but she didn't put it away in her vest. "How likely is it that we'll be met at the top by another guard?"

She was right: that had been the easy part. I'd forgotten. "Fifty-fifty. There hasn't been one the last few times. I'm hoping I'm considered trustworthy."

"Fine. When the door opens, don't run out, but don't dawdle."

For the first time it occurred to me that if it went to hell, I could say Frances forced me to do this. I wondered if I would. If I asked Sherrea, what would she recommend? Would she say that life was precious, and that I should save mine if I could? Or would she say things about honor, and commitment, and the greater good?

Or would she say, in a voice that wasn't hers, *You gotta learn to serve, and let your own self be fed by the spirits*? She'd said I had to do something about my evil ways. *Well, Sher, here I am*. I wished I could have found something less drastic.

"Get ready," Frances murmured, and I tried desperately to remember, and re-create, what leaving this elevator had been like when it wasn't a matter of somebody's life or death.

The doors opened, and I strode out. No one. No one at all. All this relief would be the ruin of me. Frances moved up and touched me on the shoulder. No talking now; we'd talked the floor plan to pieces back on the island. I nodded. She disappeared down the hall while I knocked on the familiar door, dark wood, heavy and polished. A voice called from beyond it, and I turned the cool chrome knob and stepped through.

The room was the same, dark and close, with its desk and draped window and high-backed chair. The light fell, neat and constrained on the desktop. The white hands in the light were Albrecht's, and the pale, fleshy face dim above them.

How had I done this before? Had there been a routine, a series of actions that made up the dance of trade? I stood with the box in my hand, my mind blank, my heart slamming in my ribs. The box, the box. I lifted it, set it on the desk, and with my index finger slid it across the wood to Albrecht.

"What is it?" he said.

"What you asked for. Open it."

I realized belatedly that I hadn't needed to make the tape look like an original. If I was right, he would have settled for a dub, and it would have been reasonable for me to claim that a dub was all I could find. But he pulled the box (cardboard, this time) open, and I watched his hands, his face, for any sign that I'd failed.

In the mellow light of the desk lamp, I thought it was still convincing: the block lettering for the title, the running time, the distributor's name; the scuffing and fading of the print where fingers would have worn it. The label glue didn't even smell. I'd missed my calling; I should have been a forger. When Albrecht played the tape, he'd see a title sequence that gave surprisingly little evidence of its low-tech origins, and five minutes of non-specific establishing scenes assemble-edited from six different B-horror flicks. By minute seven, I calculated, he'd know this wasn't the movie he'd paid for. But by then, I'd be gone.

He closed the box. His hands didn't have the acquisitive curl I was used to seeing in them. But again, if I was right, it wasn't simple acquisitiveness that had driven him to seek this out.

Frances, have you found your damned monster yet? I would have to leave her there. If I left without her, before she found Worecski, they'd let me go unhindered, unconnected to the thing about to happen. As it was, the business reputation that was making this possible would evaporate; I'd never sell another tape to Albrecht; I'd have to leave town for a while; but I could survive that. Now Albrecht would open his desk drawer and pull out the leather bag.

He stood up. "Come with me."

My tongue froze to the roof of my mouth. "Why?" I asked.

His expression was neutral, as any good bargainer's would be. "You don't think I keep that much in here, do you? Come along."

So much for maintaining our routine. There was nothing I could do, except follow him and stay alert. He worked a latch on a door set into the paneling behind the desk, and light shot out all around it. I squinted and stepped through.

"Sugar?" said a voice I knew, a woman's. "You all through— Sparrow!"

She wore a narrow dress of midnight-blue silk that draped like water running over her skin. Her lips were bright coral-red, and her eyelids were smoky. Her shining white-blond hair fell unbound all around her lightly tanned shoulders and decolletage.

"Hello, Dana," I said, and was surprised that my mouth worked. "Fancy meeting you here."

Her gaze snapped to Albrecht. "Sugar, what's— Is this— What's going on?"

"Just a little business, sweetie," he said, his attention on the cabinet he was opening. "Don't you worry." But she'd used a name for me he'd never heard. Or had he? Myra and Dusty had known it.

It was a large room, exquisitely appointed. Dana was sitting in a pose that suggested she'd been lying down a moment earlier, on a cream-colored couch. It was one of two, set in an L shape. A carved Chinese table stood in front of them, scattered with things: a carafe of dark red wine and two partially filled glasses; the remains of a small meal for two; a little silver-stoppered vial half full of something white; a heavy necklace of silver and turquoise medallions. The lighting came from recesses in the ceiling. The air was cool and dry. There was a sky-blue carpet on the floor three inches deep, and a rack of stereo and video gear topped with a twenty-five-inch monitor.

My eyes kept going, past the rack to another shining wood door and the man standing straight and stiff next to it. I didn't recognize him at first. He wore a high-collared white jacket and black trousers. His blond hair was scraped back from his face, and he looked even more cadaverous than usual. He was trying desperately to look at nothing, and the effort, I could tell, was almost more than he could bear. Cassidy. Uniformed, clearly in Albrecht's employ, he was having to witness his boss's seduction of the woman he was in love with. I turned back to Dana and found her watching me.

"Is this one of life's little jokes on the two of you?" I asked. My voice was unsteady, but not much. "Or did you use your connections to get him the job?" Connections. I'd realized that Dana had them. I just hadn't realized they'd been to here.

Dana flushed. "Honey . . ." She shook her head.

I looked again at Albrecht, who was pouring himself a drink from a decanter he'd taken from the cabinet, and then back to Cassidy. His deep-set eyes were wide, meeting mine, even wider than the circumstances would warrant. For an instant, I didn't understand. Then I did what I should have done long before. I turned around.

There was a fifth person in the room. He leaned at ease against the wall, where the opening door from the office had hidden him as I came in. He was tall and lean, with sandy brown hair that fell forward into eyes so light-colored they were nearly colorless. His white shirt was open over his pearl-gray cotton trousers, and his feet were bare. His smile was full of big, even teeth.

"Howdy," he said. "I do believe you must be Sparrow."

Frances, I thought in that long moment when I couldn't so much as swallow, *I found the monster*.

Mick had said he was strong, fast, and bugfuck crazy. I could see it, feel it, *smell* it on him, the madness that, when he had to, he could probably disguise as something else. Now he didn't have to.

He crossed the space between the wall and me in three strides, grabbed up my stiff right hand in both of his, and shook it, hard. "Mighty pleased to meet you, after all this time. I've heard an awful lot about you. Heck, for a while I thought I might miss you completely, but here you are at last." His smile grew, if possible, wider, and he turned it on Dana. "Your friend don't talk much. You didn't tell me that."

"I'm sorry. I just haven't had anything to say," I said. I barely recognized my voice. I sounded like someone talking to a growling dog. "I missed your name."

"Oh, no, you didn't." The smile had changed. I was not going to be able to bluff my way through this. "I didn't tell it to you. But you know what it is, don't you? These folks have been calling me Fred, but I want you to call me by the name my momma gave me." He still had hold of my hand. He squeezed it. "Go ahead. You call me by my name." He squeezed it 'til the bones pinched together.

"I really don't—" Harder. A little catch of sound came out of my throat. I saw a movement from Dana, that might have been her fingers going to her mouth.

"Say it," said the monster, his face close to mine.

"Tom Worecski," I said. He let my hand drop. I was afraid to flex it, for fear that he'd notice he'd left it attached to my wrist.

"Good for you! Now, you go sit on the sofa there. Babe, come over here and give us a kiss."

As she passed me on the other side of the table, Dana's eyes cut away from mine. She went to Tom and put her arms around him. He didn't turn his face to her, but she kissed his jaw and his neck and the hollow of his collarbone while he smiled at me. It wasn't Albrecht's seduction. It was Tom's. I wondered whether anybody would care if I was sick on the rug.

Albrecht set his glass down on the cabinet. "God damn it, Krueger, she's not—"

"A.A., if you keep your mouth *shut*, not only will I let you live, I'll *think* about not walkin' you through Nicollet market buck naked with your dick in your *fist*. You got that?"

Tom had raised his voice. Albrecht's face, innocent of sun, flushed to magenta, then went bloodless. "You need me. My staff won't listen to you."

"We been through this before. I need you like a goddamn dog needs shoes, A.A. I figured if I let you run all the little shit, it would keep you out of my way. But if that's not workin' anymore, I can find some other asshole to run the little shit. So you just sit behind your big desk and buy movies that you think'll help you get rid of me, and stay the fuck out of my way."

He was stroking Dana absently, as if she were a cat on his lap. She had her face turned into his shoulder; whatever expression was there, none of us could see it. Albrecht watched Tom and Dana with a look that reminded me a little of Cassidy. I was glad I had my back to Cassidy.

"It's not *Hellriders*," I said to Albrecht.

"Nobody ever thought it was," said Tom. "But we didn't want to discourage you right off, if you thought you needed an excuse to come up." He frowned over Dana's head, and gazed around the room as if he missed something. "So where's Her Highness?"

"I beg your pardon?"

"Don't fuck with me. You know what I'm talking about."

My hands closed in reflex over my knees. The right one hurt. He saw it; it made him happy again. "Well, shit, Myra and Dusty work for me, you know. When Franny had her little joke on Myra the other night, don't you think Myra would've told me?"

"She told you who it was?"

"She didn't have to. Dusty told me some of the stuff Myra said when she wasn't Myra, and I knew right off. There ain't anybody jaws on like that but Franny."

That didn't explain how he knew someone had come up with

me, or how he knew I wasn't really there to sell A.A. Albrecht a
faked videotape. The only thing that did—

"I expect she's listening at a keyhole," Tom said cheerfully. He
stared at me as he added, louder, "So, Fran? You come in here,
or I'm gonna break this kid's neck. You know I can."

Maybe she wouldn't care. But I thought I ought to tell her, at
least, that he hadn't started yet. "I'd hate that," I said. "Besides,
you haven't finished my hand." *Stall. You've lost the advantage of
surprise. Frances. At least pick your moment.*

"Thatagirl," Tom called out, "come on in and have a seat. Hell,
we got us enough folks for a party."

I twisted around on the couch. The door beside Cassidy swung
slowly open to admit Frances, alone, with her pistol. Why hadn't
she shot—ah, of course. She wasn't here to kill Tom's body. The
head fight had begun already; I could see it in Frances's tight-
closed lips, the net of squint lines around Tom's eyes.

I wanted desperately to know the range of a Horseman's
powers. Because I'd thought of another solution to the problem of
isolating Tom Worecski. Frances could eliminate Tom's options
for switching bodies. Bang, bang, bang. Bang. Maybe she'd
meant to all along, and it was my bad luck I'd ended up here, as
one of Tom's options.

"Someone gave us away," I said to Frances.

"I was beginning to think someone must have. Everything was
going according to plan." She kept her eyes, and the pistol, on
Tom.

By logic, someone in the room ought to have wrenched it out of
her hand by now. No, if anyone approached her, anyone who
wasn't Tom, she could shoot. Tom could *order* one of them to get
the gun. I began to think I ought to be doing something besides
sitting and watching, but what could I do? I wasn't supposed to be
there. I wasn't part of this fight. It had nothing to do with me. I
was caught between the two of them.

"Go sit beside your friend, babe," Tom said, and Dana let go
of him. Her face, when she had her back to Tom, was vacant with
fear. She sat down close to me and clung to my sleeve, where Tom
couldn't see it.

"Put it down, Franny. It's not gonna do you any good."

"Oh, I don't know. A loud noise, some nasty stains—it would
have a certain nostalgia value at the very least." The room was
cool, but there was a light gloss of sweat above Frances's
eyebrows.

"Huh. *I* thought they were the good old days. But I figured you'd got religion or something. All the fun we used to have, and here you are, with a self-righteous stick up your ass, out to blow my brains out for bein' just as bad as you." He took a step forward, grinning, teeth clenched intermittently. "And you know that's true. I've never done anything you didn't do."

I'd heard that before, from Mick about Frances. She'd denied it. And I remembered what Tom Worecski's death sentence was for. I must have moved; Tom's gaze flicked to me and back to Frances.

"You didn't tell anybody?" he said. "Oh, my. Let you who are without sin cast the first stone."

Frances also grinned; like Tom, she seemed to be doing it at least half because of the pressure. "If I'd washed my sins away first, I wouldn't have been able to minister to the rest of you."

Tom snorted. "You loved it. You always figured you had a right to run the world. You thought being part of the committee that was gonna blow it to hell was no more than you deserved. You wanted to show those bastards who hadn't had the sense to get together and elect you Goddess."

"That's not true." Frances spoke without heat, as if he'd misstated the time and she was correcting that. But the heat was there, underneath, unspoken, a slow tide of it. "You had to lie to get me to sign on. You never once planned to hold the country hostage, but *I* believed it. I thought I was working for peace. I may have been criminally stupid and blind as a cave fish, but I didn't think we meant to actually drop the Big One."

"Shit, Franny, then you were the only one."

"A loner to the very end." Her right hand was trembling, barely.

"Is it true?" Tom asked the air. "Was she really pure as the driven snow, even though she executed half the damn launch sequence her own self?"

"We were supposed to hold and wait to abort," Frances snapped, her face white. Some of it was surely whatever Tom was doing to her head. But she looked like a woman watching a rerun of her worst nightmare. She had done it. She had lived with it all these decades. And she'd dedicated herself to seeing that the people who'd shared the blame wouldn't live with anything anymore. I'd been right all the time, to be afraid of her.

"I'll bet the jury's done deliberating," Tom said. "Awful sorry I couldn't get twelve of 'em, but one good one oughta be enough for this. Whattaya say, Skin? Innocent or guilty?"

In Albrecht's darkened office, someone moved hesitantly toward the door. It was Mick Skinner.

Frances took a step forward—no, it was a stagger, a widening of an unstable stance—and flung her left hand up to her face. The pistol wobbled and sank. Cassidy, glancing at Tom, moved toward her. Then the hand over her face dropped, and showed the blackness of her eyes, and her clenched teeth. She brought the end of the silencer to bear on Cassidy. I heard Dana suck her breath in; but Cassidy stepped back.

Tom had used Mick, the shock of him, to break Frances's concentration. Then he'd struck at her, hard enough to cut her loose, for a moment, from her muscles. But Frances was in fragile command of herself now, and Tom stood relaxed for the first time since Frances had come into the room. He'd struck and let her go. It was a gesture of contempt.

Mick looked like someone enduring the course of a natural disaster. His once-neat braids were coming loose, coils and streaks of hair stuck in the sweat on his forehead and jaw, and his clean-lined features were marked with weariness and emotion. Sweat striped and dotted the chest of the T-shirt he wore. He must have come from the island on foot, and quickly. At Tom's command. His hands opened and closed at his side. "Guilty," he said softly, looking at Frances. And, in an echo of himself, "My family was in Galveston."

"I was going to tell you," said Frances. Her eyes were on his face; her voice was low and unsteady. "By deed, if not by word. Feel free to reproach me, but you won't catch up to what I've done to myself. I've had more time, after all. But what about you? What will you have to reproach yourself for?"

"You ought to die." Mick sounded half strangled.

"So should your ally, here. Leave us out of it. You didn't inform Tom of my arrival out of sheer righteous indignation. Christ, I wish you had. Then maybe you'd have kept all these civilians out of range of my comeuppance. Besides, Tom hadn't told you I was one of the ones responsible for the Bang, had he? He wanted me to convict myself. He knew you'd hurt more that way. So why did you tell him we were coming? What superior philosophy made it necessary to warn the snake about the scorpion?"

Mick was silent.

"Or was it not philosophy at all?" Her voice was softer now. "You can walk away from him, Mick. Now. I can hold him that long. Take Sparrow and get away from here. There's nothing he can do to you. If he told you otherwise, it was a lie."

"That's easy for you to say," Tom broke in, cheerful. "Ol' Skin, his experience tells him different."

"I tried," Mick said. "He sent Myra and Dusty after me. I dumped my body and rode Sparrow, figuring I could hide out that way, just until things cooled down. But they found me. I got away from them, but I think I was supposed to. He can find me anytime he wants, Fran, and now he can find Sparrow, too."

"No," Frances said, and in her voice was the deep sadness I'd heard when she'd told Dusty, *I have a damnably long memory*. "He just has a hold on you. The longer you stay, and the more dirty things you do for him, the better the hold will be."

But I had looked up, uncontrollably, at Tom.

"That's right," said Tom, to me. "Mick got you away from them the first time I sent my kids. No love lost between Mick and Myra and Dusty, I'll tell you. The second time, Franny got you away. But while that was going on, I'd sent Mick himself."

Mick, in the archives, saying, *I came back for my jacket*.

"You bastard, that's not true," Mick said. "You didn't send me."

"That got a little screwed up," Tom continued, as if Mick had never spoken. "Worked out all right in the end, though. I've never been able to get anybody on that goddamn island before."

This time there was no protest from Mick.

"My God," Frances sighed, "can you hear yourself? Playing Ming the Merciless, gloating over your explanations to the captive hero?"

Tom looked surprised. "Who says you're the hero?"

"*I* do. How can you be so small, Tom O' Bedlam? How can you have lived so long, and still be so small?"

"I run a city," he said, his lip curled. "You're just a little killer."

She looked mildly insulted. "I'm seeking vengeance for the whole Western Hemisphere. I think that's positively grandiose."

Tom leaned into the cushions of the couch and smiled. "Hell, I missed you, Franny. I'd have elected you Goddess."

"Don't start," Frances said softly.

"It don't hurt to ask. There's enough here for two of us." His voice, too, was soft. Albrecht, in the act of pouring himself another drink, made a little noise and turned. "Fran, I know you. I know you better'n anybody. I know Skin here thinks he's got your number, but he's just a goddamn puppydog." And that made

Mick flinch, and look to Frances. "But it could be the good old
days all over again. I know what you want, Franny."

His voice, his face, had turned surprisingly sweet. Frances
watched him gravely, the line of her dark brows straight, her lips
pressed tightly together. The head fight was over. This was the
clean, insidious pressure of words and a shared past.

The rest of us sat or stood quite still, waiting for our futures to
be decided. I had seen Albrecht's face when Tom proposed to turn
half his city into a courting gift. I had seen Mick's face. Mick,
who a few hours ago had made love to Frances. Cassidy's
expression was of uncomprehending, enduring despair, the look
of a man who didn't expect things to ever be good again. And
Dana, beside me, might have been carved out of ice. She hadn't
raised her eyes from the Chinese table since Frances's pistol had
pointed at Cassidy. There was no blood under her faint tan, and
her fingers twisted and ground at the silk over her knees.

Chango, was I going to go quietly to the slaughterhouse? *My*
side had the gun. If my side was still *on* my side. I wanted out of
here. She wanted . . . something.

"I don't understand," I said in as conversational a tone as I was
capable of. I wasn't sure what I was hoping for, besides a change
of subject. "Why did you decide you had to bring me in?"

Tom paced slowly to the other couch, and sat down. He was at
right angles to me now, and his right knee brushed my left one. A
smile grew on his face, in increments. "Because Mick said you
were a good fit. He and Franny must have told you all the fun we
used to have? I wanted a taste."

"Take a bite of this, then," said Frances calmly. She raised the
pistol in both hands, firing position. The silencer had a perfectly
round black eye that looked into mine.

I wanted to scream. I moved instead. Before I knew I meant to,
I found myself rolling over the back of the couch and breaking for
the door that Cassidy guarded. The gun made an ugly, flat sound.

Cassidy reached the door first—and yanked it open. "Go!" he
mouthed. His hollowed-out face was twisted with anguish, like a
man facing the medusa. I'd have to take him with me. Otherwise
Tom Worecski would dissect him alive, and Cassidy knew it. I
grabbed his arm as I hit the door.

It turned into a snake, strong and contrary. No, still an arm, but
twisting through mine, jerking it up until my shoulder joint
blossomed with fire. His other arm closed around my jaw. He
giggled next to my ear.

I couldn't see him, but I could see the part of the room I'd just eft. Frances stood with her gun not quite aimed at us, wearing a near cousin to Cassidy's expression. Dana, half crouched on the sofa, stared wide-eyed at us. Albrecht had pressed back against the wall, his hands over his face. Mick was still in the office door, one arm reaching, as if he could stop whatever was about to happen. And Tom was sitting, empty, on the couch.

Empty.

Cassidy's voice said, beside my head, "I told you, Franny, I could snap the kid's neck. Wanna watch?" Then he sucked air in through his teeth, as if something struck him.

I pulled and pulled, and only hurt myself. I didn't stop trying to pull away. If I could have torn off the arm he was holding, I would have.

"You know what I want, you say," Frances said in an unattended way, as if she'd sent the words to her lips and tongue with no instructions for tone of voice. "After all these years—all this overly long and self-indulgent life—there's only one thing I want. And the most unnatural circumstance on the face of God's creation is that I might be here, with a gun in my hand and you in front of me, and still be denied that one thing."

Frances's eyes were round and pitch-dark, as if the pupils had eaten the irises. I didn't think she was seeing us. I thought she might be walking in some nightmare desert landscape inside her head, where she was converging on Tom Worecski with all her conscious mind, her wit, her honed and focused will. Cassidy's body was still, and tensed hard. Tom was moving through that landscape, too. The gun muzzle swung and steadied, and I saw again a foreshortened view of the silencer.

I don't think I heard the gun. It would have been dramatic, but however dramatic the moment may have been, I don't think that was part of it. No, I didn't hear anything, or see or feel anything. I stopped—

—and started again on my hands and knees on a field of sky blue, with Tom's voice ringing out across the room. "What is that? What the fuck *is* it?"

"Cass?" Dana's voice came, thinly, from the same quarter. And again, stronger, "Cass?"

My shirt, where it lay over my shoulders and back, felt funny. It stuck to my skin. I turned my head and found the blood shining under my chin. I couldn't get my breath. I was afraid to look behind me.

"Cassidy!" Dana screamed finally, and crossed the carpet in a headlong stumble, to fall to her knees next to Cassidy. Next to his

body, behind me. You had to have known, beforehand, that it wa_
Cassidy. I shivered once, twice, and realized that I wasn't goin_
to stop. "You bastards," Dana gasped, "you fucking *bastards!*"

"Wanna try again, Franny?" Tom's voice, from the couch, wa_
harsh. "Wanna see how many more civilians you can go throug_
before I get bored and pull your guts out through your face?"

Frances stood in front of me, her feet wide apart, the gun i_
both hands pointing to the floor. She was staring at Tom as if he_
eyes would never move again.

"Let her go, Tom," Mick said, barely loud enough to hear
Perhaps anything louder would have gotten out of his control
"Let 'em both go. You proved you could beat her. She can't sto_
you. Let 'em go."

"What's the goddamn *thing*, Mick? You've ridden it. Yo_
didn't tell me about it."

". . . It's a *cheval*."

"Bullshit it is! They don't have any brains."

I stood slowly up. Dana was curled on her knees besid_
Cassidy's body, crying: great, heaving sobs with no self
awareness in them. Her hands were closed over her face. Now
when there was no one there to feel it, she didn't touch him.

Mick's sigh trembled. "It's a long story, Tom. Please let 'e_
go. I'll tell you all about it. You don't want them."

Like Frances, I looked at Worecski. His eyes moved betwee_
us.

"Don't I? How long a story is it, Skin?" Tom jerked his hea_
toward Frances. "Go take the gun away from her."

Mick came walking slowly, shakily over. I think he expecte_
Frances to shoot him. Instead she stared at him, the gun still i_
both hands; then she pulled the clip out smoothly and handed th_
gun to Mick. Tom laughed.

"That'll do. Now, here's how we're gonna play it. Skinner'_
gonna tell me his long story. Then I'll decide what I want to d_
with the two of you, and I'll come round you up. Whatcha think
Skin? Fifteen minutes? Is it that long a story?" He threw his hea_
back and laughed. "Jesus, Skin, if Scheherazade had looked lik_
you, her old man would have offed her the first night."

Then he sat up and turned to Frances and me. He didn't loo_
like a man who'd just laughed. "Ever seen a rabbit after a dog'_
caught it? Run, you little rabbits. I'll be right behind you."

7.1: You get what you pay for

Had we known that Tom, in this one thing, was perfectly trust-worthy, we'd have taken the elevator.

Instead we ran as we'd been ordered to. We plunged down the fire stairs in the near darkness of the emergency lighting and the sealed-in heat of the past day. At first we tried to pause at landings, watching for an ambush, waiting for the sound of a shot. We gave it up after a dozen floors. After all, what did it get us? A chance to return fire? With what? But the strain on our nerves was as great as the strain on our legs and lungs.

By the time we reached the foot of the stairs we were both wringing wet. Frances had twice come close to falling. She leaned on the door at the bottom of the stairwell, her head flung back, the breath shuddering in and out of her lungs. "I'm sorry," she said. "I thought I ought to say so, while I had the chance."

"It doesn't matter." And it really didn't. She'd killed—my friend? I didn't know, I couldn't tell, I wasn't sure what a friend was. I could have asked him whether we were friends, if she hadn't— But she wasn't responsible; cats kill birds, and rattle-snakes bite, that's what they do. She only wanted one thing in the world. I wondered if she wanted anything else now.

"What's out there?" she asked. "Should I be prepared for the unusual?"

"I don't know. Maybe not. It's the Hall of Broken Glass."

A thin burst of a laugh. "Crystal Court. What happened to it?"

"I don't know," I said again. "The whole first floor is empty, except for the guard desk. I think the mess has been left as a no-man's-land. We'll be exposed, crossing it."

"Well, that'll be a change. Let's do it."

We came out of the stairwell quickly. I led, because I knew where the door was. Frances knew where the doors used to be. Weak pools of light overlapped across broken tile floor and drifts of glass and plastic shards, and shone through gaping frames that had once been storefronts, rimed with the remains of shattered plate glass. In the center of the room the twisted wreck of an escalator lay, wrenched free of the sagging second-level balcony and heaped on the floor like the spine of a metal dinosaur. I had a badly preserved bit of videotape of an old television show that showed this space full of people, the escalator turning and turning. I'd watched it once, and never again.

The floor crunched and rang under me as I ran, loud as a siren. I could hear Frances behind me; then suddenly I couldn't. She'd slipped and fallen to her knees. I skidded to a halt, darted back, grabbed her arm, and pulled her up and forward. She got her feet under her in time to keep from being dragged.

Two shots, I thought as the door loomed ahead of me. *One for each of us. I should hear them any minute now. He's had his fun.* Then we were through the door, and the air was warm and humid and smelled like food and alcohol fumes and sweat and cooking smoke and not at all like the rooms at the top of Ego. The trike was still there.

"This is crazy," Frances said, fumbling the latches open. "As soon as we roll away, he's lost us, he can't . . . Oh, God." She scrubbed fiercely at her face with both hands. It printed her cheeks with little smears of blood. She must have stopped her fall with her palms, back in the Hall of Broken Glass. "Of course—Tom doesn't give a damn if he loses us. We can't hurt him; why should he care if we get away? He must be laughing himself into a seizure right now."

She helped me into the back and scrambled into the driver's seat. Whatever she thought Tom was doing right now, she hadn't slowed down. As for me, the mindless strength that had gotten me out of Ego shut off the moment the weather shell closed over my head. Waves of trembling passed over me, and to stop thinking of Cassidy I had to stop thinking at all.

Spirits, he hadn't even gotten a good exit line. No lines at all; no more trusting, uncomplicated, ill-considered actions; no more startling moments when the fine mind shone through a break in the alcoholic clouds. The fine mind was on a wall in Ego—

Stop thinking.

And Dana, who was still alive, still there, who might come to envy Cassidy because nobody could stay on the good side of a madman forever. And when she found herself deep in the nightmare, who had the means to drag her safe out of it? What friend did she have—

Stop.

The trike was rolling; buildings passed overhead. Frances's shoulders were raised, as if she were ducking something. We shot through an intersection, and I saw headlights catch fire, swing in behind us.

"Dios te salve, María," Frances spat. "Tell me that's coincidence."

She turned, and turned, and did a savage cut-and-cut-again through the remains of a hotel's covered driveway. We sailed, nearly airborne, into the street and around the corner. A few streets later we had headlights behind us.

By the third time, we'd been forced south all the way to the Exhibition Hall. Frances slipped us out of reach by darting down a highway exit ramp—the toll collector saw us coming and fled the booth—then lurching off it and straight up through the tall grass of the embankment to the street above. I couldn't hear her words over the engine, but the tone held a rising edge of fury and panic.

Ego's dark silhouette rose over her sister towers ahead of us, banded near the top with its ring of lights, its two antenna masts rising like horns from the roof. . . .

"Radio!"

"What?" Frances shouted.

"They've got radio! Nobody else does because nobody can afford to power a transmitter. But Albrecht runs the commercial stations! A few roof spotters with binoculars, talking to a central point, plus the receivers in the cars—"

"Oh, God," she groaned. "I'd gotten used to civilization being dead. I suppose you don't know of anything to foul their signal?"

"Sure. One good electromagnetic pulse—got a nuke?" I said, with unnecessary force.

"Thank you."

"Transmitting on their frequency would do it, but I'd need the wattage and the antenna height. No go."

"And I can't exactly lose them in traffic," Frances said bitterly, with a gesture that took in the empty streets around us.

"No," I answered slowly, because I wasn't sure that what I'd had was a useful idea. "But if you can lose them long enough to get to the Night Fair, I defy 'em to track you through it."

A moment; then she said, "And from there I can bolt for old I-394 and simply outrun them."

Thinking about something else was as good as not thinking at all. All I had to do was not run out of something elses. "How are we fixed for pin money?"

She didn't answer; she was in the midst of a nauseating bit of maneuvering. But from the quality of the non-answer, she thought it was a damn silly question.

So I added, "Running costs. I want to stop at my place and pick up a couple of things."

"I'll let you use my toothbrush."

"Will you let me sell your near-mint CD of *Sergeant Pepper*?"

"Aha. I am enlightened. But how do we keep them from finding us between here and the Night Fair, O Solomon my partner?"

"Underground parking garages," I replied.

She ripped out a U-turn past the fender of our current pursuer, and spared a second to glance over her shoulder at me. "You terrify me. But we have to amputate first. Pray that my memory is good."

I didn't understand what she meant until she did it. She turned suddenly, at speed, into a driveway between two apartment buildings—but it wasn't a driveway. It was wide enough for two people walking abreast, for bicycles, for the trike. But not for the car on our tailpipe, whose driver must have seen the sculptured break in the concrete curbing and trusted it to be what it looked like. The noise behind us was horrible.

Frances killed her headlights and wove through two blocks' worth of alleys. "Good," she said. "It *was* still there."

"You didn't *know*?"

"I wasn't sure. Which of the ramps can we still get into?"

I banished from my mind the death we hadn't died, and set to navigating.

We twined through the Deeps from the roots of one tower to the next. Between them, when we had to cross streets, we coasted, the engine idle to keep sound to a minimum. Once, under the Dayton family's building, we drove into a pit party, mingled nightbabies and street-meat dancing, drinking, and cockfighting under strings of lights and the low concrete ceiling. They scattered, and we wove through like a needle in burlap. The band didn't even stop playing.

We surfaced at last across from one of the Night Fair's gates, the one she'd brought me to that first day. She stopped the bike in the shadow of the overhang and studied the street. It wasn't empty; there was too much spillover from the Fair for that. "Careful," she aid—to herself, I thought. "They must be frantic by now. They'll ave told him that they've mislaid us, and he'll . . ."

"What?" I asked.

"We really have to get out of here," she said lightly. "Because f we're still here to fish for, he'll poke a hook in the best bait he an find and dangle it. The friends we left behind, say."

I opened my mouth to tell her that I wouldn't be tempted to rade my life for Dana's, and closed it again. I suppose I would ave said it if I had been sure either that it was true, or that it vasn't. Instead I said, "Mick sold us out."

"Think of my ongoing concern, then, as my way of rubbing his ose in it. *Now, soldiers, march away; and how thou pleasest—*" he put the trike in gear and crossed the street as quietly as the ngine would run.

The Fair was full of commotion and whatever level of frenzy ould be sustained over the course of a night. I'd never wondered vhy I could be comfortable here and twitchy in a group of four eople. The answer, now that I thought about it, was easy. The treets and stalls of the Night Fair were the opposite of intimacy. 'o be one of four was to be a focal point; to be one of hundreds vas to be anonymous as sand on the shore.

"Is it always like this?" Frances asked, barely avoiding an ncoming water truck.

"Oh, yeah—" But it wasn't. Not the density of people, but the ;alvanic current that ran through them, the sound of the voices, he intensity of motion: these were different. These said, *Warning, lert, something needs attention, system failure.*

Both Mick and Dana knew where my apartment was. Mick new what was in it. "Hurry," I said.

Frances looked back at me. Whatever she saw made her turn the rike into an instrument of chaos.

We couldn't get closer than half a block from my building. We lidn't need to. The top floor was a torch that could probably be een on the island.

I kicked the weather shell open and was past Frances and into he crowded street before she could stop me. She caught up with ne. I fought her, and screamed at her, until with force and ractized economy, she hit me in the stomach. I folded up on the avement in the little clearing we'd made in the disaster-watchers. Aly very own disaster. Had the ones who started it even thought of he tenants? The old man who sang so badly, the people who'd had abbage for dinner. Was anyone dead? But it had to be fire. Because nothing could harm the archives except fire.

I gasped for air, and took it in mixed with smoke and sparks and floating black ash. The fire was loud, louder than the noise of the crowd. There was an explosive cracking, and someone above me said, "There goes a beam!" and the rising voices and comments that burst out told me that the top floor had fallen in. I lifted my head—and saw, half obscured by the people around me, a head of curly hair, rose-pink in the firelight. The crowd shifted; I saw him full-length for a moment, in gray suit and silvertones, smiling like a blindfolded angel at the blaze. His companion smiled, too, trailing her fingers absently through the hair at the nape of his neck. Dusty and Myra Kincaid. Sated, for the moment, with cruelty.

Frances took my elbow, pulled me to my feet, and took me bent over and staggering, back to the trike. I clung to it when I found it under my hands. There were two pumper trucks in the street, their crews heaving like galley slaves, but the water from the hoses only reached to the fourth floor. If the fire followed its present course, soon that would be the top of the building. Frances's arm closed around my shoulders. I ducked away.

"All right," she said. "I forgot. I thought this time . . . Can you get in by yourself?"

I could. Her voice had been level; so I was surprised when I looked up and saw her beside the trike, a thin track of tears marking the dirt and soot on each cheek. I lifted my fingers to my face, to see if it was wet, to see if this was something catching and not crying at all, because why would Frances cry over this? But my face was dry. Well, of course. Water vaporized in fire. The whole inside of my head was dry, and quiet.

She said things to me as she roused the trike: They would be watching for us here, and we had to run now if we were ever going to get away. It sounded sensible. I don't know if she expected an answer.

The next thing she said was scatological. "Roadblock," she added. Through the windshield I saw that we were quite far from the Night Fair, and that she was right. And it wasn't the last one.

Sometime later we were parked in a dark place, with Frances sitting hunched in the driver's spot as if she'd been gut-shot, her arms folded tight around her. "While he ran us through downtown like icons in a video game, he sealed up the City," she said. Her voice was the ruin of the one I was used to. "Maybe we could get out on foot. Maybe, but we couldn't get far. Dear God, dear God, why didn't you let me kill him?" Then she shook herself, and sat upright. "Stop that. Well, Horatio, I need another idea." She looked over her shoulder.

She wanted me to think. I shook my head, to tell her I couldn't do that, that cause and effect and the manipulating of them were beyond me because they were part of the stream of time, and I didn't want to go there. Maybe she thought I just didn't have any ideas. It came to the same thing.

She sat very still for a long while; then she put the trike in gear. "Back to the island, if we can. Maybe China Black will bury us in the basement for a year and a day, or however long it is before Tom finds some pleasing distraction that isn't us."

I don't know why Worecski hadn't ordered the bridge stopped up. Maybe some property of the island prevented it. Or maybe his roadblock was on the span connecting the island to the opposite bank, where there would be no place to turn off, no escape. But in the near end, the suspension bridge was unoccupied. Frances drove slowly, her head working from side to side, until finally she said, *"There,"* and turned off. Either we were expected, or Frances had found the street by sheer force of will.

China Black's gate looked different in the dark, its weathered wooden slats higher, closer set, forbidding; Frances drove fifty feet past it, cursed, and backed up. It didn't open when we turned in. Frances left the trike to idle as she went up to try it, and finally to pound on it. There was no response.

She stepped back a pace from the gate and addressed it in a clear, carrying voice, bright as buffed chrome. "I understand the reluctance—the wasps' nest having been knocked down, I don't suppose I'd want to be standing next to the fool with the stick, either. But at least have the decency to minister to one of the victims."

It worked like an incantation. After a moment the left half of the gate swung inward a little. It was China Black herself who'd opened it; the eyebrows caught the light as she looked past the panel at Frances. Then she slipped through and pulled the gate to behind her. The black, high-collared thing she wore, I decided, was a robe.

She reached the trike in two long strides and peered in at me. "You're hurt?" She stretched out a hand for my shoulder.

Of course. The blood. I'd forgotten I was wearing Cassidy's colors on my shirt.

The passionless, ironical observer that was master of my head wasn't mastering my body. I was as surprised as anyone when I jerked away and folded forward in the passenger's seat, clutching

my hands to my face as if to close off all the senses that worke
there.

"*No,*" Frances said, and I felt China Black's hand snatche
away. "It's not h—the blood isn't Sparrow's. But yes, that's th
victim. All I want is a way out of town, or shelter until the mes
I've made settles."

The foolish physical reaction was gone already. "You wouldn
have so much trouble," I muttered, straightening up carefully, "i
you didn't talk about me in the third person."

But China Black was already shaking her head. "I can't. Th
island was safe only as long as he wanted nothing on it. We hav
no defense against the kind of force he will bring; we are too few
and those are not our skills. We cannot protect you here. We ca
only die with you. And forgive me, but this is not our fight."

Frances lifted her chin. "News, it seems, travels fast. I though
the car phones were all gone."

"Rumors travel fast. That you are here, and desperate, confirm
them, no?"

"Can you at least help us leave?"

Another head shake. "I don't know enough. I'm sorry. Bewar
of the river; you can be caught at the old dams and locks, and the
may be watching at the bridges, too. But if you escape, there is
place you can go." China Black recited the directions: south
farther south than I'd been since I'd first entered the City.

"You didn't warn us about Mick," I said.

"I wasn't sure until tonight, when I found him gone. Forgiv
me."

"Is Sherrea here? Or Theo? I'd like to say goodbye."

It seemed like a stupid thing to want, but neither of them looke
at me oddly. "They've both gone," said China Black. "They, too
are at risk, because they were seen with you. They left not lon
after you did."

"Of course." I had nothing more to say.

Frances stood very straight, with one hand on the trike. "I'r
sorry to have turned surly," she said to China Black, "when
ought to have been thanking you for sheltering me. Someda
someone will put Tom out of his and the rest of the world's misery
He might even manage to do it himself. But I won't get anothe
chance."

"Life is full of second chances," China Black said sternly.

"I don't deny it. But thank you, anyway." Frances swun
herself back on the trike and closed the shell around us. Chin

Black stepped backward when the engine started. Frances saluted her with a raised hand and pulled out of the drive.

The east was turning milky; it was there to see as we recrossed the bridge, heading for whatever haven we might happen on. Another dawn in Frances's company. I'd spent more time with Frances than I'd ever spent with Sherrea at a stretch. I didn't think that, by itself, constituted friendship.

I hoped Sherrea was safe. She'd tried, after all. She'd told me to change my wicked ways long ago—*days* ago. Forever. To forget myself, and serve whatever came my way, needing it. There was very little now to forget. And something, I supposed, to serve. How many days ago? Five? Six? I'd called her from Del Corazón, and I'd threatened Beano with—that's right, it had been . . .

"What day is it?" I asked Frances.

A pause. "Thursday, I think. No, it's tomorrow now—Friday."

"Turn right at the next street."

She glanced back at me. "Is this a decision-making device?"

"I've had an idea. No, *that* way. Now, go straight."

A short cautious time later, we had stopped in the shadows behind Del Corazón. We might be too late. We couldn't be—that would be closing the last gate, the ultimate injustice in an unjust world. Fifteen years of life used up, wiped away; if I found out I was fifteen minutes late for the only unselfish thing I'd ever thought of doing, it would be more than even I deserved. I yanked on the cord that rang the back bell, and waited, and yanked again.

The door flew open, and the door frame protested, metal on metal. Beano stood inside, white as diluted milk, in tight, torn jeans and a T-shirt that seemed likely to die of exhaustion crossing his pectorals. He frowned when he saw me. He began to swing the door shut.

"No," I said, my voice breaking. "Listen to the deal first. Then make decisions."

"A deal?" Beano asked. "Or a screw job?"

"A deal. Can we come in?"

I don't think he'd seen Frances until then. "Who's she?"

"A package I want to deliver."

"Fastened with tape," Frances said blandly, "and not with string. Don't look at me; I have no idea what's going on."

"Can we come in?" I repeated.

After a moment Beano said, "I'm busy."

"I know. That's why I'm here." And I met and sustained his rose-colored glare.

"It *is* a screw job."

I shook my head.

I think he let us in out of unadulterated curiosity. He hurried us through the back rooms to the shop, where the air was thick with old and new incense. Frances sat, one ankle across the other knee, on the corner of a little table stacked with denim and leather pants. It would have been a convincingly casual pose, if she hadn't spoiled it by watching me. Behind her, hanging from a nail, was something made of knotted silk cord, like the web of a wealthy spider. Beano went behind the counter and leaned on it. That told me my place. I was the supplicant; I was to have judgment passed on me and my offer.

"So?" he said.

Out of habit, and a desire to make everything normal again, I began to think of how to ask for what I wanted without revealing how much I wanted it, or how much it was worth. I stopped myself and swallowed all the words I'd formed. This was not the time.

"We've crossed the City bossman," I said to Beano's unreceptive face, because I didn't think I could explain about Tom Worecski. "And he wants us so badly he'd drink the river if he thought we were at the bottom of it. I want to buy passage for her"—and I nodded at Frances—"past the roadblocks and safely out of the City."

"What about you?" Frances asked, her voice sharp.

"How'm I supposed to do that?" Beano asked me. We both ignored Frances. She wouldn't like it, but I hoped she'd put up with it.

I took a deep breath. I might be too late. . . . "Right now, someplace around here, people are unloading barrels of methanol that were never within shotgun range of a tax stamp. Like they do every Friday. She can go out by the same method the barrels came in."

Beano had been relaxed when I began. He wasn't relaxed anymore. "Or City finds out about the 'nol? That's not how it works. City's out there. You're still in here." He straightened up, and his shoulders and chest seemed suddenly to occupy the whole side wall.

"I told you it wasn't a screw job," I said. "If she gets out safely, I'll pay for it."

He stopped glaring. His head pushed forward, tilted, like a bird watching for insects in the grass. "Will you," he said. His eyes were red and heavy-lidded, like a vampire's after a good meal.

I nodded, but I did it meeting his gaze, and it was enough.

"I have a question in the queue," said Frances.

"Just you," I told her. I supposed I would have to look her in he eye as well.

She answered, gently, "The hell you say."

I could lie; I could tell her we'd have a better chance if we split up, that I could find my way out by myself, or had a place to hole up. Like any good lie, it had a little truth in it. Smuggling one person would be easier to accomplish than smuggling two. It took less room, and it took less convincing of the people doing the smuggling. So I could say it. She might buy it, and go quietly.

"This is how it's got to be," I told her.

"Why?"

Curse the woman. She could put more irony, more force of will, more threats and promises and personal anguish, into that one word than anyone I'd ever heard of.

"One of us has to stay. I don't have anything to lose. Everything I had to offer anyone, everything I've spent my life and feelings on, is gone. I'm over, I'm done with. I shouldn't have been started in the first place, you know that."

"That's terribly affecting, but you left a part out. Why does one of us have to stay?"

I took another breath. "Because somebody's got to pay for it."

Frances frowned. Then something changed in her face, and she slid off the table and addressed Beano. "The tri-wheeler in back is mine. I built a lot of it myself. Everything works. It's full of pre-Bang toys you won't find anywhere else, and I had every intention of staking my life on its reliability. It's worth passage out of town for two, and a great deal more. Will you take it in trade?"

Beano smiled at her. "Good thing you offered. The boys with the barrels are gonna want something. They can have the trike."

"If you hadn't mentioned it," I said, exasperated, to Frances, "he might not have thought of the trike."

Frances rounded on me. Her face was bloodless. "You can't do this. You *can't*."

"Of course I can. It's none of your business." I said to Beano, "Safe passage for her out of the City. Deal, or no?"

"I'll check." He stopped in the doorway to the back rooms, and said, "Don't go away." Then he closed the door.

"You made it my business," Frances said immediately.

My gaze went where I'd been keeping it from going, while Beano was in the room: the shelves of the display case. The set of bone needles was there. "No, I didn't. I wish I'd just lied about it."

"I'd have figured it out. I will *not* do this."

"Look, it's not as if I'm going to die."

"Aren't you?" she said, and there was such a look in her eyes that I stepped back a pace. I realized suddenly that she didn't have to change my mind. She could replace it. She could walk out of here in my body, with hers under my/her arm. If I'd realized it surely she had, too.

She had. I saw it in her face. Then her eyes closed tight; she steepled her fingers over her nose and mouth, turned, and walked into the shadows near the front of the store.

"That would be a Tom sort of trick, wouldn't it?" she said pleasantly. "I could just bludgeon you into doing what I want."

"Neither of us would get out of town."

"That's probably true. I suppose this way or the other yields up the same thing. Including the bludgeon. But do you know," she said, and she dropped her hands and looked at me, her self-possession in tatters, "I'd forgotten exactly what Tom was like? That sucking evil that pulls you into it, that bends light, that declares itself the center of the universe and you an impurity, there on sufferance—no, that's not right. That makes it sound exclusive to Tom. I didn't know I'd changed, Sparrow, because I didn't have my own kind to measure myself against." She stopped. I couldn't tell if she'd forced herself to, or if she couldn't force herself to go on.

I had to make three tries at saying anything before I succeeded. "Then maybe you won't throw it away after all."

The silence was four heartbeats long. I counted.

"Ah. I didn't think you'd figure it out."

"Anybody who was paying attention would have noticed that you were snuffing *every* Horseman who helped push the Button. You've been dropping artistic hints all night."

She sighed unevenly, which might have been laughter. "And you were there when I told China Black I'd have to leave one alive, after all."

"Yeah. But I think you picked the wrong one."

She walked back into the light, and stopped within arm's reach of me. I stayed where I was. "Is this," she said, "your way of making me reconsider my choice?"

The conversation was too intense to bear, had been for a long time; and I was tired. "Yes. No. I don't know."

Beano opened the door at the back of the shop. "They like it," he said. "It's a deal."

I'd known they were going to like it. I'd known Beano would talk them into it. "Fine," I told him. "As soon as I know she's clear, you get paid."

Beano frowned at that, but I glared back, and he finally shrugged. It was only time.

Frances's hand lifted, then dropped. "This is a hard thing you want me to live with," she said, doubt in her voice again.

"You've had a lot of practice," I reminded her. "You'll manage." And I walked away, to the farthest back room, to wait.

The City sat on a network of maintenance tunnels, some of which went back to the beginning of the previous century. A few had been turned into fallout shelters, during the years when those seemed like a good idea. Others were used as passways for steam piping and electrical conduit. Taken together, and allowing for detours around blocked and collapsed portions, they reached from the Night Fair to the river. That was the way the alcohol came in; and that was the way Frances went out, to the river and a boat with a false lower deck. Usually the crew filled the space with merchandise, taxed and otherwise, for the trip back. Frances ate into their profit margin. They were glad of the trike.

Beano told me all this when he came into the back room, a folded and sealed square of paper in one hand. In the transom above the back door, I'd watched the course of the day; the glass had faded to blazing white, and the air in the room had turned hot and motionless. It was still hot, but the light through the transom was the last of it. Beano held out the paper.

The wax held the impression of a thumbprint, and the letters 'FR" quickly scratched with a fingernail. I was confused for a moment, until I remembered that Frances's last name began with an "R." I broke the seal.

The message was in a small, angular hand, and the ink was very black. It read:

"What hills, what hills are those, my love,
Those hills so fair and high?"
"Those are the hills of heaven, my love,
But not for you and I."
       Nor the other hills, either. At least, not yet.

                                                            Frances

It was better identification than the thumbprint and initials. crumpled it and handed it to Beano. "You'd better burn this. I they knew she'd been here, you wouldn't live to see the end of it."

He took me literally; he lit the oil lamp on the table and burn it over that. Then he came and squatted next to the chair I'd spen most of the day in. His face gleamed evenly all over with sweat like wet marble. In the skin under his eyes there was a faint flush of pink, like fever. He wore the same clothes he'd opened the doo in that morning; the T-shirt was black with sweat down his ches and under his arms.

"You've run up a big tab," he said softly. He touched a lon fingernail to the blood on my shirt. I felt the nail go through th cloth and dig slowly into my skin.

Deciding is not the same as being reconciled; and reconciled i nothing like being willing. In self-imposed isolation all day entertained with the thoughts I couldn't muffle, I'd had time fo reconciliation. But my stomach churned anyway, and my hear pumped at a speed to support any desperate action I wanted t take. I stood up. Beano stood, too, half a head taller, stark with muscle.

"That's the Deal," I said.

He licked his lips—unconsciously, I thought. "Nothing's free," he agreed.

I closed my eyes, waiting for whatever it was going to be When nothing happened, I opened them again.

Beano was smiling. "Whattaya say you make a dash for th door?"

"Why?" I whispered.

"It's more fun that way." He turned and walked purposefull toward the back.

I meant to pay my debts, honorably, without protest. But couldn't stand against that last flicker of hope. I bolted for th shop and the front door.

He caught me there, slapped me up against the wall, pinned m to it with a hand around my neck. The fingers of his other han trailed down the side of my face, traced my jaw, and caressed thei way down my throat. "What's this?" he asked. He lifted Sherrea' pendant into my field of vision. "Present from your mom?"

I couldn't breathe past his grip. I couldn't answer. He twiste the cord around his fist and yanked, and the cord broke. I hear the pendant hit the floor.

He found out, eventually, that I was not like other people. I didn't seem to trouble him much.

Card **8**

Surroundings

The Devil, Reversed

Gray: The dawn of spiritual understanding, loosening of the chains of slavery to material things, conquering of self-interest or pride.

Crowley: Renovating intelligence. His magical weapon is the secret force, the lamp. His magical powers are the Evil Eye and the witches' sabbath. The Child of the Forces of Time. A secret plan about to be executed.

3.0: Where the serpents go to dance

I left Del Corazón on my feet, by the back door. It wasn't pride; there was no one watching, besides me, and my interest in heroic gestures was at an all-time low. Beano had gone away somewhere, and the building was quiet. No, I would have preferred being taken out on a stretcher, but there was no one to do it. And I really wanted to leave.

It was as if my body were a parcel I was carrying for someone else. It was heavy and hard to hold on to, and worse on both counts with each passing minute. But I was obliged to carry it, I'd get in trouble if I dropped it. I made an honest effort for half the length of the alley, in the dark, holding myself up on the sides of buildings. There was noise from the streets all around—I was close to the Night Fair, after all—but the alley was empty.

I think I tripped over something, but my memory of the evening is blessedly imperfect. I might just have dropped the parcel.

A little later I was lying facedown and having trouble breathing. I don't think I was in the same place. I turned my head and got more air, laden with the smell of garbage from nearby. I don't remember any noise; someone must have turned the sound off.

After that—or before that; these are islands of awareness in a foggy voyage, and I'm not sure of the order in which I reached them, or whether they were really there—I remember being terrified that Beano would find me. Then I recalled that I was safe from Beano. He was paid off. It was the other people I owed who were dangerous. Like Cassidy. Of course he was dead; that was the heavy thing on his side of the scale, that I was having such trouble balancing. He didn't seem angry about it. He looked sad, in fact, and I wondered if I'd told him about the apartment

197

burning. I meant to ask him why he didn't have a hole in his face, but I don't know if I did, or if he answered.

Curiously, none of those islands had pain as part of its shoreline. The first one that did involved, again, not getting enough air, and being in darkness. But this time I was on my back on something level and hard, and the smell was of livestock and clean straw. I heard the rise and fall of voices at a distance, and suddenly a thump, something striking wood, very close to my face. Reflex made me flinch. That, in turn, started my nerve endings speaking to my brain. I'm fairly certain that the endpoint of that memory isn't random, that I passed out.

Sherrea's voice—Sherrea's?—shouting, and a bang like a screen door, and a fresh breeze. I opened my eyes on a black satin sky full of stars and the dry-brush streak of the Milky Way. Somewhere under that sky was my body, which was as full of pain as an orange is of juice. But I didn't have to live in it. I recognized the effect of some painkilling drug, and something else; a distant relative of the healing process, in that it relieved suffering that healing couldn't handle. I closed my eyes again.

". . . broken," Sherrea was saying not far away. "Can you fix it, Josh?" There was a frantic edge on her casual words.

I was marginally aware of cloth being drawn back, of contact with one of my hands. "Oya Dances," said a new voice, softly, as if there was a terrible thing described in it. "LeRoy, quick, get Mags out of bed and tell her to prep. I'll meet her in the surgery. Sher, fingers here—that's it—and monitor the pulse. Do you know CPR?"

I was glad I wasn't there. It sounded scary.

For a while my mind kept working while my body was giving notice to quit, which is a sensation I don't recommend to anyone. Memory, dream, and drugs collaborated to open doors that I wouldn't have so much as walked past, had they been real doors, and had I been given a choice.

Behind one was a roomful of water, where I swam, badly, looking for an exit. It didn't help that the water was full of people floating. They were naked and limp; their limbs waved like seaweed. Their eyes were open on nothing. Mick as I'd first met him, tall and athletic, with a bullet hole that went all the way through him. Dana, her pale hair clumped and writhing around her face, more alive than she was. Theo, his glasses on his nose despite the water, his head at a quizzical angle. Cassidy, a little blood trailing behind him like bright red thread and a half smile on his lips.

Another opened on the third room in my apartment, the archives, all the precious contents shelved and tidy. As I stepped in, I saw more clearly: CDs fused to their plastic boxes in strange half-liquid curves; amplifiers and cassette decks blackened and brittle, their chassis warped, their cases leprous; videocassettes oozing together; the books transformed into neatly ranked flaking bricks of charcoal. The smell of burnt things was nauseating. Then, item by item, each piece of hardware powered up by itself. LEDs and digital counters lit like opening eyes on all sides. Fans came on, and stuttered and shrieked, their lubricants cooked away. The color monitor was the last; it burst into life with the refinery gun battle from *White Heat*, made grotesque and technically impossible by the spiderweb of cracks on the face of the picture tube. Flames licked out of the vent panels of everything.

And there was the door that opened onto Frances—Frances?—sitting beside me, holding a glass to my lips and saying, "Eat your opium, dear; there are children sober in Africa." That might even have been real.

But the strangest was the flat, white world, like a sheet of paper, with nothing on it but a motionless line of pictographs like the ones from native southwestern cultures, stylized silhouette figures in black. I seemed to see them all from above. I was the one on the left end of the row, I knew, the one that might have been a dog or a rabbit. I couldn't see the other end; I don't know why.

The second figure on the left was a woman, her arms and legs at lively angles, wearing a headdress. Or possibly a halo of fire. "Oh, it's you," she said. "What are you doing here?"

"I don't know," said the dog/rabbit/I.

"It's a debased age," she said. She sounded disgusted, and a little like Frances. "You're not supposed to simply land on the doorstep like an unlucky relative. You'll have to go back."

"I don't know how."

She clicked her tongue. "I could do it, but we'd better begin as we mean to go on. It's time you met him-her anyway. You'll love this."

She wasn't the next pictograph in line anymore. Instead there was another, curved and capering, two projections like horns or feathers poking up from its head. It was holding a flute.

"Ah! Ah! Not now!" it said, dismayed and delighted. "Indeed, you are a cub of mine. Sorta. And your timing sucks! You're welcome anytime, as long as you only come when you're called. This is your head speaking. Now beat it!"

As the white surface broke up like a bad video signal, I thought, *That probably* is *what my head sounds like*.

A decent continuity finally reasserted itself. I became aware of that—the feeling that the things around me were real events, in chronological order—even before I began to receive commentary from my senses. Then I felt the passage of air over my hair and face and shoulders, and smelled, faintly, an unlikely combination of growing things and rubbing alcohol. I heard footsteps and stirring cloth and a clink of metal against glass, and voices far away.

Opening my eyes required deliberate effort. When I did, I knew the room was part of an old farmhouse. I'm not sure why, except that it reminded me powerfully of where Dorothy woke up at the end of *The Wizard of Oz*. It even had checked curtains, open to the sun.

I was lying in a narrow bed between smooth, thick sheets. I'd been undressed, washed, and bandaged; probably several times by now, I realized. That made me uncomfortable, but I was too exhausted even to twitch.

I turned my head a little, and met the inquiring gaze of another person. He was built like a block of red sandstone, not particularly tall but wonderfully square. His hair was black and white in equal measure, and his broad red-brown face was lined on the forehead, at the corners of his eyes, in two brackets around his wide mouth. He wore a faded cotton shirt rolled up to the elbows and faded trousers. "Are you really awake," he said in a voice surprisingly light for the shape of him, "or are you still out walking?"

I opened my mouth, but nothing came out.

"No, you're back. Probably not for long, which you shouldn't worry about. I'm Josh Marten, head people doctor around here. Sherrea said I should tell you right away that she's here, and your friends Theo and Frances as well, and that they're safe."

I closed my eyes in relief, because I'd just begun to wonder, and didn't think I had the strength to make the words.

He crossed the room and laid a hand on my forehead. But it was a cool, dry hand, and I was too tired to mind. He took my pulse at my throat. "I think you're done making me work so hard. Answers to other questions I'll bet you have: You've been here three days. None of the damage was permanent, thanks to me. And this is about the best you'll feel for a while, because when your painkillers wear off, I'm going to stop giving them to you during the day. You're going to hate that, but it's better than making an opium fiend of you. Now, go back to sleep."

I closed my eyes and slid out from under the burden of thought.

When I woke again, there was a battered upholstered chair pulled up to the foot of the bed, with Frances in it. Her feet were up on the seat cushion, jammed against one arm, and her knees were propped on the other. Her head tilted sideways against the chair back. She was sleeping. The crescent moons of her eyelashes, under her straight black brows, looked like obscure mathematical symbols. Her mouth was closed and severe even now. One hand was curled around her ankles; the other arm trailed over the side of the chair to brush the floor. I was willing to bet her feet had gone to sleep.

Her eyes opened, as if I'd made a noise. "Good afternoon," she said, a little hoarse. "As you see, they didn't throw me overboard and keep the bribe. Though you might be wishing they had."

I cleared my throat. "No. Why?"

She unfolded her legs with a snap. "Then I take it you haven't started to hurt yet."

She was wrong; I'd had long enough to realize that that was what had made me wake up. "Waiting for the note was a formality. He would have done it anyway," I said.

"Would he? What in the Devil's name did he think you'd done to deserve it?"

"Behaved like an asshole about three times too many."

"My, my. They have the death penalty for assholeism now?"

"I told you he wasn't going to kill me."

Frances leaned forward, her elbows on her knees, her chin propped on her laced fingers. "No? Then who was it who almost did? Doctor Brick Wall out there spent four hours over your unpromising-looking carcass saying things that will probably damn his soul to hell by whatever faith he subscribes to. Many of them he shouted at you. He seemed to think you weren't helping."

"I wish I'd been there. Sounds pretty funny."

In measured cadence, she said, "It was not funny."

I didn't want to disagree with her. She seemed to have temporarily run out of things to say.

After a little while I ventured, "He said I couldn't have any more dope, didn't he?"

"He said that. And before you ask, I am not here to smuggle in a pipe of hash. But I'd be delighted to distract you with stories."

I must have put the question mark on my face.

"What I had in mind," she said, answering it, "is the tale in one part of The Rescue of the Protagonist from Durance Vile, a tragicomedy. Since I'm here and Sherrea isn't, I claim dibs on first telling. Don't you want to know how you were got out?"

I thought about it. I realized with a kind of gentle disappointment that I didn't, really. I was out, and they had been exercised enough about it to get me out, which was nice. That seemed to be it. But it would be rude, I decided, not to let her tell me.

It may have taken longer than it seemed to work this out. Or some of it may have showed in my face. Whichever it was, it made Frances look at me strangely. "If you're tired, I'll go away."

"It's all right. Tell me."

The look didn't quite disappear, but she began. "So. After sitting quietly for two hours in the dark on the sweet soft throne of a tar barrel and breathing in lungfuls of dead fish smell, I'd figured out my plan. I would have my methanol pirates take me straight to China Black's safe place, where I would extort an irresistible amount of ransom money from the locals, and send it back in lieu of my note, to Beano. I meant to count out five thousand pounds or make some blood flow—do you know that song? The pirates, unfortunately, refused to accept changes in the script. They *would* boot me off just past the checkpoints, and they *had* to have a note to send back. I think they were afraid that if I stuck around, I'd talk them out of the trike."

She sat a moment, her hands clasped lightly before her. "Do you know how hard it was to write that note?" she said in a new voice.

"It was very good," I told her. "I knew it really was from you."

"That's not what I mean. The arrival of that note would start something I didn't want started. I knew that. In the end, I couldn't do anything about it. But I wanted you to know I tried."

"I told you, he would have—"

"Done it anyway. If true, it still doesn't change the way it seemed at the time." She raked her hands through her hair. "So I made the damned cross-country trek here, where I found Sherrea and told her where you were. She coupled your name with a few choice bits of verbiage. She knew better than I did what you'd called down on your head. Then she worked out the Great Escape.

"You ought to *try* to appreciate it properly," Frances added with a sigh. "Maybe you will later. I thought it was the stuff that caper movies were made of, but what do I know?"

"I can't try until you tell me about it."

"That's better—it almost sounded like you. The plan was a variant of the plague trick. Sherrea and a fellow named LeRoy put three rather startled calves in a livestock trailer, hitched up the pickup, and headed in on I-94. No particular attention paid to them, since they were going *in*. They went to Del Corazón, found you, and hid you under the false floor in the trailer. Then they put the shockingly realistic latex sores on the calves and headed for the Cedar Avenue checkpoint."

At that she stopped and looked expectantly at me.

"Sores?" I asked.

"Anthrax," she said, savoring the syllables. "Spreads like wildfire, fatal, communicable to humans. Nobody searched the trailer. The only problem was that when LeRoy finally pulled off the latex, all the hair underneath came off, too. The calves are out in the pasture shooting accusing looks at anyone who comes near."

"You're right," I said. "It would have been good in a movie."

Frances leaned forward again and gave me the strange look; then she stood up. "Go back to sleep," she said.

This time it didn't work. For one thing, I hurt almost everywhere. And I was nagged by the feeling that Frances had wanted entirely different responses from the ones she'd gotten. I couldn't think what they would have been—I'd been polite and attentive and cheerful, if not very emphatic—but that didn't keep me from trying.

The next week seemed like one long series of disabilities and allowances made for them. I couldn't remember ever having been bedridden before, or even very sick, so they all came as a surprise. Going to the bathroom was the most unpleasant; I insisted on hobbling across the room to the water closet long before I was really able, even if it meant having to lean on someone as far as the door. The alternative, after all, was much worse.

Eating was a trial; I had a loose tooth and stitches inside my mouth on the left side. Being bathed by someone else, as it turned out, was simply impossible once I was conscious. I was able to let Josh change dressings at first, while I was still too weak to get all the way through the process by myself. After that, I took care of it. I'd never realized how close to the full range of motion getting dressed required, until I did it when it seemed that none of my muscles would move through their full range of motion without pain. But I did it.

Josh insisted I call him that. He said since the only thing he had to call me was "Sparrow," he was forced to give up on proper doctor-patient formality, but he would feel better if I would return the insult. He told me he learned his craft by apprenticing himself to a woman who had gone to med school and had a pre-Bang practice as a surgeon. He told me his wife had died two years ago and that he still missed her; that he had three children, ages sixteen, nineteen, and twenty-one; that he preferred vegetable gardening to flowers; that the accomplishment he was proudest of was learning to play the guitar at the age of forty-six . . .

In short, he flung his life open in front of me without even seeming to notice he'd done it. I sat numb, patient, and politely silent under the fall of information, intending to forget it all as soon as the words stopped sounding in the room. I needed to do with his life story what he had done with the names: equalize us, achieve parity, balance debit and credit in the accounts of the Deal.

I couldn't do it. The ring on his left hand reminded me of the wife I'd never met. Some skill of his in the sickroom made me wonder whether he'd acquired it during his apprenticeship. A row of flowers outside the window reminded me of him in negative. There was a slow corruption of my principles going on, that I could feel, but that I was helpless to stop.

He never mentioned what he knew about me, which I didn't understand at all. He'd examined me when Sher brought me in, and he knew I was aware of that. That part of the wall of my privacy was already torn down. Yet he never raised the subject, as if it were still private, as if we were on opposite sides of that wall. What value did he think the knowledge had, when both of us possessed it?

Theo came to visit me several times. I found I almost couldn't talk to him. I remembered sitting in his room in China Black's house, feeling as if we were the only people in the world who understood the language we were speaking that day. We had traded secrets and painful admissions in that language. Now, looking at him, I felt as if someone had plucked the whole vocabulary out of my brain. I didn't think it had had any words for explaining what had happened to me, anyway. Theo looked hurt when the conversation faltered. After a while he stopped visiting.

When I could walk that far, I took to sitting on the front porch of the farmhouse. There was enough to see from there to keep my mind busy and out of trouble, and when there wasn't, I usually dozed off.

The front porch looked out on a makeshift village square with the corners filed off. It had one large tree at the center, and a scattering of smaller ones. There was a pump and a trough, and a few benches, and a charred brick firepit. There were also flowers—less thickly planted than in China Black's garden, and

less disciplined, but with something of the same feel nonetheless.
It was pretty, and there was almost always something to watch:
someone doing something to a flowerbed, or pumping water, or
rocking a baby.

Other houses surrounded the square, in a confusion of styles
and sizes. Some had been built there, some moved there from
other places. Behind the first ring of houses, partially visible from
my chair, was another. These, too, were a confetti of styles and
materials, including cloth-and-tubing domes and some complex-
looking tents. I put the number of dwellings I could see at about
two dozen. If there was anything beyond those, I didn't think
about it.

One afternoon Sherrea came and sat with me. She'd been a
regular visitor to the sickroom. More than that, she'd been an
irregular volunteer nurse there, since her hands, for no clear
reason, were among the few I could tolerate for the relatively
impersonal services. But our conversations there had been short,
and had brushed lightly over their subject matter.

Now she greeted me and sat on the porch floor at my feet, her
arms wrapped around her knees and a half-empty mug in one
hand. I could smell the tea, but I wasn't sure what kind it was. The
undisciplined mass of her dark hair dwarfed her sharp-featured
little face. She wore a huge, busy-patterned cotton tunic bound
with three different sashes around her hips, black leggings with
holes in both knees, and sneakers with the toes cut out. It was all
a concession to country life; none of it trailed behind her, after all.

I hadn't realized that we'd been sitting in silence until Sherrea
said, "Did you take a vow not to ask questions, or what?"

"Huh?"

"Oh, *that's* a question. Don't you want to know where you are,
or who these people are, or why I brought you here, or *anything*?"

"Sure, if you want to tell me."

She set her chin on her knees and stared at me. "What happened
to your head, Sparrow?" she said. "What's going on in there, that
nothing comes out anymore? Or is there nothing to *come* out?"

"My head's fine." A thought shot to the surface: *I know; I've
met it*. But it was gone before I got a good look at it.

"It is not. You never used to tell anybody anything, but at least
you had a personality. Now you're even locked that up. I'm your
friend, you idiot! You can be rude to me!"

I closed my eyes and leaned back in the chair. It was a hot day,
and a damp one, and inhaling was like breathing soup. "I don't

have anything to be rude to you about. And if I've locked anything up, it's more than I know."

She sighed. "Maybe that's true. Maybe you don't know you've done it. In which case, you did it because some part of you had to. In *which* case, you have an even screwier sense of personal property than I thought you did."

"That's a non sequitur," I said, smiling.

"The hell it is. What do you think you own?"

Sweat trickled under my shirt, cold as ice water. "Nothing."

After a moment she said, "That's what I mean. You own exactly what everybody else owns. Your body, for starts. Nobody can make any claims on it but you. You can choose to give control of it to somebody else, temporarily, like you did back in the City. Which, by the way, took more guts than sense. But it took a lot of guts. But when that's over, your body's still yours, you haven't given a bit of it away.

"And you own your mind. Everything you think is your property, and it's yours whether you build a fence around it or not. Nobody can cross into it, nobody can make you change anything in it, and nobody can hurt you there, unless you let them. Whatever Beano did to your body, he bounced clean off your mind and didn't even leave a dent. Unless you put him inside the property line yourself."

I'd opened my eyes, and was looking at the porch ceiling. "You should bring all this up with Frances. A Horseman's perspective is probably a little different."

"I *did* bring it up with Frances," Sher said caustically. "I thought somebody ought to. Funny thing is, she agrees with me. According to Frances, her victims' minds are bulletproof. She can replay their memories, but those are just recordings. They're not the person, they're just what the person draws on sometimes. She says if she wanted to make someone hate blue, or like rhubarb, or want to shoot the dog, she couldn't do it. She can kill minds, but she can't change 'em."

"But she can steal bodies. That's hard on the first part of your theory."

"And I could strangle you dead, right this minute. That would be stealing, too. I'll give you half an exception for the Horsemen, but after that I'll say it again: They can kill ya, but they can't own ya. And until you're dead, you belong to you and nobody can change that. You don't have to lock your brain in a box to be sure of it."

She stopped, and I dropped my gaze from the ceiling to her face. "Okay," I said.

She threw her mug at the lawn and stomped off the porch.

As my endurance came back, and my flexibility, I began to walk instead of sit. Outside the second ring of houses (my estimate had been low; there were thirty-nine), I found barns and sheds and stables and workshops. Beyond those were pastureland and cultivated fields. Grain did its foot-rooted wind dance there; corn thrashed its jungle leaves; beans waggled long green or purple or yellow fingers; summer squash ripened furiously in a pinwheel of tropical-looking vegetation. Here, too, there were always people, cultivating, hoeing weeds, spreading things, raking things, trimming, harvesting. It all seemed as ritual as a pre-Bang Catholic mass, and as intelligible to outsiders.

One morning, when I'd gone farther than I had before and was feeling the effects, I sat down in the shade of a tree next to a field. Five people were hoeing up and down the rows of something I didn't recognize. One of them reached the end of the row nearest me, looked up, smiled, and came over.

"Hi," she said, dropping down onto the grass. "Sparrow, isn't it? I'm Kris." She pulled her straw hat off to reveal a brush of hair the color of the hat. She tugged a bandanna out of her pocket and wiped her face with it; then she unclipped a flask from her belt and poured some of the contents over the bandanna. She draped that over her head like a veil and jammed the hat back on. "Funny-looking," she said with a grin, when she saw me watching the process. "But it does the trick. The evaporating water keeps your head cool."

"Looks like hard work," I said, nodding back out into the sun.

"Goddess, it is. Especially this part of the year. Harvesting isn't any easier, but it's more fun, and you have something to show for it right away. Every year about now I start wishing it was winter."

This was a reasonable line of conversation, not too personal. "What is that out there?"

"Sugar beets. We voted to do 'em this year instead of tobacco, thank Goddess. Don't get me wrong—I love to smoke. But I'll pay for my tobacco and be glad to. It's a good cash crop, but the hand labor is murder, and no matter how careful we are, we always have trouble with the tomatoes when we grow it. Turns out we'll make as much on the beets, anyway, so I can afford to buy my smokes."

"Oh," I said. Every word of that speech had made perfect sense, but I still wasn't sure what had gone on.

Her grin broke out again. "That's right, Sher said you were strictly a City-dweller. And we were supposed to be patient when you walked through the basil and fell in the flowerbeds."

"You've been lucky so far. The state I've been in, the flowerbeds could have fought me off."

"Yeah. What does Josh say, are you doing all right?"

My own fault; I'd introduced the subject. "Fine." I stood up. "I should be getting back, I think."

"Me, too—back to swingin' dat hoe. Ugh. You coming to the whoop tonight?"

"*Whoop?*"

"We've never figured out a better name for it. In the town circle. There'll be some drumming and dancing and singing and shouting, and food, and a bonfire . . . what can I say? A whoop."

"I don't think I'm quite up to dancing."

She flashed white teeth. "We'll pretend you're an ancestor. Sit by the fire and we'll feed you and ask which song you want to hear next."

"I'll see," I said.

I didn't think I'd be there. But when I got back to the farmhouse, I found the kitchen in a state of cheerful uproar, and the inhabitants united on the question of where I was going to spend my evening.

"Better take it easy if you don't want to wear out before the whoop," said Mags, who was poking holes in a piecrust. She was a plump, wide-eyed, snub-nosed Latina. I would have thought she was about sixteen, if Josh hadn't told me that her son was twelve. The son, Paulo, was shelling beans at the table. He was tall for his age, dark and thin, and stared at me solemnly every time I appeared.

"That's all right. I thought I'd stay here."

"Don't be a dink. You can't stay here, and if you did, you wouldn't have any peace, anyway. Everybody goes who's not actually dying. If you stay away, they'll think you've got leprosy. Paulo, put those in to boil, *gallito*. Oh, and slice those peppers into rings for me, please."

"She's right," Josh called, from somewhere beyond the screen door. "You want them to think I did my best, and failed?" He pulled the screen door open and let it bang behind him. His head and shoulders were wet from the pump, and he carried a tub of butter. "As long as you don't polka, you'll be fine."

Their cheerfulness was oppressive. Their assumption that there was nothing that made me different from anyone else in the place except, possibly, my injuries, was alarming. "Nobody will mind," I said. "I'm not really part of the community."

Josh turned his head to one side and looked at me, as if he were trying to read me like a thermometer. Then he set the tub down, pulled a stack of flat-bottomed bowls from a shelf, and began to fill them with butter. "If you say you're not," he said, "then you're not. And no one will insist otherwise. But there's a difference, you know, between being a member of the community and acknowledging that you're part of that community's shared experience.

"I know this will sound crazy to you, but showing up tonight—even for a little while—and eating our food and sharing our fire will be taken as an expression of gratitude. No one insists that you be grateful, either, but it would be a nice gesture."

"I am grateful," I said, feeling a stirring of distress. "You saved my life."

Josh's hands paused over the butter. He raised his eyebrows and opened his mouth, closed it again, then said, "No, never mind. The wrong lecture at the wrong time. Will you come tonight?"

I tried to imagine what I was committing myself to. Would it be more like lunch at China Black's house, or like the Night Fair? Either one seemed, suddenly, equally frightening. "I'll come," I said, because I knew I had to.

"Good," Mags said. "Then put these in the oven for me, will you? Put a tray under them or they'll dribble all over. Josh, you better bring those clothes in off the line."

I took Mags's advice and lay down in the back bedroom that had changed from the sickroom to Sparrow's room in the household language. I wondered what would happen if another invalid turned up.

The shadows were long and the sunlight deep gold when someone knocked on my door. I opened it to Mags, who pushed a folded pile of clothes into my arms.

"I just remembered, you don't have much variety in your wardrobe. You can wear these tonight. Actually, you can keep 'em. Large Bob said the only way he was ever gonna fit in those pants again was if he stopped eating entirely."

"I can't—"

"Yes, you can. Say thank you and close the door."

"Thank you," I said. "Very much."

I set the stack on the bed and looked at it. I didn't mean to keep them, but I didn't see how I could avoid wearing them tonight. It was a pity; the things I had on were Josh's, which meant they were huge and had been washed and worn until they were soft as flannel. I didn't look forward to clothes that hurt. I shook out the first thing on the pile.

It was a pair of black trousers with a stretchy drawstring waist and pleats at the top, made of brushed cotton twill. Underneath them was a cotton shirt, in a style I'd seen the interesting Indians wear in movies. It had an open collar and a low yoke, and wide sleeves gathered into cuffs. The shirt was wine-red, and the buttons on the cuffs and down the front were silver. It looked festive but restrained, and the whole business, once I put them on, felt as if I were proposing to go out in pajamas. Mags had understood about clothes that hurt.

I wish these people would stop understanding everything, I thought irritably. Something in my throat hurt, but I swallowed, and it went away.

The village square—excuse, the circle—was illuminated with lanterns hanging from all the lower tree branches, clusters of torch candles around the plank tables, and the bonfire. It sent almost enough light through the front windows to read by. I went to the kitchen and out the back door, and stood leaning on a porch pillar in the dark half of the night.

"Scared?" said Josh. I hadn't seen him sitting on the steps.

"I . . . Yes, actually."

"Sher said you weren't a social animal."

My hands opened and closed on nothing. Words pushed their way out of my mouth, unbidden and unwelcome. "Maybe I am, and there just aren't any other animals like me."

"What kind of animal do you think you are?" Josh asked, sounding mildly surprised.

I inhaled with my teeth closed. It made a hiss. "You know," I whispered.

"What *you* think you are? Nope. I know what *I* think you are."

"And what's that?"

"A customized human being."

"Well," I said. "That was easy."

Josh stood. I was on the porch and he was on the ground; he had to look up to meet my eyes. "It *is* easy," he said. "Identity magic is the oldest and easiest kind there is. It's what language is for."

"Anybody gonna help carry this stuff?" Mags yelled from the kitchen, with volume enough to be heard inside and out.

"Damn," said Josh; then, loudly, "You betcha!" He thumped up the porch stairs, past me, and into the kitchen.

Paulo and I each had charge of a pie. Josh got the beanpot, swathed in toweling. We tramped across the lawn to the sawhorse tables, and put our contributions down next to everything else.

People smiled at me, and waved, and introduced themselves. It was like China Black's and the Night Fair both. I couldn't decide if it was the worst of both or not. The people who introduced themselves often told me how long they'd known Sherrea, or how they came to know her, or asked me how I had. Sher, it seemed, was universally acquainted around here. It was the first time I'd thought to wonder how she came to know about this place, and what it was to her. I was very polite to everyone.

I wandered toward the bonfire, wishing I knew how long I ought to stay. Then a flash of light on a face at the corner of my vision startled me, and I turned to look.

Theo was walking next to me, and the light had been glancing off his glasses. "Hey," he said.

I stopped walking. I'd been talking to strangers all evening; I could do this. I had only to gather my much-tried manners and put them to work again. "Hello. How are they treating you?"

"Great. I think. Only there's nothing to do. I keep thinking about whether Robby's surviving without us."

Ignore the strange feeling in the stomach; rely on the manners. "I expect so. And you'll be able to go back soon, won't you?"

"To what?" Theo asked. "Occupation under Tom Worecski?"

I frowned. "But that's what it was before you came here."

"It's not—never mind. Look, I'm gonna ask somebody tomorrow if there's anything electronic they want done around here. D'you want me to volunteer you, too?"

"No." I almost turned and left, but I remembered: manners. "No, thank you. I'm not doing that anymore." Then I left.

Tom Worecski had had the archives burned. That had damaged that part of me, but it hadn't killed it. Something else had done that, something I couldn't name, that had seared away the connection between who I was and what I knew. I still knew electronics, I still had languages and *language*, all the things I'd woken with out of that parody of birth fifteen years ago. But they didn't belong to me. *Nothing*, I'd said to Sher. I owned nothing. My body was on lease from the past, a machine I'd rented and lost the paperwork for, and I had no idea where my mind had come from. All the things I knew might have been stolen from someone else.

I managed to stay in motion, and so avoid having to talk to anyone else. I saw Frances for a moment, at the opposite end of a table. What, I wondered, did all these nice people make of her? *So well spoken; lovely person, actually, for a mass murderer.* She returned my look with a grave, piercing one, and I moved on again.

I didn't see Sher until much later. There was music at the edge of the bonfire: guitarists, singers, a fiddle player, a mandolin, someone with a clarinet, and a shoal of drummers who sounded as if they'd played together in the womb. Someone offered me finger cymbals, but I declined. At the edge of the light, people were dancing.

On the opposite side of the hodgepodge circle of musicians and audience, I saw Kris, the woman from the beet field. She sat on the grass with her arm around another woman. They were both smiling, alternately at the musicians and at each other; they whispered in each other's ears; they laid their heads on each other's shoulders. The other woman kissed Kris on the cheek, halfway between her cheekbone and her jaw. Josh had removed the stitches from the inside of my mouth just a few days ago, in about that spot.

I stood up abruptly and walked into the dark. I ended up on the other side of the big central tree, leaning against it, staring up into the branches. The candle lanterns hanging there had almost all gone out. I concentrated on my breathing, on letting my chest rise and fall, on seeing if I could take in exactly the same volume of air each time. The day and everything in it seemed to have conspired against my composure. But it had survived, and with a little attention would continue to do so. This had been a bit of testing for real life, that was all.

"It's all right," said Sher, beside me, in a wrung voice I'd never heard from her before. "Nobody wants you to hurt. It just seemed so strange—you were so different. But if you have to shut us all out or break . . . . then shut us out."

I put my hands over my face for a moment. Then I let them drop. "I'm sorry," I said. "I don't know what you mean."

I heard her breath run unevenly into her lungs. "It doesn't matter. Never mind."

The farmhouse was close, but I would have found it anyway. This body I was leasing had always had good night vision. I closed the door of my room behind me, folded the borrowed clothes, and went, eventually, to sleep.

The next day I hunted through the fields until I found Kris, and asked her to put me to work. She was in one of the smaller garden plots this time, a long straight stretch between the dairy barn and the horse paddock.

She got up off her knees and banged her hands together to get the dirt off her gloves. "Sure. What are you good at?"

"Nothing," I said. It was a useful word lately. "I'll have to be trained."

Kris grinned and waved at the rows. "Then you're doomed to learn to weed. C'mere." She pointed. "That's an onion. Don't pull it out. Anything that doesn't look like that—see here, and here—is a weed. In this row, anyway. You're trained. Off you go."

In half an hour the cramped, unfamiliar position met my healing injuries and joined forces against me. I was sweaty, too, even though the work wasn't strenuous. But it was just what I wanted. It slowed down thought, and channeled it into unfamiliar paths, ones my life to date hadn't sown with mines. I was surprised when I reached past the last onion sprout and found that it *was* the last.

"Good work," Kris said. "The next row is lettuce. It looks like this."

A minute into that row, and Kris pointed to the thing in my hand. "That's also lettuce."

"Oh," I said. After that, I did better.

Eventually I could figure out for myself which were the weeds. At that point, Kris moved on to the next garden plot, and I had the first one to myself. It was hypnotic work, with its own loose rhythm and a set of physical techniques both precise and trivial. The way a slow, smooth pull would bring a weed up by the roots and a jerk would snap it off at the surface. The way dandelions had to be pulled by all their leaves at once. The machinery of my arm moving out and back, reach, pull, toss. I could do this. I knew where this skill came from, and whose it was. Mine, mine. Wherever the rest of me was stolen from, this was mine.

Via Kris, who had taught it to me. Then was it Kris's skill, after all?

And someone must have weeded China Black's garden. Whoever it was, I shared this knowledge with her or him.

I'd stopped in midmotion, still crouched and kneeling, the latest thing I'd pulled still in my hand. It was a thin-stemmed little plant with short oval leaves climbing in pairs up the stalk. At the end was a cluster of star-shaped flowers in an aching, vibrating magenta.

I had pulled one of these before—in China Black's garden. "Sparrow?" Sher's voice came to me, from the end of the row.

I couldn't breathe, except in little bursts that seemed to catch halfway down my throat. I had pulled one of these when, angry with Sherrea for something I'd done, I hadn't listened while she told me again: *You don't belong to them. You don't now, and you never did*.

The origin of my body and my mind didn't matter. I, the part of me that learned, that called on my memories, that knew I'd pulled a plant like this before, that had moved this hand to do it, was fifteen years old and innocent of evil or good. Neutral. From here forward, I was blank tape; what would be recorded there, and when, and why, was up to me.

I couldn't *breathe*. I'd dropped the plant; I closed my dirty hands over my face as if I could find and tear away whatever was keeping the air out. My whole curled body shook with gasping, with the high, thin sound it made.

"Oh," said Sherrea, very close now. "Oh, *hell*." I felt her arms close around me, lightly for a moment, then very tight.

I was crying. Once I realized it, it got worse, until I couldn't stop it, until I wondered if a person could die of it. I was catching up for all the things I hadn't cried for: for Cassidy; for Dana; for my own pain; for the archives with their sweet glowing window on the past; for the lost, desperate look on Frances's face when she thought she was at the end of her life; for Theo, cut off from his father and his home. I cried because Josh still missed his wife, and because Sher was crying. I cried because all the things I'd never felt before had come and settled in, and since the surface there was new and delicate, they were all painful.

"Sparrow," Sher said damply. "It's okay, it's okay."

She was right, actually. I turned my face into the cloth on her shoulder and went on crying.

Card **9**

Hopes

The Star

Crowley: The Daughter of the Firmament, the
    Dweller between the Waters. Hope, unex-
    pected help, clearness of vision, realization of
    possibilities.

Waite: Immortality. Truth unveiled. The Great
    Mother communicating to those below in the
    measure that they can receive her understand-
    ing.

t was not unlike being invalided all over again. The effect wasn't widespread; the number of people who knew about my emotional collapse was limited. But for several days Sherrea, Theo, Frances, and Josh all behaved as if I was likely to either erupt or evaporate without cause. I expect I needed it.

I needed forbearance from myself, too. It hadn't been a perfect catharsis; my instincts were still in place, and I had to struggle against a passionate desire to slip back into silence. And my memory was still good. Now that I had a nice, scraped place on my soul to scour them across, the crueler things I'd said or done to protect my privacy came back to me.

The worst was that same night, in the kitchen. Mags was replacing the gasket in the faucet, and I was sharing the lamp oil, reading *A Tale of Two Cities* at the kitchen table.

"Why are you called Sparrow?" Mags asked suddenly. "Did you name yourself? Is it symbolic? Is it a reference to something?"

I could tell her about waking up on the side of a levee in a tangle of brush, sweating already in the morning sun, and seeing a buff-gray breast and a round black eye bobbing on a twig above me. The word had appeared in my head. That was when I recognized language, that I had it; and that I had no past, that I recalled, to have learned it in. It was my first moment of self-knowledge. How was I supposed to know that Sparrow guarded fire for the Devil?

Cassidy had told me that.

"No," I said suddenly, "it's just a name."

"It doesn't fit you, you know."

Sparrow guarded fire for the Devil. Shortly after he'd said that,

he'd made me a gift of something and I'd felt trapped by it. Bee
I'd finished his beer. And because of that violation of m
principles, my valuable principles, I'd made him believe that
didn't care about him.

"I mean, sparrows are little and round and brown."

The last conscious thing Cassidy had done in his life was to tr
to make me a gift of mine. "They work for the Devil," I said, m
voice breaking up like a clod of earth in water. "Excuse me."
bolted out the back door.

By some miracle, there was no one in the town circle. I stoo
leaning against the big central tree, my forehead on my clenche
hands, and wept again. This time the storm was silent, and angr
And this time I had to do it alone. However well I told it, no on
else would understand the size of my wrongdoing or my grie.
There had been a person who'd felt entitled, for the value of
swallow of beer, to deny a friend. It didn't seem possible to shar
a life with that person.

The night continued to move around me, the tree continued t
hold me up, the earth didn't open under my feet. Instant oblivio
wasn't offered to me. I would just have to go on.

But I noticed, eventually, that there was an uncommon lot o
verbal tiptoeing happening around me. It was Frances who was th
first to be polite and self-effacing one time too many. I can
remember her exact words; I remember that the sentence was eve
more ornamented and less linear than usual. I said, "I tell yo
what: I'll lock myself in my room, and you can slip notes unde
the door. That way you can think about what you want to say fo
days before you say it."

Frances's eyes opened wide. "Hullo," she said, grinning
"you're back!"

Theo slid gradually into quoting from movies again, because h
couldn't help it. I understood how that worked. After all, I'
avoided seeing Theo for weeks because I couldn't look at him an
not think of VU meters and mixing boards. Sherrea simply forgo
and cussed me out one day. After that, without comment, w
picked up the rhythms of genuine conversation again, genuin
argument, and silences that weren't loaded with anything.

So there was no discomfort, when I went out to the stable
looking for a pitchfork, in finding Sherrea propped against th
fence of a nearby paddock. There was a certain amount o
strangeness, however. She was feeding handfuls of clover to
camel. A two-humped, dark brown, disreputable-looking camel

"How in the name of . . . *everything* did that get here?" I said, in lieu of the sentence I'd been planning to say.

"Isn't she hot stuff? There's not a thing we can do with her, but the camels keep hanging on, and they're so weird we can't bring ourselves to trade 'em off to somebody who needs 'em."

"There's more than one?"

"Oh, yeah. A male, two she-camels, and a calf just this spring."

"But where from?" I asked again, holding out my hand.

"Put some grass in it, or she'll just bite you. The land we're on used to be the zoo. Whenever you're up for a serious hike, you can see the old buildings—they're over that ridge a ways. They're ruined, though. It's kind of a sad place. When the Engineers set up camp, the tropical animals had already died, and some other species, too. The last tiger died two years ago, and everybody was miserable, even though we all knew it was gonna happen eventually."

"A *tiger*?"

"Yeah. He was beautiful. But we just couldn't find out enough about taking care of tigers, and what we could find out, we couldn't always use. But the moose and the wild horses did okay on their own, so we let 'em go feral. And you'll see snow monkeys in the woods, if you watch. The musk oxen were our big success, though."

The camel looked adoringly at me from under vast, sand-colored lashes, and tried to tear a piece from my sleeve. I pulled another hank of grass and offered that instead. "They're still here?"

"No, it's too hot for 'em here now. We were losing too many to disease. But we found out about some people north of Winnipeg who're doing kind of what the Engineers are doing here, and they said they'd take 'em. So we had a musk oxen drive up to the border. It was great, except people started singing 'Git Along Little Musk Ox' when we'd stop for the night. Now we hear the herd's increasing again. I figure that's one for the good guys."

"Who are—?"

The camel bit me.

"She's really sweet," Sher said as I rubbed my forearm. "You just don't want to ignore her."

"You're darn right."

The camel pulled her lips back blissfully once more.

Josh's brand of tiptoeing wasn't verbal. It wasn't even tiptoe-ing, really; it was a different kind of caution, another sort of

concern for my mental state, and it manifested itself in watchir
me. I'd known he was doing it, but I hadn't known ho
thoroughly he was doing it until he stopped. I brought it up o
evening, in his surgery, where he'd had an emergency call. Larg
Bob Beher had broken his left wrist; I assisted at the cast-makin
(Josh's principles of doctor-patient formality were, based on th
example, a little slippery; Large Bob referred to the doctor :
"Josh, you sonofabitch," and Josh addressed the patient as "M
Beher, you horse's ass.")

We were alone, and I was gathering up the last ends of plaste
gauze and the pan of chalky water when I said, "Did you think
was going to kill myself?"

Josh looked up from his dishpan full of scary stainless-ste
implements. "I wasn't sure. I didn't know you before, you see
But I knew while I was sealing up the outside of you, tha
something inside was broken. Then, when you . . ."

"When I did my imitation of a garden hose all over the carr
patch," I said.

"Whatever. I couldn't tell if that helped or hurt. Acceptance
despair sometimes looks like that, too. That's why people ofte
say of suicides that they seemed so much better the day before.

"I couldn't have done it. Frances would have been furious, afte
I kept . . ." I took a moment to decide if I was really going to d
what I thought I was. "Josh, do you have any beer?"

He looked affronted. "I have an icebox, don't I?"

"I'll tell you the whole story if you want to hear it. But I don
think I can do it yet without drinking some beer."

"These things take practice," he agreed. "How 'bout th
porch?"

So we sat outside in the dark, reeking of pennyroyal to keep th
mosquitoes off, with three bottles of home-brewed beer apiece
and I told him what I was and how I'd managed to end u
blood-boltered in his front yard. Josh whistled and invoked goo
in all the appropriate places. When I was done, he took a long
meditative swallow of beer and said, "What are you going to d
now?"

I hadn't expected that. "I don't know," I answered after som
thought. "Do I have to do anything?"

"Maybe not. Probably not. But in the larger scheme of thing
we're close to the City. We do a lot of trading there. This seem
like the kind of business any sane person would leave unfinishec
but you may find that it won't leave *you*."

I finished my third bottle. "Maybe I ought to go."

"Where?"

"South again? Or I could try Mick's idea, and head for the border."

"Not the border," Josh said. "You wouldn't get across openly, anyway."

"Have they closed it?"

"No. But they'd ask for your health card. And when you couldn't show them one, they'd give you a physical. Then they'd take you out back and shoot you."

"Oh. Not fond of unusual foreigners up north, huh?"

He finished *his* third beer. "Besides, you might not have to go anywhere at all. Then what'll you do?"

"Prune the raspberries?"

He laughed. "Be careful what you ask for." Then he set his bottle down on the porch and leaned forward in his chair, looking out at the village circle. "Has anyone explained to you about hoodoo?"

"I know about hoodoo," I said, a little sharply.

"Really? Well. Ask Sherrea," said Josh in an odd, pleasant voice, "about this town."

The tone put my back up. It occurred to me that Josh could have meant it to; he might not have been all-knowing, but he had a respectable average with me. "She said it used to be the zoo."

"That probably had something to do with it, but that's not what I mean."

"Will she know what you mean?"

"Oh, yeah."

"Do I have to ask her tonight?"

Josh opened his eyes wide. "You don't *have* to ask her at all."

Frances would probably have had an elegant and corrosive response to that. I only sighed and took six empty bottles back to the kitchen.

The next day the weather was beautiful, in a way it rarely was so close to midsummer: warm, but full of fresh wind and high, white clouds. Theo and I spent almost the whole of it in a shed-turned-machine-shop, overhauling a generator. We came out, sweaty and filthy, and discovered the tail end of what we'd missed just as the sun touched, blinding, on the treetops. Theo scrambled to the top rail of the fence and sat with his face to the dazzle, his eyes closed. I didn't have the energy to climb; I just leaned.

"This is okay," Theo said. "You know, for the boondocks."

"Philistine," I said contentedly.

He twisted on his rail and looked down at me. "You like it
don't you? Here, I mean."

"I don't . . . know. That is, yeah, of course I like it. But if
you're saying, am I going to stay here, then I don't know."

"There's not enough tape here," he said to the field before us.

"No. But I don't know what to think about that anymore
either."

"What's to think about it?"

"Maybe nothing. But I don't want to suck my living out of the
past like a leech, Theo. I'm afraid of it. I'm still affraid of all the
stuff I woke up knowing. It was put there to be useful over sixty
years ago, so why should it be any good to anyone now?"

"It's *been* useful," he said, ruffled, "and it *is* useful. So who
cares why?"

I sighed. "I do. Because I've been useful, Theo, and I am
useful, I think. But I popped to the surface fifteen years ago wide
awake and full of trivia, and now I want to know *why*."

"Zeus and Damballah?" said Theo in a determinedly neutral
tone, as if he thought someone ought to bring it up.

"Oh, sure. Or how about—was it the Blue Fairy? Who zapped
Pinocchio? No strings on me." I stopped, because that way lay
self-pity, and I was trying to kick the habit.

"I always thought you were more like the Scarecrow," said
Theo. "You know—'If I only had a brain.' "

"This from the man who watched *Guns II* six times. What do
you want to do?"

He knew I wasn't talking about the next ten minutes. "Get
everything at the Underbridge to work at once."

"Then I guess you're not an atheist."

"Hell, to do that, I'd have to *be* God. I'd like to record those
drummers who played the other night. Man, if I'd had a DAT
recorder . . ." He sat quiet for a moment; then he peeled all his
brown hair back from his face with both hands. "I want to go
back, Sparrow. And I can't. And I *hate* it." He did, too. It was in
his suddenly harrowed voice, the desperate closing of his fingers.
Those things sealed my mouth and robbed my mind of comforting
phrases.

"Well, hey," he said suddenly, slipping down off the fence.
"We're young, we're strong, and we know how to wire a
quarter-inch phone plug. Something'll come along."

"Any minute," I said. I looked up at the sky, held out my
hands, and added loudly, "Preferably in Hi-8 format, with a copy
of *Casablanca* loaded." I turned back to him. He was smiling, a

ttle. "You've got grease all over your nose, from pushing your glasses up."

Theo was staying in LeRoy's house across the circle from osh's, a two-and-a-half-story log building so new it still had the heated smell of cut wood. When we reached it, Theo led the way around to the back porch. There was a pump beside the steps, and a big jar of soft soap on the porch railing. Theo pulled his shirt over his head, which, I found, made me uncomfortable. I sat on the top step and pretended to be absorbed in brushing dirt off my jungle boots.

"Pitch me the soap?" he said. I had to look at him after all. He'd been going without his shirt intermittently, it seemed; he was lightly browned, and freckled across the shoulders. It still made me uncomfortable, I decided. I threw him the soap jar, and he traded me his glasses for it. He cranked up the pump, stuck his head under the water, and let out a reverberating, gurgling shriek.

"I think," said Frances, strolling around the corner of the house, "the water's cold."

"You wonder why he'd do a thing like that," I said.

"No, you don't. If he's in the same condition you are, there's no mystery at all. What were you doing, building an oil tanker?"

"He was worse, actually. We were wrestling a Honda generator."

"It won?"

"Probably a moral victory. But it runs now."

She sat on the step below mine. "So," she said, watching Theo douse his head again, "what are we going to do next?"

I stared at her, keeping my mouth closed with an effort. Then I wrapped my arms around my knees. "I've had this conversation twice already in the last twenty-four hours. You people ought to coordinate better."

"Did they mean the same thing I do?"

"I don't know."

"Then how do you know you've had this conversation? I mean," she added, before I had time to object, "that I want to know how you think my future ought to influence yours, and vice versa. I like it here, but eventually, being in striking distance of the City would rot my mind. I'd have to take another shot at him, and there's no point. As you pointed out, shortening the running time on my life story would be ungrateful. So I'll leave, sooner or later, and sooner is probably not a bad idea.

"Given all that, are you staying, or going?" She pulled her own knees up to her chest and looked at me.

"If I go, do I have to go with you?"

"Christ, no, but you're welcome to. This is my Byzantine wa
of telling you so."

It was one solution. It was a good one, in fact: guaranteed t
remove me both from Tom's reach, and from the thorn-hedg
maze of reminders of my past mistakes. It didn't help Theo, bu
maybe I could come up with a way to do that, too. "Can I thin
about it for a while?" I asked.

"No," said Frances, "I expect you to fling yourself onto th
back of my horse without so much as a clean handkerchief. C
course you may. Please do."

"Oh, *shit!*" Theo wailed. "No towel!"

"No, no towel," I agreed.

Frances shook her head at me. "You're not a very nice persor
I'll get you a towel, Theo. In the meantime, pretend you're a dri
irrigation system."

Theo pushed the streaming hair back from his face as France
went in the back door. Wet-headed, without his glasses, he looke
like a stranger. "She's doing better, I think," he said.

"Frances? Better at what?"

"That's right, you were busy not noticing everything. She'
rattle off the speeches, but they were all bitter. And she wouldn
fight back."

"Wouldn't fight back?"

"I don't know how else to put it. I think she felt responsible fo
what had happened to you."

I frowned.

"Well," said Theo, "*I* know you can be stupid without anybod
else's help, but maybe she didn't. Anyway, you were pretty muc
wired in series. You got better, she got better."

I didn't say anything, and it was just as well, because France
came out with a towel and sailed it at Theo.

"LeRoy wants to know if you'd mind having corn fritter
again," she said to him.

Theo looked at Frances in disbelief. "Mind? I mean, do you?"

"That's what I told him. But he wanted me to ask. Saints an
angels, if there's one thing people around here seem to know
about, it's food. The place must have been founded by an exile
cooking school."

"You're staying here, too?" I asked, surprised. "At LeRoy's?"

"Attic. Why," Frances said, aggrieved, "does everyone put m
on the top floor, as if I were likely to have a nasty accident with
a chemistry set?"

"Maybe they're hoping the stair-climbing will cut into your natural vivacity."

She narrowed her eyes at me. "Have you been listening to me for too long?"

"Sparrow, is that you?" LeRoy's voice preceded him to the screen door. He opened it and poked his long amber-brown face out. There was a streak of flour in the cropped black fleece of his hair. "Mags asked me if I'd dig out some old schoolbooks of mine for Paulo. If I can find 'em, will you take 'em back with you?"

"If you don't mind them a little seasoned with machine lube."

"Nah. Someone threw the physics book in a vat of Coca-Cola once, from the looks of it. Frances, is it okay if I look around in the attic?"

"It's your attic. Can we help look?"

"I don't know," LeRoy said, a little desperately.

When we'd all tramped up to the attic, I could see why. Frances occupied one end of the floor space: a camp cot, a crate with a few books ranked neatly inside and a candle lamp on top, another crate used an an open-fronted dresser and filled with folded clothes. It was spare and obsessively neat.

The rest of the attic contained what looked like the pasts of the past three generations of every family in town, in boxes, in overflowing trunks, in storage cabinets made from the crawl space under the rafters, and a two-door closet built into the end wall. "I thought this was a new building," I said, rather faintly.

"I moved it all from the old one," said LeRoy. "There wasn't time to sort it."

"Yes, there was," Sherrea said as her head appeared on the landing. "If you hadn't put it off until the day before we needed to tear the old place down. *Santos*, what are you all doing up here?"

"Looking for a needle," Frances said.

"Huh. I was going to invite myself to dinner."

"Great!" said LeRoy. "As soon as we find these books."

"We'll starve," Theo sighed.

The possibility seemed to send Sherrea into action. She pointed each of us at a box or cupboard, and took one for herself. I got the two-door closet.

The floor was stacked with magazines, and if they were sorted, it was into an organization that I didn't understand. *Car and Driver*, *Popular Electronics*, *Wigwag*, *The Utne Reader*, *Air and Space*, *CoEvolution Quarterly*, something called *Dirty Linen* . . .

I felt as if I'd fallen, with a bad toothache, headfirst into a cand[ ]
box. The urge to sit and read was unbearable.

Not that the magazines were the only things there. I pulled o[ ]
a smelly wool quilt, three fluorescent tubes, an electric fan with [ ]
blade missing, a fat-bellied painted reed basket, a stack [ ]
stamped-tin ashtrays bearing the legend "Reynolds Radiator: [ ]
Good Place to Take a Leak," and an enormous framed brow[ ]
photograph of a beaming blond woman, from around the mi[ ]
1940s. I sneezed and raised my eyes, daunted, to the closet shel[ ]

There were some books there, the bindings disguised by [ ]
barely arrested cascade of newspapers and an inverted pyramid [ ]
cardboard boxes that, if anything in that closet had seemed to b[ ]
arranged by intent, I would have called a booby trap. I recognize[ ]
that. I pointed it out to myself, almost in so many words, i[ ]
mingled amusement and dismay. And still my hands went out t[ ]
ruffle under the heap of newspapers, to try to draw the books fror[ ]
the very bottom of the stack.

Newsprint slid, one fold, then two. The boxes trembled an[ ]
rocked. At last, inexorably, in the same style as avalanches filme[ ]
for documentaries, the boxes tipped forward and poured the[ ]
contents and themselves over my head and shoulders. I think [ ]
yelled.

I stood finally at the end of a long drift of mixed pape[ ]
sneezing. The mess eddied gently around Frances's knees, wher[ ]
she sat cross-legged in front of an open box. "Just think," she sai[ ]
mildly. "It *could* have been paint. . . . *What's that?*"

Lying between us, face up, was a bent and battered postcard o[ ]
a city by night. The buildings were illuminated and rich against [ ]
blue-black sky, lovely and unimaginable in their use of power[ ]
Once people had lit the outsides of skyscrapers, and turned ther[ ]
into sculpture and monuments when their insides were empty.

Then I recognized the pillar of glass in the middle, reflecting it[ ]
sisters and the cool night sky on its flanks, crowned with a hal[ ]
ring of little white lights. I was looking at my City.

No, I realized, after a glimpse of Frances's face—I was lookin[ ]
at hers. The City as she'd left it, whenever she'd left it to do he[ ]
nation's bidding and ride the bodies of strangers. The city, maybe[ ]
that she'd been innocent in, blank tape herself.

"But what's the big gold one?" I asked aloud.

"Pardon?" she said, looking up blindly.

"The one with the top lit to a fare-thee-well. That's almost a[ ]
big as—"

I realized it as I said it, but Theo answered me anyway. "Cripes. It's the Gilded West."

Frances laughed, just a little. "The *second*-tallest building in town by popular fiat; did you know? My mother always claimed, when it was lighted, that it looked like an electric shaver."

"No," Sherrea said, peering over Frances's shoulder. "It looks like a skull. See? From this side, anyway. Those shadows are the eyes—"

Theo had crouched in the multicolored reef of papers and was stirring through them. "Here's another one—and another one. Look at this! The Tent Farm with the roof still on. Cool. And that building's not there now."

"The Multifoods Building. And City Center," Frances told him, her voice steady. "Both desperately ugly. They will not be mourned." But I could see her face. I wandered over, as if to look at the postcards, and touched my fingers lightly to her shoulder.

"Here's another one of the Gilded West after dark," said Theo. "It looks like a toad in this one."

"It's the other side," Sherrea said. "Bullshit. Where's the toad?"

"Right here. There's the two front legs, and the body, and the two red lights on top are the eyes."

"*Santos*. It *does* look like a toad."

Frances tipped her head back and met my eyes. Her expression was an unstable mix of hilarity and distress. "Thank heaven," she said, "the Norwest board of directors are no longer with us."

Sher had both postcards, skull and toad, in her hands and was studying them. "They're both death symbols."

"Oh, happy bankers," Frances sighed. "No wonder the building's standing empty now."

"Noooo . . . Theo, hasn't your family got it? Why's it empty?" Sher tapped the edges of the cards and fanned them like her tarot pack, her brows drawn together.

"I'm not sure. Something about security, I think. And maybe just that they're so close in size, and somebody didn't like the competition. It's not really empty. It's got stuff stored in it."

I sat on my heels next to Frances. "What kind of stuff?"

"Groovy stuff. I'd have gotten it all by now, except you can't exactly take most of it out in your pockets. Uninterruptible power supplies, the four-hour ones; about three dozen heavy-duty storage batteries; some charge controllers; a whole pile of halogen floods—hey, they must be replacement bulbs for the outdoor

lights. Take that look off your face. Just because the place isn
lived in doesn't mean it's not guarded."

I'd forgotten LeRoy, and was startled when he said, "Y'know
if we're not going to find the books, we might as well hav
dinner."

Sher said, "LeRoy, it's your house, but don't you think w
oughta put this back in the boxes, at least?" She flourished th
postcards. "Hey, can I hang on to these?"

I stood up and worked my way around the pile to the close
again. The books I'd tried to get at on the shelf were still there.
pulled them down. *Modern English Grammar, 7th Ed*. *Window
on Western History*. And, binding and page edges irregularly tan
Adventures in Physical Science. I stared at them, and at the pile o
paper on the floor, and the postcards in Sher's hand.

"If you want to send a message," I said softly, frowning agai.
at the books, "try Western Union." But no telegrams wer
forthcoming.

I wound up delivering the textbooks to Paulo and coming bac
to LeRoy's for dinner. Theo and Frances had been right about th
corn fritters. Conversation was easy around the table during th
meal; but as we finished, Frances leaned toward me and said in
low voice, "I think I'd like to get embarrassingly drunk, in goo
company. Would you mind? And Theo and Sher, too, if they ca
stand it?"

Sher contributed a bottle of Iron Range malt whiskey. W
climbed to the warm, barely sloping roof of one of the hay shed
and sprawled there, drinking from the bottle and watching th
emerging stars and talking, erratically, about nothing particular
The whiskey was smoky and full on the tongue, and the roof slop
faced south, away from the City.

The bottle had gone around a few times when I dropped m
gaze from the sky to the roof. Sher, Frances, and Theo wer
picked out in monochrome by starlight and a half moon, th
uneven rickrack lines of heads, shoulders, and knees dusted silver
The moody voice of a clarinet rose behind us, from somewhere i
town, asking rhythm-and-blues questions that didn't need a
answer.

Frances held the bottle on her chest and said thoughtfully:

"Now all the truth is out,
  Be secret and take defeat
  From any brazen throat,
  For how can you compete,

Being honor bred, with one
Who, were it proved he lies,
Were neither shamed in his own
Nor in his neighbors' eyes?"

I said, "Who—"
"W. B. Yeats," Frances sighed. "There's nothing like the Irish
or times like this."
"Bottle," said Theo, and Frances passed it.
I looked at them, and thought it was no wonder that I hadn't
subscribed to the concept of friendship. The silliest exercise I
could imagine would be to squeeze these three profoundly
dissimilar people under the umbrella of the single word "friend."
But, it seemed, I'd been silly. "Bottle," I said to Theo.
"But of course, my little chickadee."
" 'Sparrow,' you asshole. That's a good Fields, though." I held
the bottle up to the moon. "To us," I said, very softly, and drank.
The moon was high when we slid, graceless but undamaged,
down from the roof. Frances was still collected and fluent, but I
thought the whiskey had worked; the wild taint on her words since
she'd seen the postcards was gone. It occurred to me, my own
feelings rocking more freely than usual on the surface of the
liquor, that I'd probably just attended a wake.
We walked Frances and Theo back to LeRoy's house. I turned
to the town circle, and the sight of the farmhouse and its wide
front porch. Then I said, "Sher?"
"Well, don't shout. I'm right next to you."
She was, too; I'd thought she'd started toward her place, but she
hadn't moved. As if she'd known I was going to ask.
"Tell me about the town," I said, feeling the twitch of fear in
my stomach that goes with the beginning of any risky enterprise.
I had good night vision, but I longed suddenly for a full moon
instead of a half. Something—the moon, a star, a last lit window
in a house—reflected for a moment in Sherrea's right eye and was
gone. "Why?" she asked.
"Josh said I should."
"I wanted to know, back when you were still sick, if you'd
taken a vow not to ask questions. Now you ask 'em because
you're told to?"
I felt the same rush of irritation I had with Josh. "When have I
ever done what I was told?"
Around us was a fury of crickets, but I thought I heard her draw

breath. "Always," she said. "Because it's the easy path, and the one you're least noticed on."

I had a powerful longing to turn and go. "Tell me about the town, Sher. I want to know."

"Why do you want to know?"

I thought of the camel, and Josh saying that the character of the town might have a little to do with the zoo. And Frances' frivolous comment about the cooking school. "Because I *like* here. I'd say you don't have to tell me if you don't want to, but you didn't want to, you'd have told me so and gone to bed b now."

"Sparrow," she said in an odd, unsupported voice. "Why d you want to know?"

I did turn then, and took three steps toward the circle. Th movement shook a thought loose. The postcard lying on the floc in LeRoy's attic, face up in front of the only person in th community who had seen that view before. And the books w were looking for, stored where they would set off that cascad when moved, just as the cards in a tarot deck, if you believed worked that way, always came off the stack in the right order.

And Theo being a friend of Sher's, and me knowing both o them; Sher being friends with China Black; meeting Frances o the bridge; Mick finding *my* body in the first place. Further back that I had come to this City, and stayed, and further yet, that I' been brought to life at all. We, the tarot cards, had come off th deck in order.

I faced Sherrea, queasy with nerves. "Because I think I kno half a secret, and I can't keep it properly until I know the res Because whoever's shuffling is stacking the deck. Why did Jos ask if I knew about hoodoo, then tell me to ask you about th town?"

For a moment she didn't answer. Then: "Maiden, Mother, an Crone. I didn't think you were gonna do it."

"Do *what*?" I said, my patience frayed.

"Prove you knew enough to understand the answers, dipshit, she told me happily. "I'm gonna fetch a candle. If I tell you t wait under the big tree, will you trust me to come back and answe you?"

So I stood under the big tree and waited for her. I could see th stars between the heavy branches. The grass of the circle, faintly reflective with dew, was a little lighter than the sky.

I was still queasy. It was as if my stomach knew something m reason didn't, about what I had asked, what I was about to fin out. It was hard not to go straight to the farmhouse and lock the door behind me. I sat down, leaned against the trunk, hugged my knees, and tried to think of nothing.

Then I looked up to find Sher standing over me. "*Santos*, this isn't even the hard part," she said.

"I don't know what it's a part *of*."

She dropped down on the grass in front of me. In her hand was a little lantern, glass framed in tin with a squat white candle inside. She set it down between us and lit it, and a pleasant piney smell began to spread around us. "I'll make it easy. Heck, maybe I'll even make it boring. What do you know about hoodoo?"

"It's magic. Crowley's definition, about making changes in conformity with will."

"Do you believe it works?"

"No," I said, before I quite thought about it.

"Good. Because it does, and that's not how." She let me wrestle with that for a moment, her face impassive and erratically underlit. "We're living in a closed system. Energy can't be created or destroyed. That's true of mental energy, too, and spirit, and emotions—all the stuff that magic and religion are about.

"People who work with those kinds of energy, the unmeasurables, have been called hoodoo doctors. Somebody's got a lousy love life, or is being worked against by somebody else, or wants to find a better job—it's sort of like going to the medical doctor when you're sick." She grinned suddenly at the farmhouse and said, "G'night, Josh. Anyway, they go to the hoodoo doctor, who does the spell and asks the *loa* to help the customer. What's really happening is that the hoodoo doctor, who has a lot of energy and can get hold of more, moves it into the system in favor of the customer, and asks some of the major components in the system to keep things stable."

This all sounded reassuringly like what must have been in the science book I'd delivered today. Too reassuring to be the whole of it. I fastened, in a kind of reverse self-defense, on a lurking inconsistency. "Where *are* the *loa* supposed to come into this?"

Sherrea shook her head. "Trust me, you don't want to hear that yet."

"Then what you just told me isn't true?"

"I'm trying to explain it in order so it'll make sense. Look, hoodoo isn't sticking pins in an apple. Hoodoo is all the energy and attention you bring to what you do. Everything you do. The work of your hands, done with all your attention, becomes a container full of energy that you can transfer to somebody else.

Baking bread is a hoodoo work. So's putting in a garden. Or fixing an amplifier, or teaching someone else to. *If you do it right*, with your whole head, and an awareness of where it came from, and where it's going when it leaves you. The process it's part of. And you have to be concentrating on moving energy, not money."

"Then this is a hobby business?"

"There's a difference," she said with exaggerated patience, "between getting money for what you do, and doing it for money. If you don't do it for love, or because you think it needs doing, get out and let somebody else do it. If nobody else does it, maybe that means it shouldn't be done."

A moth had come to knock against the lantern. There were fireflies in the flowerbeds, and something, an owl maybe, shot out of one of the upper branches and disappeared into the darkness. I thought about the City, about the structure and rules of all its exchanges. I remembered the ones I'd taken part in, right up to the last one. "This sounds really nice. But people don't live like that. They want what they've paid for. They want things evened up. Nothing," I said, almost against my will, "is free."

"That's right—that's your damn religion, isn't it? And the rest of the congregation is full of people like Albrecht and Beano." She was angry. Her expression was hard to read in the unnatural light, but her voice was full of it, and the set of her shoulders, outlined against the sky, was stiff, as if she might lever herself up and go away.

"Don't," I said. "Standing by the principle has become a reflex, I guess. Besides, I've hurt myself with it. If I give it up now, I'm saying I hurt myself for no good reason."

"It was a good reason," she said, very softly. The moth was louder than she was. "You're both alive and here. You had to pay at his rates, in his currency. There wasn't time for anything else."

I dropped my gaze to my crossed ankles and left it there.

"Anyway, as long as you keep the energy, all kinds of energy, moving through the system, *everything* is free. But as soon as you block some of it off, take it out of circulation—*wham*. The payback is enormous. You kept your self, your energy, out of every damn thing you did, and you're still paying for it. Albrecht is stuffing energy in boxes and hiding it in his basement as fast as it comes in, the asshole. And *everybody's* paying for it.

"When the whole system is screwed up like that, you need more than a hoodoo doctor. Straightening things out for individuals isn't enough anymore. So what you need is a gang of people whose job is to keep the energy circulating, to show other people how it's done, and to make sure both of those go on even when the gang isn't there." Sher leaned back, set her hands on her knees, and looked at me.

"Do you think you're through?" I asked. "I'm waiting for the answer to the first question. What does this have to do with the town?"

"Oh, work a little bit, Sparrow. It'll do you good."

I think I knew, really. I just had to line the facts up in my head. A community of people who made food and entertainments for each other, who had no store or even any regulated system of barter. A town that had given a herd of musk oxen an escort north, and done its best to keep tigers alive. The people who saved my life because, just then, it needed doing. "Oh," I said, and, "The whole town?"

"That's right," said Sherrea. "Welcome to the Hoodoo Engineers."

That wasn't the end of it; I had questions, she had clarifications. But not much later, I walked alone back to the farmhouse.

Or not quite alone. For company, I had my sense of something almost seen, something hovering over me, something that would be revealed eventually, whether I liked it or not. I'd thought it would be in Sherrea's explanation, and I'd been afraid of it. Now I wished it had been. It was spoiling my appreciation of the fireflies.

Card **10**

Outcome

The Tower

Waite: The ruin of the House of Life when evil has prevailed, the rending of the House of a False Doctrine.

Gray: Change or catastrophe. Freedom gained at great cost.

Crowley: His magical weapon is the sword. His magical powers are works of wrath and vengeance.

10.0: Dancing for a rainbow, sweating for the sun

I dreamed that night, for what seemed like all night. I wanted several times to wake up, and maybe even tried to; but I could no more wake up out of the world I traveled through that night than I could have woken up out of the real one.

I'm sorry. That was a bad choice of expression. However I say it, I couldn't wake up.

It began with the pictographs, black on white. I had forgotten them, or forgotten to mention them to anyone. I was on the left end once more, and next to me the woman with the headdress was saying to me, "There's not time. It's not your fault, Wind and Rain it's not, but you'll suffer for it all the same. You can't be taught the dance in a fistful of suns, never mind this little slot of darkness."

The creature with the flute beside her responded, "What's to teach? Box step, two-step, cha-cha-cha. Every living thing knows it already. Hey," it hollered at me, "you know those little bugs in your body? The teeny tiny ones that tell everything what to do? Tell 'em I said to lead!"

"You might try being something other than a handicap for once," she told it. "You old liar."

"You," it said with sudden dignity, "are no fun. What business do you have talking about dancing, the mood you're in? Get thee to an alehouse. Time's a-wastin'. We're outta here. Music, music, music!"

Three dimensions. It wasn't a sudden transition, but until then it had been a paper-flat world. Dream logic. The creature with the flute still was, and wasn't anymore, and was clutching my wrist and flinging me. Someone else caught me, and flung me again. I could hear the flute, but I couldn't see it. But even more than the

flute, I could hear drums, the crisp rolling voices of the drums
from the village circle. I could see the drummers, male and
female, gleaming with sweat, bare-shouldered, their lips drawn
back in grins of exertion and delight. Someone else caught my
arms.

Jammers. I was the balky axle in their wheel. They were
stamping and clapping to the drums, their eyes rolled back in their
heads. "Step! Step! Step!" they chanted. Their skinny arms and
bony elbows were like the bare branches of trees, jerked in the
wind of the beat. They held me down. The drums hammered at
me, cut openings in my skin, laid their rhythm-eggs in the bloody
wounds and sealed them up, to wait for hatching. That was the
first time I wanted badly to wake up.

The Jammers capered around me and herded me on, through the
illuminated, benighted Deeps. The buildings were lit like the
street scenes in movie musicals, with flashing marquees and neon,
with electricity pouring unheeded everywhere. It *was* a movie
musical; the cast of thousands leaped and wiggled and stepped,
unsynchronized, through a soundstage Nicollet Market. Both
Mick Skinners were there, or rather, both bodies. So were Dana
and Cassidy. A skeleton went by in a silk top hat and tailcoat,
pausing only long enough to thrust its skull through the ring of
Jammers and click its teeth at me.

I'd been looking at the Jammers all wrong. I'd been thinking of
them as unhealthy, underfed living people. They were beautifully
preserved corpses, of course. How silly of me. They danced very
well.

Two long-fingered hands, rose-brown next to the Jammers'
graying skin, parted the rim of their wheel and reached in to me.
I let my wrists be taken, let myself be pulled out of the ring.

The hands were attached to a woman whose blue-black hair
shivered over her shoulders and down her back to her ankles. She
was naked. I stared helplessly, because here in the dream-street I
couldn't look away, or go away, as I would have in waking life.
It was such a strange-looking body. The soft, substantial fleshi-
ness of the breasts, shifting and trembling like nervous pigeons
when she moved; the smooth padding of stomach and thighs and
wide-set hips. She wasn't fat, but looking at her, I thought of
butter and cream and molasses, and other rich things: velvet and
satin, gold poured out in dim light, the lapping of warm water on
the skin. She drew me close and kissed me on the lips.

Then she moved away, and a figure stepped out from behind
her. This was a man, dark-skinned, and naked, too. The shoulders

were as straight as mine, but broader under the red cloak fastened
around his neck; tiles of muscle marked out the chest, and were
blurred under the thin pelt of curled black hair. He had no distinct
waist; his body narrowed from the chest to the hips, tapering and
pared as a knife blade, and the hair grew over it, thinning to a
stripe over his belly and widening again at the groin. His penis
hung relaxed in the black brush of it, limp and wobbling. His legs
were black-haired and bony-kneed. I couldn't imagine walking in
that body. I couldn't imagine walking in hers.

I had seen them both somewhere before. Where . . . ah.
Stylized, on the walls of China Black's *hounfor*.

He also took my hands and drew me close, and kissed me on the
lips. Then the picture jumped, as if someone had cut out too many
frames in the splice. He closed one large milk-white hand around
my neck until I couldn't swallow, until my breath sounded like a
saw going through a board, and slammed me back against the
wall. And Beano said, "Nothing's free. . . ." And though I
didn't really feel any pain, that was the second time I wanted to
wake up, and much more urgently than the first.

Continuity, even by dream-logic, broke, as if the projectionist
had started the wrong reel. I was in one of the vegetable gardens,
alone, wrapped in a perfect silence that never really happened in
the fields. The row at my feet was half-weeded. I knelt and went
back to work. Reach, pull, toss. Reach, pull, toss. It had a
rhythm. It had a sound, a series of sounds—and I began to hear the
drums, somewhere distant, speaking to the motion of my arm.

I stood up (as I did it, I heard that, too, allowed for in the
drumbeat) and started walking toward the town circle. It was full
dark when I reached it, but the torches, the lanterns, the bonfire,
broke the darkness up into pleasing sections. The drummers were
in an arc of the circle by themselves, playing fiercely, the big
drums between their knees, the smaller ones propped on their
thighs. The rest of the circle was clapping and swaying, and
singing responses to one strong voice whose owner I couldn't see.
I slid through a gap and stood inside the ring.

The dancers were in the center, stamping, tossing their heads,
working their shoulders. The strong voice, I found, was Sherrea's,
singing in a language I didn't know. And I knew so many. The
ring of onlookers had receded behind me; I was surrounded by
dancers now. None of them touched me, but none had to. The
force of their movements, and the rhythm they moved to, were
like an assault.

I felt the rhythm pulling at my muscles. I felt my head yanked

back and my spine arched as if someone had hooked my breastbone
and was pulling it up on a rope. My legs were weak and weren't
answering my brain. And in all the split places of my skin, in the
blood running its closed path beneath, in the straight, hard bones of
my arms and legs and in the bone cask of my rib cage, the wasp-eggs
of the beat were hatching out.

That was the third time, and the strongest. What I would have
run from the third time wasn't pain. It was the coming of the thing
I had waited for all night, the thing Sherrea hadn't talked about.
The number of hoodoo is nine, because it is three times three, and
three is at the heart of everything. Something said that, as an
aside. I wasn't listening properly.

The eggs hatched out in a stream of—I don't know, I don't
know. How does the charge controller feel, when the current
comes down the line from wind or water or photovoltaic cell, and
it holds it back, feeds it steady to the battery? Is it hot like that,
thick and hot and sweet in the mouth and the muscles? Is it clean
and brilliant as a breath of ozone after lightning? Silly. It's
hardware. It doesn't know. I knew.

I lifted my foot, and the power surged in me as if a turbine had
spun. Any motion did it. Stepping, leaping, twisting like the
upward reach of a lick of flame. Any motion. Would it work in
one of those other bodies, the woman or the man? I couldn't
imagine it. Not those borrowed suits of flesh. Just this pure
envelope of energy, engulfed and blinded in a rising tide of white
light.

Sherrea was in front of me, dressed in white. She sang out a line
and voices all around me answered. I laughed and dropped to my
knees in front of her. She held out a mirror.

I knew my own face. I had always used mirrors, to make sure
I was unobtrusive, to be sure I looked as much like the people
around me as I could manage. And so I knew my face, not as
mine, but as a mirror and a blurry print of others. Now I knew I
had to search this reflection for the real skin and bones, eyes and
nose and mouth. Working, Sherrea had said, with the whole
mind. . . .

As I found it, I built a replica of it in my memory, so I could
find me again without the mirror. A high, smooth forehead fenced
with thick, black hair; black eyebrows that arched high and even
over large, long-lidded dark eyes; a thin, high-bridged nose and a
thin, long mouth; an angular, almost fleshless jaw and chin. Bones
and features, bones and features, and not much else. No extras and
ornaments. The bones were tired of staying still.

In my right eye, I saw a spark. A reflection in the black pool of the pupil, a light; a little scene. I opened my eye wider and came closer to the mirror.

A riverbank, and a reflection off metal—there was a figure lying spread-eagled on the riverbank. It was transfixed with swords, the white metal bright in the new sun. The feet, the knees, the belly, the breasts, the hands. On the sand, silver-blond hair spread out in starfish arms, wet and clotted with dirt. One long bright sword stood upright in and through the open mouth, below the shocked, wide-open eyes.

It was Dana.

I was sitting up before I was awake, swaying and shaking. If I'd made a noise, it wasn't enough to bring anyone else.

It was morning, late, and no sounds in the house; Josh, Mags, and Paulo had probably gone off about their respective businesses. It was hot, and the air seemed to weigh me down like rocks where I lay. I stood up and sat back down again. Oh, what a lovely headache. And my whole face ached, skin and bone. It had been a while since I'd been hungover, but it had never given me nightmares before.

I put on some clothes and wandered to the kitchen. Halfway there, I heard someone knock on the screen door, so I continued on a little quicker.

It was Sherrea. "Hi. Are you just up?" she asked through the screen.

"Um. D'you want breakfast,"

"No. Look, could you skip breakfast, for now, and come out here for a minute? I want to tell you something."

I'd just opened the icebox; I shut it again. "Something's wrong."

"Not really. Could you just come?"

I stepped out on the back porch, and her eyes grew wide. "What?" I said.

"You look—I don't know. You look funny. Not really funny, but. . . ." Then she shrugged. "Forget it."

The sky was white-blue, and studded in the southwest with muddled scratches of cloud. It was thick air to breathe, and motionless. Around front, on the steps, I found Theo and Frances. I wondered if I should feel ganged up on, or if they'd missed breakfast, too, at Sher's insistence. They looked up at me, and Theo's brows pulled together; Frances stared, her lips open as if she'd forgotten them, and said, "What did—" and stopped.

"Oh, *what*, already?"

"You look," Frances said slowly, "most remarkably like you."

"You look a lot like you, too. Won't any of you guys make allowances for an ugly hangover?"

"Stop," Sher said, "or I'll forget some of this. And I think I'm in deep shit if I do." She took a huge breath. "Okay. I had a dream last night. And I have to tell it to all of you, and all at once so I don't leave something important out."

Theo, Frances, and I exchanged glances, but we knew better than to say anything.

"I was down in the Deeps," Sher began, "just the way they are now, and it was early in the morning, with all the shadows on the streets. I can see dark clouds between the buildings, and little flickers of lightning between them. I'm just outside of Ego when this woman comes hurrying down Nicollet toward me. She's almost running. As she comes closer I can see she's frowning, as if she's worried. The wind picks up all of a sudden, and paper and leaves are flying around. She comes straight up to me and says, 'There's no time. Go straight home and give this to your friend. Hurry.' And she hands me a postcard.

"It looks like one of the ones we found yesterday, with the buildings lit up, and the Gilded West right out in the middle. But the building that Theo asked about, that you knew the name of, Frances—"

"The Multifoods Building."

"Right. That one wasn't there." She stopped.

We waited.

"Don't you *see*? It's now, but with the buildings lit up."

"Okay," said Theo. I thought so, too.

"Why us?" Frances asked.

"Because," said Sher, thoroughly exasperated, "she said 'your friend.' She didn't say *which* friend."

"And you thought maybe we'd be able to tell, when we heard it?"

"I guess if I did, I was wrong. Blast it root and bough."

Across town, from the northward road, we heard the sound of a rough-running engine. "Huh," said Sher. "Company."

"That's odd," I said.

"You just haven't noticed before. The neighbors stop by to swap favors or pass news along. That sounds like Skip Olsen's truck."

"Maybe the wind was up last night," I said. "It was a great night for dreaming."

"You had one last night?" Sher asked intently.

"A whole raft of them. Terrible ones. There was a lot of hurrying in mine, too."

Across the circle, two people were walking toward us. One of them was Josh; the other was a white-haired man ten years older, in a straw cowboy hat. He carried something in one hand. "Sparrow!" Josh called when he was in hollering distance. "Meet Skip Olsen!"

By this time they were at the porch rail. Olsen stuck out a veiny brown hand; I extended mine, took his, and shook it. It still required an effort. Olsen was smiling. "I'd never heard of you," he said, "but this was sent sort of in care of the town, so I figured if I drove by and asked, they'd all know you. Damnedest bunch for knowing everybody else's business." Olsen laughed, and Josh laughed. I reached out and took the package Olsen held out to me.

It was a scuffed white cardboard box, like a gift box, not quite as long as my forearm and a little less than half as thick. It was tied closed with brown twine. Printed on it in ballpoint pen was:

Sparrow
c/o the zoo
Apple Valley

There was, of course, no return address.

Josh took Olsen into the house for tea. I stared at the box. It didn't weigh much.

"Don't open it," Frances said roughly.

"Why not?"

"Sparrow, don't be an idiot. Don't open it."

But I'd already pulled the twine off. I lifted the lid.

Like all gift boxes, it had a piece of tissue paper in it. I folded that back. Inside was a thick tail of hair, silver-blond, tied off with a thin black velvet ribbon. One end of the tail was uneven; the other was straight and freshly cut. That end had been dipped about three inches deep in something that there was no use believing was anything but blood.

I didn't drop the box, because it weighed hardly anything. I moved very carefully to the top step and sat down, still with the box between my hands, still staring at the contents.

Because neither Theo nor Sher would know, and because Frances might not remember, I said, "Dana's." My voice seemed to come from the other side of town.

Frances reached down and almost, but not quite, touched the darkened end of the tail of hair. "And whose is that?"

"I'll never know, will I?" I said, looking up at her. "Unless I g⟨
and see?"

Her hand drew back sharply. "No. He can sit like a spider in th⟨
middle of his web and starve, or thrive, or whatever he wants t⟨
do. You aren't going, I'm not going, nobody's going."

I picked up the box lid and held it out to her. "Then he'll com⟨
here, won't he? Would that be better?"

"How did he know?" Theo asked.

"We weren't a secret," I said, my voice cracking. "Somebod⟨
takes the cucumbers to market, exchanges a little communit⟨
news, it gets overheard or passed on—he's probably known fo⟨
weeks."

"I'll go," said Frances, her mouth tight.

I turned my face up to her again. "But you weren't invited."

I watched her eyes change as she realized I was right. The bo⟨
bearing *my* name, the threat to *my* friend. "You can't," she said
as she'd said at Del Corazón. "You can't. She might not even b⟨
alive by now, for Christ's sake."

"Again, there's only one way to find out." I put the lid carefull⟨
on the box. I had dreamed of Dana. Of the Ten of Swords, mean⟨
for me. Maybe this was the meaning of all that hurrying.

"We need another damned plan," said Sherrea.

"I wish you wouldn't say 'we.' I don't need one to get in; thi⟨
time I know he's expecting me. He'll probably leave a light on."

"Wait, wait." Frances dropped cross-legged on the floor an⟨
jammed her fingers into her hair. "What do you want to accom⟨
plish?"

I thought about it, and for a wonder, they kept quiet and let m⟨
do it. "I want to get Dana out. If you're asking what I'd like fo⟨
my birthday, hell, I'd like to make it possible for Theo to go back
And I'd like to keep Tom Worecski from ever doing this again."

"Then you'll have to kill him," said Frances.

"Will I? You're the expert." I felt bad when I saw the color g⟨
out of her face. I hadn't meant it to hurt.

"Sparrow," Sher said suddenly in a terrible voice. "What di⟨
you dream?"

I tried to recite it as fairly, as clearly as she had hers, but she'⟨
had a more coherent original to work from. She closed her eye⟨
partway through, and drew her knees up and rested her forehea⟨
on them when I was done. "Oh," she said, muffled. "Oh, no. I'v⟨
blown it. We've run out of time. I'm sorry," she said, and raise⟨
her head. She was red-eyed. "You don't know *anything*, because

I started too late, and now it has to be done whether you're ready or not. It'll kill you. Oh, *what's the fucking date?*"

The rest of us sat awed by the whole terrible-sounding, unintelligible speech. But Josh's voice, from the front door, said, "June twenty-third. Saint John's Eve."

"Well, I'll be plucked and basted," I said. "It really is my birthday. What a coincidence."

"Don't you understand?" Sher cried. "There *are* no coincidences here. You were made by the *loa* for this. Everybody else has a soul that's part of the continuity. Yours is brand-new. You're a custom-made item for breaking up a jam in the energy flow, and *this* is the jam, and the time. Tomorrow is Midsummer. The celebration of the sun, the energy source. Of *course* it's supposed to be done then. And you're not ready!" She buried her face in her knees again.

Josh stepped out onto the porch and laid his hands on her shoulders. "Don't take it all on yourself."

"Who'm I supposed to share it with?" she groaned, but she raised her head and wiped her eyes. "You're right. That won't accomplish shit."

It had accomplished something, actually. "This is what that reading was about, wasn't it, Sher?" I said. "The one you did for me back in the City. *There's gonna be blood and fire, and the dead gonna dance in the streets.* Right?"

She nodded, slowly, probably because she didn't like the sound of my voice. I wouldn't have, either.

"I'm a quick study. Let's see if I have this right. You're saying that the *loa* animated a *cheval* to use, eventually, to bust up something . . ." Even as I said it, the answer occurred to me. "Albrecht's monopoly, right? And they turned me loose to grow up and get ready for this. Now here they are. And the message is: *We made you. You owe us.*"

Sher shook her head.

"Sure it is. This may kill me, you said. But they have a right to do that, because I belong to them. I was right, Sher, and you lied. I don't own anything. And nothing is free."

Frances and Theo were watching us. I don't know how much of it made sense to them. But I wasn't talking to them.

Sher found her voice at last. "We're reading the same book, but your translation sucks. Okay. If that's true, you don't have a choice. But you're going to find out that nobody is forcing you to do this. I'm trying to make you *want* to do it, because if you knew as much as you ought to know by now, you would. *Santos,* the only person who's leaning on you is Worecski. But your damned stupid life was a gift. And I meant it last night when I said that the only reasons to do a thing were out of love, or because you knew it needed doing." She stood up, her shoulders very straight. "If you decide to go to Ego, because of Dana or Worecski or whatever, let me know. I'll help. *Out of love, and because it needs doing.*"

She was down the steps and six paces away before I could move, or knew I wanted to. I vaulted the railing, landed in the flowerbed, and lunged for her arm.

"I take it back. I can't replace it with anything yet, but I take it back."

"Why?" she said, her face pinched.

"Because . . . because I don't know anything about your damned *loa*, and I can't say whether they would do what I just said they did. But I don't think that *you* would."

She stared at me, her chest rising and falling. "Not bad reasoning," she said finally, "for a dipshit. That reading I did for you—it had Death in it. D'you remember?"

"Yeah."

"It doesn't mean dying, in the tarot. It means change, transformation. I think that's what it means on the Gilded West, and I think that's why Theo's family took it over and closed it up."

"Symbolic barrier to change."

"Hell, no—an actual barrier. Hoodoo works on the symbolic level to do something to the actual. I think closing up the Gilded West was a hoodoo work. And I think my dream was a request that we undo it. That we light the building again."

Theo, behind me, said, "I could do that."

"What?"

"I could light up the Gilded West. The stuff's all up there. All I'd need is some initial input of power."

"No," I said. "You're not going back to the City."

"I'm not going back to Ego. I don't have to. Except I have to get some charge. I might have to steal juice from next door."

"Frances," I said slowly, "how do I stop Tom?"

"You know very well how you stop Tom. You lock him in his head, and you kill the head."

"What would happen if he were locked out?"

"What?"

"Would he live if he didn't have a body to ride?"

"Of course not. He's not a blasted poltergeist. But how do you propose to do it?"

"I don't know," I said. "I don't know how to get Theo his first shot of juice, either, without getting it from Ego. But I don't like that, and I don't like the thought of killing someone else's body to get Tom Worecski."

"He's probably already killed the host mind," Frances said, just as Sher said, "Of course not. It screws up the symbolism."

"It what?" Theo asked.

"If hoodoo works on the symbolic level," Sher said, impatient, "then what does it mean, symbolically, if you steal power from the thing you want to get rid of to fuel the process that gets rid of it? And you can't kill the body that Tom's in because you don't have any more right to it than he does. You wouldn't get rid of him, you'd become him."

"Probably literally," I said, "based on past experience."

"Present company is unexcepted, of course," Frances broke in pleasantly. "Save a little tar on that brush for me."

Sherrea, to my amazement, blushed.

"It doesn't do to forget that I'm one of them, too," Frances added. She looked, abstracted, at her hands; then she said, "I've smothered her. Like smothering an infant with a pillow, though it took longer. I've been four years in her body, and she was not, God help her, a strong little soul."

"You're right," Sher said. "I *had* forgotten. But you can have a great time hitting yourself over the head later. It's irrelevant to what we've got to do."

Frances slid one daunting eyebrow upward. "Where were we then? Sunk up to the undercarriage in a symbolic pothole. Unless one of you has a metaphysical shovel?"

She hated this, I could tell. She didn't have even the tolerance for hoodoo that I did. She hadn't spent her life in the streets surrounded by it, making deals with it, using its forms as polite social fictions, its person-principles as swear words. If Sher's carryings-on about energy had any truth in them, Frances's power was from the past that gave birth to her. She wouldn't think of asking favors from the *loa*.

"Oh," I said weakly. "Well, of course."

"I'm glad *you* think so," said Frances. "But you could be a little more help to the rest of us."

"What's the use of having a god in the machine if you don't holler for it to come out now and then? Sher, if the Hoodoo Engineers are more than a communal living experiment—are they?"

"Finish your sentence," she said harshly.

"Can they mess with the weather?"

"It's slow."

"And can you ask the *loa* for favors, and do they deliver?"

"*Santos*, Sparrow, what—"

"Will they, for instance, provide a well-timed, incredibly melodramatic wind storm in the right place, if asked nicely?"

Sher was still staring at me, but Theo whistled, and said, "Far out! You could maybe even make it work. Except—how much time do we have?"

"A whole day," Sher said dryly.

"Bummer. I couldn't mount a windmill up there that fast without a dozen people. And you'd be able to see it from Ego, anyway."

"So we need a really small windmill," I said.

Theo shook his head. "Then you lose vane area. You'd need a tornado—"

"If we're asking anyway, why not ask big? Let me think." I rubbed at my forehead with both hands. "If—*if* we got the wind . . . we'd want an eggbeater turbine, the kind with the spin around the vertical axis, and we'd have to mount it . . . Chango, we'd have to build it first, because I don't know where we'd find one."

"New Brighton, Hopkins, or Saint Louis Park," Frances said.

"What?" said Theo and I, more or less in unison.

"Honeywell was building Darrieus turbines for the Army, to power mountain listening posts. The eggbeaters, right? Carbon fiber and plastic, and small, to avoid flyover detection. I can tell you where the plants were. Better yet, I can show you."

I looked at Theo. "We've had an eggbeater turbine in the neighborhood all this time?"

"Somebody might have already hauled 'em away," Theo said reluctantly.

"If we'd known about 'em, *we* would have. Can you make it work?"

"If we can find one," he said. "If I can get it mounted. . . . Sher, does it mess with the symbolism if I borrow some stuff from the Underbridge?"

"Hurrah for Tom Swift and his chums," said Frances. "Now, what about Worecski?"

"I don't know. That's not my specialty." I turned to Sher. "What do you use to contain a spirit?"

Sher thought about it. "A *govi*. A soul jar. People who think

hey're under hoodoo attack have the *houngan* bottle their spirit
and keep it safe for 'em. I think it's bullshit."

"Well, you know my views on the subject."

She flushed. "Thanks."

"No, my views are that I haven't the faintest idea what's going
on, so I'll try whatever anyone else thinks will work."

"I don't know if it'll work. I don't know if we have time to
make one. Shit—"

I put out my hand and touched hers. "Oh, come on. Maybe I'll
be reincarnated."

"I hope not," she snapped, and stalked off across the town
circle.

"I'd better get going," said Theo. "I have to start gathering up
gear. Can you spare Frances to help me hunt down the turbine?"

"Wait a minute," I said, startled. "We haven't—"

"Yeah, we have. Sher's gone to do the research for her part. I
have to go do mine. I mean, it sounds like we're short on time."

"Theo, if . . . Look, something's going to go wrong. Maybe
everything. You stand to lose a lot if any of the pieces fall on you.
I think you should stay out of it."

"I've already lost a lot." His good-looking face had a set, hard
look that I hoped wasn't permanent. "I want a chance to get it
back."

"This may not be any chance at all."

"You want to do it instead?"

He had me. And he knew it; I saw it in his eyes. "This is not
The Magnificent Seven, Theo. This is real life."

"Is it? You make it sound like *A Fistful of Dollars*. Go ahead.
Tell me you're gonna clean up the town single-handed."

I had to drop my eyes from his. "I can't. I don't know how to
be in two places at once."

"So you need me to do the work in the Gilded West.
Somebody's got to, and I know how."

Of course; it needed doing. Theo, who didn't seem to have a
religion, had always lived by the principles of this one.

"Just . . . ye gods, Theo, just stay away from Ego."

"I'll try," he said. Then he clasped my hand quickly and headed
off in the direction Sher had gone.

Which left Frances. "What shall I do, boss?"

"Help Theo find a turbine, I guess."

"And then?"

"Come back here."

"No, I don't think so."

I didn't, either. "Why the hell do people have friends?" I burst out.

She didn't misunderstand the sentiment. "As I'm sure Theo would say, it's a bummer, man. But you can't keep us from our future any more than we can keep you from yours. Place your troops."

I sighed. "I'd feel better, actually, if you could stick to Theo. He'll need help with the installation, and if he gets in any trouble—" I shrugged. "He's not exactly John Wayne."

"Luckily for you, neither am I; John Wayne was an actor. All right, I'll be pit bull for Theo. Which means, I think, that this is good—pardon me, *au revoir*."

"You won't be back?"

"We'll send word if we find the turbine. But if we do, I think we'd best go straight into town with it."

She stood gravely in front of me for a moment; then, lightly, she put her arms around me and let go again. She looked to the sky and said fiercely, *"And how thou pleasest, God, dispose the day."*

Then she left.

It was Saint John's Eve; it was my birthday; it was, whether I was prepared or not, whether I liked it or not, the day of my introduction to the master of my head, my *maît-tête*, my patron in the system.

I was lying blindfolded in a room, not my own. I hadn't had anything to eat all day. I was wearing white. I knew that because I'd put it on myself, on Sherrea's instructions. I knew about electronics. I knew nothing about the soul. I could only follow instructions.

Outside, the drums were playing, and had been for an hour.

I heard footsteps, several, and felt hands on my shoulders and under my knees. Whose hands? Oh, little gods, big gods, whose hands were they, that I was giving myself into? I could pull away, I could yank off the blindfold, I could say no. Sherrea hadn't lied to me this morning: I could say no.

I jammed the syllable back down my throat until it was less than a whimper, only a tautness between my lungs and mouth. I was lifted up and carried outdoors, into the hot, windless air and the endless chirring of crickets. The drums wrapped around me like flannel.

My attendants set me on my bare feet suddenly, with a bang, and I staggered. I was on grass. I smelled candle wax and burning wood and people. I was held by my upper arms on both sides and

awn forward, and gripped and drawn forward again. I was being
ssed, I realized, down a double row of hands.

They weren't strangers. None of the people who participated, who
ved me from this point to the next one, would be strange to me.
sh would be here, whose hands had held my life and not dropped
and given it back to me for free. Kris might have just passed me
, dirt under her stubby nails, teeth flashing in a firelit grin. LeRoy,
o had picked me up broken and delivered me here, and Mags,
o had fed and clothed me. These were the people who had lifted
d carried me from the old condition of my mind to the current one.
ould trust them to move me safely one more time.

Even under the blindfold, the light had grown strong. I heard
: shook-canvas sound of the bonfire. A small pressure on my
oulders urged me to my knees, and finally full-length, face-
wn, on the grass. Above me, but not far, as if she might be
eeling, I heard Sherrea's voice. It was the voice of a kick-ass
uja. My friend Sherrea looked like a waif, and sounded like a
verness turned gun moll. She cried when I hurt. She was gone.
is was a *bruja*.

"Close the circle. Legba Attibon, let it close and sit by the door.
 we invite, let you admit. Legba of the stick, you are always
elcome."

On all sides of me, voices answered, in a language I didn't
ognize.

"Who knows this person?" Sher asked.

"I do," said a strong and ragged chorus of voices. What person?
e?

"Keep what you know in your heads, then, good and bad. Hold
there, fix it in your eye, see it clearly from all sides. Because
is person is bound for death, where the self is withered and
ashed away, where even names are cut like wheat and eaten.
is person will cross the river that never runs, and on the other
de, if you can't give back the soul that you remember, this
rson will be truly dead, and go forever nameless in the dark."

Hands again, that brought me to my feet. I was pouring sweat
 the heat of the fire and the hot night, dazed and weak from
anger and from fear. The hands pushed, and I stepped forward
to ice water. I was off balance; the other foot joined the first, and
ell to hands and knees into cold so intense it simply stopped my
erves. If I had known what I ought to do next, I'd forgotten it.
Then warmth on each arm—hands?—pulled me forward. My
ngers closed in grass; I dragged myself, my feet useless as
shaped granite, and fell, facedown once more, on the ground.

Sound broke out like full-scale war. Yelling, drums, all ▪
noises that can be made with the fingers and palms. It felt so go
to be warm. It felt wonderful to be lying limp as wet newspri
unable to rise, and to know that the condition was temporary.

In fact, I had to sit up almost at once, my legs under me, ▪
head erect. The hands insisted. The hands cosseted and comb
and smoothed, and where they passed, I was dry and free of a▪
lingering chill. My skin seemed to have been remade a
reinstalled. My heart gave a single, shattering bang and began
beat strong and evenly, and I wondered if it had been stopped a▪
I hadn't known. At last, the fingers traveling over my hair and fa
drew the blindfold away.

My eyes burned and watered with the light. The bonfire w
behind me; before me was the great central tree of the town circ
surrounded in ramparts of candles. There were candles, too, in t
hands of the people who formed the circle that enclosed me. The
were enough people that it might have been everyone in town. ▪
one stood close enough to me to have removed the blindfold t▪
lay abandoned on my knees. Nowhere in the circle was there a bo
of water large enough that I could have stepped or fallen in it.

"You are born into the light," said Sherrea, and I saw her
last. White cloth ran unbelted from her shoulders to her ankles a
left her arms bare. Her hair was uncovered and massed like
thundercloud around her head, around her stern face. The ste
waif's face, with an indented place at the corner of the mouth
if a smile was stored there, with a lift of the eyebrows that said
her voice, clear as words, "Is this wild, or what? Isn't this hot

"You who kept the soul and spirit plain, come and set it in
place again," she said to the circle at large.

There was a big black ceramic pot at her feet. One by on
people came from out of the circle to put things in it. It was
singular, startling procession.

Josh began it. He wore an African shirt so large it might ha
roofed the sheep pen; he pulled from somewhere in it a paperba
book. It was the copy of *A Tale of Two Cities* that I'd been readi▪
at his kitchen table. He dropped it into the pot with a look at r
so full of mingled things that I couldn't begin to sort them out

Kris followed him, with—it was. I almost laughed aloud. A le
of lettuce, and a wink.

Paulo came, with both hands cupped closed around somethin▪
He held them over the mouth of the pot and opened them, but t▪
contents went up, not down, and glowed for an instant, go▪
green, against the dark sky. A firefly. He looked dismayed for

moment, then caught my eye. For the first time I could remember, he seemed very much the opposite of solemn.

LeRoy dropped in a spare bit of wiring harness I'd made him for the truck. And said, "I have a memory that isn't mine."

"Give it," said Sher.

From a pocket, LeRoy pulled a video-8 format cassette. I couldn't read the label, but I knew it by the colors and their arrangement. It was achingly familiar. *Butch Cassidy and the Sundance Kid*, the best buddy movie ever made. Theo, Theo. Oh, *santos,* I was going to cry, and in front of everybody.

Then Sherrea leaned forward with something in her hand. A piece of paper . . . No, a card. The Page of Swords. Joan of Arc, with her boy's hair and man's armor, looking down to hell, up to heaven. The card flexed, fluttered, and was gone, into the mouth of the pot.

"You are reborn and remade," Sherrea said, "and only the strongest and most true went into the making. Now you have to wake. Stand up and receive the spirit of your head."

I had to do it by myself. I was weak; my legs trembled under me, and my hands shook. But I stood. Sherrea came to me—so small for such a kick-ass *bruja*—with a glass bowl full of something clear. Water? She dipped her finger in it, and the smell rose: alcohol. With her finger, she drew something on my forehead.

Someone must have fed the fire, because I was blinded with light. Empty whiteness rose around me from my feet to my shoulders to my chin (I saw Sherrea's face for a last moment, through the thickening haze) and finally closed over my head.

Me, the dog/rabbit, patient and silly in black on white. The dancing flutist with the two feathers, or antennae, or ears. And the woman with the halo of fire. There was no line of other pictographs, and I felt the lack of dimension more strongly than ever.

"If you want anything," said the flutist, "just whistle. You know how to whistle, don't you?"

"I've seen that one," I said.

"You ain't seen nothin', kid. Just whistle. You're gonna miss me when I'm gone, but accept no substitutes. Just put your lips together and blow. Don't let your deal go down."

"You know, that almost made sense."

"It will pretty soon. Or you're dead meat."

"Where are the others?" I asked it.

"That's all we have time for! Tune in next week!"

I might be dead next week, I tried to say, but it was too late. I opened my eyes on the ground, where I'd landed in what I recognized in hindsight as a boneless, uncontested faint. No one in the cluster of people around me seemed to think I ought to be embarrassed. I had a vague impression of some ritual things being done quickly; then Josh and Kris put a shoulder under each of my arms and half carried me back to the farmhouse. Not long after they'd stretched me on my bed, Sher poked her head, then the rest of her, in the door. She was back to the torn leggings. I felt much better.

"I don't know if that will help," she said. "But it was a damn good try. You take a mean initiation."

"Thank you. I think."

"There's usually pronouns in it, though."

It was a moment before I figured out what she meant. Then I laughed.

"We tried to fix your identity to your body, so that you'd be more likely to hold out against Tom. And we made this." She lifted up an oblong glass bead, the size of the end of my thumb. "It's not exactly a *govi*. It's sort of your doppelganger."

"Strong family resemblance," I agreed.

"Your psychic doppelganger, dipshit. The idea is that you buck Tom off, and this doesn't; you trap him in this and break it. It's a decoy body."

"Do you think it'll work?"

She sat down, hard, on the edge of the bed. "No. But I can't think of anything else to do. *Santos*, I wish we had more time."

"We're available for a limited time only," I said, three-fourths asleep.

"What?"

"Nothing."

"They've got the turbine; the note came from Theo an hour ago. He says he'll see you in Oz."

"Ha ha, Theo. Sher? In the . . . thing, this evening. There wasn't anything from Frances."

"She said, in—I think it was an Irish accent—that there was only one thing you'd ever given her that she could hold in her two hands, that she hadn't eaten. And that the one thing would be perfect for the pot, but it was also the first thing you'd given her, and she thought the sentiment would be more use to her than the identification would be to you."

I laughed again. "That's very Frances-like of her. Sher, why does China Black have silver eyebrows?"

"She got in trouble once, she says, because her eyebrows moved. She was afraid it would happen again."

"Silly," I said, and fell asleep.

0.1: Who plans revenge must dig two graves

he wind had come up, and swept a domed lid of overcast across
e night as far as I could see. Which, given the towers in the way,
asn't far; but I'd seen it over the road into the City, too. In the
ight Fair, vendors would be keeping an eye on the sky, a hand
n their shutters and awning cranks. If the wind didn't blow the
ouds away, there would be rain. Which was no guarantee that
ere would be a whirlwind.

LeRoy had driven me to the edge of the Deeps. I'd spent the
de looking out the passenger's side window of the truck, to keep
om looking at him. Even so, I could tell that he was glancing
ver every few minutes, when the crumbling pavement gave him
ave. Whatever he wanted—to ask if he could come along, to ask
e to give it up, to cuss me out for undoing his work in getting me
ut of the City in the first place—I wasn't strong enough to stand
gainst it. So I'd kept my face to the glass and the growing
arkness, and hoped that the cloud cover meant that the Engi-
eers, or random luck, were giving us what we needed.

Josh had wanted to come, too. I'd talked him out of that, at
:ast. I didn't want anyone else there if Tom Worecski managed to
acktrack along my trail. LeRoy was risk enough. I wondered if
eRoy realized that I hadn't made any provisions for getting out
f the City. Something could happen that would leave me alive
nd in danger if I stayed. But how could I say when and where I'd
eet him, or what to do if I didn't? Besides, alive and still in
anger was the least likely possibility.

I had a clean shirt, Large Bob's nice trousers, the glass bead on
chain around my neck, and not much else. Nothing that might
erve as a weapon. I had maybe been rash there. But I didn't know
nything about weapons, and I didn't want to hurt myself. Or have

someone take the gun or knife or whatever away and use it to hu
me. That, at the moment, seemed more pressing than symbolisr

It wasn't déjà vu; I *had* been here before, in the street, looki
up at Ego. But the appropriate haunted-house sky was missing th
time behind the building's halo of little lights. And Frances was
with me. She was in the Gilded West, with Theo, waiting for
brisk Jehovan miracle. For Oya Iansa, Lightning Woman, patro
of revolution and change, whose dancing brings the wind.
wondered if she was the pictograph who sounded like Frances.
hoped Theo hadn't taken too much gear from the Underbridge.
an electrical storm came with the tornado, the club would be fu
of dancers under the long windows. Oh, gods. I wanted to be c
the sound balcony. I wanted to see Robby, and hear Spangler sa
"fuck" one more time. I wanted it so badly I hurt.

Enough. I shook myself and went to Ego's front door.

I could see the camera, watching from its bracket on the ceilin;
and past it, the guard desk. I looked into the camera's eye ar
nodded, schooling my face to something like confident blanknes:

The guard was one I didn't know, young, brown-haired, with
sunburnt nose. He looked up when I stopped in front of the des!

"They know I'm coming," I said.

"Can I have your name, please, to—"

"They don't need my name. They just saw my face on th
monitor upstairs." I tilted my head toward the camera.

"I have to call to authorize—"

"Please do."

He went into the little room with the window in the door, an
I followed silently after. When I came in, he was on the intercor
saying, ". . . didn't give a name, sir." I reached gently aroun
his shoulder and took the desk mike away from him.

"Hello, Tom," I said. It would come through clearly; I kne·
how to talk into a microphone. "I thought I was invited."

There was a beat of silence. Then the drawling voice, sayin;
"Well, God damn if you aren't. Come on up. You know the way.

The guard stepped back, watching me. He seemed skittish.
handed him the microphone and headed for the elevator.

I didn't know what I was going to do. We'd discovered, whe
we put our heads together, that the only thing we could plan wa
the lighting of Ego. Helping Dana, thwarting—or eve
avoiding—Tom, were too full of variables. I could only gc
because I had to go, and stay alert, and do the next thing, whateve
it was. Everything depended on what happened next, and wha

happened after that, and after that, and I had no idea what any of those would be. I was waiting, almost literally, for a sign. Improvisation wasn't what I was good at. What *was* I good at? What was I made to do?

Theo would light the Gilded West, if he could, at the request of Sherrea's gods. What was I here for? To bring Dana out. To stop Tom Worecski. I doubted I could manage either one. I was simply moving in the direction that seemed right, and hoping that at the appropriate moment, something would tell me I'd arrived.

"This isn't just the power monopoly," Sherrea had said before I climbed into the truck. "That's just a symptom. D'you understand?" It had meant a lot to her, I could tell: her hands were closed hard on my shoulders, and her face was uncomfortably close to mine. She wouldn't have forgotten if it wasn't important. Once, I would have smiled and told her yes, I understood, sure. This afternoon, I'd stood quiet under her hands and finally shook my head. She'd remembered then, let go and stepped back. But I'd seen the fear in her face.

Oh, spirits, if Frances wasn't John Wayne, *I* certainly wasn't. Why hadn't I just stood at the front door and cut my throat?

The elevator door opened on darkness. The elevator itself was still lit, so the power hadn't gone off. I stepped out, holding the door open. It pinged furiously; I jumped and lost my grip. The door closed and left me in a perfect absence of light. I wish I'd thought to bring a candle. But how could I have expected that here, where electricity ran like water, there wouldn't be enough light to see by?

I could find the office by touch; there weren't that many doors. But I could probably find other things, too, if I was meant to. I took two steps, my fingers trailing along the wall. "Tom," I said on a whim, "this is stupid. I can turn around and leave."

In the ceiling, a speaker crackled. I'd been right. He'd seen too many movies. "That elevator ain't comin' back."

"I know where the fire stairs are."

"Sure, you do. But I'm awful sorry about the lights on those stairs. Seem to be on the blink. You sure you want to go down 'em in the dark, nice and slow?"

That might mean that he had put something in the stairwell. Or it might only mean that, once I headed for it, he would.

"And speakin' of fire, what did you think of the one I lit for you last time? Huh?" He laughed, a high, scratching giggle overhead. *How about a little fire, Scarecrow*, I thought, but didn't say. *The horse you rode in on, and your little dog, too, Worecski*.

I found a light switch under my fingers and flipped it, but nothing happened. Shut off at the breaker box, probably located in Ego's heels; and I was in her hair. Either he'd just ordered it done, or the paging system was on a separate circuit.

I reached the door that opened on Albrecht's office. Would Tom be in it? Or Albrecht, or both? If the lamp was on, I'd be blind. I opened the door a finger width at a time.

The office was dark. And unnaturally silent—of course. With the power off, any fans or air-conditioning exclusive to this floor would go off, too. From the perfect lack of noise, I figured Albrecht's floor must have had its own independent everything. If Tom was in the room, I ought to be able to hear his breathing, if I could only keep my own quiet.

I bumped lightly into the desk, and let my hands drift in the area where the lamp ought to be. It was there. I tried the switch because it had to be tried, but nothing happened. I worked my way around the desk, stopping to listen every two or three steps, holding my breath until the pulse in my head deafened me. In time, I made it to the door in the paneling that led to the big, bright room that had been the stage for Tom's last drama.

It was as dark as the office. And the cool, dry air had been replaced with suffocating heat and damp. No venting, no air-conditioning. I could feel sweat springing to my skin already, like condensation on a glass. I took a step into the void, another—

And couldn't quite stifle the sound I made when something brushed against my face. I staggered backward. Nothing happened. I reached out and found something between my fingers: plastic—long ribbons of it—hanging from the ceiling like loose-curled vines.

What I had to stifle then was a stream of epithets. It was videotape. Half-inch videotape pulled off its reels and draped like party streamers as far as I could reach.

Light fluttered through the room, and I thought at first it was a reflection from somewhere. But in the afterimage I realized what I'd seen. The blinds had been drawn back from the wall of window glass, and the first pale flickering of lightning had passed through. Lightning. What about wind? That wasn't my part of the show. I couldn't spare either hope or fear for the weather now.

But it had given me that moment's illumination. In it, I'd seen thickets of tape, veiling the room from one side to the other. Albrecht's collection, it must be, everything I'd found for him, everything he'd commissioned from anywhere else, all originals,

cause he'd insisted on that. I closed both fists on handfuls of
pe and began, methodically, to pull it down.

The furniture was gone. When I reached the place where the
vo couches had been, I found only empty floor. A stab of
ghtning showed me the marks in the deep carpet left by the
ouches' feet, and by the Chinese table. *He might not be here at
'l*, I thought suddenly, alarmed. A cluster of tape slipped through
iy fingers to the floor. He might have left this here for me, and
: sitting somewhere below, imagining the scene, laughing. If so,
: could have left something else as well, something lethal.

No, it felt wrong. Tom Worecski had a wonderful imagination;
had the proof of it right here. But I didn't think he'd want to miss
ie effect he'd caused, even if he had to limit himself to judging
y the noises I made. I gathered up an armful of tape and yanked.

Bleaching white light shot into the room from the window and
'as gone, with the crash of mangled air on its heels. I staggered
nd fell, and jammed my knuckles into my teeth to stop sound and
ir.

Dana was hanging from the ceiling. The afterimage was printed
n my vision wherever I turned: head down, naked, her bare arms
angling among the twists of videotape, the ragged remains of her
lond hair sticking out around her face, her mouth dark with dried
lood, her eyes wide and empty. Her throat had been cut.

There was another flash, and I didn't have warning enough to
ook away, so I saw her again. I would have to see her to get past
er. I ought to get her down from there; but oh, gods, gods, I
ouldn't do it. What did you burn candles to Erzulie for, Dana? To
ave you from someone like Tom Worecski? Had she been alive
esterday, when I held her hair in a box? I couldn't tell, not from
ne lightning flash to the next. A broken mannequin, a ruined
ashion doll—but all the while she'd been alive, she had been real,
nd I hadn't noticed. Now it was too late.

The need for stealth, it seemed to me, was gone. "Where are
ou, Tom?" I said aloud.

"This way," he answered from behind a screen of tape, in the
ame tone I used: flat, stripped of frivolity or even character. It
'as his live voice, not another ceiling speaker. I moved cautiously
orward through the plastic. It stuck to my skin where it brushed,
o the glaze of sweat there. I could feel my shirt clinging wet to my
ack, the trousers catching damply at my thighs and calves.

"Why did you send for me, Tom?"

"Mick told me your little story. He said you couldn't remember
eing a Horseman, but I figured you for a liar." He was moving;

his arc was taking him toward the right, away from the window, putting me between him and them. Did he think I had a gun?

"It's true. I don't. I never was a Horseman."

"Oh, bullshit. The fuckin' *chevaux* were just meatbags. Some body'd have to operate 'em. So, are you Mitchell, that little as wipe? He thought he was Mister C. I. fuckin' A. He'd love to tr to take me out."

"I told you what I am." There was no reason not to talk; th rustling of the videotape would have told him where I was. He invited me up. He thought I was a Horseman. He wanted anothe head fight, wanted to prove to another of his kind that he was th master.

"Or Scoville, maybe? Christ, what a pussy. And Chichena hated my guts—are you Chichenas?"

On the other hand, if I'd run out of things to say, there was n reason to go on talking. When he was done playing with me, he' strike. And then I'd see if my doppelganger worked.

Theo was in the Gilded West, right outside that window. If h got lucky and a toy cyclone danced on the vanes of his turbine, it didn't tear off the top of the building and crush him in th rubble, he would light up the night. It seemed terribly silly an distant. Why had we wanted to do it? What good was it going t be to anyone? I just hoped he could get away safe. Frances woul help. I skirted another clump of tape.

"Sparrow, look out," someone said, low and quick. In front o me I saw a movement, a lighter spot in the dark like a face. ducked right. There was a spit of flame and a dry, deafenin crack, and I felt something tear a hole through the flesh of my le shoulder. My scream and the gunshot reverberated together in th room and were gone.

I'd fallen to one knee; I stayed there, bent over and gasping. clutched at my shoulder, but my hand wasn't big enough to clos over both the entrance and the exit wounds. Blood ran down m right wrist into my sleeve. So much for the clean shirt. Apologie to its owner when—no, it didn't look as if I'd have the chance t make those. It had never occurred to me that *he* would have a gun that he would choose to fight with something other than his head I was an idiot. I was not good at this.

Lightning came and went in a quick, rhythmless dance. Th room was pockmarked, in the flashes, with the image of the rai that patted against the window glass. The couches had bee moved to this end of the room, and Mick Skinner occupied one o them. His had been the warning voice. He sat very straight, hi hands pressed together between his tight-closed knees, his hair tangled and filthy, his pretty stolen face hollowed out and blank. Tom stood in front of him, a pistol in his hands aimed professionally at me. Behind him was the other door into the room, where Cassidy had died.

"Surprise," Tom said. Then he moved closer, and I heard the frown in his voice. "God damn—you're *not* Frances. Shit, I didn't figure she'd miss a chance like this."

I sucked air in, quivering, uneven. It hurt, it hurt, and my stomach cramped with fear. I pressed my lips against my upraised knee to hold back whimpering and bile. Then I turned my head just enough to say, "No . . . I'm me. You didn't . . . you didn't send for her."

"Hell, no. I thought this way I'd get Frances's head and the *cheval* body. I always did like one-of-a-kind shit. But Franny was supposed to try to sneak in on you. That'd make you a Trojan horse, huh? That's just the kind of joke she always liked. She turn yellow, maybe?"

"Lost her . . . sense of humor."

He was too dangerous not to watch. My breath stumbling loudly through my open mouth, I lifted my head from my knee and my gaze from the floor. Tom's face was bright with sweat in the lightning flicker. "Well, one out of two ain't bad."

I tried to send a look of appeal to Mick, but he couldn't see it for the backlighting, or he didn't care. It was time to say something brave and witty, and do something creative. Nothing occurred to me. It seemed I hadn't seen enough movies after all.

But Frances had. The door banged open under her kick, showering splinters from the frame. She'd gotten a handgun from somewhere, and was taking aim while the door was still swinging.

Tom dropped to the floor like a felled tree and fired three shots, all of which hit Frances somewhere between the shoulders and the knees. She sagged back and slid down the door frame. I could hear the drag of air into her lungs.

"Stupid bitch," Tom muttered. He scrabbled across the floor and kicked her pistol out of her reach, farther into the room. "Did you think I'd believe this shit? I knew you had to show up."

It was more than I had known. I wanted to say so, but my tongue was frozen.

"So go for it, Franny," Tom went on. He got to his feet, grinning. "That horse is gonna die. Make the jump, girl, just like you wanted me to. Only this time I've got the gun. Ain't nobody

to ride but your pals, and if you ride 'em, I'll kill 'em. Unless you
want to try to take me again."

"You said you'd let her go," Mick spoke from the couch. He
sounded as if he'd been shot, too, as if he had only one lung
working. "You said you'd showed her, and now you wouldn't
have to kill her."

"And I wouldn't have had to, you little prick, except here she
is. She needed showing again. What was I supposed to do? Let her
kill me instead?"

"You promised me—if she got away from you, you'd let her
go. You promised." Mick rose, shakily. What had happened to
him in the last weeks? What had Tom done to him? Whatever it
was, why hadn't it given him a sensible distrust of promises from
Tom Worecski?

Frances hadn't moved, but I saw her eyes open and squint in the
blaze of lightning. Rain was projected on her face, the image of it
running down the glass. I wondered if I could get to her discarded
pistol unnoticed.

Tom faced Mick, his whole face alive with anger. Then it fell.
"You're right. I broke my promise." Tom dropped to his knees on
the carpet and held the pistol out to Mick. "Kill me. Kill me,
goddammit. If you can bring yourself to do it, then I must deserve
to die."

Mick took the pistol. The big window rattled with the thunder.
"Oh, I can do it," Mick said in a trembling voice.

I thought, *No*.

Then Tom sagged to the floor and Mick smiled. "Jesus, what a
sucker," he drawled, and put the barrel in his mouth.

"No!" Frances screamed, but it was drowned by the double
crack of thunder, inside and out.

Tom stood up and shook himself. "Shit," he said. "Shouldn't've
done that. There was still plenty of fun in him."

He'd been weak, that was all. Mick had cared for Frances; he'd
even cared, I realized, for me. But he'd been too weak to stand
against a thing like Worecski. And I'd been too weak to save him.

Frances's head dropped back against the door frame, and I
heard a little despairing noise from her. Her eyes were tight shut.
Mick had slid in a heap to the carpet, smearing the white couch on
the way. The pistol lay on the floor between his body and his arm.

"One down," said Tom. "Come on, girl. Jump for it."

Slowly, Frances shook her head.

The bead of glass at my throat was cool and hard. My head was
swimming with heat and loss of blood, and my legs were shaking

under me. But neither gun was in Tom's reach. So I took a last shuddering breath and flung myself untidily at him.

His arm came up across the side of my face like a log. There was no reason why someone who could do what he did should be so strong. He hoisted me up in two handfuls of shirtfront and shook me. I hit him as hard as I could in the stomach with my right fist, but the angle was bad, I was weak, and it wasn't hard enough. He grunted and bared his clenched teeth, and pushed me backward into the wall. I sobbed when my left shoulder hit.

He wasn't going to fight with his head. If he didn't, I hadn't a chance against him. But the alternative to this pointless battering was to sit quietly and wait for him to kill me. That seemed wasteful.

I staggered upright and went for his throat with both hands. Tom grabbed my wrists' and forced me back to the wall again, pinned me there. His eyes, so close to mine, suddenly widened and cut sideways, toward the door.

"Jesus Christ, Frances, what's holding you back? I thought for sure— But if you were ridin' this, it would fight better. What does it take, Franny?"

I wondered if she'd heard that. If he was right, she and I would both be better off if she'd ditch her principles and ride.

I could see the pores in his face in the lightning flashes; I could smell the sharp reek of his sweat and feel the moist heat of him. I twisted, felt torn things in my shoulder pull farther apart, and bit off a cry.

"Now I remember," he said, his voice mild and cheerful. "You don't like to be touched." And he leaned forward and forced his mouth down hard on mine.

My teeth were already clenched; it was too late to clamp my lips between them. The hierarchy, from weakest muscles to strongest, is: lips, tongue, jaws. At least he couldn't get past my teeth. He pulled his head back and laughed softly; his breath fanned my cheek, as warm and damp as the air. "Your head is sayin' no, but—hell, your body's sayin' no, too. Guess I'll have to change your mind."

Somewhere in my brain, I probably had the equivalent of jaw muscles, that I could have closed and kept closed. I didn't know where they were. Tom Worecski had ridden me once before; but the circumstances had been such that I didn't remember what it had been like. I expected something like the blinding shock of Frances's assault, a forced mental entry like a mortar shell. I didn't expect Mick's easy falling in and out, like blinking, like a switch toggled. All my expectations were worthless.

Tom was a gelid, poisonous presence inserting itself through the soft places in my personality, trickling in like dirty water through a crack. He was a flavor of decay in the back of my throat, a rotting-vegetable slickness under my fingers, the rustling sound of beetles scurrying. And it was all done slowly, slowly, so that I had time to understand what was happening to me. So I knew exactly what sort of tenant would occupy the rooms of my body once I was forced out.

I struggled. I did it physically, flat against the wall, unable to so much as get a knee up between us; and mentally with even less effect.

Suddenly I was alone again. Tom still pinned me in place, but he'd jerked back a little. He was glaring. "What the fuck you got on you?" he said. "What is it?"

He let go of my left wrist. I went for his face with my freed hand, but before I reached him he slammed his right shoulder into my damaged one. The sensation was, for several seconds, literally blinding. My knees buckled, but Tom's grip kept me from falling.

The chain must have showed a little inside my shirt collar. He hooked a finger in it and flipped it to the outside. The glass bead glittered between us in the crazy light, and he caught it. As soon as he did he knew it was important, by the way I behaved.

It was like Beano all over again: slapping me against the wall, twining fingers through the cord—no, chain—around my neck. But this couldn't be Beano's. No miasma of incense. Gunpowder stink, and the smell of blood, which at Beano's had come later. Oh, *santos*, Sparrow, keep your *mind* on it, don't pass out now. I blinked, trying to clear the smudginess from everything.

"Voodoo shit," Tom spat out. He fingered the glass bead. "Was this supposed to fool me? Figured you were gonna stick a few pins in me? *Shit*." He yanked, and the chain cut into the back of my neck and broke. The bead slid off and dropped to the floor. He moved his foot, moved it back, and I saw the scattering of bright dust in the mottled light through the windows. Something ran from the corner of my eye to my jaw. It might have been sweat.

"All right, now," he breathed. "Let's party." And he began again.

Water action. Filthy liquid filling me up slowly, dissolving me, toxins rushing into my mouth, my nostrils, my ears, filming my eyes, devouring the connections between me and my senses. He'd taken control of my gag reflex already, or I would have obeyed it.

Only twenty-four hours before, my friends had acted out the gathering-together of a tangle of energy, the naming of it: *Sparrow*. Now Tom O'Bedlam consumed it, strained its juices between his teeth, picked the meat out of it with delicate, epicurean delight. Mick and Frances had told me that the host personality could be starved or smothered gradually, or killed outright. They didn't tell me it could be eaten.

I couldn't feel anything. I could still hear: thunder, rain driving against the window, the two of us panting in unison. I could see; he hadn't taken the optic nerves yet, or the muscles that moved my eyes. Over Tom's shoulder I had a view of Frances, her head turned against the door frame, her face drawn in loosely with pain. But only loosely, as if it was a leftover expression, as if what had caused it was gone or nearly so.

Maybe she would find that white, flat place. Once Tom was done with my battered body, maybe I would, too.

There was a roaring in my ears, growing steadily. It was in the room, too; the window glass was rattling.

Then the building cracked in half. I heard it.

There was light like white air burning, like a welder's arc against the eye, like the light in the old military films of nuclear tests. Tom/I screamed; and did it again when the light didn't wink out. It was his scream in my throat, but I felt it. Somewhere along the tunnel I was disappearing down, there was a remote control for that much of me, if I could just find a button and push. . . . No, it was *lips*. *Just put your lips together*. . . .

Silly. Say goodbye. The sound was one I'd heard in movies, when a train thundered down upon the camera like doom.

"*Put your lips* . . . Nothing to lose.

. . . *and blow*.

I had lost sight and hearing. But white fire filled the bottom of my blindness, lapped around my ankles, surged up to my knees, my hips, my rib cage, sliced between Tom's fingers and my neck, and closed over my head. I thought I heard a shriek, but sound wouldn't have carried in that medium.

I didn't know if it was a flat world; there was nothing in it. It was white. It wasn't warm or cold, welcoming or repellent, sweet or cruel. It was not the place I had come to before. There was nothing in it. No helpful pictographs, no street signs. The natives knew their way around.

Bait, I thought furiously, in a state of nonawareness. *You wanted me for bait*.

It worked. There were no words formed. The answer was just a part of the void that meant something.

Your timing sucked!

My timing was perfect. The lightning froze him in the midst of possessing you, my whirlwind lit the building and destroyed the barriers that kept me out of Ego, my possession of you consumed him. There was no other possible order.

What did you do to Worecski?

Nothing. I rode you. He was no business of mine, except that you were concerned with him. It was his bad luck that I arrived when I did, and that it's true what they say, that "Great gods cannot ride little horses."

Tom . . . wasn't your business?

You know my business. If you don't remember, ask my little sister. Your friend the witch.

You never said you couldn't get into Ego.

There is no technical manual for the spirit world. You will never know everything.

Why me? Why was it ever me?

Your left foot is in the past. Your right foot is in the present. You hold steel in your left hand, and flint in your right. You are the dancer between the old world and the new, because I made you to be so.

Fuck you! I deny you!

Do you deny your hands and feet?

Silence, in that volumeless space that had never admitted sound.

Let me go back, I said. *Frances is dying.*

I'm not keeping you here. Go.

I opened my eyes on a room bathed in watery golden light. The Gilded West was still gilded. The wind still roared outside. I was lying on my back. Tom lay three feet away in a half curl, one hand flung out loosely on the carpet, his eyes open and motionless.

"Anybody home?" I croaked. "Are you dead?" There was no response from whatever was left of Tom Worecski.

I crawled to the door, and Frances. Her breath still fluttered in and out of her parted lips, quick and shallow. Her eyes opened.

"Oh, *why* did I do that?" she whispered.

"Shut up, Frances."

"Don't be silly; you wouldn't be able to tell who I was. He didn't used to be a very good shot, you see. The nerve of the bastard, practicing up. It's not fair."

"Frances, *please*—"

There was a sound, from on the floor—from the inert body of Tom Worecski. I should have known; it was in all the horror movies. One last resuscitation. But in this movie, the heroes weren't going to be able to kill the monster one more time.

The sandy head lifted from the floor and turned its frantic ice-pale eyes on me, and its mouth said, "Who are you? What's . . . where am I?"

"Good grief," Frances sighed. She sounded weakly amused. "He didn't kill the host."

"Are you sure? I mean, that he's not—"

"We can . . . could always spot each other. He's not there."

I looked back into those nearly colorless eyes and tried to see them as the eyes of a stranger. For a moment I couldn't think what to say to him. Then I called on my memories of the same experience. "You're safe. Nothing's going to happen to you. I'll help you in a minute, but please—just wait, okay?"

I knew it wasn't going to work. He stared at me, and at Frances who had most of her blood, it seemed, on the outside of her.

"Don't—" I began, but of course he turned his head and saw Mick, too. He would now have hysterics, and there wasn't time for them.

Perhaps Tom had let him surface to scenes like this before. He didn't have hysterics. He folded back up on the carpet with his hands over his face, in a pitiful attitude of submission and hopelessness. Eventually, I think, he passed out; I didn't see him stir.

I turned back to Frances. "Now, shut up and mount up."

"What?"

"Ride, damn you. I'm not half as near to dying as you are. Mount up and we'll both get out."

She smiled, almost. "And then what? Shall I steal another body once we're out? Or just stay in yours forever?"

"What's wrong with Mick's solution: taking someone who's getting out of the living racket anyway?"

"Why should it be better to steal people's deaths than their lives? It's a rite of passage. How do you know that Mick's suicides weren't harmed by what he did?" She winced, and shifted slightly against the molding.

I wanted to fetch a couch cushion to prop her up, but I was afraid she'd die while I was away doing it. I looked around for anything else I could use, and saw her near hand, palm down, on the carpet. Showing between her fingers was a bit of black leather thong strung with a black onyx bead.

"Not strictly sentimental, after all," she said. "I had to be able to find you. You can have it back now, if you want. Oh, Christ, don't cry."

I swallowed, with difficulty, and it didn't help. "Frances, please. Ride me out of here. If you don't . . ."

"You'll kill me?" she whispered, grinning.

"Probably," said a harsh voice above me, "by talking you to death. Get out of the light, you idiot."

I ducked and rolled sideways, expecting a blow that never came. Then I recognized the broad shape leaning over me, and the voice. It was Josh. His face was set like concrete. LeRoy was right behind him, hauling gear, his eyes huge.

"It's too late, Josh," Frances said.

"I love a challenge." He stuck a needle in her arm.

"Oh, no fair, no fair," she whispered, shaking her head. Her eyes closed.

I knelt frozen on the carpet and stared. "Is she . . ."

"She's passed out. Now shut up."

"Josh—what are you doing in here? It's not safe—"

He jerked his head toward the window. "The building's lit up."

"Are you *crazy*? The place is full of—"

"LeRoy, plug up the hole in this and give it a sedative."

I would have felt it less if he'd slapped me. He knew it suddenly; he was very still. "I'm sorry. I—" He shook his head and turned back to Frances.

"Not a sedative," I said. "LeRoy, get that guy out of here." I nodded at the sandy-haired stranger who'd been Tom Worecski. "He's alive. Give him the sedative. He'll go nuts if he wakes up. Tom was riding him."

"My," said Josh, his back to me, his gloved hands full of tools, "there's one alive. Was that an oversight?"

"I didn't—" Then I realized that Josh hadn't suggested it was *my* oversight. I wondered who he blamed.

During the exchange, LeRoy had torn the sleeve off my shirt and examined my bullet hole. "I'm sorry," he said. "I have to take the shirt off."

It was good of him to remember. "Go ahead."

He did it with a minimum of fuss or contact, and dressed the wound the same way. His hands were shaking, and cold, but deft nonetheless. He produced a hypodermic from apparently thin air—I wondered if I'd blacked out for a few seconds—and I shook my head.

"No, LeRoy, I'm serious." I hadn't finished something . . .

"I know," he said, just loud enough for me to hear. "It's not a sedative." He wielded the needle like an expert, which I suppose he was. "It'll take a minute. But don't do anything stupid, okay?"

I didn't think I could. Whatever message the needle delivered, my body was saying, *Let go*.

For a few minutes, I might have. Then I was standing, supporting myself against the window frame. At last, I saw the Gilded West. It was the skull side, a little irregular where a few of the floods had failed to light. It *was* gilded, the fantasy palace of the postcards, the monument of Frances's childhood and the hoodoo work of Sherrea's gods all at once. A bridge between the old world and the new.

A bridge between the earth and sky. Hanging twisting and quivering from the clouds above, its pointed foot dancing delicately just out of sight on the other side of the building, was a howling cone of wind. Oya danced before my eyes, and I understood, looking at her, why change, in the cards, was called Death.

Josh and LeRoy were at work, supplementing the light with a pair of battery lamps. I couldn't see Frances. I moved, slowly, toward the office door, the one I'd come in through.

Wet hands closed around my face and lifted it, and Theo said, "Where is he?"

It *was* Theo. That was why I'd needed to keep going: to find Theo. His thick brown hair was streaked with rain and curling on his face and neck, his glasses were spattered with droplets, and he smelled strongly of burning cable insulation. I sighed and shut my eyes.

Theo shook me, very hard, and said, "Sparrow, where is he?" His voice was raw.

I opened my eyes again. Theo's face was laced through with horror, an expression so different from any I'd seen him wear that it almost made a stranger of him. I turned to find the cause of it, back the way I had come.

It was there. It must have been the same thing that had hardened Josh's features and words, and made LeRoy's hands shake. I had known it was there, and with unnatural camera angles and restricted depth of field kept myself from having to see it all.

The room was washed in the pale golden light that Theo had turned on, cast by the Gilded West: Death, the patron of change, the destroyer of the established order, looked in the window. What had been terrible in the dark was unbearable now. There had been change enough in that room to wake me up screaming for the rest of my life.

Theo shook me again, and I dragged my eyes away from Dana, from Mick, from the huddle of people who were trying to keep Frances from following the same route. "Sparrow!" Theo said. *"Where's my dad?"*

"I don't know. He wasn't here when . . ."

LeRoy's booster shot kicked in at last, and I could think again. It was a bad time for it. *You know my business*, she had said. I did. The Hoodoo Engineers had called her, Mr. Lyle and China Black and all the people who knew it was time and past time for change had called her, to break the stagnant hold of Ego on the City. The hold of A. A. Albrecht. *She*, in turn, had called me.

Not Legba the gatekeeper, male and female, to whom I was supposed to belong; it was Oya Iansa who'd come in with the light from the Gilded West, the goddess who brought revolution and the falling of towers. Oh, of course I was hers, not Legba's. Out of all the things in that bunker, she'd preserved and awakened the one with the technical knowledge she wanted. I wasn't a practical joke; I was the whirlwind.

And my friend's father had been standing in the path of it.

10.2: Mister Death and the redheaded woman

"I have to find him." Theo turned back to the office door.

"You said once . . . that you didn't like him."

Theo looked over his shoulder at me. The answer was in his face: that if I had been born instead of grown, I wouldn't have said that.

I followed him out into the dark hallway. I couldn't do anything about Frances. But I would not lose Theo.

"Where are we going?" I whispered.

"He has a bedroom one floor down."

If this had been a movie, he would have said, "*We're* not going anywhere." I was glad it wasn't. "Did—do you live here?"

"Not for years. I moved out a little after my mom died." Tom had been honest about the illumination in the stairwell. Theo pulled a candle out of a jacket pocket and lit it, and we started down in that narrow field of jittery light. "I visited, though. Mostly to fight with him. And I always thought I hated that, but I kept coming back. I guess it was better than not seeing him."

The candlelight offered emotional armor that even darkness couldn't have provided. "Do you . . . do you love him?" I said.

"He's my father."

"Does that mean you love him?"

"It means I can't tell," said Theo.

The power was working on the floor below, and the stairwell door was unlocked. Theo opened it a crack and light blasted out, followed by a rush of slightly cooler air. He blew out the candle. When our eyes had adjusted, we stepped into the hall.

"Theo!" I whispered suddenly. It sounded like escaping steam in the silence. "Was there a guard on the front door?"

"No."

"Didn't you wonder why not?"

"I *still* wonder why not, man. Maybe he went to check out the tornado. You want to stand here 'til he shows up?"

"I should have brought a gun from upstairs," I muttered "There's got to be a guard someplace."

Theo shrugged. "Neither of us knows from guns."

"You can't tell that from looking at us."

He gave me an encompassing stare. "Right now you wouldn' scare me if you had a cannon."

He was right, of course. I was suddenly aware of myself ir every undignified detail: smeared with blood, soaked with sweat blinkered with tangles of hair. And half-dressed besides. LeRoy had used a lot more bandage than he'd had to, but I felt the skir on my shoulders, arms, and stomach cooling as the sweat dried, and shivered more than was called for. I found I couldn't mee Theo's eyes.

But Theo's mind was elsewhere. "We gotta do this on attitude," he continued. "Think Mel Gibson in *Monte Cristo*."

"Sure. Could we also do it on paranoid willingness to hi anything that moves with the nearest heavy object?"

"I've got no problem with that."

Theo, my patron saint may have killed your father. If so, I made it possible. I didn't say it. It wouldn't have helped.

Theo stopped halfway down the hall and set his hand on a doorknob. He glanced up at me; for a moment I thought he'c speak. Then the moment was gone, and he opened the door.

There was a lamp lit on the nightstand, and a bulky figure on the bed; there was the sound of harsh, irregular breathing. It wa: Albrecht, gray-skinned, slack-mouthed, aged by ten years, sick But alive. Theo hunched over the bed as if looking for some microscopic, encouraging signal.

I couldn't find any resemblance between Theo and his father Maybe he looked like his mother. That would be interesting, to be able to see your nose on someone else's face, and know it was only the outward sign of an interior connection, a similarity in the blood. And the emotional connection: Was it different from friendship? What did Theo feel now? Would I feel the same, if i were Theo lying stricken on the bedspread?

I heard something click to my right and looked up. Dusty, my nemesis from the Night Fair and the Underbridge, stood in the connecting door to the next room. He wore a knee-length black robe that was too big around for him, and his shell-pink hair wa: in disarray. I'd never seen him without the silvertones; his eye:

were narrow and deep-set and very dark. He held a long-barreled pistol in both hands. "Hey," he said, "it's Sonnyboy and the Whatchacallit."

I stood very still at the foot of the bed. LeRoy's injection and a bolt of fear combined to make a buzzing noise in my head. I waited for a sign from heaven.

Theo hadn't moved, either. His back was to the connecting door. Did he recognize—yes, he'd known Dusty as one of Tom Worecski's henchmen. Theo's eyes widened, and closed; his lips pressed tight, and his shoulders rose as he filled his lungs in a rush.

"God damn it," Theo said, heated and drawling, still facing the bed, "I thought I told you to watch him!"

My teeth snapped closed, an involuntary motion. I knew that voice.

Dusty's head turned, just a little, and he frowned. "Boss?"

Theo scowled over his shoulder. "What the fuck were you doin'? How long has he been like this?"

There was a little of the bad truck driver from *Rainbow Express* in it, and some of Jack Nicholson in *Easy Rider*. But it was mostly the voice of Tom Worecski. *Monte Cristo*, indeed, Theo. But it would only buy a few minutes, nothing else.

"Like what?" said Dusty. He took a step closer, and the gun barrel wavered.

"If he dies, I'm gonna have your ass for breakfast. Go call downstairs for a doctor." Theo made a little business out of checking his father's pulse. Careful, careful—the body language would be harder than doing the voice. But of course, that was why Theo hadn't moved from the bedside.

Dusty was still frowning. "What happened upstairs? And who's 'hat with you?"

A muscle stood out in Theo's jaw. "You gonna do what I tell you, or you gonna stay and chat?"

It wasn't quite right, and I thought Theo knew it. Did Dusty? He lowered the gun. "Sure thing, boss," he said, and went out into the hall. Theo let his breath out.

From the hallway door, I heard Dusty say softly, "Hey, Sonnyboy!" and I turned and saw him framed in the doorposts, sighting down the gun at Theo. I had just enough time to take the step that put me in the line of fire.

I heard three shots as Theo knocked me down from behind. Dusty wavered in the doorway and dropped the gun. I saw his

face, an interesting mix of bafflement and annoyance, before he
fell into the hall and was still.

Myra Kincaid now stood at the door to the next room. She wore
a raincoat loosely belted over, I suspected, nothing, and her dark
cherry hair fell untidily in her eyes. She looked relaxed, half
awake, and held a pistol in a negligent grip, settling as I watched
to point at the floor. *Santos,* I thought, with an upwelling of
hysteria, where were they finding all these damned handguns?

"My brother was a mad dog," she said. "But I expect I'll miss
him, anyway." She sounded appallingly like Vivien Leigh in
Gone With the Wind. "Tom's dead, isn't he?"

"Yes," I said before Theo could perjure himself. I slid out from
under him, and he sat up with a lurch. I got to my feet and
managed not to sway too much. The pain in my shoulder was like
a blunt-ended hammer that shook my whole body, and it felt as if
adrenaline had raised blisters on my nerve endings. But all the
while, my eyes never left Myra. The gun made her master of the
room; she didn't behave as if she knew it. "I hope you don't feel
you have to avenge him."

"If Tom couldn't kill you, I surely couldn't. Dusty, not being
very bright, hadn't figured that out."

Innocuous voice, but something out of alignment in it, in the
very air. I looked into her eyes and knew she was a good deal
more than half awake. Why had she just killed her brother? What
was I supposed to say? Here was a cobra, out of her basket. What
could I possibly play to make her dance?

"Worecski's gone," I said at last, "and Albrecht's finished. The
market for bravos and assassins just dried up. Where will you go
now?"

Her eyelids lifted a fraction. "You'll let me go?"

Attitude, I thought, gathered mine around me, and replied, "I
think you'd better."

"I want safe conduct."

Good grief, who did she think I was? What did she think was
happening here? "Going fast will be just as effective. Never
coming back will be even more so."

Myra shook her head and smiled. "I'll do that. Honey, you
haven't got a clue, have you?"

"I beg your pardon?" I asked with an effort.

"That's all right—it works anyway. But if I'd known you were
one of hers, I wouldn't have had shit to do with this. That was
another thing Dusty wasn't too bright about. 'Course, neither was

om. I wonder what would have happened if I'd let Dusty pull that
igger."

I understood, at last. I was alive, and Tom was dead; so I must
ave killed him. If I could do that, I was too dangerous to
hallenge. Myra had given me her brother in exchange for her life,
nd was impressed by my mercy. I had a strong desire to go away
nd be sick. "You'd better leave now," I said.

Sne nodded and dropped the gun in a pocket of the raincoat. For
moment she froze, her hand in the pocket. Then she lifted her
ead. Her face seemed harder and older, and her lips were twisted
nd pouting, even as they smiled. Her eyes were rolled back and
nowed nothing but white.

"Tell my fierce and virtuous sister," said a dense, caressing
ontralto through Myra's mouth, "that Pombagira sends her
ongratulations. And reminds her that she could not have done it
vithout me."

Myra Kincaid and the spirit that rode her walked to the door,
tepped over her dead brother's legs, and was gone.

"Sparrow?" said Theo shakily from his place on the floor. "If
nything like this comes up again, let's split town, okay?"

"That's a great idea. I wish you'd had it sooner."

"It wouldn't have worked this time."

"You're right." I stumbled back against the bed and slid to the
loor beside Theo. "Go tell Josh that as soon as he can spare the
ime from Frances, your father needs him. Hurry."

My eyes were closed, but I could feel him crouched beside me,
ooking into my face. "What about you?"

"And when he's done with everybody else, I could probably use
little help, too."

I heard him run down the hall. Good. The rush was for
Albrecht, though; I could have told Theo that I was in no danger.
he fierce and virtuous sister still had a use for me.

Tom Worecski has his revenge, and a kind of temporary
mmortality. It might have been different if there had been a body
o stand over, dispose of, remember. And it might have been
lifferent if I hadn't seen the endings of too many horror movies.

But in my sleep I wait for the sequel. In my dreams my loved
nes come close and I touch them, and his smile stretches their
nouths, his voice comes out. Over and over. And when, awake,
see my loved ones, try as I will, I can't seem to separate love
rom terror. It's the perfect revenge. He would have been
lelighted.

I don't dream about flat white spaces and pictographic dancers
I don't hear the voices of spirits. I don't miss them. And I don
fool myself into thinking they're gone. I just haven't foule
anything up badly enough to require their intervention, that's al

I've written this at Sherrea's request. Or is it a request whe
someone drops twenty-five pounds of manual typewriter and
monstrous pile of paper beside your plate at dinner, then asks i
you'd rather do it in longhand?

"Do what?" I said.

"Your version of what happened to the power monopoly," sh
told me, as if I ought to have known.

It was, and is, a very large typewriter. Finally I asked, "Doe
it have to rhyme?"

She said she wants a record of it for the Engineers, but I thin
she also means it to be therapy for me. Or maybe she doesn't. Bu
I've treated it as if it was; I've tried to faithfully reproduce th
person who woke up on the river flats, and understand, an
forgive. I've made progress on the first two.

Even so, I think this must be three-quarters lying. I can't hav
remembered everything; and the process of trying is like recon
structing a dream. You put the connective tissue in where it neve
existed, because without it, you've got, not a narrative, but
string of senseless images.

I don't trust memory, anyway. Why should I? Memories
however undependable, ought to be the stuff left on the sand whe
the tide of experience recedes. As long as they're part of tha
process, there's something valid about them, something that tie
them to real life.

But what if something exists only as a remembrance, that wa
never an experience? What if it even leaves artifacts in the mind
English, Spanish, French, and a thorough knowledge of semicon
ductor electronics? These, in me, began as pure memory, untrou
bled by life or the sensible continuity of time. The experienc
came later.

What if Sleeping Beauty woke behind the briers alone, in th
dark, to the knowledge that the curse was not sleep but waking
and that family, childhood, fairy godmothers and all were dream
spun to amuse a virgin mind in mothballs?

She/he/it would have no choice but to make something of th
awakening. I do, as best I can.

Theo and I, in a rash moment over a flask of cherry brandy
resolved to restore the old municipal telephone system to replac
Albrecht's graft- and bribery-powered party lines. After thre

months of learning experiences, we have half an exchange up; but it's interesting work.

I found that Loretta, the old woman at China Black's house, was right: communal hydro generators, regularly spaced along the riverbank, are a reasonably cheap and reliable method for getting power to most of the City. We have four running so far.

Now that the power monopoly is broken, a surprising amount of photovoltaic technology is turning up. Surprising to me, anyway. Last week a storm took the roofing off a house on the south end of town and revealed three solar panels hidden in the rafters. I went down to direct the salvaging of them, and felt like an archaeologist who'd found the library at Alexandria intact.

People come to me for things like that, and for information, and training. I'm learning to talk to them. I'm learning to live with being recognized on the street. A frightening number of people know who I am, and even what I am, and I have to get on with life as if that didn't matter. Someday maybe it won't.

I said this was therapy. I think Sher wanted me to see that my life is not a finished story. I already know that, but maybe she doesn't realize I do. Such a surprising number of people left alive at the end, our narrator included. Do they just stop then, suspended with one foot hanging in midair, one breath half drawn?

"You may tell them," Frances said, "that Little Nell lived." She was lying on her back under the Hoodoo Engineers' big tree, eyes closed, hands limp on the grass. I'd told her about writing this.

"Oh, a tragedy," I said.

"And that as soon as Little Nell recovers from having her intestines shortened by an inch, she will be a much more interesting person, and it won't be safe to say things like that."

"Or necessary, I suppose."

She raised her eyebrows and her eyelids at the same time.

"I'd thought that you'd want to leave."

Frances looked up into the boughs and smiled. "Maybe. Eventually. But not until I run out of amusements. It should be damned amusing to be underfoot and in the way while you build the New Jerusalem. I want to write my name in the wet cement."

I look forward to that.

I liked the idea of a Dickensian ending. But I don't know yet who marries, who dies, who has offspring and how many. Theo's father survived the stroke, but his health is uncertain; he's as fragile as Frances and, unlike her, will remain so the rest of his

life. I think he and Theo have said things to each other they
weren't used to saying, and that it did them both good; but I wasn't
there.

I couldn't say why Sherrea believes the story isn't done. I know
why I do. It's because Myra Kincaid was right: I haven't a clue.
There is a whole class of answers to life's big questions that, when
examined closely, proves to be nothing but another set of
questions. I now know my origins, body and soul. That's like
knowing that magnetic tape is iron oxide particles bonded to
plastic film. Wonderful—now, what's it *for*? What does it *do*?

It does, I suppose, what it has to. It does what it loves to do, or
what needs doing. It helps others do the same. So I do that. And
sometimes, lying on my back in an inch of cold water with a
socket wrench in my hand, or teaching someone how to use a
soldering iron, or constructing witty segues between songs on the
balcony at the Underbridge, I can feel it, very close: the power and
clarity and brilliance, the strength and lightness, that I had once in
a dream, a dream of dancing, a hoodoo dream. Maybe in
time—nine months? nine years?—I'll finally have a clue.

I've found a videotape, a home dub that someone kept, of
several weeks' worth of a TV comedy show. I like it. It's funny.
But my favorite part, the part I play at the Underbridge when the
windows are colorless with dawn, when Theo has fallen asleep
with his head on the mixing board, when Robby is marching up
and down the dance floor with a broom on his shoulder, is the end
of each one. Then the woman whose show it is walks out to her
audience and the cameras in a ratty pink chenille bathrobe,
grinning, and says, "Go home! Go home!"

She's made as much sense of the world as she can for one week.
She hands it off to the audience. I love her then.

Go home! Go home!

And the house lights go up.

About the Author
Number Three—Collect 'Em All!

Emma Bull was born in 1954, well before anyone in the United States could have imagined the creation of designer pizza or the cellular car phone.

She began her career as a writer of adventure fiction in junior high with a really execrable spy novel that she wrote in a series of those little homework assignment notebooks. Somebody got shot every third page (they were small pages, too), and she regularly forgot what the homework assignments were.

She's the author of *War for the Oaks*, a contemporary fantasy set in Minneapolis, and *Falcon*, which is science fiction and almost Minnesota-free. She lives in Minneapolis with her husband, Will Shetterly, her two addled cats, and an electric mouthbow.

As a soundtrack for this novel, the management is pleased to offer: Rare Air's *Primeval*, a heady, assertive album that we believe will nicely complement the text; Richard Thompson's *Amnesia*, a mature vintage with excellent staying power (it doesn't hurt that the management's copy contains two of the Great Man's own guitar picks); and 3 Mustaphas 3's *Heart of Uncle*, which is . . . oh, trust me, have a slurp. Or you could sample *Another Way to Travel*, by Cats Laughing, which the admittedly biased management thinks is pretty tasty.* Beyond that, see you at the Winnipeg Folk Festival.

---

*The management sings with them, actually. For information on *Another Way to Travel*, please write to: Cats Laughing, Box 7253, Minneapolis, MN 55407.

**From the writer of Marvel Comics'
bestselling *X-Men* series.**

CHRIS
CLAREMONT

The explosive sequel to *FirstFlight*

GROUNDED!

Lt. Nicole Shea was a top space pilot—until a
Wolfpack attack left her badly battered. Air
Force brass say she's not ready to return to
space, so they reassign her to a "safe" post
on Earth. But when someone begins making
attempts on her life, she must travel back into
the stars, where memories and threats linger.
It's the only way Shea can conquer her
fears—and win back her wings.

___ 0-441-30416-8/$4.95

For Visa, MasterCard and American Express orders ($10 minimum) call: 1-800-631-8571

**FOR MAIL ORDERS: CHECK BOOK(S). FILL
OUT COUPON. SEND TO:**

BERKLEY PUBLISHING GROUP
390 Murray Hill Pkwy., Dept. B
East Rutherford, NJ 07073

NAME_____

ADDRESS _____

CITY_____

STATE_____ZIP_____

PLEASE ALLOW 6 WEEKS FOR DELIVERY.
PRICES ARE SUBJECT TO CHANGE WITHOUT NOTICE.

POSTAGE AND HANDLING:
$1.50 for one book, 50¢ for each ad-
ditional. Do not exceed $4.50.

BOOK TOTAL	$ _____
POSTAGE & HANDLING	$ _____
APPLICABLE SALES TAX (CA, NJ, NY, PA)	$ _____
TOTAL AMOUNT DUE	$ _____

PAYABLE IN US FUNDS.
(No cash orders accepted.)

383